The Sha'Daa Series

Sha'Daa:
Tales of The Apocalypse

Sha'Daa:
Last Call

Sha'Daa:
Pawns

Upcoming Volumes:

Sha'Daa:
Facets

Sha'Daa:
Inked

Sha'Daa:
Toys

Moondream Press
An Imprint of Copper Dog Publishing LLC
537 Leader Circle
Louisville, CO 80027
www.copperdogpublishing.com

Ordering Information:
Special discounts are available on quantity purchases by corporations, associations, and others. For details, contact the publisher at the address above.

Printed in the United States of America

Credits:
Sha'Daa™: Last Call created by Michael H. Hanson
Managing Editor: Michael H. Hanson
Creative Director: Helen Harrison
Edited by Edward F. McKeown

ISBN: 978-0-9798652-2-0

Library of Congress Control Number: 2014902999

Fiction: Horror, Fantasy

First Edition: November 2010
Second Edition: April 2014

SHA'DAA: LAST CALL

CREATED BY:
MICHAEL H. HANSON

EDITED BY:
EDWARD F. MCKEOWN

FOREWORD BY: CATHERINE ASARO

AN IMPRINT OF COPPER DOG PUBLISHING, LLC

Contents

Dedication

This book is dedicated to:
The late James I. Wasserman
and
Those who love us and have given us the space
and time to write and dream.

—*The members of Team Sha'Daa*

ACKNOWLEDGEMENTS

No man is an island, entire of itself.
— John Donne

I'd like to take this opportunity to thank the small army of individuals who are responsible for this shared-world series making it into print:

All of the many wonderful authors who have come on board (and continue to do so) for this exciting project.

The late **James I. Wasserman,** for daring to dream and write within and upon my twisted playground.

Howard Wasserman, for allowing and supporting the continued inclusion of his late son's excellent chapter *Horsemen.*

Edward F. McKeown, Sha'Daa Editor/Co-Writer, whose fierce drive and professionalism have kept this project on track through some very tough times.

Author and Scientist **Catherine Asaro** for writing the Foreword to *LAST CALL.*

Graphic Artist **Helen Harrison** for her excellent cover art.

From the depth of my heart, I thank you all.

Michael H. Hanson
Sha'Daa Creator/Co-Author
Piscataway, NJ
2014

by Catherine Asaro

OKAY, HERE'S THE DEAL. THE EARTH is about to end. Yeah, I know, you've heard it before. You don't take it seriously, right? Better watch out. Sha'Daa is coming. And you *do not* want to mess with the soul-sucking demons, Evil Gods Of Death, and other assorted riff-raff who run this particular show. Once every ten thousand years, the Earth has the mother of all bad hair days. It's coming, and you can't run, you can't hide, and you can't stop the chaos.

But you sure as blazes can enjoy reading about it. In the pages of this anthology, you'll find a tight, creative set of stories that in the process of chronicling the nefariously relentless attempts of their villains to end the world, are somehow simultaneously entertaining, dark, funny, and clever. Tying it all together is the ever-present Johnny, or more simply, the Salesman, an enigmatic fellow who turns up benignly — or not so benignly - to aid humanity in surviving the Apocalypse.

The anthology resembles the proverbial onion, with translucent layers half-hiding, half-revealing what lies below, each peeling back to reveal a new aspect of the work, and all layering together to create a multidimensional experience for the reader. Energized by the talented duo of Michael H. Hanson, creator of the Sha'Daa universe, and Edward F. McKeown, the editor of the Sha'Daa series, these anthologies offer a rich addition to the literature of dark fantasy. Reminiscent of Lovecraft, the stories bring a sleek, modern sensibility to that genre of horror, not to mention a good dash of humor that crops up in unexpected places.

Rather than an onion, though, perhaps a better comparison for this book is a puzzle. The stories are pieces in a jigsaw, but this is no ordinary puzzle, because each of those individual pieces is also a complete picture itself. When they are all fitted together, they form a larger picture, the story of the anthology. Within that mosaic, the Salesman has his own tale, one that connects every story in the book, his presence blending with the narrative. Interwoven with Johnny's plot is the story of Bak, owner of the Triple-Six Tavern, the cosmically interstitial watering hole where Johnny hangs out between each story. And finally, the overall saga of Sha'Daa itself is the theme tying all these tales and meta-tales together with its entertaining assault on life, the universe, and those of us readers lucky enough to find this book.

It's a remarkable idea and a tribute to Hanson's creative foundation and McKeown's inspired editing that such a complicated concept works so well.

And the best part is that when the Apocalypse is done sweeping through the universe — when it's all said and done between the covers of this book — we'll still be here to enjoy the result.

Buzz Kill

IT WAS SHAPING UP TO BE ONE HELL OF A night at the Triple-Six Tavern. That is saying a lot considering it's always night at the Triple-Six, a huge non-Euclidian cavernous establishment seemingly chiseled out of black granite and Escher absurdity.

At the moment, a dozen distractions were occurring simultaneously. Two huge, horned, Baccravian males, looking like upright rhinos with six-fingered hands on the end of gargantuan arms, were engaged in a wrestling match in the bar's grudge pit. With each fall, minor earthquakes rocked the floor and set beer mugs rattling. Over at the gaming tables to the right of the bar, screams, yells, snarls, and grunts of pain marked every lost or won hand. Maribel's brothel tents on the raised levels behind the main bar were doing a prodigious business, a line of male and female patrons leading all the way back to several of the entrances on the far side. In the main table area, a squad of 14th century Janissaries chugged beer with men and women from a 24th century British SAS Plasma Rifle Squad. The dance floor at the lowest level was currently home to a dozen Slythe Demons who were clearly in the middle of one of their more esoteric skin-shedding rituals. A frighteningly realistic Elvis impersonator rocked through the final chorus of *Hound Dog* on the main stage while three dozen regulars leaned, pressed, stuck, or fluttered against the front of the extremely long bar counter. The most eccentric of them all was the tall, cadaverous, shadowy character in dark trench coat and fedora who sat sipping a frothy tall one directly across from the Triple-Six's short, muscular owner and head bartender, Bak.

"It's the end." Trench Coat said in a singsong voice. "The end of it all. Humpty's tipping. He's gonna fall."

"Yah, yah, yah," Bak chuckled, fondling the priceless fist-sized translation sapphire that hung upon his bulging chest from a thick gold chain. "Every time you come in here you say the same things, Johnny. It's the end. The end is nigh. Entropy is king. Invest in war bonds. Finish the backyard bunker. Beware the bogeyman. The redcoats are coming…"

A thunderous crash marked the end of the behemoth grudge match and the shock wave unbalanced Bak. Instantly recovering, he couldn't help but notice that his friend hadn't budged at all, the monstrous vibrations flowing over him like so much rainwater.

Johnny polished off the ale and slammed his stoneware mug down. "How about a refill? My credit still good?"

Bak snorted in amusement and poured his moody patron a fresh one.

"You've been coming here, what, two… three millennia?" He asked. "In all that time you've never asked for a second drink. What's up? Life on the door to door not paying off this week?"

Johnny laughed hollowly and took a deep quaff.

Bak got called to the far end of the bar to help with some drink orders.

The Elvis clone (at least, Bak thought he was a clone) broke into a slow one, singing the sweetest version of *Love Me Tender* Bak had ever heard live.

"So tell me Johnny," Bak wheedled when he returned. "You got some inside info for me tonight or what? I haven't had this much business in, well, ever. Maribel's employees are ready to strike if they don't get an hour's break. What's the real deal? Is another world war about to break out? Don't tell me a new dark savior was just born?"

Johnny looked up, making eye contact with Bak for the first time since he arrived. The dark pools of his orbs always raised the hair on the back of Bak's neck, like they were twin windows into some inescapable black hole. Johnny smiled, revealing for the shortest of moments a single glistening gold tooth among an otherwise perfect set of bright white teeth.

"Sha'Daa" Johnny whispered.

"Ohhhhhhh shit."

I Kill Zombies

By Edward F. McKeown

TIMOTHY LOVED COMICS AND FANTASY novels. His favorite of all the hard-bodied, butt-kicking, leather-wearing bad girls defending the world from the undead was the hottest: Raven Blackstone. Black-haired with icy-blue eyes, she carried a pair of .44s and some guns too. Raven haunted Tim's teen-age nights, doing things with him. Truth be told, he didn't have too much of an idea what those things were. He'd only turned fourteen and was a shy, quiet child, save in his dreams. In those dreams, he waded through zombies, werewolves and vampires at Raven's side. His magic sword made short work of slicing off any zombie's head.

As Raven would say in her dark, husky voice, "Always go for the head."

Raven's current nemesis wasn't a creature of the night, but Tim's mother, who disapproved of the lurid comic book covers and even the novels that were, after all, mostly just a bunch of words, though in the books Raven did things they didn't draw in the comics. *Pity that*, Tim thought, thinking of Raven's drum-taut body. Still, his mother hunted the books and comics, dragging them like trophies before the general, his father, during his rare times home.

"Just be glad he likes girls," his father would say. This always led to a yelling match between his parents about feminism, respect and how Tim was getting a twisted view of who women were. Tim understood little of this and from what he gathered, neither did his father.

"Tim," his mother said. "Real girls aren't like this. They don't bend steel bars, kill hundreds of people-"

"Monsters, Mom, Raven hardly ever kills people, unless they're evil."

"Nor," his mother continued as if he hadn't spoken, "do they have sex with everyone in sight."

As the latter charge seemed to have some validity, Tim didn't attempt to mount a defense.

"I'm just afraid that you're so obsessed with this tramp-stamped, killer bimbo you're going to miss what real girls are like. Girls like Bethany, down the block, who likes you."

"Mom!" Tim protested.

"Well, she likes you. She's even said that she wanted to go to the movies with you."

"I don't like her. She's bossy, always thinks she's right. She's nothing like Raven."

"Thank God for that," his mother said. "Listen, I know your father thinks it's ok, but I would prefer you not read this garbage."

"Are you telling me I can't?"

His mother looked down at him. "No, I'm not. I want that to be your decision. Think about what I said. And be nice to Bethany, for heaven's sake. She may not bend steel bars, but she broke a board in her green belt test."

Tim, who had never tried to break anything, now found another reason to resent Bethany.

Aware of his mother's disapproval, Tim decided to handle it like an adult, using grown-up methods of lying, hiding and cheating. His aunt had given him a book light for Christmas, and it became his lifeline to Raven after lights out.

Sometime he would drag out his other secret prize, a long, sinister dagger his father had taken off an insurgent in Afghanistan during one of the "special ops" he ran. "Don't tell your mother," he'd said with a wink.

Tim knew his father loved him, but he also felt that his father was disappointed in him. That maybe he'd wanted a different son. Someone bigger and tougher, who didn't lose to the school bully. Someone who looked like the powerful wrestler his Dad had been in high school. Instead, Tim was tall and skinny, with his mother's delicate features. Maybe if he was bigger and tougher they'd be closer….

Accompanied by these gray thoughts, Tim made his way up to his bedroom. He drew out his special stash of Raven's sexiest adventures. One cover was his particular favorite. Raven stood tall in a swarm of zombies, one of whom had clawed her skintight leathers off her gorgeous, tattooed hips, exposing the pink perfection of her backside. She had a pistol stuffed in one zombie's eye. Her face was calm and fierce under its helmet of black hair.

He also pulled out his father's dagger. Tim liked to hold the hilt of it sometimes when reading, as if he could feel a zombie's neck parting under the lusty swing of his blows.

Tim devoured the comic, for all he'd read it dozens of times. Once again, Raven had been lured into danger by her treacherous boyfriend, a vampeal who Tim despised. She was battling the King of the Zombies as his ravenous hordes tried to devour her hometown.

Near midnight, the book light started to dim, and Tim's eyes became heavy. He fell asleep with Raven on his chest.

Awareness came back to Tim slowly. He sat up in bed, the comic and light sliding off his chest onto the bed. His room was filled with a dense, orange vapor.

Oh my God, he thought, *the house is on fire.* But there was no heat, no smell of smoke. Yet he could see nothing of his room beyond his bed. He thought of calling for his parents, but he suspected he was dreaming and didn't want to call for his father like a child frightened of the dark. He realized that the sheathed dagger was beside him and grabbed it. Its hilt felt hard and real in his hands. This was like no dream he'd ever had. He hopped out of bed and slid his feet into slippers.

Tim headed for the door of his room. But after a dozen steps, he realized something was wrong. His room wasn't this big. He turned but couldn't see his bed anymore.

"GREETINGS, MY NEW SERVANT," a voice boomed.

Terror shot through Tim. The voice was icy, cruel, with a filthy quality to it, as if its source was so diseased it could only pour vileness on the listener.

"Who's there?" Tim squeaked. "Mom, Dad, help!" He pulled the ancient dagger.

"DESPAIR, SERVANT. THEY CANNOT HELP YOU. THEY CANNOT HEAR YOU. WEAK, SMALL, HELPLESS ONE, YOU ARE MINE!"

"What do you want?" Tim called, turning in a circle, peering into the fog. His mouth hung open and he was breathing so hard he thought he might faint. Abruptly, he thought of Raven, and how she always controlled her breathing when she was in trouble. His breathing slowed and a measure of calm returned.

"YOU WILL KILL," the giant voice commanded.

"Kill who?" Tim whimpered. The awful voice was like a rasp on the skin.

"YOUR FATHER."

"What? No!"

"HE IS A LEADER OF YOUR SHADOW FORCES. HE WILL BE CALLED TO BATTLE OUR ARMIES. HE MUST DIE."

"Never."

"YOU WILL HAVE NO CHOICE."

"That's cheating and you know it," a new voice said.

The orange mist dispersed.

Tim found himself standing on the street outside his house, yet the world looked somehow unreal, almost as if it was a set. The sky above was black and starless. Street lights blared an unnatural yellow, cutting harsh shadows on the street.

But the two figures were what caught Tim's attention.

The farthest from him struck him dumb with fear. It stood twice Tim's height, a skull-like face with eyes like wounds stared at him. Swirling black fabric moved around it, though there was no wind and its bony, clawed hands clutched a staff. The being, its thin lips drawn over ghastly teeth, glared at a man standing between Tim and it.

The man stood facing the monster casually, as if it was an everyday occurrence. Tall and broad-shouldered, he wore a grey trench coat and a wide-brimmed fedora. The streetlights cast his face into hard shadows, but his eyes glittered from under the brim. His hands were jammed in the pockets of the coat.

"You," the monster said. Its voice was reduced in power and now held a mix of fear and loathing.

"Yes me," the man said. "Don't try this kind of crap with me. I may be a slave to the Sha'Daa, but you know what I can bring down on rule-breakers. This is a duel. The boy's entitled to a chance to fight for his soul. You chose the setting of the combat, his dreams. He chooses the weapons."

"His soul will be devoured. His hands will end the lives of his parents," the creature intoned.

"Maybe," the man said. "That's why we run the horserace."

He walked over to Tim, who was pinching himself trying to wake. "Knock it off, kid," he said, his voice gruff but somehow sympathetic. "You're still asleep but this is none-the-less real. You have to get a grip."

"Who are you? I want to go home."

"You are home, kid. You're in your bed. Your parents are asleep down the hall. Listen to me, son. There's a war breaking out at midnight tonight. It will be fought all across the world over the next 48 hours. Good and evil collide tonight across the dimensions. It ain't fair and it ain't right, but you've ended up on a beachhead of that war. They know your father's in charge of special ops, in a little-known section that deals with unusual events like this. They want him dead.

"What I am isn't important. As for who I am, well I'm called Johnny, the Salesman. My charge is to serve in the Sha'Daa. I make trades, providing humans with objects that can help them." He cast a glare at the monster. "I'm also empowered to deal with cheaters."

Johnny turned back to the boy. "You're challenged, Tim. You need a second and a choice of weapon. Remember: this is a dream. There are things possible here-"

"Raven," Tim gasped, "if she was here…"

Johnny turned to face the monster. "The challenged elects for magic sword and Raven Blackstone will serve as his second."

"So it shall be," the monster said and vanished.

Johnny turned back to him. "Quickly, kid. I've got something you're going to need." From inside his coat he produced a small silver cylinder. "It's a dose of anti-zombie serum. Twist the red top and place the other end against your skin. It'll inject the serum into your blood. But you have to trade for it."

"All I have is this dagger."

"That's what I need. It's old. Older than your father knows and it's going to be needed elsewhere. Do we have a deal?"

"Won't I need it?"

"You have your magic sword."

With a start, Tim realized he wasn't in his underwear anymore. He stood clad in thick leathers and bits of body armor. He reached up and the magic sword's silver hilt rode in the place he'd always imagined it, over his right shoulder.

"Do we have a trade?" Johnny asked.

Tim handed him the dagger and Johnny gave him the serum injector. "Good luck, kid." Then he too disappeared.

In his place, Raven stood facing Tim, wearing her usual blue halter top and beltless hip-hugger leathers. Two pistols sat snug in holsters under her arms and a pouch with extra ammo and weapons rested on her rear.

She walked up and wrapped her arms around him, pulling him up on tip-toes. Her lips were hot and soft against his. Too stunned to think, Tim felt his arms circle her bare back. Her breasts pressed against his shirt front where his jacket hung open, the feel and scent of her overwhelming his senses.

"Hmmmn, good," she said. "Do we have time to get horizontal and take care of that virginity problem before the battle?"

"Huh?" A dozen sensations struggled in his body, derailing his brain. He was conscious of being stiff as a board against her thigh.

A blood-curdling shriek sounded behind them, perhaps the only thing that could have penetrated his hormone-soaked brain.

"Guess not," Raven pouted.

From between his house and the neighbors', zombies shuffled out, arms outstretched, vacant faces drooling. "Braaaaaaaiiiiiirnnnssss," they moaned.

"Run," Raven demanded. "Follow me."

They took off.

Tim cast a longing look back at his house, but the zombies were between them and it. The undead came after them, not quickly, but they didn't tire either. Raven and Tim jumped over fences and shrubs, zombies weren't agile. Tim's sword banged his ear a couple of times, something it hadn't done in other dreams.

They cut down an alley and ran straight into a clutch of zombies. Raven pulled her big bore pistols and shot the two nearest. Tim swept out his sword, but this was not one of his idle fantasies.

The zombie lurched at him; its rotten leaf smell filled his nostrils.

Tim screamed and hacked madly. The sword worked as it had in other dreams, cutting through the zombie as if it was paper. He hacked until the zombie fell then fell back, his breath tearing in and out. Remembering the others, he looked up, but only Raven stood there, both pistols smoking and destroyed zombies by her feet. She looked at the one he'd downed. The head, still intact on the armless, legless torso, snapped at him.

"In the mood for some exercise?" she asked. "What happened to "always go for the head?" She snapped a foot down, shattering the skull under her boot.

Tim stared at her.

Raven looked about. "Let's get off the street."

He followed her up to the door of a nearby house. The lock didn't slow her as she casually wrenched the doorknob off.

"Raven," Tim said, still numb and dazed. "I've always wondered how you do that. How come you're so much stronger than a man?"

"Good, clean living," she shot back. "Now do you want to get off the street or do you want to keep hanging out like zombie veal."

They walked in and Tim ran past her to the sink. He grabbed a glass from a cabinet and filled it with water, draining it one go.

"Good idea." She took the glass and filled it, sipping more moderately. "Don't overdo it. We'll have to run again."

Tim followed her into the living room.

"Nice," Raven said as she sank onto a sofa with a sigh and patted the seat next to her. "May as well be comfortable while we figure this out. So what's the plan?"

Tim stared at her. "Huh?"

"Come on, Tim, snap out of it. I'm the muscle and god knows, the body, but you're the brains of this outfit. What's the plan?"

Tim's thoughts returned to what Johnny had said. "I'm in a duel, Raven. In the middle of a battle called the Sha'Daa. The monsters, real monsters, are fighting me through one of our adventures."

"So, things should work as they usually do. We find the leader of the zombies and dispatch it, fighting our way through its minions."

"It's a big town, Raven. And if I lose here…."

"Something will turn up," she said. "It always does."

"Meanwhile we're surrounded by the undead."

"Well, it's quiet now," Raven purred. Her hand slid over his shoulders.

"Look, I mean like- making out with you was always my dream, but there are things out there trying to eat us. If they succeed in this dream, they own my soul and body and they'll make me kill my parents."

Raven shifted and pulled him close, resting his head on her chest. "It's ok, Tim. We've always beaten them before. We'll do it now. We're a good team."

"In my dreams," he said

A sound came from the back of the house. Something was inside with them. They leapt to their feet, drawing weapons.

A zombie lurched toward them out of the shadows. Lean even for a zombie, it wore bike shorts and a tattered t-shirt with a chicken on it that read, "I'm not a nugget."

"Grains," it moaned, "whole wheat, hummus, radicchio, salad…"

"Hah," Raven said. "Zombie vegetarians. I love these guys." She leveled the Colt at it.

"No wait," Tim shouted. "It wants a salad. Maybe we can talk to it!"

She stared at him. "Talk to a zombie?"

"We need to know who's controlling it. Where they are."

He turned toward the zombie. "You want a salad?"

"Saaalllaaadd…."

"Sit there," he pointed.

The zombie stared at the chair for a few seconds, then seemed to get the idea. Raven kept the Colt leveled at its head while Tim rummaged in the refrigerator. He was in luck, finding a head of iceberg and other greens. He found the biggest bowl he could and piled them in, then slathered in French dressing.

He turned to the zombie.

"Zombie want a salad?" he asked.

"It's not a parrot," Raven said in exasperation.

"Saaaallllllaaadd."

"Who is your lord?"

It seemed to consider. "Sabian the Necromancer," it husked.

"Sabian," Raven breathed.

Tim remembered Sabian, an enemy from twenty issues before. He'd ravished Raven, who, come to think of it, hadn't put up much of a struggle for a girl who could snap chains with a pull.

"Where can we find, Sabian?" Tim said waving the salad in front of him. The zombie's one good eye tracked it.

"Schhoooooolllllll."

"The high school near the mall?"

"Yes."

"Bon appétit." Tim slid the salad across to the zombie. It dove face first into the veggies.

They left the former vegan to his repast and made their way out back.

"This is the McMasters place," Tim said. "His father keeps a motorcycle out back."

"Good," Raven said. "At least something will be throbbing between my legs soon." They found the motorcycle in the garage; near it were some garden tools and a machete. Raven hefted the machete then reached into her bag and pulled at a length of silver chain, wrapping it around the machete. "Makes it more effective on evil things. The unnatural hate silver." She climbed onto the bike, then turned to Tim, the machete in her left hand. "Get on behind me. You strike right, I'll take the left." The bike started with a roar that must have alerted every zombie in miles. "Let's do this." They roared onto the street and straight into an approaching wave of zombies.

Raven gunned the bike, weaving between them. They struck at the reaching creatures, severing heads and arms at a clip.

"Tim," Raven shouted. "I'm not sure we can make it all the way to the school. It looks like the whole town's been zombified."

"Cut into the mall. There's an overpass that leads to the school grounds." Tim pointed to an off ramp that mercifully was zombie free.

Raven gave a sharp nod and sped toward the mall. Just before they reached the doors, she kicked the bike into a wheelie and they smashed through. They roared through its dark corridors, lit only by emergency lamps and the moonlight flooding down from the skylights.

Tim pointed. "Over there."

Raven pulled up to a storefront full of mannequins in bathing suits with boogie boards, and they dismounted the bike.

"Damn," Raven said, picking a piece of glass out of her side. "See if you can find a first aid kit."

"Yeah," Tim said. "You know, if we're going to be fighting monsters and tearing through things, you might want to cover up-"

"Hey," she said. "Did I ask for a critique? All you've done since you've showed up is act weird and bitch."

"Ok, ok," he said. Tim found a first aid kit behind a salon counter full of cosmetics and tanning lotions and quickly patched up a silent and irritable Raven.

"Oh, Raven," a voice said. "You should be more careful with your precious, delicious blood."

They both jumped.

Pushing between a display of beach towel and between the tanning beds, came Beltane the Vampeal, sometime ally and always bad news. He was tall, elfinly handsome and the product of a mating between a vampire and a human.

"Oh, no," Tim groaned. "Not you again."

"Can it," Raven growled, Beltane was always a sore subject between them. "We could use his help. He's strong."

"He's after your butt. Then he will betray us to the other side."

She spat. "You *never* give him a chance."

"Because he always turns on us."

"Raven, what does this jealous boy know of your needs? Your wants?" Beltane said in his most seductive voice. "The difference between us is that while we both want you, I can satisfy you."

"He just screws you both ways," Tim shot back. "He's cheated and betrayed you twenty-times. You fall for it each time. He's a louse, he's a creep, he's a vampire. HE SUCKS!"

"Why you little-" Beltane lunged at Tim, who whipped out his sword. The razor edge missed the blindingly fast vampire, who laughed and dodged back. "Too slow, Bloodbag."

"Beltane, don't hurt him," Raven cried, but she didn't reach for any weapon.

Tim grinned at the vampire. "Do you know where we are, Vampeal?"

"Where?" Beltane snarled, his teeth fully protruding now.

Tim reached for a switch on the wall. "We're in Thomasina's tanning salon." He flicked it and half-dozen sunlamps hummed to life. The open casket-like tanning beds lit up, spreading UV all over the shop.

"AAAHHHH," Beltane shouted as he began to smoke. "Noooooooo!" The vampire left a trail of foul-smelling smoke behind him as he fled back into the night.

"Tim...are you...I mean... I'm sorry," Raven began

"Why?" Tim yelled. "Why, why, WHY, do you always fall for these lousy, stinking, no goods who treat you like crap? Why can't you go for somebody nice, for once!?"

Raven cast her eyes down at the floor. "You're right. I have the bad-boy thing. The broodier and more sullen, the better."

"Honestly," he said. "You're so stupid sometimes. The worse they are the harder you f-"

Suddenly he found himself on his toes, looking at mad blue eyes over a pistol barrel. "Nobody talks to me that way. Especially not some fourteen-year-old wanker who just discovered his pecker while looking at me."

"Raven," he managed.

"Shut up," she said, releasing him. "You keep your mouth and your judgments off me from now on."

"Raven, I'm-"

The slap came out of nowhere.

"Once this is over," she said. "We're through. For now, shut up and follow me."

He fell in behind her, fighting hot tears and wishing he'd never opened his mouth.

They made their way through the silent mall, heading for the covered overpass that led to the school ground. But they weren't a team now. They were two individuals traveling the same road. Raven wouldn't look at him. They'd never fought before in his dreams and Tim had no idea how to deal with the angry zombie-slayer.

The overpass took them over an eight-lane highway choked with cars, crashed and abandoned. A few zombies stalked up and down the highway but couldn't smell them up on the glassed-in skybridge.

Once on the other side, they descended a spiral staircase. The school stood before them, dark and silent. Raven took off without speaking and Tim was obliged to run full out to have any chance of keeping up with her. Ahead of them, zombies shuffled along near the school auditorium.

"Stay here," Raven snapped when they reached the corner of the gym next to the auditorium. She pulled a flare out of her satchel and raced off. A minute later, she was back. Her face was still angry and closed; he decided not to question her.

A blast shattered the night, a Hummer in the parking lot wreathed in flames. The zombies in the area moaned and started in the direction of the burning car. Raven and Tim slipped into the auditorium.

As they pushed through the inside doors they spotted Sabian, the Zombie King, sitting on a throne set up on the stage. Arrayed about him were his guard of zombies, and worse, a skeletal lich. Its empty eye sockets and deathless grin mocking them as they approached up the center aisle.

"Ah, Raven, never far from my thoughts." Sabian's voice was rich, musical, and deep — a voice that commanded the dead to rise and overthrow nature. Powerful, with a sweep of grey in his heavy black hair, he was the image of a king.

"My lord," the skeletal lich said. "Let your guard fall on them and feast."

"No, Baleant. No such fate for my beautiful Raven."

"You're forgetting about me," Tim shouted with a bravado he did not feel. Somehow he kept his feet moving nearer the stage at every step.

"Yes, I am," Sabian replied. "Raven, how can you demean yourself this way? Consorting with a child? Is this not below you?"

"Enough," she shouted back. "We're here to end this."

Sabian shook his head at her, an expression of pity painted across his face. "No, Raven. You are here to end the charade. You are not a solider of light, you belong to our world. I have known your lips, your body; I know this to be true. You belong to me, to us, to the coming victory that is the Sha'Daa."

Raven's steps slowed at the foot of the stage. She bit her lip and her hands fell from her weapons.

Sabian waved his hands and the zombie guard fell back. His voice became soft, seductive. "Come to me, Raven. Mount the throne and sit by my right hand. We will rule together. Ignore these petty humans. What have they given you but condemnation and abuse? Live free at last in the land with no boundaries, the land of the dead."

Raven refused to meet Tim's eyes.

Horror overcame Tim and he blanched. "Raven, no. You can't. He's a bigger liar than the Vampeal."

Raven rounded on him, her eyes flashing. She clenched her fists. "What do you know?" She climbed onto the stage and glared down at him. "You're a brat. You're nothing, not even in your own dreams. I hate you! It's you that gave me this existence. You that make me what I am and then condemn me for it. I hate you, you and all your damn species. You're going to die in the Sha'Daa."

The lich laughed, a sound to freeze the blood.

The zombies stirred.

Sabian favored Raven with a slow smile as he stood. "Shall I give your companion a quick death? As a favor to you?"

"Tear him to pieces," she screamed. "I don't care."

"No, Raven," Tim cried, holding his wavering sword in front of him. Zombies shuffled up behind, cutting off his escape. "You can't do this."

She smiled. "Watch me, brat."

"At last," Sabian said, advancing to place his hands on Raven's heaving shoulders, "you have freed yourself. We will rule-"

Raven spun in his hands. The derringer she'd concealed in her hand flashed up, firing through the necromancer's chin. The top of his head popped open like a beer can. He staggered back, his eyes empty, but did not fall.

"Now, Tim!" Raven flipped backward as the lich struck at her with bony hands.

Confused, Tim hesitated

"Finish him," she screamed. "The gunshot wound won't hold him long." Her .44's cleared the holster and she turned toward the surging zombies, firing headshot after headshot.

Tim raced for the stage, but the lich stood between him and the King. a long sword grasped in one bony hand. He swung and Tim barely managed a block. Their weapons clashed in wild play.

The lich could only be killed by destroying its phylactery, Tim thought, as he faced the lich over his sword, a small, magically-warded box, where it stored its essence. Even his magic sword couldn't kill the lich while the phylactery remained hidden. Why such a powerful being served the Zombie King...

And suddenly Tim knew where the phylactery was kept and how the King ruled the lich. He kept the lich in front of him as he circled left. Out of the corner of one eye, he saw zombies closing in, falling under Raven's blazing guns but getting closer with each wave. From the other he saw the king's head closing up and awareness returning to his eyes. Tim had only seconds left and if he had guessed wrong-

He was now between the lich and the king, facing the animated skeleton. He feinted an overhand cut. As the lich raised his sword to block, Tim spun and lunged at the king, driving the sword into king's least vulnerable organ- his heart. As one, the king and lich both gave great, echoing cries. The lich collapsed but the king grasped the sword's hilt, struggling to pull the blade out.

Tim stepped back, right into the arms of a zombie. "Raven," he screamed as the rotted teeth tore into his arm. He beat at the straw-like hair of the zombie, but its teeth would not release. Behind the zombie he saw Raven fall under a wave of them, their heads dropping toward her struggling body.

Brilliant light filled the room, clean and white.

The zombie let go of Tim and stumbled, then fell.

Panting and holding his arm, Tim turned back toward the Zombie King.

His sword was glowing, emanating a pure blue flame.

The king's hands charred black and dropped off. He sank to his knees, howling in anguish as the sword ate his substance. At his feet, the lich lay in paroxysms of agony, looking like a burning ant.

With an anguished shout of "No!" the king burst into flame and for the briefest of seconds Tim could see a jeweled phylactery box in his chest, split by the point of the sword. Then the phylactery melted and the lich dissolved into black sand. A clean wind filled with the smell of sunlight and growing things swept the auditorium. Zombies turned to ash in that wind and whirled away.

Raven and Tim were alone in the room.

Tim's sword, its work completed, disappeared, its substance becoming both the light, and the cleansing wind.

Tim scrambled on all fours toward Raven, who stumbled up against the stage, bloodied and torn.

"Raven," he said, tears rolling down his face. "You're bitten."

"Oh, God, Tim. They got you too. Oh, no, no, no."

He wrapped his arms around her. "We won. They can't use me to kill my family. I don't care what happens to me."

"Tim, Honey. We have a little time left. Sun should be coming up soon. Maybe we can see it before…well, before."

Tim slipped off the stage and under her shoulder, and they staggered step by painful step to the outside. Raven was right; the sky was brightening to the east.

Something jabbed Tim in the ribs as they stood leaning on each other. He let go of Raven long enough to check his pocket. Then it came to him in a rush, the vial of serum Johnny had traded him.

"Ooohh…" Raven dropped to her knees, moaning. "I never thought it would end this way. I thought it would be something big, a demon, vampiric orgy, not a zombie bite."

Tim knelt beside her. He felt feverish, his vision blurred. "Back there, I wasn't sure for a few seconds…wasn't sure you hadn't really gone over."

She gave him a weak smile. "For a few seconds I wasn't sure either.

You've got to forgive me, Tim. I spend so much time alone, so far from everyone in the shadow lands. I lose my bearings sometimes."

"No, Raven. It's ok. You're my friend. You'll always be my friend."

"We gave them a good fight, Tim. Sorry I never got a chance to help you with your virginity. I'd have shown you something."

Tim pulled out the small injector that Johnny had traded him. One vial of anti-zombie serum. Two victims

Raven fell over on her back. Tim tried to catch her but was pulled over sprawling beside her. He struggled back up to sitting.

Raven's breath was coming fast and shallow now, and her voice was husky. "Timmy, take the antidote. Now. Then you have to promise me you'll do something for me. You have to kill me. Cut my head off. I'm not going to wander the world eating brains. Not me."

Tim looked down at her, the sharp-featured face, the fabulous body, and her brilliant blue eyes. He thought of his father and what he would do. Thought of all his heroes. Thought of the sort of man he wanted to be if he grew up...

He pressed the injector on her flat belly and triggered it. It hissed and sent the antidote into her blood.

"No. Timmy, no!"

A deep calm came over Tim. He looked into Raven's eyes. "Too late. This is a dream. You're a dream. Without that serum, according to the rules of this place, you die. Me, I still have a chance if I wake up. I couldn't lose you, not this way. Not when I had another chance. What sort of guy would that be?"

"Not your sort I guess." Johnny's voice came.

They both looked up at the Salesman.

"You won your soul when you stopped the Zombie master," Johnny said. "But there was one last test for you. One you set yourself. You needed to know if you were going to be a disappointment to your father. You chose your friend's life over your own. Your dad's done that many times."

Tim realized that Raven was gone. She'd disappeared without a sound.

"Is she…?"

"She'll be fine. She knows she's going to be seeing less of you in the future. She's ok with it." Johnny looked down at the young man still sitting on the ground. "You're going to wake in a few minutes, Tim. Your species made it through the first night. There's been a lot of fights across the world, some losses, a lot of critical wins, but many casualties. Your dad's out in the fighting. He wouldn't have been there if you'd lost. All you went through took only a few seconds in the real world and you slept through the rest of it. So did your mother, a little bit of my own magic there. So, if your kind makes it through the next day, what are you going to do in this brave new word?"

Tim stood. "I'm going to hug my mother and father when he gets home. Then there's a girl named Bethany I want to take to a movie, maybe I'll even get a kiss on the cheek."

Johnny smiled. "Good for you, kid. Hope you make it."

Let's Get This Party Started

His name is Bak, which is pretty much pronounced as "Bach." And this establishment is his property, the one and only Triple-Six Tavern. Now as far as Bak is concerned, it has always been called the Triple-Six, that is, since he first discovered it, abandoned and uninhabited some four thousand years ago. A mercenary soldier and adventurer, short, bald, swarthy survivor of an ambushed Babylonian tax patrol, Bak had stumbled, wounded, into a bat infested cave, pursued by bloodthirsty Hittites. And the cave seemed to stretch on forever, until the screaming savages finally went silent, and the sound of running water led an exhausted Bak into an enchanted cavern where he collapsed next to a glistening pool of water fed by a one hundred foot high waterfall. He awoke hours later to find that the magical waters had miraculously healed all of his wounds. A quick exploration showed him that this was no mere cave, but some long lost emperor's hidden pleasure den, with spaces and rooms and accommodations to entertain hundreds. And Bak's lifelong dream suddenly looked like it might just become a reality…

"Did I just hear you right…Salesman?"

"Oh ho." Johnny sucked down another three inches of brew. "We're getting formal now are we, Bak, my boy?"

"I…I've heard the stories," Bak said, clearly shaken. "Over the years. The rumors. The legends."

"But you never thought it was actually going to happen, did you, Barman Bak?" Johnny giggled. "Ironic, isn't it?"

"How's that?"

"You're immortal, barkeep." Johnny smiled a shark-like grin. "Surely you realized you'd live long enough to see it all happen."

"Hmph. Yah. I suppose you have a point, Salesman. So, when does it…"

"Begin?" Johnny asked, surprised. "You can't be serious. Not standing here in this trans-dimensional watering hole and sub-space cathouse?"

"So forgive me for a moment of linear thought." Bak spit out. "It happened, it's happening, and it will happen. I get it. Now, answer my bloody question."

"Okay, my friend," Johnny's eyes seemed to smolder. "And there are very few I would label as such. We are mere hours into the event. So far I've made two hundred and thirteen of my sales-trades. The strain was showing and I felt the need for a short snort and a friendly ear."

"I thought I saw your creepy outline dashing in and out of your private storage locker." Bak nodded.

"Locker. Ha, ha, ha, yes. I suppose you could call it that, my friend." Johnny polished off the mug and licked his thin lips.

"Not that anybody but you has ever been inside that perverse crevice." Bak smirked.

"Who knows?" Johnny shrugged. "Perhaps even that will change over the next two days. But now, break time is over. Duty calls my friend. I'll see you in a bit."

And before Bak could reply, Johnny hopped off his stool and strode quickly through the growing crowd of customers toward one of the many shadowy entrances and exits that covered the farthest cave wall.

Just then, the expected fistfight finally broke out between the Janissaries and the SAS toughs.

"Bors. Jaxas." Bak shouted. Though most of the furniture was carved out of black granite and had weathered worse, he signaled his recovering Baccravian bouncers who stumbled into the free-for-all and immediately started smacking heads together.

"Craps." The croupier yelled. A group of two hundred Venusian Vampires around the craps table hissed in anger. Having dealt with those poor losers before, Bak stepped up to bat.

"O-Positive on tap." Bak yelled. "First round on the house."

That instantly doused the outrage of the albino goons as they poured out of the gaming pit and rushed the bar. Bak and four of his full-time assistant bartenders popped garlic chewing gum into their mouths, tossed crucifix necklaces over their heads, and greeted their hematologically-challenged guests with warm mugs of nourishment.

"Dammit, Bak." The voice of Bak's fifth wife Maribel echoed downward from the rustling tents above. "You either start vetting the patrons for freeloaders and deadbeats or I swear we'll sell their carcasses on the zombie market for reimbursement."

The King started singing *Caught in a Trap.*

Yah, it's going to be a long one, Bak thought.

A Question of Faith

By Arthur Sánchez

"**A**ND THEN YOU HAVE THE Tucci baptism at three," Mrs. Fitzgerald said as she donned her large brown overcoat. To Father Lee the movement resembled the unfurling of a sail — cloth flapped briskly as it stretched across her healthy frame. "Lovely people, known them for ages."

"Yes, yes," Father Lee answered. "I'll be sure to remember." He handed Mrs. Fitzgerald her hat.

Mrs. Fitzgerald though wasn't finished. "Janice will be in at one so you only have to watch the desk for an hour. If you need me," she withdrew a cell phone from her bag, "*call* me."

Father Lee smiled. "Don't worry, I'll be fine." He then crossed the reception area to the door. The Rectory had been built with a tiny foyer connecting an inner and outer door. Not really a room, its only purpose was to keep out the damp San Francisco fog. Father Lee opened the inner door. "It's only an hour. What could possibly go wrong?"

Mrs. Fitzgerald gave him a look that indicated she believed a great deal could go wrong. But instead of voicing her concerns she gave him a brave little smile, placed her cell phone back in her purse, and crossed the threshold.

Father Lee let the door shut while letting out a sigh of relief. He didn't dislike Mrs. Fitzgerald. On the contrary, he greatly respected her. Every church needed a Mrs. Fitzgerald. These matronly ladies knew more about the day-to-day operations of a parish than any priest ever could and it was because he knew that he couldn't replace her that he had already decided not to try. He'd answer the phones but not the door. Let Janice deal with the visitors.

He'd just placed his hand on the "Back at One" sign when he heard a noise in the foyer. It sounded like a muffled yelp, as if someone had walked in too quickly and had to pull up short in order to avoid running into the wall.

Father Lee looked up to see the silhouette of a man in the glass door panels. The individual rattled the doorknob but couldn't get it open. Father Lee went over and opened the door.

"May I —" Standing in the vestibule was a tall, dark-eyed man wearing a wool overcoat and a fedora. He looked up with a start and gave Father Lee the same look you'd find on the face of a four year-old who's been caught trying to get into the cookie jar. "May I help you?" Father Lee finished.

The man nodded. "Ah, yes, I'd like to speak to a priest."

Father Lee paused for second. He knew he had on his black shirt, black pants, and white collar. "I'm a priest. My name is Father Lee. What can I do for you?" He stepped back to let the man in.

"A pleasure to meet you, Father," the man said as he entered the Rectory. He appeared fidgety and his eyes darted about as if he expected to find someone hiding in the shadows. Father Lee sighed. The mentally impaired could be a challenge. These people needed help, yet the city constantly certi-fied them healthy enough to be on their own. He was so accustomed to the poor souls turning up that he had the phone number of the local halfway house memorized.

"What can I do for you, my son?" Father Lee said, trying to sound warm and inviting.

The man, satisfied that they were alone, turned his attention back to Father Lee and smiled. It was a smile that made Father Lee cautious. "I'm in need of faith, Father. I was hoping you could provide some."

Father Lee nodded. "Yes, faith is something we all need. Are you Catholic? Do you wish to confess your sins?"

The man gave a shudder and stepped back as if threatened. "No, no, I ah, I just need some faith. I'm willing to pay."

Father Lee's eyes narrowed. "You want to *buy* some faith?"

The man must have realized that he'd made a mistake because a look of alarm flashed across his face. "No, of course not, what I meant to say is that I'll trade you for it." Reaching into his pocket he produced a small white goose feather.

"What's that," Father Lee asked, "the stuffing from your pillow?"

The man shook his head but didn't take offense. "This is a feather, taken from the right wing of the Archangel Michael, on the day he cast Lucifer into the pit of Hell." His voice held a smugness that seemed inappropriate given the claim.

Father Lee hesitated. "An angel's feather?" The man nodded his head. "And you'd be willing to give that to me in exchange for my . . . faith?"

"Yes," he confirmed, "do we have a deal?" He stuck out his hand, anxious to conclude the negotiations.

Father Lee felt sad for the man. He obviously didn't understand the nature of the bargain he wanted to strike. "I'm sorry but you can't trade away your faith."

This puzzled the man. "Why not? If one can sell his soul why can't another trade his faith?"

Good Lord, Father Lee thought, crazy and a philosopher. "Yes, well," Father Lee began, hoping to guide this man past his present obsession, "though a man may *metaphorically* sell his soul, faith isn't something you can pick up or put aside when it suits you. Faith is something you have despite what the world may tell you. It comes from your heart, your core, your very soul."

The stranger stared at him as if he were insane. Then, suddenly, his eyes widened and he started to laugh. "Ah, no, you misunderstand me. I don't want you to give *me* your faith. No, I want to engage your services as a man of faith. I want . . . to use your faith."

"You want what?"

The stranger sighed with frustration. "What I want is to trade you this feather for the use of your faith. Some men think that faith is something you have but not something you use. When the time comes, I want you to put your faith into practice."

Father Lee was impressed. Disturbed or not, this man was posing a profoundly spiritual question. "I think I understand what you're trying to say. There's more to faith then just belief. In order for faith to have any real value one must be willing to act on it. Yes?" The man nodded and held out the feather again.

"Why don't I," Father Lee said as he reached out and accepted the feather, "trade you something better than a promise of faith-based action. Why don't I take you next door to the community center and get you a hot cup of coffee and a sandwich? Later, I'll call the Fulton Street Mission and see if I can't get you a bed for the night. Deal?" He held up the feather expectantly.

The stranger gave him a shy smile. "Man does not live by bread alone."

"No," Father Lee agreed, and he slipped the feather into his pocket believing that a deal had been struck, "but with luck there might be some apple pie for dessert."

"Thank you but I have much to do before I sleep. Good day, Father." The man turned to leave.

"Hold on," Father Lee said, reaching out and catching the man by his sleeve. He was surprised by how cold the material felt. "What about the meal?"

"No time," the man said. "Oh, and these are for you." He reached into his pocket and pulled out a bundle of letters. "I brought in your mail."

Father Lee frowned. Mrs. Fitzgerald was supposed to do that. "Thank you." As the man thrust the envelopes into his hand, one of the cards fell and tumbled to the floor. "I've got it," Father Lee said as he picked up what looked like a party invitation. "Now, are you...?"

The man was gone.

Father Lee looked from left to right. The stranger had disappeared. "What . . ." He stepped forward and opened the door to the foyer. There was nobody there. "How odd?" He couldn't imagine anyone moving that fast but obviously the man had.

Looking down at the bundle of mail he glanced at the envelope that had fallen. It had neither a stamp nor a return address but it was addressed to him. Breaking the seal, he pulled out a card and recognized Father Vasquez's handwriting immediately. The letters were made with long fluid strokes that almost bordered on calligraphy. Father Vasquez was Father Lee's teacher, mentor, and dearest friend. He was also dying of lung cancer.

"Golden Gate Bridge. Tonight. 9 pm. Pole 69."

He turned the card over. It was blank. He turned the card over again and reread the note. Then it hit him. "Dear Lord, not . . ."

If the note had come from anyone else he would have dismissed it as a joke. Pole 69 was the single most popular spot on the Golden Gate Bridge for suicides. Father Lee wouldn't even know that morbid piece of trivia if it weren't for his work with Father Vasquez at the Fulton Street Mission. Despair and grief sometimes led to suicide. Was Father Vasquez trying to tell him that he had reached the end of his rope? During their last visit his friend hadn't seemed despondent. On the contrary, he vowed to keep fighting lest anyone think he'd gone soft on the devil. Father Vasquez believed that fighting any wrong was striking a blow against evil. He was incredibly medieval in that respect. He was also one of the finest and most steadfast men Father Lee had ever known. What could have happened to shake his resolve?

There was a sound in the foyer and Father Lee looked up thinking that his philosophical tramp had returned. This time though the inner door opened without any problem and he had to jump back in order to get out of the way. "Hey!"

The priest that stood in the doorway looked at him with sharp blue eyes. There was a momentary flash of alarm before the expression softened and the square-jawed young man appeared apologetic. "Forgive me; I did not know you were there."

Father Lee took a moment to catch his breath. "Obviously. May I help you?"

"Yes, I wish to see Father Timothy Lee."

Father Lee looked at the man. He'd never met this priest before. About twenty-five, the newcomer had sandy blonde hair and the rugged good looks of one who enjoyed physical activities. Broad-shouldered and powerfully built, he gave the appearance of being quite solid and reliable. Father Lee felt scrawny just standing next to him. "I'm Father Timothy Lee."

The young priest stepped forward and Father Lee felt compelled to back up and give him some space. The man glanced quickly around the room and unlike the previous visitor seemed a lot more confident of himself. Satisfied that they were alone he turned, smiled, and extended his hand. "I am Father Antonio Ravenna. I am here in San Francisco visiting and was hoping to see my old teacher, Father Vasquez."

Father Lee shook the young priest's hand. "A pleasure but I'm sorry to say that Father Vasquez is not here. He's being treated at St. Agnes for lung cancer. He's . . . very ill."

"Ah, yes," Father Ravenna answered. "But he is not in the hospital. He has checked himself out."

Father Lee was stunned. "What? Why would he —" The note sprung into mind – Pole 69.

Father Ravenna watched him intently. "You know where he is?" He asked, a little too casually.

Tim suddenly felt very conscious of the mail he was holding. Suicide is an unpardonable sin. Did the Church suspect Jose's state of mind? "No," he answered truthfully, "I don't where Father Vasquez is." Father Lee only knew where he would be — tonight.

This visiting priest though wasn't satisfied with his answer. "That is most unfortunate. I know you have not seen Father Vasquez in over a week but surely he told you of his plans. He has not tried to call you?"

Father Lee stiffened. How did this man know about his last visit with Jose? "No," he said, skirting the truth again, "Jose has not *called* me." He turned and placed the mail on the desk making sure to lay the card on the bottom.

Father Ravenna glanced briefly at the stack and then back at Tim. He must have realized that he'd pushed too hard because his demeanor softened. "My apologies. My desire to see Father Vasquez has made me rude. I am certain that if he had contacted you, you would have said so."

Father Lee didn't like this priest's tone. He sounded too much like a policeman. "Why are you looking for Jose?"

Father Ravenna smiled. "As I said, I was hoping to visit."

Tim also smiled. "Should I hear from Jose, I will tell him about you. How can you be reached?"

Despite the fact there was an implicit dismissal in his offer, Father Ravenna's face brightened. "That is most kind. Please, give him my card." He handed Father Lee a business card. It was completely blank except for a single telephone number. It wasn't for a phone in the U.S.

"I'd be happy to," Father Lee said as he pocketed the card.

Father Ravenna then gave him a polite nod. "Thank you. Now I will, as you say, get out of your hair." He quickly opened the door and walked out.

It had only been a brief conversation but Father Lee felt that he'd been thoroughly interrogated. Who was this Father Ravenna – and what did he want with Father Vasquez? Was he the reason Jose had fled into the night? Father Lee only had one chance before this evening's appointment to find out. He could only hope he was right.

The Fulton Street Mission was Father Vasquez's great purpose. The mission was a soup kitchen, homeless shelter, free clinic, and social advocacy group all rolled up into one. Father Vasquez called it a 'one stop shop for those in need.' It was also the most likely place that the priest would be found. Father Lee entered the mission and found himself immediately immersed in the hustle and bustle of an active charity.

"Father Lee!" Latisha Perkins called out from across the crowded room. The effusive black woman, who managed the waiting area, was Father Vasquez's version of Mrs. Fitzgerald. Younger and thinner, she had the same ability to know everything that was going on. Latisha walked up to Father Lee. "How ya doing, padre?"

Father Lee scanned the room for any sign of Jose. "Good, Tisha, you?"

The sharp-eyed woman raised an eyebrow. "You wanna try that again? You know a priest ain't supposed to lie."

Father Lee didn't argue the point. "Have you seen Father Vasquez?" He could tell from her face that she had. "Tisha, it's very important. I *need* to see him."

Latisha squirmed under his intense scrutiny. "He said he didn't want anyone to know he was here but I don't think he meant you." She pulled him aside. "To tell the truth Father, I'm glad you came. He said the hospital told him he could go home but that don't mean he's well enough to work. You think you can talk him into going home early?"

Father Lee almost laughed. Even on a good day that would be hard to do. "He's in his office?" Latisha nodded and Father Lee turned towards the administrative wing.

"He's working on another grant proposal," Latisha confirmed. "You know him, he never gives up."

Those words echoed in Father Lee's head. What changed? Why go to Pole 69? Father Lee could hear his friend's painful hacking coughs long before he reached the door to the office. "What in God's name is going on?" He demanded as he burst through the door.

Father Vasquez sat at his desk. Middle aged, gray-haired, with the ruddy complexion of an Andalusian, the priest was huddled over a stack of papers holding a bloody handkerchief to his lips. "Tim," he said as if he'd been expecting him, "so nice of you to drop by. Come in."

Father Lee shut the door, moved towards the only other chair in the room, and sat down. "What are you doing here?"

"Working. What do you think I'm doing?"

"Hiding from your doctors. You're supposed to be in the hospital."

Father Vasquez gave a dismissive wave. "Bah, what do doctors know?"

"They're trying to help you."

Father Vasquez suddenly seemed aware of the handkerchief in his hand. The flecks of blood that stained it stood in vibrant testimony to the assistance he needed. He put it out of sight. "Some things only God can help."

Father Lee knew now was the time to ask about Pole 69. "Is that why you sent me that note? Do you plan to test God?"

Father Vasquez stared at him. "Is that what you think?"

"What else am I supposed to think?" Father Lee answered, feeling he needed to defend himself. "You flee the hospital. You send me cryptic notes. What else could it mean?"

For the first time in a long time Father Vasquez did not come back at him with a ready comment. The old priest mulled the situation over and began nodding his head. "I'm sorry, you're right. Given the evidence, I can see how you might reach such a conclusion. Though, I would have hoped that you would know me better than that."

"Then what is this about?"

Father Vasquez shrugged. "I was planning to tell you tonight but I don't see why this afternoon wouldn't be as good. There are some stories that should only be told by the light of day and others that can only be believed under a cloak of darkness. I will tell you what I know now and hope that you will come to believe it later." Father Lee remained still. He'd never heard Father Vasquez speak this way.

"Let's start with the obvious, I'm dying. I don't have much longer and my life is in God's hands." Father Lee opened his mouth to protest but Father Vasquez raised a finger to stop him. "My life has always been in God's hands. This is not something new." Father Lee relented. It was a good perspective.

"No, what matters is that I've devoted my life to the service of God and the betterment of my fellow men. Tonight I intend to give my life in defense of those two very important causes." Father Lee leaned forward to comment but again Father Vasquez raised a finger. "Let me finish. Then, you can say what you think." Father Lee nodded that he would.

Father Vasquez leaned back in his chair and folded his hands across his belly. "Have you ever heard the word: Sha'Daa?" Father Lee shook his head. "It is not Latin, nor Greek, nor any other language spoken today. I half believe it is not of any language ever spoken by man. What I do believe is that it is another term for an apocalypse."

Father Lee couldn't help himself. "You're referring to the Day of Judgment?"

"Hardly. This isn't about the Second Coming of Christ; it's about evil trying to invade our world."

Father Lee's eyes narrowed. "The Bible speaks of the end of days. Does Sha'Daa refer to that?"

Father Vasquez sighed with annoyance. "Are you going to let me tell this or not?" Father Lee held up his hand in a conciliatory manner. "The Bible speaks of THE end of days. Sha'Daa refers to an apocalyptic event that occurs every ten thousand years. It's a time when demons can breach the walls of our reality and wage war against men. It is not the end of everything but it can be the end of everything we hold dear. It's a very crucial time and it's coming."

Father Vasquez paused for a moment and ran a hand through his thinning hair. "When I was in Rome studying to be a priest, I came across certain documents in the Vatican Library. As you can imagine, the Vatican has many rare and unusual books. In truth, I don't believe that I was supposed to find these tomes but sometimes God chooses our path for us. These books spoke of the Sha'Daa and they astounded me. But when I brought these books to the attention of my superiors they were confiscated. I was told that they were heresies and to forget them. But I couldn't. So I continued to research and corroborate what I had learned. I suppose it was this research that eventually drew the attention of a small group of priests who have been guarding the secrets of the Sha'Daa since time immemorial." Father Lee raised his hand like a child sitting in Sunday School. Father Vasquez relented. "Yes?"

"The Church has only existed for a little over two thousand years. How could the Vatican have evidence that predates this?"

Father Vasquez shrugged. "The original documents were not made by Christians."

"You were reading pagan prophecies?" Father Lee looked incredulous.

"The battle between good and evil predates the church, Tim. The war has been fought since the beginning of time." Father Lee nodded his head understanding. "In any case, these priests indoctrinated me into a holy order. Our purpose is to be vigilant against the demon incursions. When we detect one, we are to stand against the monsters. Sadly, as I now sit riddled with this cursed disease, I believe that I have determined the time and place of the next incursion."

Father Lee stared at him. "Tonight. Pole 69."

"Correct."

Father Lee could feel his heart sink. It *was* madness. "Jose, that makes no sense. The bridge has existed for a little over a hundred years. It spans a bay your ancients knew nothing about. How could these prophesies name this place and time?"

"Really, Tim," Father Vasquez said, trying to keep from sounding disappointed, "you speak as if you know all there is to know about prophesies. They didn't name the place or time. They described it. Why do you think I took up residence in San Francisco? Because it matched the description of the place. And why do you think I believe it's the bridge? Because the incursion will come at a place that is neither land nor sea yet is awash with despair. Tell me that doesn't sound like Pole 69? And the bridge hovers in the air – neither land nor sea. It makes perfect sense."

"And you believe that these prophesies will come true tonight?" Father Vasquez nodded. "What, exactly, is it you intend to do?"

"I intend to seal the breach."

"How?"

Father Vasquez's voice faltered. "By throwing myself into the gates of Hell I will prevent the demons from emerging."

"You're talking suicide!"

"No," Father Vasquez countered. "I am sacrificing myself so that the world may be spared a great evil."

Father Lee threw up his hands. "You're taking your own life."

Father Vasquez suddenly lost all of his self-assurance. "Maybe not," he said softly, "that's why I asked you to meet me on the bridge. I'm not sure I'm strong enough to do this on my own. I was hoping you would assist me."

Father Lee's eyes grew wide. "Are you asking me to push you?"

Father Vasquez stared at his hands.

Father Lee couldn't find the words to express his dismay at having been asked such a thing. When he finally could speak he chose to redirect the conversation. "Have you told anyone else about this?"

"Only my contacts within the order. Though, to be honest, I'm not sure they got the message. My order has had to be very secretive of late."

Father Lee nodded his head. "That would explain why, just after I received your note, a priest came looking for you. His name is Father Ravenna." Father Lee reached into his pocket and drew out the business card. With it he also pulled out the white feather he was given. Father Lee passed over the business card and as Father Vasquez examined it, Father Lee began to play with the feather. He twirled it between his fingers and stroked the incredibly soft edges. It felt like the only sane thing he'd done all day.

"This is just a phone number," Father Vasquez said as if it were some sort of joke. "And the number is in Rome."

Father Vasquez nodded his head. "He said he was a former student of yours."

Father Vasquez's eyes lost focus as he searched his memory. "I can't say that I ever taught a Father Ravenna." He then caught sight of the feather in Father Lee's hand. "What's that?"

Father Lee looked up and then smiled self-consciously. "It's an angel's feather. At least, that's what the homeless man who gave it to me claimed. Needless to say, it's been an odd day."

Father Vasquez extended a hand. "May I?" Father Lee relinquished the feather to his examination. "I would have said it was a goose feather. You say a homeless man gave it to you?"

"Traded, actually, he wanted the use of my faith."

Father Vasquez handed the feather back. "How strange. I would have thought that if the man believed in angels he would have known that simply accepting this as an angel's feather is all the faith you need."

"Excuse me?"

Father Vasquez frowned. "It's what I've been talking to you about for the last twenty minutes. It's a question of faith. How do you know that what you are holding is *not* an angel's feather?"

Father Lee shook his head. "Logic dictates —"

"Right there," Father Vasquez said angrily, "is your problem – logic is for those who lack faith. Faith is believing without the need of proof."

Father Lee held up the feather so that it caught the light. Despite all the handling it was still a brilliant white. "So, believing that this is an angel's feather makes it so?"

"As much as believing that it isn't means it's not."

Father Lee stuck the feather back in his pocket. "If we all accepted that sort of circular logic then no one could ever be called insane. There's a difference between belief and delusion."

Father Vasquez leaned forward. "So which am I: devoutly faithful or seriously deluded?"

Before Father Lee could answer there was a commotion from down the hall. Raised voices could be heard. "I asked you where you think you are going?" It was Latisha.

"I need to see Father Vasquez," a male voice answered her. Father Ravenna had arrived.

"This priest," Father Vasquez said, "is he young, athletic, looks like he could be a soldier?"

Father Lee stared at him. "So you *do* know him."

Father Vasquez shook his head. "No, but I think I know who sent him. You mustn't be found here. Quick, out the back door." He rose and walked to a door that Father Lee hadn't even noticed. Given that Father Vasquez's office was nothing more than a converted storeroom, it wasn't surprising that it had a back door. Father Vasquez produced a key and unlocked it.

"What about you?" Father Lee demanded. "Are you in any danger?"

Father Vasquez shook his head. "This man is not a threat, at least, not a physical one. But if he finds you here your career as a priest may come to an end. You must go. I'll distract him and then make my own escape. I'll meet you tonight on the bridge." Father Lee began to protest but Father Vasquez didn't let him. "If what I told you does not come to pass, I will go with you to St. Agnes and check myself back in. Now, go."

There was a crash as one of the doors further down the hall was kicked in. Latisha's voice rose in alarm. "Sir, I'm going to call the police!"

"Yes," Father Ravenna said, "do that. We can use their help." Another one of the doors down the hall was opened as Father Ravenna began to search a second room.

Father Lee shook his head with dismay. "What is happening to the world that I should be running from a priest?"

Father Vasquez gave him a humorless smile. "I thought I told you – it's coming to an end."

The dank San Francisco fog rolled in with surprising speed. Draping itself across the Golden Gate Bridge like an old blanket, it obscured everything from sight. Even the headlights of automobiles a few feet away seemed lost in a fuzzy dream. The effect was rather disconcerting.

"This is insane," Father Lee muttered, pulling up his collar against the light rain that began to fall. He didn't even know if Father Vasquez had escaped. And if Father Vasquez had, was he now supposed to stand idly by and watch the man commit suicide?

"Hello Tim," a voice called out. Father Lee turned to see Father Vasquez emerging from the fog. Bundled tightly in a heavy overcoat, the aging priest approached slowly, as if aware of the gravity of his actions.

"You made it." Father Lee said, almost disappointed.

"When necessary, Latisha can run quite a bit of interference," Father Vasquez answered with a chuckle. "So, do you still think I'm insane?"

Father Lee grimaced. "I can't watch you commit suicide. If that's what you're asking."

Father Vasquez nodded his head. "Nor will you." He turned and grasped the railing in both hands. "I don't plan to walk out on that ledge without a good reason. I'll stay right here and wait for evidence that the demons are attacking. And, as promised, if nothing happens I will admit that I was wrong and go back to St. Agnes."

"Jose," Father Lee said as relief washed over him, "that's wonder—"

"But," Father Vasquez continued, "if the breach does come, you must promise to help me do whatever it takes to seal it. Agreed?"

Father Lee saw no problem with the bargain. It was only a few minutes till nine. When nothing happened Father Vasquez would be bound by his own words to return to the hospital. "Agreed," he said, feeling more confident than he had in days. "So, what do we do now?"

"Now, you will come with me," a new voice said from behind them. Both priests turned to find Father Ravenna standing behind them. "Father Vasquez," the young man called out, "I am charged by the Holy Church to place you in protective custody. Father Lee," he gave the priest a stern look, "*we* need to talk."

Father Vasquez glanced at Father Lee before answering. "You don't have any authority here." It was bravely stated but Father Lee could hear the doubt beneath the words.

Father Ravenna was very still. "My authority comes from Rome. If you had consented to meet with me I would have shown you my papers." He raised a hand holding what appeared to be a letter.

"Fine," Father Vasquez conceded, "I understand completely. I'll just —" He turned quickly and attempted to throw a leg over the railing. But before he had a chance to climb the fence Father Ravenna was upon him.

"Father!" The younger man cried grabbing a hold of his shoulders. "What you are attempting to do is unforgivable."

"What I am attempting to do is save humanity!" Father Vasquez shouted as he struggled to break free. Father Lee wasn't sure what to do. He stared squinting at the struggling men as the wind, having picked up moisture from the bay, blew salt water in his face.

"This is a delusion," Father Ravenna countered firmly, and not without some sympathy, "sparked by a mind confused by pain. It has no basis in truth. You must see that."

Father Vasquez turned to Father Lee. "Tim, help me! We must be here when the Sha'Daa begins!"

Father Lee stepped forward but Father Ravenna froze him with a stare. "You," he said as he tightened his grip on Father Vasquez, "should have told me what you knew. He is your friend. How could you allow him to…?"

Father Lee blocked out the rest. While the younger priest lectured him Tim became aware of a throbbing sound. He realized that it had been there all along, just under the level of conscious perception. But now, as the wind whipped about them and sea spray peppered them, the sound was quite audible. It was like the beating of drums. He looked up to find Father Ravenna staring at him as if expecting a reply. "What's that sound?"

"What?" Father Ravenna couldn't believe that he hadn't been listening.

"That sound," Father Lee prompted. "Don't you hear it?"

"Look!" Father Vasquez shouted, "it's begun!"

The two of them turned to where Father Vasquez was pointing. Just off the bridge and slightly below them a bright light appeared. Father Lee's first thought was that it was a helicopter on a collision course with the bridge but he could see that the light wasn't moving. It was just hovering there pulsating with the beat of the drums.

"What is it?" Father Ravenna asked. "A boat?"

"Not this high up," Father Vasquez ventured. "What do you think, Tim?"

"I think we should get off the bridge." But nobody moved.

As they spoke a hole opened in the middle of the sky. Tendrils of mist now swirled around a central opening as the fog fought from being consumed. It was as if the world was being drawn into a black abyss.

Father Vasquez struggled in Father Ravenna's grip "You must let me do this."

Father Ravenna's resolve though was unbroken. "It's just an odd weather pattern."

Father Lee was the one to answer him. "No, it's not." He watched the roiling mass of clouds. "You know it's not. If you were sent by Rome then you know what he's talking about. You've probably even read the documents he's been referring to."

Father Ravenna hesitated before reluctantly confirming the truth. "If I had," he said, "I would have seen them as nothing more than a few interesting historical notes written by those who did not know the truth of Christ's teachings, nor the greatness of God's love."

Father Lee shook his head. Why is it that the most devout are often the most close-minded? "Perhaps they did know the greatness of God's love. Perhaps that is why they wrote their prophesies. Jose," he said turning to Father Vasquez, "how do we close the breach?" He was being forced to shout now. The wind was so great that it almost drowned out their voices.

"The prophesies said that we must be like the angels in heaven, steadfast in our resolve. We must drive the devil back into the pit of Hell."

Father Lee took this in. "And how do we do that?"

Father Vasquez blinked several times before he answered. "The documents implied that someone had to physically push the devil back into the hole from which he is trying to emerge. That is why I must leap from the bridge and drive him back."

"The documents *implied*?" Father Lee demanded.

"Now you see why I was sent," Father Ravenna interjected. "This prophesies are filled with poetic imagery – not facts and figures. A logical investigation of these documents concluded that they are no more factual than the myths of the ancient Greeks."

Logic is for those who lack faith – or so Father Vasquez had told him. Father Lee reached into his pocket and drew out the feather. And a feather, given to you by a homeless man, can be an angel's feather if you believe it to be so. It was all a question of faith.

"Sweet Mother of God," Father Vasquez said from in front of him. They all looked again.

The fog had begun to take shape. Father Lee couldn't believe it, but the hole in the fog had begun to coalesce into the unmistakable jaws of a fanged creature. It was the maw of a ravenous beast and every fiber of Lee's being told him it was evil. Suddenly, there was the sound of screeching tires followed by the sickening crunch of metal on metal. They weren't the only ones seeing this.

They turned to the sounds of more screeching tires as new vehicles came upon the scene of the accident. Though partly obscured by the fog, Father Lee could see the battered vehicles as they came to rest transfixed in each other's headlights. One was beginning to sprout tendrils of flame. One of the drivers, having climbed out to examine her vehicle, looked up in their direction and screamed.

Father Lee spun around. Out over the water, the monster that had taken possession of the fog was fully formed. It resembled a wolf. The disembodied head flexed its jaws and gnashed its teeth as a tongue, made of crimson light, slithered over the fangs and tasted the air about it. The eyes spun in their sockets to take in the length of the bridge. There was no question that it was alive — and that it was aware of them.

Before anyone could react though, the monster's crimson tongue shot out and struck the bridge. There was a shudder in the superstructure as the monster connected with one of the support towers. Then, the tongue lolled lazily over the connecting cables causing them to whine like the plucked strings of a guitar. Two snapped and went whizzing into the darkness.

Father Vasquez turned to look at Father Lee. "We must seal the portal. Tim," he said desperately, "*help* me."

Father Lee was acutely aware of the feather in his hand. It was a question of faith. "Father Ravenna is right," he declared. "You were never meant to do this."

Father Vasquez stared at him with shock and disbelief. Then, Father Lee held up the feather. Realization filled the old man's eyes. Father Vasquez turned, grabbed a hold of Father Ravenna's coat, and began screaming wildly. "I won't let you take me back! We must close the portal!" Confronted for the first time with actual resistance, Father Ravenna attempted to pull Father Vasquez off the railing. That left Father Lee free to act.

Crossing himself with the hand that held the angel's feather he kissed it once. There could be no room for doubt. He had to believe that what he was about to do was for the good of all mankind. He had to believe that armed with an angel's feather, he could drive the hosts from Hell back into the abyss. Father Lee hopped over the railing and ran out onto a girder. He could hear Father Ravenna shout: "No!"

Father Lee stumbled along a few feet as he approached the edge. Behind him he could hear a struggle. He had no time to waste. With a silent prayer he spread his arms and leapt off the edge — into the jaws of Hell.

At first it felt as if he were floating. Then, when nothing seemed to happen, Father Lee opened his eyes to discover that he was, in fact, floating. Hot acrid air was blowing up at him. Somehow it held him up as if he were a feather caught in a breeze.

"*Is this the best you can do?*" A voice that sounded like the cracking of stones called out to him. Father Lee looked down and the face of evil was now fully animated and staring at him. "*You seek to defeat me with a chicken feather?*"

Father Lee stared at the devil and felt oddly calm. "It's a feather from the right wing of the Archangel Michael," he answered. "You could not pass him and you will not pass me."

The monster glared at him. "*You don't truly believe that. You spout pretty words because you are afraid to die!*" The creature's tongue shot out and missed him by mere inches. It struck the bridge for a second time and there was the sharp twang of cables snapping.

Father Lee didn't even flinch as the foul appendage skimmed past him. Instead, he stared deep into the monster's eyes. "No," he answered, "I'm not afraid. Death is inevitable. But what you do with your life is your choice. I choose to lay down mine in defense of my world." And he thrust the angel feather out in front of him.

The beast below him bellowed in pain. The sound was so powerful that it lifted Father Lee up several feet. "*You are weak,*" it screamed. "*You will fail!*"

"But my belief is strong," Father Lee countered. "It will prevail."

Suddenly there was an explosive release of putrid air and Father Lee found himself spinning head over heels. The bridge and the concerned faces of the men standing there shot past him as his view altered from bridge, to water, to fog, to sky and back again. He was at a loss as to what to do next when his out of control spin was brought to an abrupt halt and he found himself hanging upside down facing the beast. A hand clutched his ankle. A quick glance revealed that Father Ravenna was now holding him steady.

"Hold on, Tim," Father Vasquez cried out as he reached for Father Lee's other leg.

Below him the creature writhed and moaned like a wounded animal. But a wounded animal can be extremely dangerous. Father Lee knew he had to do something before the creature lashed out again. He had to drive the demon back through the portal but so long as he had the feather he could not fall. There was only one thing to do. Father Lee brought the feather up to his lips, gave it a kiss, then he let it go.

The feather fell as if it were made of lead. It plunged straight down into the heart of the beast. The monster saw it coming and screamed in terror. Lights exploded around him. Sound ripped through him. Father Lee suddenly felt himself fall as the power that had held him up was withdrawn. With surprising relief, he felt the hands grasping him by his ankles hold tight. Father Lee looked up between his legs to see the two men steadfastly holding on to him.

An hour later, the three priests sat in the kitchen of the South Street Mission. Father Vasquez made them a large pot of coffee to chase away the evening chill and they listened as the news reported that, due to an unusually thick fog, there had been a multi-car pile up on the Golden Gate Bridge. The accident had resulted in structural damage that would take several days to assess. There was no mention of the priests even being there.

"So," Father Vasquez said, with something akin to glee in his voice, "still think I'm crazy?"

Father Ravenna stared into the depths of his cup. "No, I do not."

"What will you tell your superiors?" Father Lee asked. "It won't be easy for them to admit they were wrong."

Father Ravenna however was a pragmatist. "The truth. I am not known for my wild imagination. When I tell them what I saw it will change certain policies."

Father Vasqeuz grinned. "Good, because I can use some help. I'm not a healthy man."

Father Ravenna sat up in his chair. "Yes, of course, I will petition Rome immediately. There are several scholars who would be perfectly —"

"I'll take Father Lee," Father Vasquez cut him off.

"Excuse me?"

Father Vasquez smiled and it was the smile of man who held all the cards. "Oh, I'll take a few men of learning," he confirmed, "but what I really need is a man of faith. And there's no one I can think of with greater faith than Father Lee." He then turned to his friend. "What do you say, Tim? Feel like spending your days fighting the good fight: handing out sandwiches, filling out forms, and begging corporations for donations?"

Father Lee allowed himself a small laugh. "And occasionally battling demons for the salvation of humanity?

Father Vasquez shrugged. "It can't all be fun and games. We do have to do some work."

And for a brief moment, the kitchen of the Fulton Street Mission was filled with laughter — the laughter of three men who knew the true value of faith.

The Milk Of Paradise

BAK ALWAYS GOT A KICK OUT OF NEW patrons who'd never heard of the Triple-Six Tavern, the most legendary of brew holes. No doubt this was because, ultimately, the tavern didn't really exist at all. That is, it doesn't exist like other bars, in the here and now, fixed in one spot, one locale, nailed to a single dimension, and timeline. Though it appears to be carved out of the heart of some giant mountain, with glowing priceless crystals lining the giant domed ceiling and wondrously illuminating the interior, its foundations are imbedded in no land, no place. And to exit it through one of the many shadowy entrances and doorways and portals on its far wall is to return to that which you had left, suddenly finding yourself standing beside a closet door, stairwell entrance, or even an elevator, ordinary back barroom doors to the mundane.

The Triple-Six Tavern is actually that famous drinking hole only whispered about in quiet shadowed corners throughout the ages. It's that wonderful mystical place of welcome that so many sobering customers blurt about late in the morning, grieving over the fact they cannot remember how they had discovered it in the first place and now cannot find their way back. Karitas, the Fields of Elysia, Cheers, Trail's End, the Big Rock Candy Mountain, Houlihans…yep. The Triple-Six is the mother of all those famous bar myths, the truth behind the fiction, and the inspiration for a worn traveler's dream of respite.

As you sow...

By Paul Barrett

AS LAST MEALS WENT, IT WASN'T MUCH, but it was the best Horace Vesper could do with his limited cooking skills.

Horace removed the plastic wrapper, laid it aside, and took his place at the table, the same place he had eaten for the better part of seventy-eight years. The dinner's aroma hit his nose and his mouth watered despite knowing better. He picked up his fork and stabbed a slab of processed turkey meat.

Once, this pathetic repast would have been unthinkable. His wife Penny would have never allowed such a travesty as a packaged meal past her threshold, much less fouling her air with its imitation scents of home cooking. But that was years ago, when Penny was alive and Horace cared, a time when laughter and people filled the farmhouse.

He stuffed the meat into his mouth and chewed with his dentures, imitation teeth chewing imitation food. An apt metaphor for the imitation of life his existence had become.

He swallowed, barely tasting the food. He suddenly didn't feel hungry, but he would force himself to finish, right down to the last crumb of the apple dessert. Then he would drink his glass of beer, one of the few things he still enjoyed, and that would be it.

As he went to scoop up the second wafer of turkey, his eyes fell on the gun. A Colt Army 1860 revolver, a relic of the Civil War, passed down through the Vesper family over the years, finally to come to him. Horace had a son to pass it on to, although he doubted the ungrateful bastard would want it. Randy had left as soon as possible and hadn't looked back. Farming was a dying profession, he said. Family farms were giving way to conglomerates, and Randy refused to dedicate his life to something that would soon cease to exist.

Horace never figured out which bothered him more, that Randy ran away from his obligation, or that he had been correct in doing so.

The gun's blue barrel smiled at Horace, promising peace, something he had not known for a while. He had cleaned and loaded all six chambers, although he hoped one would be sufficient. Fourteen inches of cold metal, ready to take him from this earth to…well, he didn't really know.

As he chewed on the second piece of turkey, someone knocked at the door. It surprised him so much he almost choked on the food. Wouldn't that have been an irony, he thought. He couldn't remember the last time there had been an unannounced visitor. The landlord always called and the farm was too far out for salesmen to bother. The few friends Horace once had were either dead or in nursing homes, and Penny's family hadn't spoken to him since her death. They blamed him for keeping her on the farm.

He took a swallow of beer to clear the taste of gravy from his mouth. He decided not to answer. He would sit at the table until whoever stood at the door left. Then he'd finish his meal, take a bath, go out to the cornfield, and blow his brains out. This was not a time for company. Answering the door would change his plans, disturb his ritual, and he was too set in his ways for such disruption.

His resolve lasted for ten seconds, before ingrained Southern hospitality and natural curiosity overrode it. Horace stood and hobbled toward the door.

The unknown visitor had patience. The farmhouse was large, the dining area fifty feet from the hallway that led to the front door. Arthritis made every step an exercise in dull ache. He expected to hear a second, more insistent knock, but it didn't come.

Probably already left, Horace thought, and I'm wasting my time.

He reached the large oak door and opened it. The early evening sun hit his eyes. Horace brought his left hand up to block the brightness. A man stood at the bottom of the three steps leading to the porch, but his face sat level with Horace's. It was hard for Horace to see that face, silhouetted as it was by the sun and further hidden by a wide-brimmed hat. Few of the stranger's features were obvious beyond the fedora and a long trench coat. Horace thought of the Hollywood gangsters of his youth and wondered if the man had a machine gun concealed under his duster.

Now you're just being a silly old man, Horace chided himself. This wasn't the forties and gangsters didn't wear such getups anymore. Now they wore three-piece suits and controlled Wall Street.

Despite the strange clothing, Horace didn't sense any malice from the man. But he didn't trust his intuition. After all, he hadn't been able to sense that his own brother was going to sell the farmhouse out from under him.

"Can I help you?" Horace asked even as he closed the door a foot, ready to slam it if the man came toward him.

"Perhaps. And perhaps I can help you," the man said. His voice had an almost sing-song quality to it.

"I don't need any help," Horace said.

The man cocked his head, throwing his face deeper in shadow and reminding Horace of an inquisitive dog. "Come now, sir. Anybody who plans to shoot themselves in the mouth isn't exactly in high cotton."

Horace stepped back in shock. "What are you talking about?"

The man walked up the steps. "Sir, my time is short and I have none to spare for ignorance or denials. You want to kill yourself, and you plan to do it this very evening, right after you finish your beer. What if I told you that, within two hours time, you'll have a reason to live? And shortly after that, there's a good chance you won't survive the night?" The man smiled, and despite the shadows, Horace caught the gleam of a gold tooth.

"Who are you?"

"That is a question for the ages, but most people just call me the Salesman."

A salesman. Horace understood that. He didn't know how this odd, fedora-wearing man knew about his plans, and didn't really want to, but he knew how to handle salesmen. "I'm not interested." He started to close the door.

"You are if you want to see the sunrise tomorrow."

Horace opened the door. "Is that a threat?" He could care less about the sunrise, but he'd be damned if he'd let some crazy drifter menace him. "Because if it is, you and I have a problem, and I've got the solution."

He lifted the Colt revolver and pointed it at the man's chest, and then stared at the gun in shock. He didn't remember bringing it with him, and couldn't even recall having it during the conversation. Only now that he saw it did its weight, two pounds of metal and death, register in his hand.

The Salesman pushed back his fedora. "Ah, that's exactly what I need. And I have the perfect trade." He reached inside his coat and Horace expected a gun to come from its depths. Horace pulled back the Colt's hammer. At the first sign of a weapon, he would shoot, no questions asked.

Instead, the Salesman pulled out a spark plug.

Horace stared at the plug, long and white, with a metal terminal on one end and the familiar curved shape of the electrode at the other, and wondered if he was going senile. Maybe this whole thing was a hallucination. But he wondered if hallucinations would include motes of dust floating behind the Salesman's head, or the dry, grassy smell of mature corn, or even the uneven brown color of the man's coat.

"Wanna trade?" the Salesman said as he held the plug toward Horace.

Horace uncocked the pistol, but didn't lower it. "Why in the Sam Hill would I want to trade you an antique worth thousands of dollars for an eighty-nine cent spark plug?"

"To save your life."

"I don't care about my life, remember?"

"Then how about the life of the one you love."

Horace stared at the floor. "The only one I love is dead."

"That's about to change," the salesman said. "Look at me."

Horace looked up. The Salesman removed his hat, revealing fine blond hair that hung to just above his shoulders. His eyes were the dead black orbs of a shark, and his skin was pale but unlined. He gave Horace the impression of an old soul in a young body.

"It's a simple trade," the Salesman said. "If you don't care about your life, then what does the value of a gun matter? You're a good Southern gentleman, so I'm sure you have more in the house, should you decide to take the easy way."

"Perhaps," Horace said, not exactly sure what he was agreeing to. "But why in hell would I need a spark plug?"

"For your combine, which is the only thing that will save you this night."

This guy really is crazy, Horace thought. But he was also right about one thing. Horace had other guns. Any of them would do the trick. He didn't need the Colt. He didn't need the spark plug either, but he was ready to be rid of this lunatic. "Fine," Horace said. "It's a trade."

As Horace took the spark plug and handed over the gun, he wondered if the insane punk would turn it around and shoot him. He didn't really care. He just wanted to be either dead or left alone.

But the Salesman simply lodged the gun into some hidden pocket and put his hat back on. "One last thing," the Salesman said. "Two hours. Wait two hours before you put a bullet between your eyes. It could make a world of difference. For you and the world."

"Sure," Horace said. A wind whipped up, bringing dust and a smell of fur. The goats nattered in alarm, and Horace blinked his eyes against the stinging dirt. He opened them a few seconds later and the porch was empty. The wind died. Horace leaned out and looked around. No sign of the strange man. The six goats looked at him from their pen, as if questioning his sanity.

"Shut up," he told them, and went back into the house.

He returned to the table to find a cold dinner and warm beer. He threw the plastic tray away, then dumped and refilled the beer. As he sipped at the cold brew, he pondered the Salesmen's words. The man was insane, but Horace couldn't dismiss him out of hand, much as he wanted. Two hours, the man asked. Why not, Horace thought. He was seventy-eight years old. What was two more hours?

The wind blew against the old farmhouse, making a wailing sound, like mourners at a funeral. Horace shivered and polished off the beer. He would have no mourners. It was possible no one would even discover his body until the harvest.

Horace pulled the spark plug out of his overall pocket and looked at it. Nothing special about it. Just your average spark plug, so there was no way it would start up the combine. After all, the machine needed eight, so unless seven more people came by to trade, this plug was as useless and unneeded as he was.

With a snort, Horace stuffed it back into his pocket. Two hours. Might as well sit on the porch and enjoy his last sunset.

Storm clouds rolled in and obscured the sunset, so Horace didn't get to see it. That just fits, Horace thought as the wind rustled the trees and brought the smell of distant rain. The goats continued their nervous bleating, spooked by the rumble of thunder.

Horace looked at his watch and saw the two hours he promised had almost passed. He felt a fool for even bothering to listen to the crazy man. He stood and moved toward the door. The shotgun would do fine. A little more difficult to maneuver and a lot messier, but it didn't matter.

He had his hand on the doorknob when the sound of a motor caught his attention. Some sort of silver sports car rumbled down his long driveway, halogen headlights burning clean white through the approaching darkness. Irritated at yet another interruption, Horace waited as the car approached.

It stopped short of the porch and the lights went out. Both doors opened and two figures, a man and a young girl, stepped out. Another gust of wind blew and fat drops of rain began to fall. The two people ran onto the covered porch. Horace stepped inside the doorway and looked at them. The man seemed mid thirties with thick brown, wavy hair and close-set brown eyes. He was average height, with the beginning of a paunch showing beneath his blue Polo shirt. He wore khaki pants.

The girl standing to the man's left could have been anywhere from nine to twelve. She had hair the same color as the man's, cut short and curved in at the ends, but her eyes were blue and wide. She stood a foot shorter than the man and wore blue jeans and a shirt with a drawing of a cat holding a samurai sword.

"Horace Vesper?" the man asked.

A bright flash of lightning, thunder and the shrill cry of the goats kept Horace from answering immediately. When he did, he said, "Who wants to know?"

"My name is Franklin." He held out his hand. "Franklin Vesper."

The rain picked up. "Vesper?" Horace said. "What are you, some distant cousin?"

"No," the man said. "I'm your grandson."

Horace took a step back. Was it possible? Horace hadn't spoken to his son in over forty years, so yes, it was quite possible. He looked closer at the man. The resemblance was there, in the set of the jaw and roundness of the face. "Grandson?"

"Yes," the man said as he lowered his hand. "We need your help." He looked at the girl. "This–"

A blur of white came over the porch railing and slammed into Franklin's side, tumbling him into the girl and sending them both to the floor. With a long bleat, the goat shook its head, lowered it, and rammed its five-inch horns into Franklin's stomach.

Franklin released a shocked grunt, and the girl screamed. Horace, stunned, did nothing as the goat pulled back, horns coated in blood, and stabbed Franklin again. The girl screamed louder and Franklin's face contorted with pain, his eyes wide and breath raspy.

It finally dawned on Horace this was really happening. The normally docile Billy goat was attacking someone. Horace stepped forward. With all the strength his arthritic bones could muster, he kicked the goat in the side. Blood spattered the porch as the horns pulled from Franklin's stomach. The goat skidded across the porch and down the three steps, but maintained its footing.

"Get inside," Horace told the crying girl as he bent down and grabbed Franklin's arm. He tugged with all his strength and, slowly, Franklin slid across the porch.

The goat bounded up the stairs, head lowered for another attack.

The girl screamed again, this time in fury, as her leg lashed out and caught the creature under the chin. The goat's head snapped up and it tumbled ass over applecart down the steps. It landed on its back with a loud bleat, legs kicking.

"Get away from my father," the girl shouted, fists clenched as she stared at the downed goat. Horace kept dragging Franklin toward the house. The wounded man groaned and did his best to help, but he was almost dead weight.

The goat righted itself, and Horace noticed the other five goats trotting up, until all six stood at the bottom of the stairs. They stared up at Horace. Their eyes glowed red and Horace's knees almost gave out.

The girl stepped between the animals and her father. "Go away," she said. They didn't retreat, but they didn't attack. They milled about bleating, as if confused. Horace felt the same way.

He finally got the man over the threshold and far enough inside to close the door. "Get in here, girl."

The girl backed up, still facing the goats. It had to be a trick of what little light remained in the storm-darkened sky, but Horace thought he saw a glow around her.

She backed into the hall. No sooner had she closed the door than Horace heard the goats yammer in concert, followed by the thud of running hooves. The door rattled as the animals slammed into it. The girl turned and looked at Horace, her confidence gone and fear in her blue eyes.

"Help me with your father."

As the goats battered against the door, Horace and the girl dragged the wounded man down the short hall and into the living room, his body sliding slowly but easily on the wooden floor.

Horace knelt down, his breath short and arms aching. He ripped open the torn Polo shirt. A gasp from the girl drew his attention and he looked up to her pale face and wide eyes as she saw her father's injuries. Horace pointed through a doorway. "Kitchen's in there. Towels in the drawer by the sink. Go get them." The girl didn't move. "Now!"

Her head snapped up. A slight hesitation, then she nodded and ran from the room.

Horace studied the stomach wounds. He had been in Korea and seen plenty of similar injuries from shrapnel. Franklin wasn't going to make it without immediate medical attention.

Franklin's eyes opened and focused on Horace. "Protect her," he rasped before coughing.

Horace looked toward the kitchen, then back at Franklin. "Protect her? From what?"

Franklin said something but Horace couldn't hear. He leaned close enough to feel the man's breath on his ear as Franklin whispered, "Sha'Daa."

A chill passed over Horace's spine, although he had no idea why. He leaned back. "Sha'Daa? What is that?"

But Franklin wasn't going to answer.

"Is he dead?" a small voice asked from the kitchen doorway. Franklin looked over and saw the girl. He nodded.

She didn't break down in hysterics, as he expected. Tears flowed, which she wiped away with the towels, now useless for stopping her father's blood.

The pounding at the door ceased, leaving only the steady pour of rain.

"Come here, girl," Horace said. She obeyed, her eyes fixed on his. "What's your name?"

"Penny."

Emotions battered at Horace. Too many at once, pounding on the barriers he had erected over the years. He looked down at Franklin. The dead man appeared asleep. In that false repose, Horace saw all the nights he had peeked in on Randy, peaceful and innocent in his child's dreams.

He looked at Penny, his great-granddaughter, named after his dead wife. "That's a nice name," he choked out. "How old are you?"

"Ten."

He nodded. In the time since he had refused communication with his son, so much had happened. A boy born, that boy grown up, a daughter produced, and that boy dead at Horace's feet. So much time lost because of pride, and it all stared at him through a pair of pale blue eyes filled with tears. Horace longed to fill in the blanks. "Your grandfather?"

"He's-"

A hollow tapping stopped her. Horace looked to his left and thought he'd gone insane. The six goats stood at the sliding glass door that led to the back yard. They all had glowing red eyes. The Billy goat raised one foot and tapped at the glass in a steady beat, knocking at the door like a guest.

A raspy laugh escaped Horace. "Now I've seen it all." He stood, his legs wobbly, and moved toward the fireplace. A pump action shotgun rested near it, useful for scaring off the occasional wolf that roamed in from the forest. He might want to die, but he didn't want to go out like his grandson.

We don't want you, a voice, rich and sinister, said. *We want the girl.* It seemed to come from the direction of the animals, but Horace felt it reverberate through his head.

"I'm dreaming," Horace said, but he knew that was a lie. The Salesman had been real and so was this.

Give us the girl and we'll let you live, the voice said, as if the request were perfectly reasonable. The hoof continued tapping.

"Take me and leave the girl be."

You are of no consequence to us, an emotionless wretch and a suicide. The girl is important. Tap, tap.

"Why?" Horace wrapped his hand around the shotgun.

Because she is the virgin.

A virgin? Horace let out another strangled chuckle. What sort of madness had he stumbled into? He brought the shotgun up and aimed it at the glass. "I don't know what's going on, but you need to clear out or I'll blow your heads off." At the corner of his vision, Horace saw Penny grimace and cover her ears.

Hell is what's going on, mortal. We gave you the chance. Now die like the fool you've always been. The Billy goat lowered its foot and the goats backed away, their red eyes disappearing in the gloom.

Horace lowered the gun and looked at Penny, who still watched the glass door. "What's going on?"

Penny screamed.

Horace turned in time to see the goats hit the glass door. It shattered under the impact of six heads, spreading shards into the living room. The goats barreled in, heedless of the minor cuts they took. Penny ran behind Horace, who raised the shotgun and fired. The first goat, a nanny called Petunia, stumbled as her head disintegrated under the buckshot. Horace pumped the gun. The goat behind Petunia leapt over her body and took a full blast to its chest, which exploded in gouts of blood and fur.

The remaining four charged toward Horace, quickly closing the distance. He backed up, almost tripping over Penny, and fired again. The lead goat's front legs separated at the knees. The animal went down in a bleat of pain and slid across the floor.

Horace chambered a round but two of the goats were on him. They rammed his legs and pain shot through his knees. He fell backwards but maintained his grip on the weapon. "Run to the bedroom," he shouted to Penny.

He heard her footsteps, but she moved toward the fireplace. With no time to think, Horace shoved the gun under the closest goat's chin and pulled the trigger. The result coated Horace's overalls and face with gore. The other goat, red eyes blazing, slammed its head into Horace's groin. He had a precious second before the pain registered. He pushed the goat away with the shotgun barrel. He tried to chamber another round, but nausea racked him as his testicles burst into fiery pain. He backed away as best he could, but it was too slow. There were still two goats, and the Billy had horns. He waited the feel the life-ending puncture.

"Leave him alone," a high-pitched voice said. On his back, Horace opened his eyes to find Penny standing beside him, a poker in her hands, waving menacingly at the nanny, which stayed just out of range. The Billy stood a few feet back, as if appraising the situation. It no longer looked like the goat Horace owned. Its fur was now a greasy black color. Its eyes had combined into one large orb, and its horns had multiplied into four spiraled and wickedly pointed protrusions.

"Run," Horace said.

"No. You have to get up. You're all I have left." Tears ran down her face, but her expression revealed her stubbornness.

Pushing past the pain, Horace racked the shotgun.

With a furious braying sound never made by a goat, the Billy leapt toward Penny. Horace raised the gun and fired. His aim was true, but the last nanny jumped into the line of fire. Its stomach exploded and the animal crashed to the floor. A stench of blood and perforated innards filled the space.

Penny had not been still. She raised the poker and stabbed it toward the mutated Billy. It slammed into the steel rod. The point pierced the single eye as the goat smashed into Penny. She fell with the animal on top of her. The creature kicked fitfully. Penny struggled under the dying animal. Horace forced himself to his knees. He crawled over and pushed the beast off the girl. The poker had gone through the goat's head and a foot of steel stuck out the back. The goat gave a few feeble kicks and then lay still.

"Are you okay?" Horace asked.

The girl nodded, but her eyes said otherwise. Horace saw a future of nightmares for her.

It's not over, the voice said, anger in it so strong it hurt Horace's head. *Now you will suffer torments you could not dream.*

The goats moved again, and Horace thought that some dark miracle was bringing them back to life, but a cloud, black as moonless night, lifted from each body and coalesced into one giant cloud. Horace readied the shotgun and braced for an attack, although he had no idea what good buckshot would do against mist.

But the vapor fled, dashing through the broken glass and into the storm.

Horace sat back, his body aching. Penny crawled over and cuddled against his side. "Thank you," she said.

He wrapped his arm around her. "You're welcome."

A great-granddaughter, he thought. A person he knew nothing about, but having her here felt somehow right. Too much time had passed since he'd had family. She had said he was the only one she had left. That meant her father—his son—must be dead. That's what she was going to tell him before the attack. All they had was each other. Horace didn't know if he loved her, but looking at her eyes and seeing her determination and spirit, despite what she had been through, he suspected he could come to love her a great deal.

"We need to call the police," Horace said. He stood with help from Penny, his old bones screaming at the abuse they had been put through.

The sound started low, a rustling like wind through leaves. Horace thought the storm was picking up. As they hobbled toward the phone, the sound grew louder. A fierce freight train rumble with an undertone of plants torn by the roots.

"Is that a tornado?" Penny asked.

Before Horace could answer, the ceiling where they had been standing moments before caved in. Brick, drywall and Horace's bed crashed to the floor, loud as a mortar explosion. Horace pulled Penny back to avoid the debris that flew through the air and fell around them. Horace didn't have to wonder what caused the collapse. He saw it, but he could barely credit it. A fist, at least ten feet wide, followed through to the floor. A fist made of corn stalks, green and mature.

"Holy Jesus," Horace shouted.

The fist withdrew, but Horace didn't wait to see where the second blow would land. He grabbed Penny's hand and ran toward the sliding door.

Now you will see my true fury, the voice screamed in his head, almost knocking him over. *The curse of Baal upon you. Your soul will roast in hell this night.*

They ran across the broken glass, skirting the collapsed roof, and into the howling rainstorm. When they hit the lawn, Horace glanced back and wished he hadn't.

Lightning peppered the clouds, showing him full what had wrecked the house. It stood forty feet tall and had the form of a human, except for its head, which had a broad face, glowing red eyes, and curled horns. There were no details to its features, since the entire body was composed of corn stalks. The field that stood beside his house and belonged to the big corporation was now nothing more than a pit of mud.

A fist slammed on the house again, collapsing another section. The creature hadn't seen them yet. Horace limped toward the barn, Penny in tow. If they could hide, he could figure something out. It was only a hundred feet away, but it seemed like a mile.

They were ten feet short of the barn when the voice screamed in his head. *You cannot flee my wrath.* The rage in the voice knocked Horace over, and Penny whimpered.

Get up, old man, Horace told himself, and struggled to his feet with Penny's help. He kept running. He heard the creature approaching, a strange sound of rustling mixed with pattering rain.

They hit the inside of the barn and the rain ceased pounding on them. Horace ran several feet further in and looked around. The combine loomed in front of him.

The spark plug, Horace thought.

A sideswipe from the creature took out a huge chunk of the barn's front wall. Dried wood splintered and whickered through the air. Boards struck Horace in the back. As he fell to the ground, he heard Penny yelp in pain, her cheek and arm cut by flying debris. Behind her, Horace saw the shadowy bulk of old hay bales.

"Hide," he said, pointing toward the bales. Penny followed his hand and nodded. Horace stood and ran toward the combine. Breath hitched in his chest, but fear of failure drove him. He reached the ancient combine, its green paint flaking, blades rusting. Fortunately, the large hood still stood open from his attempts, abandoned years ago, to fix the engine. He climbed the small ladder to reach the distributor cap and yanked it off, exposing eight empty holes, devoid of plugs.

Let this work, he thought as he reached into his pocket.

Another chunk of wooden wall, this one near the barn's top, exploded inward and showered the combine with splinters and not a few corn leaves and cobs. Kernels splattered against the machine, releasing a sweet smell.

The creature appeared in the gap it had created. Its red eyes stared at Horace and his heart lurched in his chest. He froze in fear as the beast lumbered toward him. Taller than the barn, it had to smash the roof so it could get in. Despite that, Horace knew he would never get the combine started in time.

Penny appeared from behind a haystack, near the entrance. "Hey, ugly, you want me?"

The creature wheeled around, raking the roof and tearing wood like tissue.

"Come get me." She ran from the barn and across the yard. Enraged, the creature turned, arms thrashing as it cleared the barn.

Horace wasted no time. He stuck the spark plug in one of the holders, screwed it in, and slammed the distributor cap on it. He scrambled down one ladder and up the other, which led to the machine's cab. Penny's scream, audible over the pouring rain and thrashing monster, spurred him on.

He seated himself and, praying this impossibility would be as real as the rest of tonight's events, he turned the key.

The motor purred to life as if new.

Horace's shout of joy was cut short by a sudden pain in his chest. He clamped his jaw shut, threw the combine into gear, and hurtled forward.

Outside the barn, he spotted the creature near the woods but saw no sign of Penny. The monster appeared equally uncertain as it scanned the trees. It reached out with a corn stalk hand and tore a pine tree out by its roots. Exposed, Penny screamed and ran deeper into the forest. The creature tossed the tree aside like a stick.

Forehead covered in sweat, Horace aimed the combine toward the creature and engaged the machinery. Power thrummed through the cab. "Look at me, you son of a bitch," he screamed as he laid on the horn.

The creature turned to face him. As Horace drew close, it swung a giant fist at the cab. Glass shattered, spraying outward from the impact, and the roof dented, but the cab held. Blades hit the creature's legs and pulled them in toward the machine. The monster screamed loud enough that Horace's head rang, but he pressed on. Plant juice spattered the machine like yellowish blood. The legs disappeared into the machine's innards and the creature fell backwards, where it hit the springy pine trees. Trapped between trees and machine, the beast had no way to go but down. It fed itself into the machine, which devoured it like a starving dog given a steak. As the red eyes came level with Horace, they burned into his brain. *I'll still see you in Hell, suicide.*

"I don't think so," Horace said, even as another wave of pain hit him and his face went clammy.

The last of the creature fell into the ravenous blades. Corn husks and leaves littered the ground. A cloud of black fled past the combine's lights and into the night, but it seemed helpless, a thing of little power.

Horace reached over and turned the combine off. He'd rest a few minutes and then go find Penny. He needed to wait until the feeling in his left arm returned.

The cab door opened and Penny stood on the ladder in her bloody clothes, now covered with bits of green pulp. Some of it stuck in her hair.

"Hi there, sweetheart," Horace said. "I think we're okay now." Another stab of pain racked him and his vision blurred. "You're okay, at least. You're safe."

Penny looked down at him. "Can we leave now?"

"You can, but I don't think I'm going anywhere. The excitement was just a little too much for this old man."

Tears formed in Penny's eyes. "I'll call an ambulance."

Horace shook his head. "Never make it in time. It's okay. It…it was my time to go." Another pain. His breath grew short, his vision dimmer. "I do want to know one thing. Why you? Whatever that was said it wanted a virgin. Out of all the virgins in the world, why you?"

Penny took his hand. In a voice that was not quite hers, she said, "It didn't want *a* virgin, it wanted *the* Virgin."

His vision was failing fast, but he again thought he saw a glow around the young girl. "You mean…"

"Shh," Penny said, and her voice was hers again, full of tears and sorrow. "Go now to see the Father. Rest comfortably."

Horace closed his eyes. So I'm going to die tonight after all, he thought. As he drifted away, he went with the knowledge that he was loved, the understanding that he had done at least one thing right in his life.

Everybody Get Down

"**W**E'RE NOT QUITE A QUARTER OF a way into this event to top all events." Bak's pit boss bellowed aloud. "Those Terrans are fighting for all they're worth. Twenty to one odds they don't make it to the end of day one. All takers, that's all takers on The Sha'Daa."

"Word spreads fast, Bak." Johnny the Salesman spouted without fanfare. "Kentucky Bourbon. Neat."

Bak spun around and frowned at his ancient friend. It was just six hours, but the weariness reflected on the Salesman's brow and shoulders was downright palpable. Bak slid three fingers of his best to the taller man who snatched it up and downed it in a single movement.

"Damn, Johnny." Bak said. "For a relative teetotaler you're full of surprises today. Keep this up and I'll be recommending a 12-step program."

"Nobody knows the troubles I've seen, Bak-tender."

On the main stage a quartet of Dixie fiddlers were setting everyone's foots to tapping.

"Tell me about it." Bak snorted. "Since you left, the girls and I must have served four thousand drink orders, broken up fifty genocidal bar fights, funneled the gross national product of several dozen nations through the gaming pit, and mopped up the remains of at least a hundred grudge matches in the battle pit. If this is merely peripheral fallout from your precious Sha'Daa I may just contemplate early retirement."

Johnny leaned to the side and smiled in the direction of the rear of the gaming pit. Standing there against that back cave wall was a bizarre contraption roughly twenty foot by twenty foot by twenty foot in dimension. A weird conglomeration of fire-pinned gears, spinning priceless jewels, and brass and crystal workings, the massive construct vibrated and hummed like a giant cosmic beehive.

"Why Bak, you've dug out that ancient doomsday clock I traded you two thousand years ago." Johnny chuckled. "How very appropriate."

Bak smiled in reply. "The damndest thing, too, Johnny."

"How's that?"

"The moment I set it in place the bloody monstrosity up and started operating all on its own." Bak marveled. "And though it took some time for the confirmations to come in, the infernal device has locked itself into precise alignment with The Sha'Daa."

"Now that." Johnny frowned, "is something I find convenient."

"For good or bad, this cosmic tournament of yours is breaking attendance records here tonight." Bak said.

Johnny tossed back his second drink and sighed deeply. "I guess it's a good thing you installed that Olympic-pool-sized ale reservoir last month."

"Yah." Bak chuckled. "Best trade I ever made with you."

"And the first day ain't even half over." Johnny added.

"Great." Bak's lips pursed. "Thank the fates I stocked up the ice caves with supplies just last month. Maribel's got her crew on triple overtime and the damn lines to her tents haven't slacked a bit."

"I noticed." Johnny chuckled. "Funny how the baser instincts rear their ugly heads when a holocaust arises."

The fiddlers on the main stage kicked into a devilish rendition of *Foggy Mountain Breakdown.*

"We may have to start calling up some temps and amateurs to handle the overflow." Bak mused. "Might be time to reopen the caveways to Sodom, Hollywood, and Havana."

"Any one been asking for me?" Johnny whispered slyly.

"Huh?" Bak leaned forward. "Asked for you? Well, other than a couple of dozen high-rollers betting against your hopeless campaign in the game pit, nope. Not that I've heard. I'll ask around if you want, discretely of course."

"Do that." Johnny said. "I think I'm being followed."

"You!" Bak spouted then looked around to make sure no one had noticed. "Is that even possible?"

"I wouldn't have thought so until today. Now…" Johnny paused for a moment to stare off into nothingness. "I'm not so sure. In fact, the smart man would say all bets are off for the next day and a half."

"Just don't repeat that sentiment near the gaming pit." Bak grinned. "The house has pocketed enough today to put my great-great-great-grandkids through medical school."

"And on that note," Johnny stood up. "Gotta refill the sample case. Never a shortage of marks my friend."

"Yah." Bak sighed, eyeing the steady stream of new customers continuing to pour in through the rear entrances. "I'm beginning to rethink my long standing 'no cover charge' policy."

The doomsday clock spouted out a single loud gong.

The fiddlers kicked into a rousing rendition of *The Devil Went Down To Georgia*.

The Road Forsaken

By Michael H. Hanson

"The woman led the children still deeper into the forest, where they had never in their lives been before."

— Hansel and Gretel, The Brothers Grimm

ANOTHER BASTARD CUTS ME OFF. I'M still too tired to flip him off, let alone honk my horn, so I just send him my patented glare of death and sip caffeine with my free hand. Frigging six-cylinder death traps. That's the problem with my ancient '89 Honda, four cylinders and no pickup. I get great gas mileage but every prick with a little get up and go gets up in front of me.

As usual, the coffee is slightly bitter. I always stoke it with Irish Cream milk substitute and three packets of sweet and low, but that never seems to quite do the trick. Still, at one dollar a pop, this particular WaWa (roadside gas station, diner, and newspaper shop combined) offers the cheapest coffee around. I'm talking 24 ounces of stomach-cramping eye-opening wakeup juice. And there's nothing better for a 45-minute commute every morning in the state of New Jersey.

And what a pain in the butt commute this was. I live up in the northwest region in the quaint little town of Dagda, just off of Route 206. Or rather, it used to be a quaint little town. What were once hundreds of surrounding acres of forest is rapidly being over-developed. The sprawl is creeping into the farthest reaches of the Garden State. Route 206 used to be a nice quiet two-laner bisecting the wilderness. Now it's abused and overused by way too many commuters. I dread its inevitable conversion to the geriatric and cynical seediness of old Route 22. What should be a 25-minute commute turns into a one-hour ride through purgatory if you don't leave home by 6:30am.

I overslept today. It happens. I didn't hit the road until 7:30am. The inevitable bottleneck of cars occurs from Chester all the way down to Bedminster, six miles of solid chrome. This is half of my commute. The other half is on 287, a large enough interstate but still capable of gridlock as even its four lanes get inundated near the center of the state. 287 practically drops me off at the front door of my publishing house in Pithscorea, NJ.

I flip between News Jersey Radio, NPR, and Magic 98.3. Nothing of particular interest as News Jersey gives me the brilliant advice to avoid the unusually overcrowded 206. NPR is broadcasting an interview with some actor who played a doctor on that TV show SCRUBS. I flip to Magic and tap my fingertips on the steering wheel to the Black Eyed Peas classic "Boom Boom Pow."

Route 206 is scenic enough, if you like trees. Personally, the things give me the willies. Multiple branches stretching everywhere like the arms of petrified prehistoric insects. And come autumn they shed all those dreadful leaves like so much dead skin. Like I said, Mother Nature is no kin of mine.

Five more minutes of solid gridlock and I notice, for the first time, a side road on my left. At first I think it's another one of the many partially-camouflaged driveway entrances that so many upper-middle-class New Jerseyites create to hide their faux-palatial estates. A closer examination shows that it is an old cobblestone paved road that splits off about 90 degrees from 206.

"What the hell?" I think as I jerk my steering wheel to the left and floor it when the oncoming traffic lets up. In seconds I'm plowing forward at 45 miles an hour.

This avenue is only about twice as wide as my car. I'm not worried about collision, however, because the road is so straight and flat, and the sun is shining so brightly through the trees, that I've got a sightline of at least a mile.

What is this thing? Some kind of utility road, a private lane to some movie star's estate? I weigh all the ponderables but after about six miles I come to feel that this is the real thing, an old back road that for one reason or another has just not gotten much use.

Maybe it leads to a one-lane bridge, I think, as I accelerate to 60 mph. For the first time this morning I lean back in my seat and relax. The warm sunshine beating in through the windshield and the regularity of the tall roadside trees lull me into sudden complacency.

Jane would like this back road, all the foliage. She's a real nature freak, my Jane. Me? I'm a city boy stuck out in sticks because of the fickleness of the publishing industry. My company moved out here five years ago and I came with it.

I look in my rear view mirror to see if anyone else has followed my lead but I cannot see very far. Strange, I've still got the mile or more of unfettered sight in front of me as I move right along however. I shrug, must be a trick of the light.

I finish my coffee and, after looking at my own eyes in the rearview mirror, open the driver's side window and toss the empty tyrofoam cup out. "You'll never take me alive coppers." I yell with a braying laugh. This road is too cool. I know that if I go much farther on it I'll be reaching the general region of central New Jersey, hopefully not too far from where I work.

Stray thoughts float like dandelions all around me. I snatch at one. Why I'll bet this is a road just like this one where the Ghost Gang disappeared.

The Ghost Gang is one of those New Jersey Urban myths. Like the Jersey Devil it had a life of its own and was passed from elementary class to elementary class. Chris, a neighborhood kid, gave me the rundown a couple of years ago when I hired him to help me rake some leaves. Rumor has it that back in the late 1950's some biker gang out of Newark took off one hot July day for a rally outside of Pittsburgh. They never arrived, nor were heard from again. Friends of the gang waited on the Pennsylvania side of the Delaware Water Gap for two days before contacting the police. But no one had seen them since they cut off on some side road off of route 22 west. Some say dirty cops ambushed them. Others say they took off for Canada for the easy pickings up there.

I think they went home to see the latest episode of I Love Lucy.

Ha.

Like fifty or sixty young adults could have walked off the face of the earth in one shot and nobody anywhere would have found anything out? No clues? Nothing?

Chris had a petulant look to his face and swore he'd heard this story from his father who was a teenager at the time. I just smiled at the kid and gave him an extra five for the raking.

The sunlight dims for a moment then comes back as bright as ever.

Though it is difficult to tell from the low vantage point of my moving car, I come to the realization that the trees lining this road are easily three times as tall, and big around, as any I've ever seen in New Jersey. Strange that the trees lining this particular road would have been spared the lumber company's axe.

It seems to grow dim for a moment. I squint. Overhead, tree branches have spread out and formed a canopy over the narrow road. I feel a slight chill and turn my heater up a notch. There'd be snow before you know it. Have to remind Jane to pick up some road salt for our driveway.

Jane. My wife. Just thinking of her brings a smile to my face. I look into the rearview mirror and wrinkle my brow at the sight of my own unruly blond hair, blue eyes, and very pale skin. We make quite a pair Jane and me. And yes it still never ceases to amaze me all the looks we get when together in public.

A squirrel dashes across the road but is gone before I can even think of touching the brake pedal.

I scratch my neck. I've got a few freckles about the shoulders from too much sunlight but that's never a problem for my sweet Jane. She's black. No, not African-American, or Afro-American, but just plain black. As she made it clear to me on our second date years ago that the hyphen-terminology was for sociology students and politicians. She was black and that was all there was to it.

Actually she's brown, medium-golden, chestnut brown. The most beautiful and perfect complexion God ever created. And after ten years of marriage her pigmentation still graces a gorgeous canvas of lusty curves and alluring smiles. I love her as much now as the first day I met her.

Man, I couldn't wait to finish up work and get home for another Friday night of marital privacy. I'm still a little bummed I had to run out so quickly this morning. I wonder if I gave her enough...damn it.

I slam on the breaks and skid to a halt.

Dammit, dammit, dammit. The money. I forget to hit the ATM and give Jane the money she needed today. She must be furious with me. This is what I get for sleeping in and then rushing out of the house. I pull out my cell phone...and cannot get a signal. Damn. Wouldn't this just have to happen right now?

I put the car in reverse and start a three-point turn. Jane is usually home until 10am so I should be able to catch her. Traffic north on 206 at this time of the day is minimal anyway and I'd only been on this side road for ten or fifteen minutes.

I barely move four feet when my bumper meets bark. Oh, come on. I spend the next ten minutes trying every variation of backing up I can think of. It doesn't help. The road is too narrow. The car won't turn in such tight confines. I can't back up all the way to 206.

As I pull forward again, I look into the rearview mirror for a final glimpse at the optical illusion of roominess formed by the trees at that narrow part of the road.

"Maybe it wasn't an illusion?" I ask myself.

I talk to myself out loud whenever I start getting scared out of my wits. It's been a long time since I've last done this, not since Jane had her appendectomy eight months ago.

"Then what else could it be? Of course it's an illusion," I say. "Maybe the trees are moving together." I smile slyly into my rear-view mirror "Maybe they're closing up behind me. Cutting off my retreat."

I feel something shift beneath my belly muscles.

This is stupid. I'm not going to think this crap anymore.

I grit my teeth and lean on the accelerator until I am moving over 75 miles an hour. Wherever I'm going, I should get there soon. The road still seems plenty wide immediately in front of me.

I lick my lips and glance at the rearview mirror. I slam on the breaks. Son of a bitch.

I sit for a whole minute grinding my teeth. While my front view is almost endless, I can clearly see only sixty yards behind me. What the...

"You're going in circles, Mark," I say.

No way.

"Yes way. Why do you think you haven't gotten anywhere? Look at your watch. Look at your fuel gauge. Look at your odometer."

My mouth drops open. I have less than half a tank of gas left. I've driven almost a hundred miles this morning.

It's not possible. You can't drive a hundred miles in New Jersey and not get anywhere.

"You can if you're driving in a big circle...especially if the circle is circling in on itself," I spit out.

And the craziness of it all suddenly clicks inside me. Of course, I was driving in an ever-decreasing circle. It's some kind of maze. That's it. Some rich Jersey bastard created a stupid maze for his rich stupid kid in the middle of the woods and I've stumbled onto it.

I exhale. So all I've got to do is keep driving forward and I'll reach the center.

"But then what?" I ask myself.

Then I'll turn around and drive back out.

With renewed vigor I hit eight-five miles an hour. I ignore the rapidly falling gas gauge needle. I do an even better job of ignoring the rear view mirror, which seems to want to tell me something. My will is stronger, though, and I keep my eyes glued to the front. I'm going to reach the center of this ridiculous maze and then go home.

"Check your gas, Mark," I tell myself.

The needle is nearing the red empty line. I grit my teeth to keep from losing it.

There must be gas there. Right? That makes sense. What's the point of having a stupid maze like this if your friends can't get back out? Any stupid rich person knows that. I chuckle a little too strongly at my own lame wit.

My palms grow sweaty. I lick my lips until they start to chap. I'm now hunched over the steering wheel like a vulture. I've got to stay focused.

Small distorted shadows flick over the front of my car. Every time I look up, however, I only see the suggestion of some large, birdlike form that disappears beyond the trees.

A hawk? An eagle?

"Since when do hawks have two heads?" I ask myself with a shaky voice.

No. I did NOT see two heads.

And then something catches my attention. Fifty yards up ahead, and setting within the tree line at the right, is a gas stop. The closer I get to it I see it is an aged, paint-peeling, Esso Station. My first thought is that it is some long abandoned landmark. Surrounded by tightly growing trees, there is no way to pull into it, or turn around via u-turn or three-point turn. The gas pump, in all its faded, Art Deco glory, sets right up against the edge of the small road. The shack behind it looks like a one-room hovel. I pull up and am even more surprised to see I'm not alone.

The gas station attendant is a six foot six, Rastafarian with jet-black skin, a large mop of dreadlocks, and a faded Bob Marley hat. He steps out of the shack and waves to me. He is wearing an ancient, threadbare black suit that looks like it is on the verge of disintegration. The slim Jamaican taps on the passenger side window with his large knuckles. I shrug at the absurdity of it all and power down the window.

"Hey man," I said. "I'm lost and low on gas. Can you help me, here?"

"They call me the Salesman, mon," he said. "Johnny to my friends. And many be needing my wares today. Babylon in dire trouble and not all the ganja in paradise be making it better. The Idren are in need."

"Yah," I said. "Well, how about you fill it up with regular and give me some directions back to 206?"

"There's no tiger in my main tank," Johnny smiled. "Been waiting on the Esso refill man for many, many years. And you can only get out of here by going straight forward."

"There another station up ahead?"

Johnny scratched his chin in intense concentration for a moment.

"Maybe we can do business after all, mon."

Johnny spun around and walked into his shack. About one minute later he walked back out holding some kind of shrink-wrapped display kit, with an old folded map on top of it.

"I be given you this in trade," Johnny said. I made out a plastic one-gallon gas container shaped like a donut under the plastic. "It be a Car-Buddy kit, mon. Filled with petrol, a plastic air pressure gauge, and three road flares. And this is a map of these back roads. Watcha say?"

I held out my credit card be he just shook his head. "No way, mon. I don't do plastic. Tesla and Edison never made it to this neighborhood."

"Fine," I said, realizing I was about to be taken for a large wad of cash. "How much? And make it fast I'm late for work."

"I be liking your bangles, brother." Johnny said, looking at my two thin silver bracelets. I'd purchased them last year at the Akwesasne trading post near my parent's hometown of Mertier, NY. Silver bears chased each other in their metal circles.

"No way," I said. "Here's forty-five dollars in cash. It's highway robbery and you know it."

Johnny smiled a wide grin, which consisted of a mouth filled with bright white teeth, marred only by a shiny gold left lateral incisor.

"Your greenskins aren't any good here, Mark." Johnny said. "You want out of this maze? You want gas? I want your bangles, brother."

Furious, but helpless, I handed over my prized bracelets. Johnny had me pop my trunk and set the Car-Buddy kit inside before slamming it shut. He tossed the map through the open window onto the empty passenger seat, and waved to me as I drove forward.

"Irie, brother-man," Johnny said.

As I pulled away I could see Johnny lighting up a large hand-rolled joint, nearly the size of a cigar, with a stick match. Then the thought suddenly struck me. How did he know my name was Mark?

A brightness up ahead. Some kind of clearing. Finally, I've reached the end of this damn back road.

I drive out of the woods as my engine starts knocking.

I take a few deep breaths and smile and chide myself at my earlier panic. A living road, trees plotting against me, rich man's maze. I laugh. Jane would love this story, her being a vegetarian and the daughter of upper-class wealth herself. Wonder what she'll say about my missing bracelets, though. I still can't believe I got suckered like that.

I can see dozens, maybe hundreds of cars all around me. Great. I've probably pulled into some big company's rear parking lot. With my luck, there will be an anal-retentive security guard at the entrance just waiting to give me a hard time.

I pull up next to a dark-green, 1998 Toyota Camry XLE. I stare at the dash of my Honda and the needle is pretty close to empty.

I park then pick up the map and unfold it. The damn thing must be decades old! It takes me a few minutes but I finally figure out where route 206 is. Next I reason out that I have been driving on a wildly circular utility road, possibly built over a logging road from a couple of centuries back. This lot shows up as a clearing in the map, with a second utility road exiting east just a short ways away. I try my cell phone one more time but cannot get a signal. The boss is gonna kill me.

I get out of my car and look around to see where the nearest payphone might be.

On closer examination I realize I'm standing on the outskirts of an open area that is covered with dirt and small rocks. Not a glint of pavement anywhere. Hundreds of cars fill this circular clearing that is at least the size of two football fields. There are no buildings in sight. Only trees. This is no parking lot.

"Where am I, Autoland?"

I stand with my back to the woods facing inwards on a motley assortment of vehicles. Not quite knowing why, I start walking forward.

At first the cars I pass by don't look all that different from most you see on the highway these days, a variety of automobiles in varying states of disrepair and each anywhere from six months to twenty years old. The outermost thirty yards of this strange junkyard, as I begin to classify it, is made up of such cars and motorcycles.

Then I spot a 1987 Schwinn five-speed bike. Its tires, like all the other vehicles are flat, but except for some minor rusting, it looks to be in fine condition. Who the heck would toss such a nice bike out?

"Rich people." I snort. "Typical."

I'm about a third of the way into this circle of vehicles when I start taking a closer examination of everything I walk by. A 1982 Suzuki Katana, a 1981 Honda CBX, and a 1976 Suzuki RE5 Rotary. Wait. That's a 1971 Studebaker Avanti and except for some weathering it's in fine condition. Flat tires but still.

I stop and look all around this bizarre junkyard. Of course, the newer cars are on the outskirts and the older ones go inward. But I'm not even halfway into it so...

I get a feeling of premonition and start to stride forward again.

A 1973 Apple Crate bicycle, a 1966 Honda Police Special motorcycle. A sense of unreality starts creeping into everything.

A 1963 Lincoln, with suicide doors, oh man.

Years of collecting model cars and bikes with my older brothers start flowing back into my head. This place is a treasure trove.

1959 Chevy Impala, 1960 Schwinn Spitfire Bike, in black and cream no less. They're just more junk in this place. Nice junk but the same as everything else. No reason to feel weird.

And then I come to a halt. I'm just over halfway into this museum. I stare at a mound of motorcycles, almost three feet high. Most of them are either 1958 Duo Glides or 1957 Sportsters, a Harley-Davidson lover's dream. Something about them sends a chill up my spine.

It hits me. There are at least fifty Harleys in this big mound. Fifty. The number mentioned in the Ghost Gang story.

"So this is where they ended up," I say to myself. "And now this is where you've ended up, hotshot."

I try to block out all thought of the bikes and stride forward again.

A 1956 Ford Victoria, a 1949 Indian Silver Arrow motorcycle for God's sake. A 1942 Columbia Tourist bicycle, a 1940 Packard station wagon, a 1939 Ford Model C, and a 1936 Schwinn Aeorocycle. I'd only seen one of those in some old magazines.

I'm easily two-thirds of the way to the center of this circle of rusting metal and the variety of museum pieces is dwindling. It seems like every three strides are another five to ten years back in time.

A 1935 Iver Johnson ladies bicycle in blue and white, a 1931 Auburn Saloon car, a 1930 Peerless V16, and 1927 Mead Ranger bicycle.

Though I'm only walking, my breathing has deepened considerably. The warm summer air feels heavy in my lungs.

A 1925 Bantam compact car and a 1924 Indian Chief motorcycle.

I'm only ten yards from a small clearing in the center of this circle of wonder. A 1910 Buick Model 10 and a 1910 ford Model T. Oh, by all that's holy, a 1905 Stanley Roadster. This just isn't possible. No matter how mad some billionaire might be he'd never just chuck all these treasures out here like this.

A 1903 Pierce Arrow motorette, a 1903 Oldsmobile, a 1902 Cadillac Model and a 1901 Oldsmobile.

I've reached the clearing. It's about twenty feet in diameter. Nervous sweat drips down my face. The clearing is littered with rubble and bicycles and other things, which I approach to examine.

An 1895 Massey-Harris bicycle and an 1894 Trigwell Regent bicycle. And there, dead in the center of it all, jutting out from the dirt, is a spoked, wooden wheel, iron shod, six feet in diameter. I look at all the pieces of rotted wood lying about.

"A covered wagon, like the settlers used," I say. "And it got here just like you, didn't it? I wonder where the owners are?"

And then I notice something new. The silence. My haggard breathing and heartbeat had filled my ears for the past few minutes but now I realize just how QUIET it was in this clearing. This deep into forest, surrounded by trees, I should hear an orchestra of insect symphonies, but here, nothing.

"And the ground, not a blade of grass or flower or weed anywhere in the entire clearing. Nothing ALIVE that is....Mark."

The hair on the back of my neck stands up. I sense that my life is in danger.

I turn around and scan the periphery. I can see the road that led me here, and about thirty yards from it the other road the map said would lead me in the direction of my job.

Something flickers for a moment on the edge of my awareness. What?

There is movement and I rub my eyes several times. Shadows are moving over the farthest edge of the cars toward me...from the direction of my parked car. I look up at the sky. The clouds have all dissipated and the sun shines freely.

These aren't shadows.

"Motherfucker," I yell.

I sprint in the opposite direction out of the circle of antiquated metal. I keep looking back to see a tide of dark tendrils spreading over everything and slowly overtaking me.

This is real. It's not a dream. They are coming for me.

My chest hurts and I cough up phlegm. When I was eighteen and the third ranked varsity runner on my high school Cross-Country Team, I could run ten miles a day like it was nothing. Twelve years of driving back and forth to work and late nights in front of a PC has stripped me of all such past glories.

Gasping, I reach the outside of the circle then stop dead in my tracks. The shadowy tendrils are not only right behind me but also off to my right.

I turn and for the first time I realize this is not a large circle, but more of a bell-shaped clearing. It flares open off to the left.

This might be my one chance. I sprint with all my remaining stamina towards the distant lagoon of safety. I can now hear something behind me. Wispy sounds like chalk on a blackboard.

It isn't until they are within a few feet that I see what is chasing me. Long thin branches, stretching and undulating like muscular, brown snakes.

They are on my heels. I'm almost to the side where the woods open up again when a sharp cramp hits my left gut and right thigh and I drop like a sack of flour.

The branches flow over me. I can see them clearly now. They are tentacles. And they are covered with hundreds, maybe thousands of tiny jagged mouths vomiting sap and yawning hungrily.

They wrap around my legs and start dragging me in the direction I'd been running towards all this time.

I struggle frantically but cannot get any leverage to lean forward to attack the branch-vines with my hands. I'm dragged over a small rock, which I hit my head on and lose consciousness for a second or two.

I see stars but sudden intense pain from my ankles brings me back around. I scream and am able to lift my head up enough to see the vile sap burning and eating through my pants and through my skin right down to the muscle. Wisps of smoke and an acrid odor pass over me.

A tiny vine punctures the side of my neck. I drown in an ocean of arcane and sickening imagery. Something is talking to me through the vines. These vines are dragging toward a demon-god…Mannock. A hellish deity transported from a dark dimension to these woods ten thousand years ago during a holocaust called The Sha'Daa. Trapped here for ten millennia, Mannock fed upon hundreds of innocents that stumbled into the sphere of its influence. And now the cycle had come full circle, and The Sha'Daa was back. All over the Earth portals by the hundreds were opening and creatures as hellish as Mannock, or worse, were threatening all life, everywhere. The apocalypse had arrived.

As I'm pulled over a thick bush, the vine in my neck breaks off and my thoughts become clearer. I'm about to be dragged right past a small outcropping of deadwood before getting pulled into the flared out area at the bottom of this clearing.

I tense myself.

The pain in my legs becomes unbearable.

I'm near it. I'm getting pulled past it. I lunge.

I grab the still living branch of a large tree that has fallen over.

I yank myself to a halt.

Jerking upright I grab and tear at the tentacles around my ankles. The acid sap burns my hands but adrenaline blocks out most of the pain. While strong enough to pull me along the ground, these vegetative tendrils are no match for meat muscle and I rip them apart.

"AAuugghghghhhhhh," I scream out in animal rage and triumph. My legs are free.

Wild-eyed, I stand up. I can feel a crazy grin splitting my face. Trickles of blood drip down from a cut on the back of my head.

Then I see them.

My strength and my sanity almost bleed away. Almost. My knees barely begin to buckle as I grit my teeth and spin a quick 180 degrees on my heels. A new supply of adrenaline floods my limbs and I run back among the automotive corpses. I glance back over my shoulder to get a quick bearing.

Thousands and thousands of the rough brown-gray tentacles converge on me from every direction.

I start a terrifying game of cat and mouse amidst the many ruined cars as I zigzag madly back towards my Honda. I quickly realize that their sheer numbers are now impeding the tentacles. The tentacles are constantly knotting up in tangled collisions. The thousands of rasping sliding fingers are more than muffling the vibrations of my footsteps.

Three times tentacles slap around my waist and ankles but my momentum is just enough to break from their fiery embrace.

An eternity later I slam against the back of my car. The vines, a confused undulating mass spread throughout the auto graveyard, all stop moving for a moment as I gasp in great heaving breaths. A second later their confusion ends and they all flood directly toward me.

I frantically pull my keys out of my front pocket and stab at the trunk lock, missing it two times. Four vine-tentacles slap against my back and tear off the last remaining remnants of my shirt as I pop the trunk and stab both of my hands into my utility box.

An extra large vine starts to wrap itself around my waist, like a python, when I suddenly spin around, break off the strike-cap, and slap it across the top of the flare. Red flame bursts forth and I shove it against the vine on my belt.

The snake-like tentacle around my waist yanks itself backwards, but too late. In a split second it ignites as if it was dipped in gasoline. A horrific high-pitched scream issues from it and I cringe as my eardrums are overloaded.

Every other vine it comes in contact with, also explodes into flame. I quickly realize that the deadly acidic sap each vine contains has a wonderful flammable drawback.

Dozens of their fellow vines leap into the fray and desperately begin to cover and muffle out their burning brethren, trying to snuff out the fire before it starts eating away at them.

I have different ideas. I strike up another flare. With one in each hand, I start darting back and forth igniting every single vine in sight.

In five minutes they are all on fire. I am deafened from all the plant screams.

I jump on top of my car to get a grand view of the carnage. Marveling at the thousands of rippling burning tentacles, I notice that each one has acted as some kind of fuse, carrying the fire along their lengths towards the inlet at the far side of the clearing where they had tried to drag me earlier.

Green and brown smoke suddenly starts pouring from behind the trees over there. A deep earth-shaking howl smashes through my deafness and chills me to my core.

The source of the vines is on fire.

I walked back to my car's trunk, snatch up the Car-Buddy that Johnny The Salesman had given me, and pop off my car's gas cap. I look in the direction of the Hell-Howl. That hell-thing, Mannock, what if is not really dying?

I glance over to the car sitting close to me. Inside, I spot an infant's safety seat. It is empty of course. I glance back toward my car and see Johnny's map resting on the dash. The rotted stench of burning vine-tentacles fills the air and twice I have to stop to retch. I pick up the car-buddy and look at my car's gas cap one last time.

"Fuck it," I growl. I grab up the last of the flares from the trunk and move in the direction of the otherworldly howling. I think about the empty child's safety seat and a dark rage slowly builds up within me. How many of my kind have been slaughtered in this place? How many families?

A couple of minutes later I reach the point where I had earlier won my freedom. Several more feet and I turn the corner of the alcove of trees. The sight before me is almost beyond comprehension. Once again I feel my sanity slipping.

The near corner of this clearing is a shrine. The offerings lay in an ivory pile just off to the left. I slowly walk towards the massive burning primordial father tree that is the vines' God.

It towers into the air nearly fifty feet, the diameter at its base easily half of that. Though nothing green grows on it or its jagged broken limbs, there is still the air of life about it, twisted, decaying, evil life…life that is now threatened by dozens of streams of fire.

I walk within a few feet of the immense mound of human bones. One tentacle manages to break away from its burning brethren and wrap itself around my neck. I instantly feel microscopic tentacles stabbing into my ear, my skull, my brain.

"Hear me, mortal," Mannock's powerful, ancient voice speaks in my mind. "Help me and I will spare you. You will be my servant and many shall be the rewards you will reap. My powers are returning to me. Within hours I will be able to reach out for hundreds of miles. All life will become my prey."

A sudden image of Jane breaks through this nearly overwhelming spell. I reach up, and screaming, yank the vine off the left side of my head. Blood flows down my neck and I know I'll never hear out of that ear again.

Mannock is aware of me and several of its larger branches, each ringed in green flames, dips downward. I duck under the giant limbs and run forward. The foul tree-mouth is filled with a thousand tongues, rancid bile, and splinter teeth. I drop to my knees knowing I have only moments to spare.

I pop the cap off the Car-Buddy, drop one flare into the opening with just the strike-head sticking out, crack it with one swipe, and simultaneously toss it into Mannock's mouth as the flare ignites.

I drop and roll away as the car-buddy explodes and silently thank Johnny for the now timely trade.

Raging fire instantly fills Mannock. The arcane creature wallows in sickening rage and despair as the green flames relentlessly tear into it. Branches and vines everywhere undulate and snap wildly in unencing agony.

The quickly spreading wildfire tears through all the dead foliage on the ground, cutting me off from the auto graveyard and the two roads on the far side of the clearing. I stand up and stagger off, coughing, into the forest, Mannock's receding, unholy, dying mental screams driving me to the brink of insanity.

But what do I stagger towards? When I leave these woods, what will I find? A world filled with monsters, all my loved ones and colleagues dead?

I pray for my wife and grit my teeth. Whatever I must face, I'm going home.

Nesting

IT TOOK BAK A FULL WEEK TO MAP OUT the interior of this fantastic uninhabited wonderland after his miraculous recovery. The large waterfall supplied not only a drinking pool, but a natural array of baths that funneled their way to a series of toilets and urinals carved deep into the walls to the left rear of the main cavern.

A grouping of shiver-inducing ice caves filled with satchels of grains and dried sides of meat greeted him next. The overall temperature was a cool 70 Deg F and the interaction of the waterfall and exiting river crevasses constantly replenished the air. Then there was the main bar. And what a bar counter it was, four feet high, three feet deep, and stretching a full 150 feet across. It appeared to be carved out of a giant single piece of ebonite. At the sight of this Bak knew his dreams had come to pass. He could finally embrace his true fate. When he ultimately figured out the puzzle and workings of the multitude of magical doorways and portals that allowed passage to and from his newfound lair, he was ready to start building a business, a bar, the Triple-Six Tavern.

In The Chamber Of Skulls

By Sarah Wagner

"**H**OW MUCH LONGER?" SEVEN-year-old Lily Montour climbed back into her booster seat, flipping a long, black braid out of the way of the seatbelt.

"Not too much, Pumpkin. We'll be there soon." Angie fastened her own seatbelt and reached into the bag on the passenger seat. She'd bought and wrapped surprises to keep the girls happy. Well, happier anyway. Boredom came quickly after five days in a hot car driving from California to Pennsylvania.

"Thanks, Mama!" Lily ripped into her small package, chirping at her new treasure. Her bright, dark eyes flashed with glee. Her wide, open face lighting up. The best possible reminder of her lost husband.

"How about you, Grace? Are you going to open yours?" Angie didn't really expect an answer; Grace hadn't said more than three words for the whole trip. "Honey, I didn't want to leave either."

"At least you got a vote." She crossed her arms and turned to stare out the window, leaving her new present unopened on the seat beside her next to the others dressed in their delicate silver paper. Grace looked just like Angie when she was mad. Not a trace of their mixed ancestry then, just the Seneca in their high apple cheeks and black eyes.

Angie sighed. She hadn't really gotten a vote either. After Joseph died, they lost their base housing and, when she got laid off, she'd one option: run home to her own mother. It would have been easier, in a way, if her husband had died in combat. She'd always been prepared for that, could make sense of that. But no, a car accident tore her husband away.

They passed through many towns that had seen better days, their brick facades crumbling, windows boarded up, elderly folk sitting on their porches, perhaps wishing for days gone by when hope didn't seem so unreachable.

Traffic got heavier as the signs for Pittsburgh exits popped up. It wasn't where Angie wanted to be, back in the land of her youth, too many bad memories, too much baggage. She loved her mother, but her stepfather always made her feel uncomfortable. Probably some left over resentment over how quickly he'd come into their lives after her father's death when she was fourteen. The only good thing Charlie had ever done was introduce her to Joseph. His father worked security for one of Charlie's clients and because their ancestry shared ties to the Iroquois nation, to the Seneca people, Charlie thought they'd have a lot in common. Even if his reasoning was obnoxious and ignorant, he'd been right. Angie touched the dog tags around her neck and vowed that it wouldn't be for long, just a few weeks until she found a job somewhere else.

Her mother and stepfather lived just outside of Pittsburgh. Papa Charlie, as her kids called him, was a business man in the city, but Nana Kate refused to leave the house that had been passed down in her family. Each generation expanded it until it was a jumble of additions, bound together by the lemon scent of wood polish, apple wood smoke, and fresh baked bread. She didn't want to live there but visits were welcome.

Angie double-checked the large black numbers beside the door as she pulled into the drive. The house looked the same, apart from the awful blue siding, but her mother's flower beds were gone, sodded over or filled with boxwood shrubs, pruned to spires. The maple tree she'd climbed as a girl, carved her initials into, had disappeared, leaving not even the suggestion of a stump for a headstone. The old white-washed rockers were gone from their place on the front porch. Now, that warm, comforting place gathered shadows and dust.

"Please, remember your manners, girls. I promise this won't be for long. Best behavior, all right?" She chanced a glance in the rearview mirror, rewarded by one bright smile and one scowl. "Grace, drop the attitude."

"Whatever." Grace looked away, out the window, anywhere but at Angie. "This doesn't look like I remember."

Sadness welled in Angie. "I know. I don't know when it changed, but it did. Just like everything else, I guess."

Angie pulled into the driveway and parked the old Taurus station wagon. As she got out, stretched her tired legs, her mom and stepdad emerged from the house. She gasped a little. Her mother had lost weight, gone from curvaceous to deflated, from solid to gaunt.. Her eyes had a vague and distracted air as if she was elsewhere. Her mouth was drawn in a line.

"Welcome home, Angela." Her stepdad, Charlie, looked younger, more muscular, less gray, rosy where her mom was pale "Hello girls, welcome home." He held out his arms to the girls but Lily hid behind Angie and Grace muttered something incoherent.

"Girls, please." Angie sighed. "I'm sorry, Papa Charlie. They're tired."

"It is a long drive." The way he looked at the girls made Angie's stomach knot, but she couldn't put her finger on the reason. "We almost thought you weren't going to make it in time."

"In time? Am I missing something?" She looked back and forth between her mother and stepdad.

"Oh, nothing big of course. Your mother and I put together a little welcome home party for you."

"I don't think any of us are up for a party right now." Angie shook her head, shocked that her mother – queen of all things proper – had allowed him to even think about a party. Joseph had only been gone for two months; they'd just driven for two or three eternities across the country. None of them were fit company.

"Not tonight, Angela. Tomorrow at eight sharp." His firm, authoritative voice left no room for argument. "It'll be good for you."

"I don't mean to be rude, but the moving truck isn't here yet, won't be until the day after tomorrow. We don't have anything appropriate to wear and, honestly, I can't imagine having any kind of 'party' right now."

"Nonsense. Your mother has taken care of dresses for each of you. This means a great deal to us. And it will be good for you to meet these people; they could help you get established."

The crafty bastard knew damned well that Angie couldn't pass up any opportunity at employment. "Then I had better get the girls settled in and get rested. We're really very tired."

"I made up your old room." Her mom finally spoke. Even her voice seemed little more than an echo of her usual self. "I'll bet you three are hungry too, right? I have dinner waiting. Just needs heated up a little."

"Thanks, Mom." Angie took Lily's hand in hers and tried to take Grace's but she'd already bounded up the stairs ahead of Nana Kate. Someday, the girl would have to forgive her, instead of dwelling on all the unfairness. Angie crossed her fingers for her mother's meatloaf and walked into the house.

After being plied with a disappointing store-bought lasagna and chocolate cake, the trip caught up to Angie and her girls. It didn't take long for them to settle in. Angie fell asleep with Lily nestled in close on her right and Grace on her left before the last of the credits rolled on Lily's latest favorite princess movie.

When the dream came, she knew it was a dream, but it had nothing in common with any dream she'd had before. The sound of chanting filled her ears in the darkness, "Sha'Daa… Sha'Daa… Sha'Daa…." The voices rang in a melody that stirred her blood, the drums beat with some deep instinctual familiarity. She moved through the cold dark, breathing in the scent of deep earth. Closer to the sounds until a flickering glimmer of light appeared around a bend and she could see the long tunnel spreading out before her.

She heard noises behind her: a child crying, a woman pleading in a language Angie didn't understand. In the dim light, she made out the shapes of men, heading straight for her. They didn't notice her, passing right through her as she tried to duck away from them. The child they carried saw Angie and tried to reach out to her, screaming as her tiny hand passed through Angie's arm.

As the men turned into the lit chamber, Angie got a good look at them – broad shoulders, red flesh painted with symbols that frightened her, dark, clawed demons. Their long, black hair had bones tied into it.

A woman stumbled down the same path the men had taken, another painted man pushing her along with a long stick. Tears welled in her midnight eyes, running down over her smooth, red clay skin. A chill ran through Angie, goosebumps crawling down her arms. Angie felt an immediate kinship with the woman but unlike the child she did not seem to see Angie. Angie followed after them.

Light flickered from torches, licking the faces of a thousand skulls embedded in the walls, some of them human, others, decidedly not. The chamber smelled foul, old death and sulfur dancing in her nose. Men sat cross-legged, beating on hide drums. The child and the woman were bound, huddled together on the floor at the feet of a man wearing a hideous skull for a mask, a loin cloth, and thick black paint. The skull-mask frightened Angie, its foreign shape something she'd never seen before, broad at the back, tapering down to a beak-like snout, jaws lined with two rows of serrated teeth. It gleamed in the firelight, yellow with age and lovingly polished.

The masked man spoke, grabbing the child's wrist, slicing open her tender palm on one of the skull's teeth. The woman and Angie both yelled and rushed toward the man, but when the child's blood touched the ground, the earth trembled. A dark empty space opened in the center of the room. A small, iridescent pool of swirling black and blues, floating above the floor, just big enough for one long arm, with three sharp talons for fingers to reach through.

Angie woke in the dark, sweating, still feeling pulled, drawn towards that space, that arm. The word Sha'Daa echoed through her head. The girls lay asleep beside her, the soft sounds of their breathing calming her. Angie laid for a long time, awake in the dark, clutching Joseph's dog tags, visions of birdmen and blood fresh in her mind.

Lily and Grace went off exploring after breakfast, leaving Angie alone to scour the classifieds and help Nana Kate with the preparations for their 'welcome home' party. Never mind that none of them wanted to leave California in the first place, let alone celebrate it.

Every time Angie would try to ask her mother about the changes she'd noticed, the conversation stalled, shifted to some other, less intimidating subject. Angie promised herself that she'd pin her mother down and make her answer when the party ended. Charlie had done something to her, changed her and not for the better.

Angie positioned the last of the flowers on a table on the patio as Charlie called for her. Pushing her hair out of her face, she looked around at her work and smiled. The arrangements would have been much more beautiful if her mother's garden was still intact.

"You should round up the girls and get ready now, Angela." Charlie stepped onto the patio.

"I was just finishing up with the decorations." She pursed her lips as she inspected the strings of paper lanterns that bordered the large patio.

"And they're lovely too, but people will start arriving in about an hour and a half." He looked down his nose at her, ice in his gaze.

"Don't worry about us, Charlie. We'll be ready on time."

Angie turned away before she rolled her eyes. Yes, he was right, but she was thirty-four, not thirteen. Grace she found sitting in the car with her bag, reading a book. It took longer to find Lily, tucked under a pine tree, in the middle of a rousing game of hide and seek with her newest imaginary friend, Johnny.

Getting everyone washed and dried ate up most of their time, leaving just enough time to put the girl's sleek hair in braids and put their dresses on. Angie grimaced at her mother's taste in dresses. The three of them looked like matching brides in the ankle-length white sheaths. She didn't have much room to complain, beggars can't be choosers and all that.

As she zipped up Lily's dress, Angie noticed the silver bracelet around her daughter's wrist. "Honey, where did you find that?"

"Do you like it?" She twirled the end of her braid around her fingers. "Johnny gave it to me. Well, he didn't *give* it to me. He traded. That's what a good salesman does, he said."

"Traded you?"

"Yep for a pack of trick peppered gum." She held out her slender wrist to show off the too big bangle, a band of silver intricately engraved with tiny bears.

"Hey!" Grace grabbed for the bracelet. "That gum was mine, you little brat! The bracelet should be too."

"Grace. Not tonight." Angie sighed as World War Montour erupted again.

"You're mean." Lily's shoulders drooped. "But he gave me one for you too." She went to her bed and bent down to retrieve a box, pulling a second bracelet out of it. "Johnny said this one is yours." Lily handed over the silver circle with some reluctance. Grace immediately slipped it on

Concern filled Angie. "If you see this Johnny again, I want you to point him out to me, OK?" She didn't like the idea of strange men giving her babies jewelry. Gum for silver, indeed.

"Sure." Lily spun the bracelet around her wrist like a little hula hoop, oblivious to her mother's concern.

"All right, I think we're about as ready as we're going to get." She checked them all over once more, pulled her own straight, black hair, into a tight knot and led the girls out of the room.

As they stepped out of the house into the deepening evening, she heard Lily gasp. With the delicate lanterns strung up around the patio, the flowers bursting from their vases, and the torches along the tall hedge, it did look a bit other-worldly. Angie smiled to see the awe on her youngest daughter's pretty face. Even Grace looked impressed. They didn't have time to soak in the splendor as Papa Charlie's friends began to trickle into the party.

Angie quickly grew tired of people, especially with this particular group of people. Most of Charlie's friends fit neatly into two categories: snobs or lewd men who cared less about who she was than what cup size she wore. Lily and Grace stayed pretty close to her. She couldn't blame them as there were no other children at the party. Another thing that didn't seem like her mother. She started to wonder if her mom hadn't had a stroke or something.

"Angie," her mom appeared at her side as if she knew Angie was thinking of her, "you need to loosen up a bit. Mingle. Talk to people. They're here to meet you, after all."

"Yeah, I'm sorry. I'm just really not much for parties, I guess." She sighed, staring at the tall hedges that lined the patio, certain she saw something move between them.

"Nonsense," she pressed a drink into Angie's hand.

"Mom! You know I don't drink." The bourbon smelled so good, too good. "Twelve steps, remember?"

"Yes dear I know very well. Appearances, dear, just carry it and pretend. You're too tense. Please, your stepfather really went out of his way for you tonight. Now girls, why don't you come with me and I'll get you something good to eat."

Angie wanted to call her girls back but Kate had already taken their hands and started towards the house. Her mother's behavior now bordered on the bizarre.

"Lovely party," a man's voice startled her.

"Yes. Isn't it just?" She breathed in the intoxicating, forbidden smell of booze and ached to sip it. "Thirsty?"

"You don't want your drink?" The tall man smiled, light glinting off a gold tooth, as he tipped his dark Fedora. He was older then she but she found it hard to pin down his age. His eyes were deep, dark and compelling.

She shook her head. "I don't drink."

"Well then, don't mind if I do." He reached into the pocket of his long trench coat and pulled out a silver flask. "Not for me, mind you, but you never know who might need what when." The container disappeared into his coat with a wiggle of his eyebrows. "Now would you look at that? Wonder what that could be?"

He handed her the crystal glass, empty but for a small trace of white gel. "What the hell was in there?" Angie didn't mean for the words to come out of her mouth but the man acted like he hadn't heard her.

"It doesn't seem right, my taking your drink and giving you nothing in return." He put his hand back in his pocket. "What kind of Salesman would I be then?"

"So you're Johnny." She should have been uneasy around him, but something about him gave her comfort as if she'd known him for years. Maybe the engraved bears didn't mean anything, certainly he couldn't have known her ancestors were of the Bear clan, the Hodidjioiñi"g'. Plus there were bigger things to worry about. Like her mom, drugging the drink she knew Angie couldn't drink.

"At your service, Angie." Johnny took his hat off and bowed with great flourish. "And this is for you. A special key for a special lock." He put a small key in her palm.

"I don't have any pockets," Angie said in confusion.

"Put it with his picture." The man put his hat back on and grinned in a way that reminded Angie of the Cheshire cat.

"How did you know about that?"

"Doesn't matter. You keep an eye on these people, Angie. For a while, you'll have to play along. When the time comes, you'll know what to do." Johnny tipped his hat and walked off into the night, disappearing into the shadows between the hedges.

Angie stood there for a moment, dumbfounded. Carefully she slid the tiny key into her bra with Joseph's picture. No one knew she kept his picture there, next to her heart.

Setting the empty glass on a table, Angie went to find the girls who were happy in the kitchen with Nana Kate. Johnny's words kept repeating in her head. *Play along.* When her mother shooed her back to the party, she went. She stayed near the door, waiting for the opportunity to grab the girls and run.

People drifted over to her and Angie and she tried to make small talk, enough to get by, painfully aware of how keenly Charlie watched her. Several of the other guests started acting strangely, slurred words, a few stumbles, wide yawns. Angie did what she could to play along, only marginally making a fool of herself.

When the first person fell asleep on the patio, Angie made her way into the house to roundup the girls. She wasn't tired but she sure as hell wasn't going to leave her girls alone to pretend to be drugged.

"Where are you going?" Charlie intercepted her at the door, hand tight around her wrist, almost painfully so.

"To get the girls. I'm sorry but I'm really very tired. I thought I'd just go ahead and take them to bed now so one has to worry about them."

"No need. Your mother has it all in hand." He tightened his grip on her wrist, pulling her away from the door towards a lounge chair on the patio. "Here, why don't you just sit down and rest a minute. I'm sure you'll feel better soon."

It took everything in her not to wriggle away from him, from the way he and his friends were looking at her. She looked around and several of the other people were beginning to fall asleep on any chair they could get to. Others though, four of them, they were watching with keen eyes and sly smiles. She resisted the urge to fight and run. There were too many of them for her to be able to get away and she had children to protect. Johnny did say to play along, so she would do so until she found the opportunity to run.

As she laid herself down on the lounge chair, she took a good look at the people who were still on their feet. One man took his jacket off, revealing a badge on his belt and a gun at his side. Angie's heart sank. What hope did she have of getting away with her girls with a cop on Charlie's side? So she forced herself to close her eyes and go limp. She resisted the urge to spring up and fight even as large hands groped her and lifted her up. The man put her over his shoulder, meaty hands high on her thighs as he carried her through the house and out the front door.

"The girls are ready. Put her in the back. Make sure you cuff her just in case she wakes up before it's time." Charlie's voice made Angie's skin crawl.

Angie prayed to every god she'd ever heard of as the man put her down in the back of a vehicle that stank of sweat and blood. He pulled her wrists together behind her back, the clink and snap of handcuffs echoing. As the vehicle moved, she rolled and shifted, bumping into metal walls. Carefully, watching the driver through the metal bars between them, she curled up into the fetal positioning, straining her shoulders, hoping the driver couldn't hear the popping sound as she pushed and wriggled until her arms were in front of her. Deft fingers tucked into her bra, fishing out the small key.

A turn of the key and the cuff on her left wrist sprung open. Angie swallowed a squeak of victory and popped the right cuff too. Hands free, she searched the back of the van for something, anything she could use as a weapon.

A cell phone twittered in the cab and the driver answered. "Yeah, Sarge," he said, "I don't know where you got that tip, but these people are harmless. It's just a party. No sign of drugs or weapons." Tense quiet filled the gap as the driver listened. "Charlie's wife called it in? You're sure? Well you know she hasn't been right lately."

Understanding washed over Angie and her heart sank. Charlie had enough power over Kate to make her turn her flowers under but not enough to let him hurt her daughter and granddaughters. He wouldn't expect his wife to call the cops. Or to drug the one drink Angie couldn't touch. And now they knew she'd tried to stop them.

"All right, Sarge. I'll stick around for a little bit longer, but I'm telling you there's nothing here." The driver disconnected and cursed.

Angie had no luck finding a weapon in the van. She tried to figure out where they were but the road twisted and turned like most Pennsylvania roads. When the van turned off pavement and onto a bouncy, pitted, gravel road, Angie cursed. They could be anywhere in the woods, judging by the small scratches she heard on the outside of the van, as branches clawed at the metal: a park, an old farm, a quad trail. Anywhere at all.

The driver got out of the van. Voices drifted in through the driver's open window. "You're certain the information came from Kate?" Charlie asked, disbelief in his tone.

"That's what my sergeant told me." The driver replied.

"All right. We'll take the girls down and get set up. It's time to deal with Kate, she's outlived her usefulness. Once I get the girls into the tunnel, take care of it. Just make it fast. The Sha'Daa is nearly upon us."

"You got it, boss."

Angie moved to the back door, feeling for a handle, some way out, but there wasn't any, even the holes where the handle would have been bolted in were filled with putty. She could do nothing for the mother who'd birthed her, who'd tried so hard to save her. A minute later the sound of a gunshot brought tears to her eyes and filled her, not with fear, but with steel determination.

She held the cuffs behind her back and curled up as far from the doors as she could get. When the driver climbed in to drag her out, if she moved fast enough, if she could remember all her marine husband had taught her, she might be able to take the advantage.

The doors opened and the man looked surprised to see her awake. "Come on. Get out here."

"N..n..no." She stumbled over her words, hoping she still looked stoned enough that he wouldn't consider her any kind of threat.

"Come on, now, no one's going to hurt you." He held out his hand to her. "You're safe now."

"You ...you killed my m...m...mom." It didn't take any acting at all to break up over those words.

"Damn." He let out a frustrated sigh and started climbing into the van.

Angie sprang into action, throwing herself at the officer as he climbed in, off balance enough for her to knock them both out of the vehicle, landing squarely on his broad back, the wind knocked out of him. She grabbed the automatic from its shoulder holster and rocked the slide. She didn't think about it, couldn't. Just aimed for his head and fired once, twice, deep into his skull, ruining his face and splattering hers with blood and bits of things she didn't want to think about.

Angie rose, kicked off her high heels and ran, barefoot, to where her mother lay on the ground. Kneeling down beside her, Angie put two trembling fingers on the side of her neck. The cruel red hole in the center of her mother's forehead mocked her. Death had already claimed her. "I know what you did Mama. I know you did your best."

Through her tears, she noticed a small fire flickering in the distance, beyond the tree line. Angie headed for it, careful to be quiet. The fire turned out to be a torch at the entrance to a tunnel, left behind for the cop. She took up the torch in her left hand, keeping the gun at the ready in her right. She was in luck it was a Colt .45, like Joseph had trained her with.

The tunnel still had the lingering scent of diesel fuel and freshly turned earth marking it as a recent excavation. She hadn't gotten more than five feet into it when the drums started. Like a panicked heartbeat, frenetic, wild, ancient. For a brief, hysterical moment, she wondered if some future-self was standing in the tunnel somewhere, watching.

Her bare feet made little noise as she ran through the tunnel. A hundred yards in, the chanting began. Angie could only understand the one word, over and over, "Sha'Daa." Images of disfigured skulls swam in her head.

Angie realized that this part of the tunnel was older, ancient timbers holding up the earth every few yards, the dirt was looser, drier under her toes. The tunnel made a hard right and Angie peered cautiously around it. Fifty yards away, the flickering yellows and oranges of firelight cast bright shadows in the dark. Angie dropped her torch. She'd need both hands to have any hope of being accurate with the big Colt.

The voices in the chamber grew louder, the drums thundering through the dark. Angie paused beside the entry, cursing the white dress that nearly glowed in the dim light. Trying to keep to the darkness, she pressed against the earth wall of the tunnel, shifting so that she faced the entrance. Instead of a dirt wall, she found herself face to face with a misshapen skull, like the one she'd seen in her dream.

She swallowed her fear and prayed she wouldn't be seen as she peered quickly into the chamber. She could see only part of the room, three large men pounding on drums, naked but for paint and loincloths. Closing her eyes, she listened, trying to hear each drum on its own, hoping that each one had a slightly different tone, because that meant there were only four drummers. Four drummers and Charlie.

One magazine, three shots fired, she had five shots left. If destiny had any love for her at all, she had enough. Lily screamed and Angie couldn't wait anymore. She flung herself into the entrance, aiming and firing three times in quick succession, putting rounds in the orange circles she pictured over centers just as Joseph had taught her. The big .45 slugs threw them on their backs.

She turned and saw her mistake, her heart leaping into her throat. There were two other drummers racing for her. Two more shots from the Colt and down they went, though her last shot went low and hit one man in the thigh, arterial blood spurted. Death would come slower for him.

"Give me my daughters," she aimed the empty gun at Charlie. Her daughters cowered behind the stepfather, their eyes wide and horrified. Her hands shook slightly as she looked at him, naked but for a cloth and the skull mask she'd seen in her dream, its teeth gleaming wickedly in the torchlight.

"You can't stop this!" Rage filled Charlie's voice. "This is my destiny! My ancestors failed last time. I will not. You can't stop me." He grabbed Grace by the wrist and her bracelet flashed a bright, unearthly green. Charlie screamed, pulling back his hand as if burned.

"Run!" Angie screamed. "Get out of the tunnel and hide. Don't come out for anyone but me."

Grace grabbed Lily's hand and ran for the entrance. As they passed the writhing drummer, his hand grabbed Lily's tiny ankle. As the younger girl screamed, Grace's foot shot out and connected solidly with the man's head, stunning him just enough to let Lily go. The girls ran into the tunnel, not looking back once.

"I don't need them anyway!" Charlie growled.

Angie gestured with the gun.

"You'd have shot me if you had a bullet left." He leapt toward her, grabbing Angie's hand and slicing deep into it with the tooth of his hideous skull mask. "Blood for the door. There must be blood for the door!"

As the blood dripped from her palm onto the floor, the earth trembled. A small, iridescent pool opened at the far side of the skull-lined chamber.

"Not enough. Not enough." He tried to cut her again but Angie slipped her blood-slicked hand out of his grasp, dodging him.

With a maniacal laugh, Charlie swung his fist and connected. Blood poured from her nose, each drop widening the opening pool. A long, scaly arm slipped through the gate, talons clicking on the skull and stone floor. Charlie whooped with glee, dancing in the firelight, screaming, "Sha'Daa! Sha'Daa!"

Angie tore at her dress, pulling strips and packing them into her nose, wrapping her hand to stop the blood from reaching the floor. All the blood from the men she'd killed hadn't done it. Only her blood opened the doorway, the same blood that ran through her daughters' veins.

She watched the arm slip back into its own dimension, only to be replaced by a long, narrow head. The same kind of head that Charlie wore for a mask. Wicked teeth and powerful jaws snapped and reached for her. And for Charlie too.

"Why are you doing this?" She ducked and dodged to escape the knife in Charlie's hand.

"I need your blood to open the door," he said, grinning behind the skull.

"Why open it at all?"

"I will be master. I will be the king of the world with the strongest, most vicious army the world has ever known. The entire human race will bow before me."

"I doubt very much that these," she jumped over the creature's feathered head, "care who you are. I don't think you'll be master of anything."

Charlie lunged toward her, the blade cutting. Angie blocked with the empty Colt. Everything Joseph ever taught her about defense surged through her as she spun around. The creature whined as it missed Charlie's leg by a hair's breadth. Angie kicked Charlie in his broad gut, pushing him backward, just enough. Charlie grabbed her leg, pulling her with him.

But the kick had brought him in range of the monster. He screamed in agony as the monster's teeth sunk deep into his flesh. An arm joined the head as the monster pulled Charlie closer. He bellowed, releasing her. Charlie kept screaming as the jaws clamped down, tearing flesh from his calf then thigh. The monster squawked, its claws buried in Charlie's thigh, keeping him still as it jerked its head to swallow the meat.

The sudden silence as Charlie passed out pushed Angie into action. She pulled her dress over her head, tearing a strip to bind her arm, to staunch the blood that drip, drip, dripped onto the skull floor. On all fours, she sopped up the blood on the floor with her dress, praying her own blood could be mixed enough to make it useless if it couldn't be removed. She rubbed and sopped, and the gate shrank until no blue iridescence could be seen beyond the demon's head. It shrieked and squawked in pain and anger as she cleaned up more blood. It screamed in pain as the gate collapsed, separating its head in her world from its body in its own.

Naked but for bra and panties, Angie sat down for a moment in the dark of the tunnel and stared at the monster's still snapping and twitching head, at Charlie's still form as his life's blood ran out of his severed arteries in a rush.

A mist filled the chamber, pouring out into the tunnel. It smelled of sage and flowers, washing the chamber clean of the scents of blood, sulfur, and death. Shadows moved in the mist and Angie's shoulders sagged. Had she failed after all? But it wasn't demons that came to stand before her. Men, their skin red like clay, their hair bound with leather and feathers, stood staring at her, smiling.

One beckoned for her to kneel and she did so, watching them with a mixture of disbelief and awe. One by one the men touched her with pollen coated fingers, washed her in the smoke of smoldering sage, before passing through her into the dark. Each man gifted her with a memory of another life, another time, when the Great Spirit ruled and the tribe was family.

One red-skinned man remained. His hair was long, grey and braided, the feathers on his head just as silver. "Hekáés Sha'Daa." The old man touched her face, his palms red with paint, and spoke to her in a language she didn't understand, even as his words became clear in her mind. "The time of the Sha'Daa. It is not over yet. This gate will not open this day or the next. You have done well, my daughter."

"The Sha'Daa?" She asked as the man plucked a feather from his headdress.

"The time when Hell is close enough to touch. Two days every ten thousand years during which the fate of our Earth is decided by those here to fight."

"How many gates are there?" Fear spiked in her gut.

"Too many to count and not all of them as well protected as this." He tucked the feather into her hair. "May your future be blessed for all time."

He kissed her forehead and passed through her, leaving her with a memory of his own, of the last Sha'Daa when his daughter defeated the men bent on opening the gate. In his memory there were two daughters, the solid and real red skinned girl from Angie's dream and an ethereal and ghostlike Angie, several shades too pale but identical in features.

With a last look at the chamber, at the bodies there, Angie turned away and ran through the darkness to find her girls. She stumbled blindly through the dark, trying to remember how far she'd come.

"Lily! Grace!" she called into the darkness.

The girls came running, still crying, and wrapped their tiny arms around Angie's waist. She dropped to her knees to hold her babies.

"I'm sorry, mama. For everything." Grace cried into Angie's shoulder.

"Baby, you've got nothing to be sorry for." She held them close. "It's going to be all right. We're safe now."

All Night Long

"**A** MANHATTAN," JOHNNY GROANED. "Shaken, not stirred." Bak spun around and quickly went about his ministrations. "Johnny?" Bak eyed his friend nervously. "You okay?"

"Healing, hee, hee, hee," Johnny grunted with a short string of barely controlled giggles. "Insides got a bit scorched by a volcano god in the pacific."

"Whoa." Bak said, concerned. "I've never said this before, but, you want like a dip in my resurrection bath, pal?"

Johnny chuckled for a long slow minute before making eye contact with Bak. A rowdy rendition of *I Wanna Hold Your Hand* echoed from the main stage.

"No, my friend," Johnny replied with just a hint of humor. "It's a kind offer, but, well, that wouldn't really help me. I'm not as, um, corporeal as I look. This damage is on somewhat of a higher spiritual level. I just need a few minutes of non-interrupted rest, ha, ha, ha, ha, ha..."

In the rear of the game pit the doomsday clock now had one half of its interior gears, jewels, and various incomprehensible guts in full operation. At least one hundred patrons just stood back there desperately trying to decipher its cryptic noises and flashing lights.

"Okay," Bak slid Johnny his martini. "One quick note though. I've, uh, got a lead for you."

"My tail?" Johnny glared straight ahead.

"Yah," Bak said nonchalantly while toweling the bar counter. "Young guy. Human. Average height. Caucasian. Some freckles. Been in and out about a dozen times since you last left. Nowhere in sight right now. Funny thing, though..."

"What's that?" Johnny frowned.

"He doesn't use the rear passages," Bak licked his lips. "It's like he just steps into shadows and disappears. Didn't think that kind of dimensional shifting was possible within these walls."

"Neither did I," Johnny said, while sipping the last of his drink. "He could be one bad hombre."

"You're scaring me Johnny," Bak said. "Ain't nobody tougher than you."

"Flattery," Johnny smirked, "won't make me pay off my bar tab any sooner." Johnny took a deep breath and shook silently, desperately forcing back a long rack of convulsive laughter. Bak did his best to ignore the uncomfortable display. Johnny's personality shifts from somber to nearly maniacal were legendary. Johnny's shaking eventually subsided and he looked healthy and whole again.

"Bak, great clambake," a friendly voice cut in. "Bloody Mary, hold the blood and heavy on the Mary. Johnny, looking sharp, you old hunker you."

Bak and Johnny turned sideways toward a handsome, dark-haired man of medium height and build.

"Kenneth," Johnny said. "Sick of Vegas already? Or is saving mankind beneath your high-minded objectives today?"

"Huh?" Kenneth frowned. "I haven't been to Vegas since I hacked off Sammy and Dino last month."

"Wait," Johnny added. "What year is it?"

"Nineteen-sixty-five. Why?"

"Temporal mixup. My bad," Johnny shrugged. "Was talking about a later you."

"Yah. Whatever daddy-oh," Kenneth rolled his eyes at Bak then took the first sip of his drink. "Ohhhh, Bak you're platinum, baby. Now, if you gassers will excuse me, I only popped in long enough to clear out the blackjack table. Got a hot bird waiting for me in Reno. This player is scramsville." Kenneth strode triumphantly back into the gaming pit. The stage band struck up a strong Mersy beat with *She Was Just Seventeen.*

"He's here," Bak hissed.

"What?"

"Your tail. He's on the other side of the grudge pit. Hasn't spotted you yet."

"I don't have time for this," Johnny spit out. "I've got to reconnoiter a Manhattan sewer, a submarine, and a Russian airport in the next four minutes."

"There's a bolt hole in the floor this end of the bar. Short tunnel leads to a 21st Century doorway in the back," Bak said out the side of his mouth. "Move it."

Moments later Johnny disappeared from sight and Bak slid the covering floor mat back into place.

A Roman gladiator, swinging a net and thrusting a trident, rounded off with a four tentacled Cthuluan monstrosity in the grudge pit. Three hundred patrons crowded around in appreciation as dozens of side bets changed hands, claws, hooves, pincers, and tentacles.

A Mexican mariachi troupe took to the stage, taking over from the now exhausted Liverpool mop tops. Bak had to give the four lads credit. The surrounding roar of voices was a tough aural opponent to overcome. Then again, Bak always paid in gold coins, which usually made it worth the effort.

"Twenty-one," a dealer shouted from the gaming pit.

"Ring-a-ding, come to daddy," Kenneth's joyous voice retorted.

"Barkeep," a deep threatening growl stated close by.

Bak looked up. Johnny's recent pursuer had silently appeared on the other side of the bar.

"I'm looking for someone."

The Voyage Of The Eris

By T. Anthony Truax

THE PROUD, OLD LIGHTHOUSE STOOD watch over the edge of the rocks. Below it the cold Atlantic roared and crashed into the cliff base, as it had for so many years. Once a beacon to guide and welcome for Long Island's deep-sea fisherman, the lighthouse was now a "must have" photo for the tourists visiting the modern-day playground for the East Coast's elite: The Hamptons.

A crowd of reporters waited inside the dry-dock warehouse of The Montauk Yacht Club. Its poured cement floor and aluminum walls echoed and amplified the idle chatter of the mix of reporters from newspapers in New York and Boston.

Lou Brohman and his wife, Amanda, wandered into the area. The bewildered pair felt lost and out of place. Lou was amazed at the size of the warehouse. Its arching ceiling could accommodate the tallest mast of any boat imaginable. He firmly held his wife's hand as they headed toward the commotion at the far end.

"Why in the hell are we here, Mandie?" Lou groaned.

"Lighten up, Lou," Amanda replied. "You've been writing about adventure and history for twelve years, but you've never had any of your own. Besides, Allyson is taking care of everything, even our flight home."

"This is not *my* idea of a vacation. A vacation is sitting next to you by a pool and drinking Cuervo margaritas."

"You are gonna have one hell of a time mister," Amanda said, playfully punching him on the shoulder, "and you'll be thankful when we reach England."

Lou looked around the warehouse. Amanda started on again about some of the sites she wanted to see in London. Lou listened idly as he took in the scenery. Opposite the folding chairs and reporters was a massive tarp. Whatever the reporters were here for was hiding behind it.

One reporter from the *New York Daily* recognized Lou and casually approached him. "Looking for some new writing material?"

"Nope," Lou replied, "somehow I just got on the guest list and now I'm going to merry ole England."

"Two Oscar nominations and the hottest movie scripts in the business had nothing to do with that invitation, right?"

Lou smiled back awkwardly. He'd never figured out how to deal with his own success. "Just lucky, I guess."

"Luck, eh? If you really don't wanna go, trade your ticket to me. *This* many celebrities with nothing else to do but get drunk and be stupid…I could sell that story to the highest bidder and retire to Myrtle Beach."

Amanda leaned in towards the reporter, "Not a chance."

A plain-dressed man with salt and pepper hair walked to the podium in front of the tarp and cleared his throat. The newspaper reporters milled closer, writers from the boating magazines, however, recognized Buddy Harrison and quickly moved in.

Harrison had made himself into a living legend in power boating. Before being wooed away by Allyson Chrysler-Smith, he'd been chief engineer and architect for Anheuser-Busch Racing, heading up the "Miss Budweiser" powerboat program. The last boat he designed for them set the current world speed record for a sprint boat at 220 miles per hour. When it came to boats and speed, Harrison was the lone giant in the field.

"After eighteen months of designing, testing and retesting," Harrison began in his subtle, Southern drawl, "it's time for our creation to do what no other watercraft had ever done: cross the Atlantic Ocean in forty-nine hours!"

A murmur of astonishment ran round the huge room. Harrison motioned for everyone to settle down. "I would like to invite the sole financier of this record-setting project, Allyson Chrysler-Smith, to join me at the podium and unveil our creation."

The twenty-five year old billionaire-heiress approached the podium, the newspaper reporters muscled their way into clearer view. She looked like a modern day princess: straight blonde hair and a swimsuit model's appearance. Even dressed in a modest, white business suit, she glowed. Lou tried not to gawk at her, especially with Amanda at his side. She had all that and a Brown University Bachelor's Degree in business and marketing. Her not-so-private personal life was less brilliant; torrid affairs, alleged drug-use and an engagement that ended with her fiancé's suicide mere days before an appearance before a Connecticut grand jury.

Allyson smiled at the flashing cameras.

"Ladies and gentlemen," she proclaimed, "I present to you all the ship that will redefine luxury in ocean travel. I give you…*Eris!*"

The tall, gleaming bow reflected the explosion of camera flashes. Harrison had already moved away from the podium and returned to the stage with a metal tripod and several posters.

As Chrysler-Smith left the stage, the reporters settled down. Harrison directed their attention to the tripod and sketch showing the outline of the craft from above.

"*Eris*," he began, "is a four-deck yacht, standing some fifty feet tall, and is the first boat of her kind. She's built to be environmentally friendly while providing a fast, yet luxurious ride to her passengers. Her double-hull is constructed of aluminum and industrial grade molded plastic, with twenty-eight suites to accommodate the fifty planned guests for her maiden voyage. Solar panels atop the roof of the fourth deck will supply ample electricity for all of the amenities, as well as power the massive turbine engine that will thrust *Eris* across the Atlantic.

"She's aerodynamically designed to cut through the air by using higher than normal bow and a bubble-shaped glass facing on the two "above deck" floors. A similar bubble-shaped glass enclosure at the stern creates a two-deck observation area. The exterior design of the craft tapers bow to stern.

"At the speeds that *Eris*' engine, which we've nicknamed 'The Blower,' can muster," Harrison waved his arms, "sun tanning on the deck would just be a bad idea anyway."

Several reporters chuckled along with Harrison.

"What about the odd-looking stilts poking from the sides of the craft," a boating magazine reporter asked.

Harrison smiled. "The trick to getting *Eris* to achieve the speed Ms. Chrysler-Smith demanded had surprisingly little to do with engine power. To further reduce friction, the boat is designed to lift out of the water and ride on the two "skis" attached to the "legs" protruding from the hull. To prevent too much lift, hydraulically powered wings are positioned from their recessed areas within the hull and flaps, like on a commercial airliner, help control the air's flow.

"The design of *Eris* was a collaborative effort. I sought out suggestions and advice not only from experts within the boat-racing field, but I received useful information from Formula One car designers, engineers that designed military and commercial aircraft and even some friends at NASA."

A large map showing the northern half of the Atlantic Ocean unfurled behind Harrison. "Given the fact that *Eris* would be traveling at over 115 mph on a pair of steel-reinforced skis, steering will be near impossible. *Eris* will travel due east on a path parallel to forty degrees north latitude, heading directly towards Portugal, for approximately twenty five hours, then cut engines and coast to a stop within fifty miles north of the Azores.

"There will have to be about a six to seven hour cooling period," Harrison explained, "because a single turbine engine just can't make the entire five thousand mile trip with a craft this size without it. Technology will eventually catch up and eliminate this requirement, but the bar will already by set by us."

"Once 'The Blower' cools, *Eris* will head west by northwest; for the southern mouth of the English Channel. The second leg of the journey will take another thirteen to fourteen hours."

"Buddy?" a reporter interrupted, "that doesn't add up to forty-nine hours."

"You're right, it doesn't," Harrison replied. "Our final destination will be 'Jubilee Gardens,' in the heart of London, thirty miles inland from the English Channel up the River Thames."

As Harrison spoke further about the *Eris* and her unique attributes, an assistant passed out a neatly typed list of passengers. The man handed one to Lou and he read it, making sure his name was there. The list included several actors, a couple of musicians and a dozen or so of the more famous members of the Hampton's 'Brat Pack,' the trust-fund babies constantly moving from party to party and living off of their inexhaustible inheritances.

One name near the bottom caught Lou's attention: Manuel Cortez Esperanza. A life-long boxing fan, Lou had become fascinated with the Nicaraguan-born world champion. "El Presidente" was known less for his eight consecutive knockouts then for his generosity toward his fellow countrymen, since the end of the most recent civil war. Suddenly, this trip didn't seem like such a horrible idea.

"Lou?" Amanda gently called out, "come and meet the President of Nicaragua."

Lou's eyes lit up like those of a small child on his birthday as he met the olive-skinned man.

Turned out that Esperanza and two members of his team were fans of his films and writing. Although Manny, as he insisted he be called, had a thick Hispanic accent, he was pleasant and easily understood. Lou was surprised at Manny's height. Lou, who stood about six feet and two inches tall, was more that a head taller than Manny. His ring persona had made Lou think this unbeatable warrior would be more like a mountain.

"Si, I get that a lot," Manny said. "Tell me, have you met Senor Johnny?"

"No. I didn't see his name on the list. Who is he?" Lou replied.

"A most engaging fellow. He just approached me with a quick business proposition. I thought he was loco, but suddenly I found I had made the deal."

Manny turned to point the man in question out.

"He's right over here. I traded him one of my used jump ropes for a... where did he go?"

"What does he look like?"

"A slender man, a little taller than you. A real, how do you say…character? Wears a long black trench coat and has a shiny gold front tooth, like a villain from one of your American gangster movies."

"Perhaps he's in the clubhouse getting a drink. Let's grab a beer and see if we can find him."

The three headed for the main clubhouse, a mansion-like three-story structure. Amanda took Lou's arm and rested her head on her husband's shoulder as Manny told them of his upcoming title defense in London.

Eris cut through the Atlantic like a saber. The yacht had been christened with a bottle of 1959 Dom Perignon champagne by Allyson, amid flashing cameras and television spotlights. *Eris'* propeller engines roared to life and she set off on her course, due east towards the Azores.

The view from within the domed helm was quite a site: one hundred eighty degrees of pale-blue sky meeting with a darker blue, yet surprisingly placid Atlantic.

Some six hours into the trip, the first glitch reared its head: all inbound and outbound communications, even the satellite telephone, ceased working. The rest of the instruments within the helm: the GPS navigation, the sonar and even Harrison's antique brass compass, remained operational.

Harrison and his two associates only briefly considered turning back. Harrison decided they would not need the radio, so long as they maintained their planned heading and watched the radar for any oncoming blips. Nothing was so far amiss that it couldn't wait to be checked out once they reached the Azores as 'The Blower' cooled. From there, their contacts could be easily raised by cell phone.

Below the command center, Lou casually stayed off to the side and soaked in the debauchery; he hadn't seen this much partying since college. The musicians took turns playing for the passengers while the rest huddled by one of the several bars, snorting lines of cocaine or firing down shots of the finest whiskey that Allison's money could buy. A couple of them lay passed out behind one bar.

Almost every one of the actors and actresses pulled Lou aside to talk him into writing them into his next screenplay.

"I'll see what I can do," Lou would accommodatingly answer each of them, "but it's always the studio's final decision."

Lou looked across the room more than once and watched Manny hold court. Lou could tell Manny had already grown tired of this scene as well.

It seemed like every intoxicated celebrity was taking one phantom punch at him. Manny was smart. With a multi-million dollar title defense less than two weeks away, breaking a hand on the glass jaw of a drunken party guest would be a costly overreaction. He just smiled and let them walk away, unharmed.

At one point, Manny gave a weary glance over at Lou and each knew what the other was thinking: *Get me off of this boat!*

A warm hand gently rubbed Lou's left shoulder. He smiled thinking it was Amanda, but it was Allyson. As remarkable as Allyson looked on television, it didn't do her justice from two feet away. Her eyes were a little hazed over from the excessive drinking and lack of sleep. She draped her arms over Lou's shoulders.

"Are you having fun on my boat?" she asked.

"Yes. It's almost as beautiful as you are, Allyson."

She giggled and replied, "It's fast too."

Lou bit his bottom lip. "I've been meaning to ask you a question?"

"You want me for your next movie?"

"You don't need me for that. You could buy your own studio and make yourself the star."

"True, but owning the studio doesn't guarantee it would be a good movie. I need a genius like you to..."

"My question," he restarted and changed subjects, "is, why did you name this boat *Eris*?"

"Because this is my boat and that's what I am...an heiress."

"But the way it's spelled. Eris was a Greek goddess..."

"A goddess? Was she pretty?"

"Of course she was pretty...she was a goddess," Lou answered. Evidently she had no idea that in Greek mythology Eris was the mischievous and malevolent goddess of strife and discord, sister to Ares, god of war.

"You didn't answer my question, Louie," Allyson pouted, "I asked if men fought over her?"

"She started the Trojan War."

Again Allyson giggled. "You said 'Trojan.'"

"Yes," Lou sighed, "yes I did."

As Allyson turned and staggered in the direction of a buffet table across the room, he mumbled to himself how fortunate the rest of the Ivy League must feel that Allyson didn't roam *their* hallowed halls.

Up in the command center of *Eris*, Kerry Taylor had the helm while Harrison was taking a nap. Kerry had known Harrison for the better part of eight years and had either piloted or assisted Harrison on many of his racing campaigns. As second in command, money didn't buy better than Taylor.

Taylor was more concerned that the ship's communications were not cooperating than Harrison, but was somewhat put to ease knowing the rest of the instruments were functional. A little more than twenty-four hours had passed since *Eris* left Montauk and everything seemed to be going as planned: speed was steady at one hundred eighteen miles per hour, course was steady and the ride was smooth. "The Blower" was running a little hot, but its temperature was nowhere near a dangerous level. *Eris* was gliding across the top of the ocean like a skater on freshly cut ice.

Since steering was impossible while "The Blower" was engaged, Taylor just watched the engine temperature and positioning. Harrison and Chrysler-Smith had made sure that no ocean vessels would be within three miles of their course. All Taylor had to do was make sure nothing went wrong.

Taylor lifted his coffee mug and knocked some papers onto the floor. He knelt to pick them up. As he stood, he glanced at the sonar screen and saw something that was not supposed to be there. Something that *wasn't* there the last time he checked...a blip. Not just any blip, but a green blob on their heading. He glanced at his watch and did a quick calculation. Two minutes to impact, at the most, given their current speed.

"How the hell did *you* get there?" Taylor muttered. They were still another hour away from the Mid Atlantic Ridge and the ocean bottom was still thousands of feet beneath them.

Taylor slapped at the large red button: the emergency kill switch for "The Blower." Next, he pounded on the locked door behind him to wake Harrison.

"Buddy!" he barked out, "Wake up! We're heading face first into a crap storm."

Buddy opened his eyes and noticed the engine wasn't running. He sat up, opened the door and walked to the helm.

"Kerry?" Harrison inquired. The tremor in his voice frightened Taylor. "What the hell is that big-assed green blob doing on the sonar?"

"I dunno, Cap. You plotted this course. I was really hoping you'd tell me."

"There's nothing out here but blue sky and salt water. Raise the flaps on the wings. We gotta slow this son-of-a-bitch down!"

"They went up as soon as I killed the engine."

Harrison glanced at his watch, the instruments and the menacing blob, which was approaching sickeningly closer to the center of the screen. "Kerry, we can't lower the rudder and prop engines until we get below fifty!"

Taylor and Harrison both knew exactly what would happen if *Eris* hit something at their speed. Taylor and Harrison had both seen their share of fatal high-speed boat crashes to know what they were in for.

"What do we do?" Taylor demanded

"Tell the passengers to brace for collision, but do it calmly."

Allyson stood behind the buffet table, directly behind two white-coated men serving cake and champagne. She raised her voice and waved everyone over.

Manny had just made his way over to Lou, who was seated along the starboard bulkhead. Lou, with a scotch and water on the rocks in one hand, patted the seat next to him and Manny quickly obliged. Amanda appeared from the rear balcony and sat next to her husband.

"That's an excellent idea," a voice said. They looked up at a steward, a tall man with kind eyes. "Why don't you try buckling into theses chairs," he said. "They are the latest safety equipment but quiet comfortable."

"Is something-" Lou began, then realized he was already buckling in.

"I wonder if Allyson is gonna mention why they shut the big motor off," Amanda stated, also snapping her harness as was Manny. She looked up and the steward was gone.

"Are we at the Azores already?" Lou asked. He glanced at his watch but it, was almost ninety minutes earlier than he had expected them to slow the engines.

"Hi everyone," Allyson started as she steadied herself against the tabletop. "I really hope everyone is having a great time. Are you?"

The thirty or so people standing in front of the table let out lively whoops and calls in answer to her.

"Fantastic," she continued. "I want everyone to grab a fresh glass of champagne for what I have to tell you...now when we dock in London I want you all to stay on..."

The server to Allyson's left whirled around at her and forcefully drove a silver pie-cutter into her throat. Her jaw fell open and her eyes widened as she staggered backwards against the wall behind her. Blood sprayed from her severed vein and onto her guests. The front of Allyson's party dress turned crimson as blood flowed over her tanned breasts. Some of the guests screamed in fright as they looked up from their blood-tainted champagne to watch their hostess slide down the wall into a puddle of her own blood. Others actually laughed, thinking it was some type of prank using expensive movie special effects and gadgets.

The laughing stopped as the server that had just felled Allyson picked up an axe from beneath the table, turn to the other server, who was stunned stiff by what he had just witnessed, and viciously struck him above his right eye. A spray of red shot from the wound and covered his grinning attacker with dots of blood.

Panic gripped the screaming guests as they scattered in every direction, trying to escape from the blood-stained maniac struggling to force the axe from the server's skull.

Amidst the confusion, blinking blue lights began to flash. Taylor appeared in the doorway, loudly instructing passengers to find a seat and buckle their seatbelts before...

The axe struck Taylor squarely in the chest.

Seconds later *Eris'* still exposed starboard ski struck it something. *Eris* was still going more than sixty miles per hour at impact. The force of the collision bent the metal ski up and backwards and spun the entire craft downwards and to its right as the incredible momentum caused the doomed vessel to violently barrel roll across the top of the ocean. It skipped like a rock flung across the water. Chunks of the solar panels, as well as steel, fiberglass and aluminum were thrown in every direction as *Eris* repeatedly bounced off the water and viciously spun in the air before finally coming to rest on her shattered hull.

At the first sound of the collision, Lou, Amanda and Manny had closed their eyes and rode out the horrific carnival ride. They ached from the ordeal, but at least they were alive, the fighter-plane-rated body-harnesses of the thick cushioned recessed-seats having done its job. The three, still buckled into their bodymold-crash-seats, took in the eerie silence. Not even the slightest groan of agony or plea for mercy met their ears.

The tall steward who'd bade them buckle in, sloshed through the shin-high water and gently placed his hand on Amanda's trembling arm. Though his white coat was smeared with blood, by some miracle, he appeared to be unharmed.

"Madam," he said, "if you are able to stand, we must get the three of you to a life boat."

Amanda did as she was told and slowly splashed her way with her husband and Manny through the reddened seawater towards the stairs. She kept her eyes straight ahead, knowing the carnage that surrounded them. Lou scanned the room and looked for some sign of life. He saw nothing but the once white walls, now covered in blood and gray matter. Scattered and broken bodies floated face down in the rising water; no bubbles to signify life anywhere. In all his years of writing, he had never imagined this kind of horror

Once on the main deck, a second man, another server who had survived the wreck, assisted the three into an inflated, octagon-shaped raft. The dark-skinned Hispanic, also wore a bloodied white coat, but he was covered in cuts and bruises.

"Where are you going?" he called out as the first man turned back.

"I'm going below to look for more survivors. Paddle *that* way to that island and I'll be right behind you."

"The boating is sinking, you fool!"

"I need to check the suites below deck. I'll be right behind you. Now go!"

"Hermano," Manny called out and pointed to the man with the paddle, "dame un." Which in Spanish meant, *Brother, give me one.*

Manny and the other man, named Ricardo, paddled in the direction of the nearby island. Amanda clung to her husband's arm and shivered as she watched the doomed *Eris* sink, stern first, beneath the waves. There was no sign of the first man.

"Lou, I can still see it," Amanda said listlessly. "Terrified and screaming people flung about like socks in a dryer.

As the orange raft neared the island, the three men jumped over the side and pulled it onto the rocky shore. There was no sand anywhere, no trees either, just barren hills of wet stone. Manny and Lou helped Amanda, still visibly shaken, out of the raft while Ricardo went ahead by himself.

Fifty yards inland, they found a pair of massive, square-shaped stone pillars. Beyond the pillars were toppled stone walls. Lou touched one of the pillars; it was cold and wet.

"Where in God's name are we?" Lou asked.

"Perhaps," Manny replied, "we have crashed into Atlantis."

"No, you haven't found Atlantis," a voice called out from beyond one of the crumpled ruins. "I welcome you all to the lost island city of Is."

A man strode out from behind a pile of carved boulders. It was the server who had murdered Allyson. He wore the same uniform as before, but it was dry, clean and pressed. In his right hand he carried a long sword, and in his left, he held the severed head of Ricardo. He stopped about twenty feet from the final three survivors of the wreck, casually dropped the head and leaned on his sword as if it were a gentleman's walking stick.

"And then there were three," he said with a welcoming grin.

"What the hell is the meaning of all this?" Lou demanded as he picked up a large rock. "Who are you and why are we here?"

Manny moved to stand at his shoulder, his hands coming up.

"My, my...you talking monkeys have become so demanding. Why not ask your deliverer, behind you...for Elemeniah caused the boat to strike the stone, not me. I was content in killing you all one at a time. Quite ironic for the angel of safe waters."

The three turned to see the man who'd helped them off the sinking boat. He, like the man with the sword, still wore a server's uniform, dry and free of bloodstains.

"It is true," he said, "just as you, Dagon, summoned your sunken city back to the surface." He turned to them, his face filled with an ancient and limitless sadness. "I could not save those aboard the Eris. They would have struck upon Is in only a few more seconds. I could only prevent Dagon from slaying the one he came for by advancing the disaster a few seconds. A horrible choice but during the Sha'daa both demons and angels are limited. Humans always hold the balance."

"Yes," Dagon said as he drove the sword between the stones and into the moist ground, "it is *mine*. I can raise it wherever I please. Is was once a proud and prosperous city, welcoming all who came in peace and repelling those who would do the city's inhabitants any harm.

"The king of Is betrothed his only daughter to the ocean to ensure the city's safety and a lasting peace. The princess would take a lover by day and give him an enchanted mask to wear at night. This mask would bedazzle her lover to walk into the ocean.

"One day, a prince dressed in red came to Is to seek out the hand of the fair princess. She took him into her chamber, as she had done so many times before, but before she could convince the red prince to don the enchanted mask, he convinced her to give him the city. The princess crept into her sleeping father's chamber and stole the key to the city's gates. But as the prince accepted the key, the spurned ocean rose up and devoured the city. All on the island died save for the princess, whom the vengeful sea turned into a mermaid to lure sailors to their demise.

"Over three thousand years have passed, Dagon," Elemeniah said, "and little of this glory you spout has surfaced since then."

"Not so," Dagon retorted. "The princess served me well over the centuries and I also took the *Titanic* as a prize...but the task I have now been assigned will earn me the highest acclaim the Abyss can bestow, once our victory is complete."

Lou raised the stone he held in his hand.

"Son of Man," Elemeniah said, "drop that stone. So long as the demon remains encased in mortal flesh, his powers are limited. To kill him would unleash him."

"Tsk. You're no fun," Dagon said. "It seems we have reached an impasse, old friend. You cannot pass me with your mortal ward. The Gifted will not help the Council of Twelve to close the portal. In six hours the Council will be overrun by General Agaliarept and his legions once they exit the portal.

"ou cannot defeat me; for we are immortal...we could battle until this planet plummets into the sun before there would be a victor."

"Yet I challenge you under the rules of the Sha'daa," the angel replied.

Dagon only playfully shrugged. "Then our lot is cast. Let us play." Dagon waved his hand and the ground behind him shook as it rose. A second hand gesture made the risen stone flat and polished.

Elemeniah calmly walked towards the three survivors and silently motioned for them to come closer.

"What the demon says is true. All across Earth, a demonic invasion has begun and mortals are being slaughtered. It will worsen if I do not deliver my ward to the Council."

"Which one of us is he trying to stop?" Manny asked.

"I'll not say, Son of Man, for then Dagon would know."

Manny glared into Elemeniah's onyx eyes, "What are we to do then? What is this Sha'daa?"

"Embrace," he replied as he opened his arms. Elemeniah's arms grew in length and easily corralled Lou, Amanda, and Manny in a powerful, but warm embrace. Suddenly everything became clear to each of them. Knowledge flowed freely into their minds, like wine from a bottle. Dagon had to be defeated for Elemeniah, the Unmovable Mover's appointee to guarantee safe passage of "The Gifted" to England. The Council of the Twelve could not do so without besting Dagon. Because "The Gifted" was mortal, Elemeniah could not pass through and carry him or her through the celestial realm; "The Gifted" could only travel through the mortal realm.

Although many were born with a chance to become one of "The Gifted," many were led astray by the ways of the world. For the purest, it was an honor to briefly serve the highest cause and to protect the true Defender. For an imposter, a painful death was a certainty.

Thy will be done, echoed in the minds of all three as they followed Elemeniah toward the raised stone. The polished surface had sixty-four squares, eight rows of eight columns; each square was two feet wide by two feet long.

Lou looked at Elemeniah. "He wants to play checkers against you for one of us?"

"Not checkers, idiot," Dagon shouted from the other side, "Chess." Dagon's clothing had changed from the neatly pressed white and black server's uniform to a red tunic and toga. A thin golden crown was across his brow and the golden key of Is hung around his neck by a thin chain. With a wave of Dagon's hand, fifteen bewildered people appeared, each standing on a separate marble pedestal. They were the dead from the *Eris*.

Allyson Chrysler-Smith, wore a gown still stained with her blood, though her neck was unblemished. She felt her throat, then saw despair engulf her face as she realized she couldn't move from her perch. She stood on the side of the damned.

Dagon grinned and slowly nodded. A nightmarish chorus of fifteen tortured screams rose up and echoed off of the stone ruins as their regenerated flesh was methodically and painfully twisted and altered to the various forms he wished. When the screaming stopped, Dagon's minions were complete. Two black clad, demonic archers held the positions of rook; two black-skinned centaurs with spears and red armor stood as his knights; two hooded monks stood as Dagon's bishops; and, lastly, Allyson stood in the spot of the queen. Dagon had transformed her into a succubus. Her hair and eyes had become darker than the Abyss itself, and her naked body glowed red like the setting sun. Tiny horns had sprouted above her eyes and raven wings, as black as her hair, protruded from her shoulders. Before Dagon and his chosen seven were eight crouching gargoyles, each glared hungrily at the three mortals standing at the side of Elemeniah.

"Am I to choose any souls I wish?" the white clad celestial asked.

"Of course, old friend," Dagon answered.

Out of thin air appeared eight armor-clad soldiers of Is along the front line. Their spears and shields reflected the sun's light into Dagon's eyes. At that same instant, an archer appeared as one rook; two warriors in gleaming silver armor stood in the position of knights; two holy men in flowing white robes, holding matching staffs of wisdom and a book of Life, emerged in the squares for Elemeniah's bishops. Three marble pedestals materialized as well. Without being instructed, Manny stepped onto the one with the word "rook" carved into it and then froze into place. Lou and Amanda walked on to the pedestals with "king" and "queen" engraved on them.

"I protest, Angel," Dagon howled. "Your pieces were once citizens of Is and they belong to me."

"Not true," Elemeniah replied with a grin, "they lived on Is but were betrayed and died through no fault of their own. They remained true to the Mover, even unto their deaths beneath the waves. They bore the mark of *my* master in life and their souls were untouched by you and your master after their deaths. I claim them from their watery graves to play your silly game, Dagon. Or shall we summon, the Saleman to rule?"

"So be it," Dagon snorted, "I will go first."

Dagon surveyed his opponent's placement of the mortals and pointed at Lou, who stood as the king, the most important piece on the board. "Fool. You have revealed who the Gifted one is."

"Thy will be done," Elemeniah murmured.

Dagon conjured up an hourglass to keep the time and made his first move. The demon played aggressively, barking out commands and wantonly sacrificing his gargoyle pawns to free space on the board for his "power" pieces, particularly his centaur knights.

Elemeniah played a more calculated game, as if time were on his side, and rarely made a move that would endanger a critical piece without Dagon losing his attacking piece as well

When a white piece was taken, they heard, "Thy will be done" as the defeated quickly evaporated into a wisp of white light and faded as it moved towards Elemeniah. The fate of a lost red piece, however, was far more dramatic. The pedestal beneath the lost red piece burst into a raging blaze of black and purple flames. The scorching heat would quickly burn off the demonic shell and expose the screaming victim to the surrounding inferno. While the flames devoured any clothing, they didn't consume flesh. The flames tortured the person until they descended through the board and into eternity among the damned. All the while, Dagon delighted in the screaming and pleading. He even gleefully waved at Allyson, as she sank beneath the playing surface.

Over four hours into the contest, the two immortals had finally worn down each other's pieces. Elemeniah's king was in jeopardy. Dagon's centaur knights flanked Lou at either side and a single remaining archer prevented any forward movement by Lou. To make the situation more dire, one of Dagon's remaining pawns was one square from the white's back line. Amanda could be moved to take either the lone archer or the centaur, but then she would immediately be claimed by the remaining piece. Dagon himself was menaced by Manny, who blocked any forward movement. An Isian centurion stood but a single square from the red back line that Dagon could not block.

"I think it is time that we end our contest," Dagon proclaimed, "and I take 'The Gifted.'"

Elemeniah refused to acknowledge his opponent and focused on the board as Dagon commanded his pawn to advance to the white back line.

"Ha!" Dagon said. "I will trade my pawn for..."

"Not so fast, Dagon," the angel interrupted, "you've destroyed all your pieces and cast them to the Hellfire. With what shall you replace your pawn?"

"What in the name of Prana are you talking about? My pawn is on your back line and I can trade it for my succubus!"

"Fine then...open a portal and produce your lost succubus."

Dagon screamed in a frustrated rage as he realized there was no portal to the Abyss on the island for him to summon anything. His arrogant lack of planning had derailed his plan and left him with only an immobile pawn along his opponent's back line. Dagon's rage intensified once he realized that, as the red king, he could not move during Elemeniah's turn without forfeiting his contest.

Elemeniah smiled for the first time in four hours as he watched Dagon simmer. "Check."

Dagon looked about the board; none of his pieces could come to his rescue. He could not advance forward, that would bring him into Manny's line of attack, and a backwards movement would only delay the inevitable. He moved himself one square to his right, hoping Elemeniah would move Amanda directly into his archer's line of attack. The angel did not oblige.

"Allow me to show you something, Dagon," Elemeniah said. He opened his coat and pulled out a small white ceramic piece that looked like a castle's tower. He waved it at Dagon as he commanded his centurion to the red back line and made the trade.

Dagon again screamed as the soldier faded into white light and a silver armored archer took his place. Although he was not in immediate danger, now the red king was prevented from moving forward or backward. He ripped his golden crown off of his head and threw it in disgust as he cursed Elemeniah in an ancient language.

"I'm not defeated yet," Dagon barked.

He commanded his archer to advance to the square next to Amanda.

"I can still send your queen to the ferryman, Elemeniah, if you choose to press the attack."

What are you doing? Lou's mind screamed as his body remained frozen in place upon his pedestal, *You can't sacrifice Amanda! Don't do it!*

Elemeniah paused for a moment as he surveyed the board. Dagon's knights couldn't threaten Lou. Manny was poised to take the red king should he move forward and his other archer was equally poised, should the red king retreat.

"Amanda?" Elemeniah called out, "move one square diagonally and to the right...in front of Dagon."

Thy will be done.

Dagon looked at the peaceful, diminutive creature directly before him. He looked into her eyes and knew he was a single two-foot by two-foot square of marble from fulfilling his task.

"Check...and mate, Dagon," Elemeniah declared.

Dagon again roared his disapproval, ripped the Key to the City of Is from his neck and flung it in the ocean. His skin melted away, as if it were a blanket pulled from beneath him. Once his mortal body was gone, all that remained was a floating black specter that hovered over the spot where the red king had stood. It moved like a sheet drying on a clothesline in a breeze. The stench, however, of ten thousand years of rot and evil that filled the air would have been knee-bending to the three mortals, if they could move.

"I will not be defeated," Dagon hissed in a voice like a thousand snakes.

"That's not how the game is played," a new voice came.

"Senor, Johnny!" Manny said.

There, standing atop a stone pillar, was a tall man in a black coat and hat. He glared down at the demon from great dark eyes, though his mouth was stretched in a wolfish grin under his long nose. Gold blinked from between his lips.

Dagon raised his wings as if to claw his way skyward.

"In the name above all other names," Johnny boomed, "I hold you, Dagon, servant of darkness, bound to your wager and cast you from this mortal realm. Be gone, demon! Face your masters...and accept your punishment. Thy will be done!"

An unholy shriek rang out from the defeated specter as it spun, trying to escape its fate, until it stretched out and splintered into thousands of shards that floated down onto the ocean's surface and sank.

Johnny smiled wider and wider. His body seemed to shimmer and fade until all that was left was a gold-toothed grin. Then it too winked out.

Suddenly, a deep rumble vibrated across the rocks and the island began to violently shake. Lou, Manny, and Amanda felt life jolt back into each of their bruised bodies.

"Run," commanded Elemeniah. "Run to the raft."

All three sprinted as fast as their tired legs would carry them. They reached the raft, already floating in knee-deep water. The island was returning to the depths. Manny hurled himself into the raft first and then pulled Amanda and Lou over the side. The three collapsed onto the floor of the raft, and watched as the quaking island split in two and slowly dip below the surface.

Amanda looked around. "Where's the angel?"

"He can take care of himself," Lou yelled back. "Quick! Paddle away from the island!"

As the tops of the two stone pillars, once the gates of the city of Is, crumbled, fell and were reclaimed by the ocean's waves, the three survivors saw Elemeniah holding Dagon's sword on his left shoulder, walking over the water towards them. A proud smile graced his face and an inner light shone around him. He playfully kicked at the ocean's waves as they rolled by him.

"It is time to leave, Daughter of Man. The Council of Twelve awaits you at the Temple Church," he said, as he gently placed the sword in the raft.

"I...I still don't understand," Amanda replied.

"When a legion of Templar knights returned to England from their crusading," he began, "they discovered the portal to the Abyss and built a house of worship upon it to keep it at bay by making it holy ground. Being hallowed, the only way that Hell's spawn could break through the portal would be if the dimensional boundaries between the realms were weakened, like today. Fortunately, the Templars prepared for this day. Your purity of heart, Amanda Renee, will be my master's instrument to repel the demons and seal that portal until the end of time...but we must leave now."

Amanda reached for Elemeniah's open hand. Her other hand was desperately clenched in her husband's grasp. A tear rolled down her cheek as she looked at Lou's face. Amanda felt the gentle, angelic hand stroke her hair and then firmly settle on the crest of her head. As when she was in Elemeniah's embrace, a calm confidence filled her fatigued body.

"Mr. Brohman," Amanda said, "you'd better not keep your wife waiting in London too long."

"I love you," Lou said. "It's no surprise to me that *you* are the best of people. I'll see you there."

She slid her hand from Lou's grasp and nodded to her guardian as she took his hand. She felt herself rise up into the air and smiled at her husband as she floated above the bottom of the raft.

"What of us?" Manny spoke up.

"First," the angel answered, "you will take the sword of the Archangel Michael and watch over it for me while I complete my task. Dagon stole it thousands of years ago...Michael will be most pleased to have it returned. Secondly, the Azores is exactly one hundred seven miles to the east. You would be wise to begin paddling."

"You're taking my wife and leaving us in the middle of the Atlantic?" Lou challenged.

Elemeniah smiled at him. "'The Gifted' is safe now that Dagon is defeated and I will watch over her until her mission is complete. As for you, my master would not assign a task to one who could not complete it. Have faith."

With that said, the angel and Amanda floated higher into the air and sped off toward the horizon. Lou watched, dumbfounded, as they faded from his sight.

"Hey!" Lou screamed out at the same horizon. "We don't know which way is east!"

"Santa Maria!" Manny yelled, "Lou, help me paddle...quickly!"

Lou grabbed a paddle and joined Manny, who was already paddling furiously.

"Dios mio, gracias," Manny whispered as he stretched out over the soft orange side of the raft. Lou helped pull him back in. In Manny's hand was a bright orange piece of foam padding with a brass chain wound through a hole in it. Boaters used them as a key chain because they floated. Attached to the chain running through the foam was Buddy Harrison's compass.

"Where did that come from?" Lou questioned.

"This key ring is what I traded my jumping rope for with Senor Johnny. He told me that a person on a boat has to be careful and to make sure he doesn't lose things overboard because the sea does not easily give stuff back."

The two men laughed like a pair of madmen.

After regaining their composure, Lou wiped a tear from his cheek.

"Well, Manny, I guess this rowing should be good training for your title defense next week."

"I have the compass, my friend," Manny answered, "I think that makes me the Captain. Si?"

"Very well, *Captain*, see if you can use the inside of your new compass to signal that boat way over there." Lou motioned toward the horizon.

Amongst the catacombs beneath the Temple Church, a kind-faced woman dressed in a plain white smock stood at the ready in front of five cave openings. To her rear stood twelve men in medieval armor with red-crossed banners on the front of their breastplates, as the Knights of the Temple of Solomon wore nine centuries before. An ominous roar and rumble echoed from a dark corridor directly in front of them. There was a terrible blast of heat and an unholy stench.

Two yellow eyes, like that of a serpent, peered through the shadows and Agaliarept stepped into their sight. Steam rose from the gigantic viper-headed demon's armor and scaly skin as the cool English air blew around the abominable general. He looked indignantly at the twelve men and the unarmed woman before him and unsheathed his massive battle sword.

"To the Defender!" the monstrous demon cried out. A deafening roar came from the darkness behind him as the charge sounded.

"Thy will be done," Amanda whispered as she looked into the wildly approaching beast's eyes.

A powerful wave of white light exploded from her chest and drove the demonic general back into his ranks. Shrieks rose from the lesser demons as the divine light burned their eyes and scales, making them retreat.

"Stand your ground, cowards," the demon screamed out as flames burst from the scaly skin beneath his armor.

The light changed angles as Amanda's arched body rose up in the air. The twelve men silently knelt and bowed their heads in reverence. The demon-general's footing began to give way and he was pushed backward even further as a deafening voice from above boomed for all to hear. "MY WILL BE DONE!"

Agaliarept exploded as a second, more intense, beam of light fired out from the body of "The Gifted." Those demonic infantry that weren't incinerated with their general fled into the Abyss, trampling one another as they did.

The rocks surrounding the entrance flowed together to cover the opening, as if the hands of the Almighty were guiding it all into place.

The intense light subsided and Amanda gently settled into twenty-four awaiting hands. Her breath was shallow but her skin was cool and her pulse calm. A smile crossed her tired face for, within her guardian's embrace this one final time, Amanda knew all was well. She knew that the portal was sealed.

Thy will be done.

Uneasy Lies The Head

BAK'S TENURE AS THE PROPRIETOR OF the Triple-Six was not without its early hitches. The first one thousand years was a constant struggle to maintain trustworthy alliances with the suppliers, traders, and the inevitable backstabbers with whom he did business.

Centuries of trial and error, on top of his own innate ingenuity, allowed Bak to create the series of booby traps, hidden beast pits, and secret pathways that either repelled or outright killed off all armies, constables, and thugs who sought to take away that which was his, the Triple-Six Tavern.

It was not until his two thousandth year of business that Bak was able to make those mystical blood oaths and agreements which opened up the full array of dimensional and temporal portals built into the rear-most level of his establishment, portals which all had the same all-powerful geas weaved into them: that no unapproved weapon, or poison, be permitted to pass into this hallowed place. A well-compensated troop of towering toughs managed to overcome any and all attempts at strong-arming the establishment, something well-witnessed by the rear most ice cave that Bak kept regularly supplied with the corpses of impetuous mob thugs from a dizzying array of sentient beings and timelines. More recently he began to wonder if his depletion of American 20th Century criminal ranks had been noticed in the real world. Considering their lack of imagination, each mob boss would no doubt suspect his closest rival of the worst, and retaliate in kind.

By his three thousandth year Bak had married his third wife and fathered his twenty-fifth child, all of whom he made take the most powerful and deadly of magical oaths of fidelity, which if broken, would bring irresistible doom upon the perpetrator. Those that refused the oath were allowed egress from the tavern with all the gold and precious gems they could carry, never to return, living out their lives with the knowledge they had forsworn endless wealth, luxury, and immortality.

⊕　⊕　⊕

Hellbeast

By Edward F. McKeown

ELLBEAST ROARED, ITS VOICE SHAT-tering the desert quiet. Toxic smoke belched forth as it shuddered to wakefulness. Then, as suddenly as it had roused to furious life, its heart stumbled, sputtered and died.

"Fuck," Sergeant Andrew Cross said. He leaned back on the tarp protecting him from the scorching metal hull of his M88 MRV.

"*Hellbeast* we named you and a hellbeast you are." He looked in disgust at the fuel pump that had chosen the worst possible time to die in the thirty-four-year-old tank recovery vehicle.

"Last track in Iraq," O'Neill cackled. "Everybody thought it would be a shiny new Abrams and it's going to be us, the rolling wreck."

Cross glared at the young New Yorker. College kid could never keep his goddamn mouth closed and Cross was annoyed with himself for forgetting the kid was there and trashing their track. As commander, he might cuss *Hellbeast* but he didn't need a smart-ass Yankee doing it.

"Shut it, College. Get Cabera and Santiago. We are going to pull this fuel pump. Tell the tank transporter to go ahead and take off without us."

The kid's face took on its usual sullen look.

"Why don't we just leave this thing here and go with them? The whole damn Army's leaving Iraq. Mission's over. They're just going give this old piece of shit to the Kuwaitis. It's not worth shipping back to the States."

"Neither are you, shit-for-brains, but the Army will pay for it anyway. Get going before I bounce this wrench off your damn head."

O'Neill jumped off the tank and sprawled into the dust.

"Ok Sarge. No need to get tough."

"How the fuck did he ever get into this man's Army?" Cross muttered to himself, then louder, "And belt on your sidearm, Soldier!"

O'Neill scrambled back and grabbed his holstered pistol, muttering about all the insurgents being dead. He headed for the M1070 Heavy Equipment

Transporter, loaded with the recovered Bradley APC they'd pulled out of a wadi, now sat. O'Neill spoke to the driver, who nodded and wasted no time in pulling out, driving gingerly across the crushed stone road to Al Maaniyah. They'd head on from there to Kuwait.

Cross looked beyond the disappearing transporter to the dusty yellow clay town that huddled at the foot of a range of low hills. It had some unpronounceable local name that sounded like Alfalfa, so they called it that. People had probably lived on that spot for the last five thousand years, and in much the same way..

Cross sighed and stood facing the setting sun. The desert would turn cold soon. They'd risk rigging up a light to work for a while, then bed down. He'd put Cabera on the .50 cal to watch; the little Italian was the best of his crew. The insurgency had been crushed, but Iraq wasn't going to be a safe location for a long while, if ever.

As usual at this time of day, a black mood descended on Cross. It had been at dusk that an APC full of Dutch troops had wandered into his area years ago. He'd been a tank commander then, in a brand new M1A Abrams, king of the battlefield. The Dutch assholes had roared out of a draw at high speed, right into the side of his column. The sun had been behind them and the constant desert dust obscured their outline. Charlie Troop's commander screamed, "Ambush!, action left," over the net. Cross's crack crew reacted faster than anyone else. The deadly 120mm swung out and fired. The Dutch died. CNN lovingly carried every detail, carefully stroking and nurturing the blue-on-blue story each day. What good TV it made.

Board of inquiry blamed the Dutch, but it didn't matter. Dutch anti-war protesters howled in the streets and demanded he be jailed, as if the fog of war was something new to them. Cross was hot and the Army needed to bury him. He went from the tip of the spear to the pickup crew. He drew the oldest M88 in the outfit, one judged too old to bother upgrading to the new standard. His crew was like the *Hellbeast* itself, rejects and leftovers. At another time Cross would have broken them and reforged the crew into a crack team. Not now, he was as burnt out as that Dutch APC.

Cross lit a cigarette and leaned against the armored cab of the 56-ton, ingot-shaped M88. "Yep, *Hellbeast*, nobody wants either of us broken down wrecks.

A thousand yards away, Mahdi Al-Mumin stared at the American war machine. Hate for the infidel filled him, along with equal mixes of fear and frustration. He'd fought the invasion for years, tasting the bitterness of defeat as the Iraqi government troops joined, then replaced Americans in the field. Support had slowly dried up, with the Syrians shrinking under American pressure and the Saudis cracking down for their US masters. Only the Iranians remained true to the cause, though it galled him as a Sunni Iraqi to take aid from them. His father had died fighting them in the War of the Cities. But Al-Queda had fallen on hard times and he took what aid he could get.

The Americans were leaving Iraq, going out of his range. All he could fight then would be government troops. Americans did not care how many of their stooges died, so long as none of their own filled the body bags.

If we could kill these, CNN would plaster their faces on TV for days, maybe weeks. In the ultimate of ironies, the Zionists of Hollywood would doubtless make a movie about the last American casualties. *Our allies,* he thought in bitter amusement, *though if we win, we'll kill them first.* At least the enemy soldiers were worthy of respect in battle.

"Maybe it's for the last time," he swore, "but you will not leave our soil. You will pay in Allah's name for all your nation has done."

He looked at his band of eight followers, worn thin by poor rations and hard running. But the love of Allah burned in their eyes and their weapons were clean and oiled.

There was one who was not of their band. She studied him with frightened eyes. Hassan had delivered the Italian journalist to them. He'd worked as her driver for weeks to gain her trust, then lured her out to the desert where his men waited. Al-mumin's men had wanted her lush body but he had other plans for her. She would record their heroic struggle with the Americans, then fetch a pretty ransom. She was a European and houri to be sure, dressing and working as a man in offense to Allah, but she would be more useful if they treated her with respect.

He walked up to the gagged woman, fighting the urge in his own loins. It had been a long time since his last woman.

"We will wait for the dark of the moon," he said. "Then you shall have a story."

The long evening passed slowly for the Al-Queda men and Al-mumin had to discipline Hassan, who he found holding the European down and trying to pull off her pants. For lack of respect to orders, Hassan would walk point.

Now that they were moving, his men were in good spirits, joking among themselves. It was a long way to the village yet and there was no chance of being overheard.

Al-mumin held the Italiana journalist by the arm. She stumbled in the darkness, due to her bonds. She'd slowed him down and now he was near the rear of the small column. Al-Mumin cut her hands free and gestured with the knife.

"Behave, or else."

She nodded.

Abdul grinned at him as he walked past. The big man held their last RPG7. The weapon was their best chance against the Americans and he was their best shot with it. They moved rapidly but cautiously, heading toward the village, planning to skirt it and come upon the Americans.

The ground beneath Hassan suddenly opened, as if he had walked into an immense tiger trap. The smell that burst from the hole was so foul as to almost physically strike them, driving them back. The scout, too well-trained to scream even while falling, disappeared into the hole.

But then he did scream. A short, cutoff burst of terror.

It surged from the hole, huge, indescribable, irresistible and fast. Al-mumin gained only the impression under the starlight, golden scales, titanic bulk and power. Three more of his men, including Abdul and the RPG7, were flattened under the huge bulk.

A Jinn, his mind gibbered, an evil genie.

The creature, as large as a dinosaur, lashed out with teeth, claw tipped arms and tail. His men never even got off a shot.

"Allah save us," Al-Mumin whispered, backing and raising his rifle. He'd forgotten about the girl and he fell over her as he backed.

"*I am your god now,*" the voice rumbled in his head. "*You will serve me. It has been ten-thousand years since I walked the earth. My reign comes again. I need servants, food and fear.*"

The Jinn looked down at Al-Mumin. Its face was a horrible mix of human and beast. The teeth that gleamed were easily a foot long, but its eyes looked like a man's.

"*You and the woman will serve me. These others,*" it looked at Al-Mumin's crushed and slaughtered followers, "*are my first meal.*"

Al-Mumin stared up at the colossal beast.

"There is no God but Allah and Mohammed is his prophet. I serve only Allah."

"*Fool,*" the Jinn laughed, a huge braying sound, though the words came only in his mind. "*Fool, fool, fool. You do not serve Allah. Point to me the passage in the Koran that tells you to blow up women and children as deliberate targets. Allah spits on you. Heaven does not await you at death, only Hell. My hell, and you are already my servant. All that you believed, all that you fought for, is despicable to your god.*"

The weight of the Jinn's words settled on his soul, eating into it.

"Inshallah," he said weakly.

The Jinn laughed again, its voice shattering the night.

"*Come my servant, my new priest, guide me to the village. It has been long since I supped full on the terror of your kind.*"

Al-Mumin turned to the reporter. Their eyes locked.

"Run," he shouted, "Get the Americans. Run now!" He spun back, raising the AK-47. "Allah Akhbar," he shouted as he fired. "God is great."

The Jinn bellowed and charged as the slugs tore into its vast, armored body. Some bullets sparked off its plates with yellow flashes.

Maybe I was wrong, Al-Mumin thought as the bulk of the Jinn blocked out the sky and the AK-47's bolt locked back empty. Maybe I am bound for hell but Allah forgives much and tonight I die as a warrior defending a village. Inshallah.

Gabriella Murano ran flat out with gunfire and monstrous roars in her ears. When she could run no more she collapsed, gasping for breath. The monster had not pursued her. Why, she did not know. She climbed to shaky feet, fighting nausea and the band of agony across her chest. Come on, come on, she said to herself, you've run marathons.

She staggered to the top of the dune and looked about, dreading the sight of the monster coming for her. But the beast was nowhere in sight. Slowly she scanned the horizon, then realized that she was utterly lost. She wrapped her arms around her from fear and cold.

"Mother Mary," she whispered, "guide me to safety and I swear I will go back to the Church. Give me a sign."

"Don't have any signs," a voice said in Italian. "How about a compass?"

Gabriella screamed.

"Ciao, bella. Don't make so much noise. There are bad things in the desert tonight."

Suddenly a man stood on the dune above her. How he got there she could not tell. Tall and angular, he wore a long, black greatcoat and a broad-brimmed hat over straggly white hair. For a second she wondered if he was a priest.

"Who are you?" she asked, backing away in the shifting sand.

He gave a mad laugh and capered along the top of the dune.

"I have many names," he said with a grin, "and many lives. You may call me Johnny. I am," he gave a deep bow, "The Salesman."

"Do you serve the...the monster."

"Certainly not," he snapped. "Johnny only serves himself and, of course, his customers."

He walked closer. His huge dark eyes seemed to pin her in place.

"Johnny likes humans. They are fun and have such nice things to trade and he must trade. It's what he does. Now, and perhaps forever. But the Sha'Daa is a special time. Bad things walk the roads between the worlds. You met one. For the next forty-eight hours, in many places in the world, Hell will seek to break through to Earth."

"Can you help me?" she asked, her mind refusing to focus on his mad tale. "I need to find the Americans."

"I can help you to help yourself." From his coat he produced a silver compass. "What do you have to trade? Johnny must make many trades in the next two days. He must make sure that everything that humans need is where they can find it. But you must trade for it all."

Gabriella searched the pockets of her cargo pants. The terrorists had stolen all of her money and jewelry, leaving only her cameras and recorders to cover their attack on the Americans. But they'd missed one thing. Her mother's rosary, which she always carried for luck. She pulled it from her inside pocket. It was beautiful piece, silver and wood with a vial of holy water blessed by Pope Pius XII inside it. "This is the only thing of value I have besides my equipment."

Johnny looked at it and grinned, exposing a shiny gold incisor for the first time.

"Excellent, the forecast is for vampires in jolly old England. A deal, a deal," he cackled. He snatched the crucifix and handled her the compass.

"Stay on 125 degrees for six kilometers," Johnny said. "You will find what you want."

Johnny suddenly swirled his coat around him and Gabriella found herself alone in the desert. She pinched herself but she was awake and the compass was real. Slowly she set out, breaking into a jog as soon as her body was able.

"Sarge!"

Cross snapped out of a fitful sleep. Cabera was leaning down from the ring hatch where the .50 cal and M203 grenade launcher were mounted.

"Movement. Somebody in light-colored clothes coming this way."

"Don't shoot yet," Cross said. "Probably some kid from the village on a dare." O'Neil and Santiago had also roused, grabbing carbines. Cross picked up an old 45 caliber grease-gun and opened a hatch looking in the direction

Cabera pointed. There was no moon and he didn't have fancy night-vision glasses, but he could see a scrap of white shirt and the dim sound of a voice reached him. He raised field glasses to his eyes and saw a person wearing white and waving their arms.

"OK. O'Neil, start her up and let's hope that fuel pump is fixed. Cabera keep a weapon on our friend. Santiago, you watch everywhere else. I'll check this out." He hopped out of the M88 as its diesel coughed into life.

Cross jacked the bolt on the M3 grease gun and walked forward, sand crunching under his desert boots. He hoped O'Neil was smart enough not to turn on the lights and ruin his night vision.

The cold desert wind was in his face and it brought him a sound.

"Help. Help me."

Warily, Cross came on, now bending double and using the rilled sand for cover. Ahead of him someone charged over the top of a dune. He brought up his grease-gun to cover the figure, a woman, westerner from the look of her white shirt and jeans.

"Halt," he yelled. "Halt or I shoot."

She skidded to a stop.

"Don't shoot. Don't shoot," she yelled, searching for him in the dark. She sounded European.

"Hands up, walk slowly ahead," he ordered. "Is there anyone with you?"

"No, no. I need your help."

"Stop there. Kneel down with your hands on your head." Cross stood from cover and walked over to her. If she was a suicide bomber, he was toast. But he couldn't let her get close to *Hellbeast* without being searched. Watching her and the desert behind, he came up.

"I'm not Iraqi," she said. "I'm Italiana, a journalist with ANSA. I was kidnapped by insurgents."

"Shut up," He reached down and searched her roughly with one hand.

"I'm not hiding a bomb in my bra," she snapped.

"Feels like there would be room," he said.

He pulled out devices from her cargo pants' leg pockets and unhooked his red-lensed flashlight": camera and recorder. He quickly ran the light over her face. She was dark-haired, pretty but could easily be Iraqi.

"Papers?"

"Breast pocket."

He started to reach for her shirt.

"Basta," she said, "I'll get them." She pulled them out with one hand. He studied them with the flashlight. They looked right but it was hard to be sure.

"Kinda late for a stroll, Miss," he looked at the name, "Miss Murr-mur..."

"Murano, Gabriella Murano." she said. "Just like the glass."

"What glass?" Cross asked, confused.

"Can I put my hands down? I'm exhausted. I've run for kilometers."

"Okay."

She muttered something in what he assumed was Italian.

"What?" he said.

"You will think me mad when I tell you what I have to say," she said. "You will never believe me, but you must."

"Let's get back to the 88," he said. "Tell me there." He helped her to her feet, holding her by the arm, not from chivalry but to feel if she was going to suddenly move.

"Yes, to the tank. You have a big gun, yes?"

"We're not a tank. We're a recovery vehicle, a kind of a tow truck for tanks."

"But guns, you have guns?" She looked up at him as they walked back. He put on the red-lensed flash on so they could see their footing better.

"Enough," he said. "Tell me about these insurgents. What do you know? Who's out there? What did you see? How many? Where? What weapons?"

"Yes, yes but they are all dead now. Killed. A monster came from the ground. It was as big as a house. It killed them."

"A what?" he laughed. "A monster. Lady, the only monsters around here walk on two legs."

She looked up at him.

"Until tonight, you were right."

Cross shook his head.

"OK, keep walking." Desert must have cooked her brain, he thought. No point in asking her more about the insurgents. Either she was mad or a liar. Or both.

They reached the M88. Cross opened the door and they climbed in.

Cabera leaned down from the hatch. He whistled and a cheesy grin broke out under his mustache.

"I see you found a date."

O'Neil looked like he was going to injure his neck craning around from the driver's seat. Santiago, evidently thinking her a Latina, said something in Spanish.

"Eyes on the desert," Cross snapped. "Christ, you'd think you guys hadn't seen a girl in years."

"Sí, pero ninguna tan bonita cómo ella," Santiago said

Gabriella grinned at Santiago. "Ciao."

"I could translate," Cabera offered hopefully.

"She speaks English and WATCH THE FUCKING DESERT!"

Everyone snapped back to their posts.

"You are very loud," Gabriella said.

"Maybe I'll scare off the monster."

"No," she said. "It is bigger than this tank. Huge, with arms and four legs. I see that you do not believe me. Caspicso, I do not believe me either and I saw it. I only ask this. It said-"

"It talked?" Cross said.

"In my head. How you say?" She looked up at Cabera and rattled off something in Italian.

"It spoke directly to her mind, she says," Cabera's face was a study in suppressed humor.

"Telepathic," O'Neil threw over his shoulder.

"Si, si," Gabriella said. "Bono, Telepathic."

"It said it was going to the village. I think it ate the Al-Queda men. Otherwise, you might be dead. They had a rocket launcher. The leader distracted it with his gun, but no good. It lives. It will come to the village."

Cross leaned back on the bulkhead.

"The obvious answer is a trap," he said, looking at Cabera.

Cabera shrugged.

"Why get us all juiced up and armed then try to jump us? They can't know exactly how we'd come, so how would they know where to place a mine or IED?"

"What harm?" she pled. "Come to the village."

This is nuts, Cross thought. Aloud he said. "OK, we'll come, but we are taking the long way around. We'll come in from the East. And lady, if there's a trap, I swear I'll slit your throat."

"Yes, yes," she said. "I hear this already from the Al-Queda. We go now."

"O'Neil, back us out of here and head east. Keep sharp, everyone.

It took them an hour, with Gabriella fidgeting and fuming every minute until they backtracked and came at the village, paralleling the road but not on it.

A broad flat hill faced them, backlit by the town's few lights. O'Neil raced *Hellbeast* up it and stopped just below the crest, giving them a good view of Al-fal-fera.

Cross stared in disbelief at the thing raging in the center of the town square. The beast looked like a cross between a Tyrannosaur and a brontosaurus. With a shock, he realized there were two almost human-looking arms over the four legs. One held a small, pitifully struggling figure and even as they watched, the huge head dipped and jaws met in the suddenly still body.

"Do something!" Gabriella shrieked.

Cross shook himself into action.

"Santiago, illuminate that thing. O'Neil get us in there." Hellbeast's searchlight lanced through the night to catch the startled monster in it. It revealed the townspeople around it, most caught against a long hall at the end of the square.

"Cabera, the villagers are too close for the grenade launcher. Use the .50 cal."

As the M88 roared toward the true Hellbeast, its big .50 cal cut loose in controlled bursts both to protect the villagers and the .50's barrel from overheating. The effect on the monster was immediate. It reared backward, almost somersaulting as the .50 struck. The pitiful fragment of a villager dropped from its claws. With surprising speed for something so big, it raced away down a side street, flattening its body like an infantryman. The act warned Cross that he was not dealing with a mere animal.

"After him, College Boy," Cross shouted. "Get him."

They hit the harder pavement of the square and shot forward but had to screech to a stop as panicked villagers raced toward them. O'Neil barely avoided running them down.

Cross opened the side hatch. "No. Get out of here. Move out of the way. For Christ sake get out of the way."

Villagers, some only partially clad in white bedclothes, screamed in Persian, trying to climb on the M88. A young boy with huge, white-rimmed eyes scrambled up the front. Tears streamed down his brown face. "Jinn, Jinn," he screamed

"Look out," Gabriella grabbed his shoulder from behind.

The monster had come out of a side street. In its arms it held a small pickup truck.

"Cabera," Cross yelled, ducking back into the armored hull. The crying boy shrieked and leapt off the M-88. Villagers ran, trying to escape the square.

The monster flung the pickup as Cabera pulled the .50 around. He managed to fire both the grenade launcher and the .50 as the pickup struck the M88 with the wet crunching sound of metal. Cross was flung painfully into the wall, landing on Gabriella just as Cabera's lifeless body fell into the M88, his upper body crushed and bloodied.

A second greater shock hit the vehicle. The hellbeast threw itself on them, its claws scoring and shattering the armored glass of their vision slits.

"Motherfucker," Cross shouted. He yanked his old M-3 grease gun off the bulkhead, jacked the bolt to load the .45 cal rounds. Hot, fetid breath blasted him, and he looked up to see the monster's huge face leering down at him from the hatchring. Cross screamed and pulled the trigger. The weapon stuttered out its clip into the hideous face. He was rewarded with a titanic howl of pain and the beast twisted away, crashing into a building and raising a cloud of dust.

"O'Neill. Turn left. Bring her about to face it." He dropped the clip and replaced it, scrambling up into the hatchring. But the .50 cal and grenade launcher were both twisted metal. *Hellbeast's* desert paint was chipped and scored and most of the exterior equipment had been torn off. As Cross watched, the beast shook itself out of the devastated house as the M88 swerved to face it. He heard Santiago and O'Neil firing pistol and carbine from their driving slits and added a stream of lead from the grease gun.

The monster howled again and Cross could see it was streaked with glistening, rusty fluid. Blood, he reasoned. He looked down, seeing Gabriella, her own face streaked with red.

"Get me those," He gestured frantically at spare clips for the submachine gun. Gabriella scrambled up with a handful of reloads.

The beast roared and flung a building timber at Cross, who ducked back inside the M88. The beam shattered on *Hellbeast's* armor.

"He's gonna charge," O'Neil yelled. He fired the9MM Beretta out the slit. The pistol's pitiful popping seemed only to underscore their impotence against the raging beast.

Cross hastily changed clips, and poked his head up. The monster's head tracked toward him. Then it seemed to look beyond the M88. It turned and raced away, the massive, scaled back poking up above some of the smaller buildings.

Cross turned, hoping to see a platoon of Abrams tanks coming to the rescue. All he saw was the flame of sunrise spreading in the East.

Gabriella joined him in the hatch.

"It fears the sun."

"God knows it didn't have reason to fear us," Cross huffed, leaning against the ring as pain and bruises asserted themselves.

"You hurt it," she said. "You hurt it."

"Not enough," he said looking at the crushed .50 and M203, "and we've shot our bolt."

The villagers wailed and waved their arms over the thin bodies lying in the square under sheets and tarps. One corpse lay under an OD tarp and a tiny American flag. O'Neil, Santiago, Gabriella, and Cross stood over the body. In the bright light of day, it was impossible to credit last night's nightmarish battle but for the destruction all around.

Cross got some shovels and handed Gabriella one. The other two men took the bloody tarp. They walked it to the village edge and dug the grave, planting Cabera under a crude cross. Graves Registration would recover the body later but they couldn't leave the corpse above ground in the heat.

The others looked expectantly at Cross, and he realized they were waiting for him to say something.

"I'm not much good at this," Cross said. "My dad was a preacher man, Southern Baptist. He'd have known the words. Me, I ain't been to church for a long time.

"All I know is that Hell came to Earth last night. Cabera saw it and he turned his weapon on it. So I guess you could say he died doing God's work and I hope God will welcome him in for it. We now know there is a hell, so I guess there must be a heaven too."

"What are we going to do, Sarge?" O'Neil asked, all his usual sullenness long fled. "The radio's smashed and the antenna's tore away."

"These people," Gabriella said. "There are too many wounded who can't be moved."

Cross looked at Santiago.

"What do you say?"

The stout Mexican shrugged his shoulders.

"We are in the final days. Jesus will come for us all soon." He pulled a silver cross on a chain from inside his shirt and kissed it.

"There is no priest here to confess me but I have spoken my sins to Jesus and he forgives me. I fear nothing now. We are all in God's hands."

Cross looked down at Cabera's grave.

"Can't say I feel good leaving that thing alive after it took one of mine. Besides, we came to this shithole country to help these people. So, I'd say we stay and help."

He looked at O'Neil.

"What do you say, College Boy? If we stay, I want it unanimous."

O'Neil looked startled at Cross' question, then grinned "Guess it takes a Hellbeast to kill a Hellbeast."

Cross turned to Gabriella. "Tell the village headman to take as many people as he can and head for Al Maaniyah. There was an Iraqi battalion there a week ago. We'll stay here and do what we can. When you get there tell the commander what's what and to send all he's got."

"No, I am staying," she shook her head.

"The hell you are."

"I am a journalist. This may be the biggest story since the atom bomb. I must stay. The village headman can tell the Iraqi commander."

"A desert goat-herder?" Cross waved his hands. "He won't listen to him."

"He will listen as much as he would to a European woman," she shot back, eyes flashing. "With so many witnesses, he will come. Not believing, but he will come. You did."

"Crap," Cross said. "I could have you tied up and dumped in a pickup. I don't like reporters, lady. I'll do it."

She smiled at him. "Then who will record your heroic defense of the village?"

"We ain't after medals," Cross shouted. "I just want to help these people."

"Then you should not deprive me of my right to help in my own way."

"Nimble-witted women are the bane of man's existence," Cross muttered, as he stalked off.

Gabriella looked at Santiago and O'Neil.

"Do you really think we'll get medals?" O'Neil asked.

Most of the villagers had departed in a crude convoy of the few operating vehicles and carts. Cross spotted the small boy among them. The child's father had died in the jaws of the hellbeast but his mother had survived. The little boy looked at Cross with empty eyes as the pickup drove off.

Some of the women stayed to tend the badly wounded. Fifteen of the men under the headman's son, Hamzah, produced rifles and AK-47's. They garrisoned the town's largest building, which had become the hospital, and the area by the minaret, which Cross selected for a watchtower.

Cross was no clearer now on what to do about the monster. The .50 had hurt it, but none of their remaining weapons had a fraction of its hitting power. They had some grenades, but no way to fire them and they were not the throwing kind.

He looked at Gabriella. At another time he might have enjoyed the view. She was hot stuff, but it wasn't doing him any good here.

"Any ideas, people?" he asked, leaning against the Hellbeast and lighting a smoke. Gabriella put out her hand. He passed her a Marlboro.

"The thing, did it read your mind or just speak to you mentally?" O'Neil asked.

"What's the difference?" Cross asked.

"We can't surprise it if it reads minds. But if it just speaks mentally."

"The terrorist," she said, "he surprised it when he decided to shoot and it did not sense us last night before we attacked. But it did know he was a terrorist. It lectured him about the Koran."

O'Neil scratched his head. "So it knows something about our world but doesn't seem able to read minds."

"Think about killing it," Cross said, dragging on the cigarette.

O'Neil shrugged.

"Our weapons hurt it, but we don't have enough firepower."

"Run it over," Santiago said.

"I dunno," Cross replied. "It's bigger than the M88 and faster. We might be a bit heavier, but I ain't sure of that."

"You have a plow blade," Gabriella said. "Can you dig a hole?"

"Never big enough or in time," O'Neil said. "And why would it fall into it?"

"Come on, come on" Gabriella said, slapping the back of her hands together. You are the American cowboys. Time to ride to the rescue."

"The only other thing we got is a..." O'Neil stopped as a thought struck him. "Fuck," he said.

"What?" everyone chorused.

"God damn," Cross said. "It might just work."

"What?" Gabriella demanded.

"You know," he grinned at her. "You were right. It's time to cowboy up."

As the sun set to the west, Cross and Gabriella stood in the town's lone minaret, watching the three roads that led from the foothills into the town. The Hellbeast would likely use one of them, rather than struggle through the uneven, brushy countryside.

Below them, six townsmen stood on the nearby rooftops, talking and smoking nervously, fingering their rifles, occasionally looking up at Cross. Their leader, Hamzah, spoke quietly with then. Hamzah sensed Cross' gaze and raised his hand, thumbs up. His teeth flashed against his dark beard.

Everyone else was in the big government building that now served as their hospital. The last defense would be made there.

The town's generator has been destroyed last night. A few electric lights run off some portables held back the night rapidly pooling around them. The M88's engine coughed into life. The evening sirocco whispered coolly to them.

"There," Gabriella's voice trembled as she pointed. Cross whipped up his field glasses and saw the Hellbeast striding out from the foothills as the last sliver of sun disappeared.

"Heads up," Cross shouted. "Heads up."

The creature advanced on all fours, making good use of cover as it came toward them. Hull down behind the low hills, Cross thought. It would have made a good tanker. The Hellbeast paused just outside of town, seeming to study it.

Cross kept a country song playing in his head, hoping that O'Neil was right and the beast could only receive thoughts broadcast at it, rather than snatch them from their minds.

"Mamas don't let your babies grow up to be cowboys..."

"Humans," the voice rumbled in their minds. Cross and Gabriella flinched, the natives below cried out, Inshallah or Allah Akhbar.

"*Do not resist me,*" the voice intoned. "*It is the time of the Sha'Daa. My kind is returning to reclaim this world after ten-thousand years of exile. All over the Earth, the old passages are opening to us. Join me, dance in the darkness and live. Resist, and die in agony.*"

Cross concentrated on the lyrics. They could do nothing until it came closer. "Them that don't know him won't like him and them that do sometimes won't know how to take him..."

Suddenly Gabriella screamed. "It's a trap. They mined the outer roads, but the big weapons are destroyed. Spare me and I will serve you. I don't want to die."

"Bitch," Cross roared. He struck one precise blow, tumbling Gabriella out of sight. He looked down at the villagers with their long rifles.

"Shoot."

A ragged volley crackled from Hamzah's men, stinging the monster.

"*Die, fools!*" It roared and charged, straight down the center road.

Cross stepped over Gabriella, heading down the stone stairs three at a time. He made it down to the doorway just as the Hellbeast strode into the town square. The smell of it bit at his nose.

He raised his grease gun and fired a burst. Then Cross pulled a whistle from his pocket and blew.

The M88 *Hellbeast's* engine roared and its searchlight flashed into the monster's eyes. But the machine at the far end of the square did not move; only its winch did. From under the sand where it had been buried, and off the buildings where it had been hung, the M88's heaviest cable snapped from hiding. Like a giant lasso of steel, it closed about the throat of the huge monster.

The monster lunged away and was brought up short by the cable. A savage jolt raced through the cable, rocking the tank recovery vehicle. Suddenly, the M88's engine stumbled and the winch stopped its massive pull.

"No," Cross shouted. He leaned out and cut loose at the monster's head. The cable hung loosely about its neck. If it slipped further, they were doomed.

The monster covered its face with one arm and flung a wrecked motor bike at Cross. He ducked into cover as it struck the doorway. He leaned out again, just as Gabriella fired the shotgun Cross had left for her in the minaret. She screamed furious Italian curses at the hellbeast.

"*Traitor,*" the hellbeast roared in their minds, glaring up at Gabriella. "*You led me into this trap. I shall scour your flesh from your body.*" His immense tail rocked back.

"Gabriella, jump," Cross screamed. He'd hit Gabriella a good one, so the pain would block any leaking thoughts of the deception from reaching the monster. He hadn't wanted to do it, but she'd insisted.

"Try not thinking of a pink elephant," she said. "It if thinks, we die."

Gabriella dropped the empty shotgun and leapt from the minaret to a rooftop just as the monster's tail crashed through the minaret. Cross hotfooted it through tumbling debris, heading for the town's central well.

The M88's engine roared back to life as the fuel pump cleared and the winch snapped up the slack. The monster was pulled off its feet, crashing into a store and exploding the glass window.

"Everyone, fire," Cross shouted. "Aim for the head and arms." A storm of stinging shots blinded and enraged the hellbeast, weakening its arms as it clawed at the garroting cable.

The M88, braced by its bulldozed blade the same way it would be when lifting a tank, jerked and shuddered but did not move as the winch drew the beast to it. The monster lashed out with its tail again. The ram of bone and reeking flesh whipped over Cross' head, so close its passage tumbled him to the ground. It smashed the building next to him. Hamzah and his men vanished into a cloud of dust and rubble.

Cross rolled away as the tail swung back. Christ, he thought, who would think it could reach so far? The beast laid about with its claws and turned everything in the street into a missile hurled at the inexorable M88. But the winch still turned. If the beast succeeded in hitting the winch… On the other side of the street, Santiago popped up with a carbine, firing at the hellbeast's head. It flinched and the beam it threw passed wide of the winch. With a roar the monster tossed a beam at Santiago, and the Mexican and his carbine flew in separate directions. But the winch again pulled the hellbeast from its feet and began to drag the monster.

Cross ran up the other side of the street, watching Santiago crawl feebly away. He saw Gabriella break from cover, duck under a swing of the hideous tail and grab the downed trooper's arm, dragging him on.

"I may get to like reporters yet," Cross said to himself.

The hellbeast fetched up against the M88 and struck at the winch, bending it. Cross started firing bursts from his M-3 grease gun. The beast's head lolled back, its giant tongue bulging as the winch drew it tight against the 54-ton M88. He could hear O'Neil screaming "Sarge, Sarge" and the popping of his pistol as college boy fired from inside the tractor.

Cross raced around and clambered up the front of the M88, his grease gun locked and loaded. As he peered over the cab, the hellbeast saw him.

"*I will grant your every wish,*" its thoughts beat on him, redolent with pain and despair. "*Everything you want. Power over your kind, women in every variety, riches. Tell me, tell me what you want.*"

Cross stood on the M88's deck.

"I want to see your head over the mantelpiece back at the family ranch. Won't have to hear from Gramps about that grizzly he killed any more." He raised the submachine gun, sighting on one monstrous eye.

A weak fury washed over Cross. The beast's eye focused on him.

"*You have won this round, human. But there will be other times and other places. You will suffer...*"

Cross pulled the trigger and the grease gun sang its song all the way through its thirty round clip. The hellbeast's body spasmed in agony, rocking the M88, but Cross kept his feet. The monster slumped limp and lifeless and the cable started cutting into the huge neck.

Cross glared down at the fallen hellbeast and spat.

"Fuck with the best," he said. "Die like the rest."

From atop the remnants of the ruined Minaret, Johnny looked down as the triumphant soldiers and villagers cautiously approached the slain hellbeast.

"Well played, humans," he laughed, a mad grin peeling his lips from his overlarge teeth. "Oh, very well played. But the Sha'Daa rages unchecked for the next forty-eight hours across the face of the world. If the others of your kind fight well, your species may live to see another day. Johnny will see." He laughed again and in a twinkle of the eye, was gone.

Party Harder

THE DOOMSDAY CLOCK IN THE GAMING pit was now operating at almost 50% capacity. Three hundred patrons, an eclectic mix of odds makers, gamblers, clergy, and anarchists stood hypnotized by the contraption's otherworldly operations. A series of bone-jarring gongs blasted outward from it, which instantly set off a frenzy of cross-bets, wails of laments, accusations, fistfights, and desperate prayers.

On the main stage the Vegas River-dance troupe was tapping and skipping to *The Russian Dervish*.

"Light me," Johnny said.

Bak looked up at the haggard eyes of The Salesman. Johnny had an unusual churchwarden pipe in his mouth. Carved from a huge chunk of pure dark blue sapphire, the 16 inch long pipe mimicked the shape of a porpoise beautifully.

Bak lit a stick match. "I didn't know you smoked, Johnny. Not that I'm complaining. You know the were-breeze doesn't allow smoke to pool or fill the air. Best investment I ever made…"

"There's a lot you don't know about me Bak buddy." Johnny exhaled the thick sweet smoke. "Which is why you sleep like a baby every night. Trust me."

"Listen," Bak blurted, "about that guy following you. He…"

"I met him," Johnny sighed.

"Whaaaa…," Bak said, startled.

"Back in the real world," Johnny nodded. "He finally came out of the shadows. Didn't give much up but told me enough."

"Yah," Bak cut in. "He approached me after you last left. Told me not to bother lying. That he knew you had come and gone. Told me to tell you he'd be back. Then he just disappeared. One second he was there and the next, poof. So, what's up?"

"As the big clock shows, The Sha'Daa is roughly half over," Johnny said.

"Half over?" Bak said slowly. "So you're saying ain't no one or nothing actually conquer the old planet yet? That's incredible."

"Absolutely incredible," Johnny nodded. "Humanity just never ceases to amaze me. Every time I think they are the most despicable, lowly race of creatures ever spawned by the universe along comes one who rises to the chal-lenge, displaying virtue, and honor, and bravery undreamt of."

On the main stage the troupe was now dancing to *Andalucía*.

"And here you are doing everything in your powers to help them," Bak smiled. "You never told me why."

"Don't get nosy," Johnny sniped.

"And this ghost of yours," Bak said.

"Calls himself, Prana," Johnny said, exhaling more smoke.

"This Prana guy, he's not such a badass after all?"

"Oh quite the contrary my friend," Johnny chuckled. "If this boy becomes a player the end of the game is an instant outcome, one way or the other. Nope. Our good Prana is an anomaly in the greater scheme of things, one which I may never truly comprehend…assuming I survive."

Bak slid a Guinness across the bar that Johnny quickly sucked down.

"Gotta hit the store room. Talk to you soon," Johnny said.

"Hang in there, Salesman," Bak shouted to his friends' receding back.

"I don't care how hot you are in Los Angeles right now," Bak heard Maribel's voice echo down from the brothel tents. "It's two hundred gold pieces for three hours work, and not a second less. Now plant your flat butt, red head, and collagen-injected lips back on that mat and put them to work, Lohan!"

Iron Girl

By Mallory Makepeace

"Life is either a daring adventure or nothing at all."
— *Helen Keller*

ONLY FIFTEEN MINUTES WERE LEFT until the triathlon's start and Lyssa kept bending over to thumb a knot out of the center of her right calf muscle. It had been bothering her ever since she and her single Transition Crew, Megan, got off the shuttle bus they had taken from the Kona Makai Hotel on Walua Road to the race staging area at Kailua-Kona Bay. Though it seemed to take forever, Lyssa finally got through the body-marking line, and quickly stripped off her visor and sneakers before handing them off. Megan, mother goose that she was, didn't want to leave poor Lyssa by herself but there were a few more details to work out at the officials table as a few folks were still not completely on board with Lyssa's unusual entry in today's field. Competing, with no handicap assistance, was simply beyond the comprehension of some. Hell, Lyssa thought. The Kanebo Corporation had taken out a special one million dollar policy on her. What more did the damned race officials need? Lyssa gave her calf one last high pressure rub. She knew the minor cramp was simply stress, over the fact that Kanebo was going to pay her a substantial bonus if, and only if, she managed to finish in the top five percent of the field. The price of corporate sponsorship and the wondrous, high-tech prototype race suit she'd been entrusted with. She knew it helped that everyone told her she looked like the actress Angelina Jolie, useless information to Lyssa who could form no picture of her own face. Pretty ruled the sighted world it seemed.

"Ten minute warning." A race official shouted over the intercom system. "Tri-athletes to Dig Me Beach."

A rapid series of coded pulses flickered across Lyssa's abdomen. She quickly stood up and walked toward the main beach area. Small pulses across her left and right shoulders continuously changed her heading. The GPS units were working perfectly and Lyssa knew that to any passerby she appeared as just one more tri-athlete approaching the race start.

The field consisted of exactly three hundred men and three hundred women who rapidly converged toward the narrow stairwell that led to the ocean where the swimming leg would start. Television camera crews surrounded the athletes, focusing specifically on the pros and a few pre-selected age groupers. The vast majority of them were faint sensory echoes that Lyssa easily avoided. For a moment her suit's sensory net seemed to pulse and freeze, but then recommenced operation. The Kanebo techs warned her that intermittent microwave transmissions potentially could give her trouble even though the components in her suit were supposed to overcome the problem.

The surface of Lyssa's body, covered by the suit, was a tactile eye, aware of any and all objects and terrain in close proximity. Short, sharp electrical jolts indicated direction changes, as every square inch of the course was mapped out ahead of time in her suit's computer, and constantly reevaluated via satellite and her suit's miniature GPS units. More impressive than all of this technology combined, however, was Lyssa's mind. A polymath with total recall, she retained an unheard of autistic talent. Never having seen anything in her life, she had the ability to mentally visualize three-dimensional impressions of objects she could touch and feel. After weeks of practice with the complex race suit sensors, Lyssa visualized, with uncanny clarity, a grey 3-D virtual map of the landscape and moving people or objects all around her. This hybrid human-machine sense, combined with her own innate athletic ability, made her the perfect candidate to complete this unheard of achievement, a visually and aurally impaired athlete partaking in and completing a triathlon with no partnered-assistance from human companion or guide dog, whatsoever.

Three times Lyssa came within a foot of some of the "challenged" athletes in this difficult event, first a wheelchair racer, next a single amputee with a curved, carbon fiber prosthetic leg, and finally two blind athletes, one a man with a guide dog, and the second a woman, with a male, sighted race-companion. A familiar vibe emanated from both and Lyssa quickly turned from this pair, hoping that her thin disguise of new hairstyle, cut and dyed blonde, and the darkened swimming goggles would work. She was determined to hide her own handicaps from every fellow athlete until the very end of the race.

Without warning, just twenty yards from the start, a tall figure stood before her, forcing her to halt awkwardly in the sand. Her anger flaring, Lyssa began to reach for her customized, GW Micro Braille reader to tell the schmuck off, when two large, long-fingered hands grabbed her own. A blaze of tactile ASL commenced. Even more surprising than this breach of visual/hearing-impaired handicap etiquette was his ability to talk via TASL. Lyssa had never met her match in this form of communication, but this man (his gender instantly betrayed by the shape and texture of his hands) moved his fingers at an unbelievable rate.

"Lyssa Furon, my name is Johnny." He gesticulated rapidly into her hands. "We have little time. I am The Salesman. I am here on an urgent mission. This is the time of The Sha'Daa. Nothing must stop you from completing this race. The repercussions would be horrible. I know you have no reason to believe me, but you have been chosen by fate to be the savior of the planet. Do you remember when you were eight, and first ran your hands over your step-aunt's face and it flashed into your mind, her large nose, and thin eyebrows, and wart near her upper lip? And that windy day in the park when you were thirteen and you could suddenly SEE all of the fig trees about you? And then your first sexual encounter with a man, and the unusual images that formed in your mind of male anatomy that both shocked and thrilled? Your mind is like no other on this planet, Lyssa, and so you are the only one who might complete this challenge."

Lyssa's mouth opened in shock.

"Your true abilities, unknown by so many, will serve you well today. I fear, however, that near the end of this challenge, you may falter. Take this."

Johnny placed a small, marble sized, cellophane wrapped clump into her right hand.

"If things become overwhelming, take this and chew it. It's not any kind of performance enhancement drug. It will not ruin your great achievement on this important day."

Lyssa hesitated. This was madness. A total stranger confronts her right before a race and expects her to take some strange food item? Slowly, surprising herself, Lyssa quickly pocketed the item in her right hip pouch. As bizarre as this whole incident was, something in Johnny's ASL "voice," the naked urgency communicated through his strong, confident hands persuaded her to hold onto it.

"Now. To complete our transaction I need but one thing from you. Your bracelet." Johnny said.

If Lyssa had vocal cords she would have gasped. Her bracelet? Surely Johnny was crazy. Made of a now rusting stainless steel, the ugly little medical ID that declared she was deaf, mute, and blind was her only heirloom. A gift from her stepmother at the age of three, she had despised it for years. And then, after a decade of unwavering assistance, teaching, and love, she saw it as a symbol of her unending bond to the woman who had never given up on her, and had opened this curst child's mind to the beauty of the surrounding world. Lyssa Furon, Albanian war orphan and adopted daughter of her single, Greek mother Helena Furon, had grieved mightily on her eighteenth birthday, as Helena had passed away that morning, from complications due to pancreatic cancer. On that day Lyssa had sworn she would never be a victim or a cripple the rest of her life. And now ten years later she found herself reliving that grief in horrid detail.

"You must make this trade now, Lyssa." Johnny squeezed into her hands. "I cannot force you."

Something in Johnny's unspoken voice persuaded her, and Lyssa did that which she could never have imagined possible. She gave this total stranger her aged I.D. bracelet.

Just as Johnny began disengaging his hands, Lyssa, on impulse, pressed forward and instantly ran her hands down the sides of Johnny, his front, and then his face and head. The Salesman made no move, patiently allowing this intensely personal examination. A bright, monochromatic image loomed large in Lyssa's highly unusual mind, that of a tall, slender man of indeterminate age, with clean-shaven hawkish face, amazingly dressed in suit, trench coat, and fedora on this hot and humid day, but seemingly untouched by and unaware of the extreme weather.

"You must prevail." Johnny pressed into Lyssa's hands. "The fate of all depends on it." And then he was gone. Lyssa spun around, thinking for a moment that Johnny had merely let go of her hands, but no, her suit sensors, and her own innate ability to feel the presence of others told her that the Salesman had disappeared.

Without further hesitation Lyssa turned and entered the line to the stairwell down to the ocean. The encounter with Johnny had lasted no more than thirty seconds.

A god of death rose up through the dead skeleton of a sleeping volcano known by most Hawaiians as Kohala. Ten thousand years had passed since his last corporeal transubstantiation, yet his mind had peered into this dimension from time to time, sometimes appearing in the dreaming minds of the descendants of those humans who'd repopulated these islands in 400 A.D. Their shamans had named him Kuahana, the god who kills men, and Ku, the maker and architect of war.

Silent, invisible, Ku hovered over the chain of islets and eight main islands known as Hawaii, and marveled. Never in the one million years since this portal first opened had he been witness to such a wealth of sentient flesh and blood. During many of the previous Sha'Daa's, spatial and temporal alignments had been such that the portal within Kohala could not be breached or challenged. And then over dozens of others the barriers of distance and the vast surrounding ocean left but little in the way of native animal and plant life to conquer and feed upon. Several times, however, in the most recent of Sha'Daa's, during the past 80,000 years, humans had settled and spread across the still-growing island chains. Some faced the Sha'Daa challenge and thwarted Ku's efforts. Others, including those in the last Sha'Daa 10,000 years ago, failed and perished.

Ku hungered as he had never done before. Beneath him, spread across this island empire, lay a host of humanity numbering well over two million. Humans had advanced greatly in the interval, and the population of the Earth had expanded beyond imagination. Looking about himself Ku gawked at oil tankers plowing through the ocean, and jets burning through the air.

If Ku succeeded in the challenge, his armies would finally face a worthy enemy. But that was a precipitous thought, and Ku now laid his mind open to the full nature of what competition would decide the fate of these isles. Since Kohala first breached the ocean's surface 500,000 years ago, Ku was bound by the laws of The Sha'Daa to abide by a competition – forced to gamble his forces onto the field of battle to determine whether or not he and his hordes would be allowed full and unrestrained access to these isles for a period of forty-eight hours. Beneath him, a group of six hundred human warriors had gathered to compete in some strange conflict.

"Very well," Ku thought. "I accept this challenge."

As the players gathered near water's edge, Ku began creating his first host of horrors.

Still confused by her bizarre encounter with Johnny the Salesman, but struggling to maintain focus for the grueling race she was about to start, Lyssa adjusted the jet-black wraparound swimming goggles she wore.

The bright summer sun had climbed rapidly above the horizon when the cannon was fired and six hundred athletes swam forward into the ocean.

The buffeting of elbows, hips, knees, and forearms was furious early into this 2.4 mile rough water swim. Four times Lyssa was nearly hit in the face by someone's foot but managed to avoid the strikes at the last moment. She kept a strong pace, confident after hundreds of hours in the Kanebo sim room. The potential for injury, or worse yet, an abrasion or tear in her race suit, was alarmingly great in this packed mass of bodies, but her competitive spirit had been lit. Slowly, Lyssa began to advance her position through the field.

The ocean had turned into a frothing mass of swimmers tearing through the foot-high waves like ravenous sharks.

Lyssa slowly moved forward and past her immediate competitors with long, powerful, freestyle-strokes. Not needing to raise her face forward and above the waterline for constant course direction adjustment, she was able to achieve near one hundred percent efficiency in form and movement. The turnaround point was still a ways ahead, but so far things seemed to be moving along just fine. Other than a strange tangy taste to the water, Lyssa was completely unaware of the horror that was befalling dozens of her competitors.

Without notice the right heel of the swimmer directly in front of her struck Lyssa's forehead, hard. She felt herself beginning to pass out…

Ku laughed as swimmer after swimmer died in violent convulsions. The first wave of terrors, Huaka'i Po, the Night Marchers, were invisible harpies that flew down into the waters and surfaced beneath and amid the many tightly grouped swimmers. At first unseen, their ancient song of death and destruction seeped into the ears of those in close proximity. And then, those that paid it any heed, were quickly captured by the spell. The god of death focused his attention on one impressive swimmer, a large man near the lead. Entering the blonde haired athlete's mind he saw through the mortal's eyes.

Jake Eger knew he had a great shot at making top three today. Kissing his wife Agatha, and their two-year-old son Jeremy, goodbye at the airport in San Francisco yesterday had been tough, especially after one solid year of training that had taken up much of his personal time at the expense of his family. But the drive to succeed and win had pushed Jake for years, and now, just months from turning thirty, tearing through the water like a torpedo, he felt like payoff was only hours away.

Jake glanced up for a moment to double check his bearing. What was that weird ringing? Almost like music. Jake managed to block it out all the way up to the turnaround point. He made it around the marker buoy and commenced the second half of the swim. This transition to an opposing current allowed for a momentary lapse in concentration.

"Just what is that music?" Jake thought.

Directly in Jake's path was a gorgeous mermaid with long flowing red hair, pale skin, and green eyes. Naked with an erotic and shapely human torso, she smiled at him. As Jake started to smile in reply, this sailor's myth transformed into a monstrosity of fangs and multiple tentacles that wrapped painfully around his arms and legs. A large beak with razor teeth dipped and bit deeply into Jake's skull. His final thought was hope that Agatha had mailed his most recent life insurance policy payment out on time…

To surrounding athletes it appeared that Jake had stopped moving, perhaps to massage a cramp while floating. Those that paid more than a moment's notice saw he was convulsing and bleeding profusely from mouth and nose, and then were also overtaken by the harpy spell.

Race officials at the first transition point suddenly found themselves scratching their heads when at the end of the 2.4-mile swim only three hundred athletes emerged from the water to commence the bike leg.

Emergency standby lifeguards and ambulance services began confirming that half the original pack had drowned. Reporters, photographers, and video crews started swarming around Dig Me Beach trying to make sense out of the confusion.

Lyssa felt sand under her hands and knew she had made it back to the shore. A bruise had started forming near her left temple. Through sheer force of will she'd kept from passing out. The second half of the swim had been a lot tougher as the chop and currents picked up. Lyssa accidentally swallowed salt water on what seemed like a trip on a water treadmill back to shore. She crossed the timing mat at personal record pace and vomited.

Lyssa fought panic as the micro antenna embedded in the right hip of her suit had trouble locking in on her destination, the transition area behind the King K hotel. Finally it kicked in and she navigated her way to her bike-to-run transition bag, which lay in the waiting hands of Megan Forrester. Megan helped Lyssa with her cycling shoes, jersey and helmet, before pushing the carbon fiber Noboyuki race bike forward. Before patting Lyssa on the back for luck, Megan signed frantically in ASL.

"Jesus, Lyssa, you cut your forehead." Megan said while cleaning and slapping a small adhesive bandage over the small bruised cut.

"You're doing great and ahead of pace." Megan said. "Something weird is happening though. Half the pack seems to have gotten held up at the water leg. Many of them were definitely hurt. There's even a rumor of fatalities. I don't know why the race officials have not stopped everything, but until they do, just keep it up. I'll see you at the run transition station at Keauhou. Good luck."

A quick hug and then Lyssa started out slow to get her bearings. The next 112 miles were technically going to be the most difficult portion of the entire triathlon. For the average cyclist, bicycling represented a relatively equal mix of vestibular balance, vision, and a feel for gravity. Lyssa may have had two strikes, but she felt more than confident to the task after the many simulated disasters and near disasters she had been subjected to in the sim room. Having experienced the worst of what could happen to her, she had become so overly sensitized to the constant data input feeding through her race suit that her reactions were quite nearly prescient.

The first eight plus miles on bike winded through the town of Kailua-Kona and up onto the Queen Ka'ahumanu highway. Lyssa took the initial climb out of the saddle to work her way further up in ranking early on. Her legs felt fresh as she increased her pace on the Queen K. Within ten minutes she found herself passing more people than expected. But it was upon entering the lava fields where she crossed "the wind line" that everything took a turn for the worse. Gusts up to 50 knots began buffeting riders and a number of men and women constantly crashed in front of her. The fourth time this happened Lyssa illegally swerved across the road's centerline to avoid the fallen rider. Luckily no judges spotted the maneuver to cite her.

This extreme buffeting and falling riders continued for twenty odd miles. Lyssa primarily used her bike's small chain-rings on the gently rolling terrain of no more than two to four percent grade. More so than in the swimming leg of the race, Lyssa had to bite down on her feelings. All these crashes had to be the result of unprofessional and overaggressive cyclists as much as it was the wind.

Lyssa sequestered that ever-present anger and resentment that had lapped on the shores of her psyche since her birth. Weird fluctuations in air temperature flickered at the edge of her awareness, but otherwise were ignored as Lyssa constantly adjusted for course changes. Already she had emptied and tossed both of her water bottles. At mile fifty-five Lyssa began the long climb to Hawi. The wind was head-on as she wrapped around the north tip of the island. She hated to admit it, but she sensed that her reserves were low. Ignoring this weakness, she leaned into the headwind.

Lyssa remained unaware of the macabre terrors that ran rampant among her competitors.

Two riders several yards in front of her were hit by a strong wind gust. The one on the left yawned to his right. Just then a news van drove past on the shoulder. For a tenth of a second Lyssa's suit's sensor net shut off and just as quickly rebooted.

"Damn microwaves." Lyssa thought.

Lyssa suddenly realized that the two bikers had collided and were on the ground immediately in front of her. She swerved, but too late. Her right wheel struck the outstretched leg of a male biker, throwing her from her own bike to hit the ground, rolling off of her left hip. Her right thigh struck the man's handlebars and sustained a nasty but superficial gash that immediately started to bleed.

Ku exulted. Everything was going to plan. The humans seemed completely unprepared for this challenge. It was as if there was no concept of racial memory. Had they truly forgotten the nature of this fatal competition after another ten thousand year cycle?

But Ku had to win in competition and so he sent forth a wave of his lesser intangible emissaries, to strike the minds of the race officials, suppressing any thoughts of stopping the triathlon. The race would not end unless the athletes themselves gave up.

After the survivors left the water, Ku released his invisible Mujina, Medusan horrors that dove upon the cyclists. In moments, these sickening creations flew down amidst the many athletes struggling for victory. One after another of the triathletes crashed to the road, or worse, collided with one or several of their competitors, causing disastrous pileups.

Unable to keep himself from savoring the carnage, Ku infiltrated his awareness down into the pack of athletes and entered the mind of the lead female athlete in the race.

Katherine Rafferty, Irish National, gritted her teeth and leaned in to another short bike sprint. She was absolutely sure she had the female category lead nailed down well and good, but wanted to put as much extra room between her and that skinny witch from Kenya, Emily Kolenjin, as she could.

Ever since the turnaround station at Hawi, a flickering golden light kept appearing on her right periphery until she could no longer ignore it. Turning for the briefest of moments to check it out, the strange floating globe of beautiful light quickly morphed into the image of an angel. Katherine's eyes opened wide when the apparition sprouted five-inch fangs and leaped upon her. Her last thoughts were of her daughter Mary, and how for the first time mommy would not be able to give her birthday kisses in two weeks…

To everyone around Katherine it appeared she simply lost her line, and careened off the main road and into the ditch. Those few cyclists that slowed down for a quick look instantly took notice of the strange golden lights and were themselves doomed.

For one hundred and twelve miles the attrition rate on the second leg was staggering. Three pace-vans with video crews, not to mention three cable network overhead helicopters were doing their best to chronicle what appeared to be the most disastrous iron man competition in the history of the sport. Dozens of ambulances had long ago converged on Dig Me Beach. Several more were rushing to various parts of the bike course as desperate cell phone calls kept jamming the 911 switchboard. Endless phone, shortwave radio, and e-mail transmissions to race officials continued to go unanswered. Why was the race still going on?

Lyssa had quickly recovered from the bike crash, breathing again after she realized her suit was not ripped. At the turnaround feed station at Hawi, Lyssa managed to replace her bottles, fuel herself, and began an all too brief tailwind descent over the course of ten minutes.

The remaining half of the bike leg back across the lava fields was an exercise in agony. The cut on her right thigh stopped bleeding, but the pain came and went in waves. Also, the damage to the suit sensors around her left hip created a 'blind spot' that she constantly had to be wary of lest a biker appear out of nowhere on her eight o'clock. The important blessing in Lyssa's mind was that her bike had not been irreparably damaged. The front tire continued to skew slightly to the left, but other than that Lyssa was still in it to win it. Sucking down more water she leaned into the headwind and gritted her teeth. Forty-nine more miles loomed ahead like eternity.

Fifty surviving cyclists, a roughly equal mix of men and women, managed to make it to the bike-to-run transition point at Keauhou.

Lyssa brought her Noboyuki to a halt, stripped off her helmet, and grabbed a bottle of Gatorade out of Megan's outstretched hand inside the change tent and quickly gulped it down. Lyssa then frantically tore off her bike helmet and footgear to rapidly put on and lace her running shoes. Megan slapped stinging brown salve onto Lyssa's wounded thigh and followed it up with anti-bacterial ointment and a gauze pad thoroughly wrapped in an ace bandage, but not so tight as to cut off any arterial flow for the remainder of the race.

As Lyssa stood up Megan stuffed a small energy bar into her mouth. Megan then grabbed Lyssa's hands and tactile signed frantically.

"It's crazy, Lyssa." Megan said. "The news is reporting casualties. Deaths. The police and ambulance services have their hands full. Everyone has cornered the race officials but they're not making any sense. They keep refusing to end the race. I think you should stop."

Lyssa leaned forward and gave Megan a passionate but much too short kiss. Megan knew what finishing the race meant to Lyssa. But Megan had not met Johnny, The Salesman. His words echoed in Lyssa's hands. She didn't know why, but everything happening told her that the Salesman had told her the truth. She had to finish this race at all cost.

Lyssa broke into a quick jog. Her suit's sensors were picking up far fewer competitors in her immediate vicinity than expected, but she quickly tossed such distracting thoughts away and focused on covering the next twenty-six plus miles as quickly as she could.

The third leg had begun.

Lyssa emerged from the bike-to-run transition into a blast furnace of the most horrendous heat she'd ever experienced on a triathlon course. The sun was high in the sky and the humidity felt like it was one hundred percent. Even the damned asphalt was radiating waves of baking heat. Already halfway to full exhaustion, Lyssa was finding it near impossible to acclimate to the shocking increase in temperature. She practically staggered to the first of the well stocked aid stations on the running course, only slowing down long enough to grab and put ice in her mouth, and a sopping sponge that she squeezed over her head. The station was abandoned, more proof that something terrible was underway.

Three times Lyssa checked her Braille timer wristband. At the oceanfront turnaround near the six-mile point she did a one hundred and eighty degree turn and headed back towards town. Like the last six miles, the next would be on mostly flat road where she felt mildly confident she could maintain this record pace.

When she hit Palani Drive, though, she knew all bets were off.

Ku was two thirds of the way to victory. If no human finished the challenge, then he and his legions of horror would strike this treasure trove of flesh and innocence.

The rampant spilling of blood filled the air with invisible clouds of dark mana that Ku now fed greedily upon. He began to gain mass and substance at an exponential rate. By the time all of the human athletes met with defeat, he would be corporeal, and free to rend and kill at the head of his waiting army.

Ku released the last of his horrors, the Lapu, upon the surviving athletes. Invisible like their brethren, and far more insidious and subtle, they quickly flew downward. The death god of gambling sent his mind down among the victims so he could experience every drop of terror and fear.

Bill Aata, native New Zealander, six foot tall, bronze skin and hair, built like a Greek god, had the lead. He knew something was wrong from the lack of staff along the road and much of the crowd seemed to have fled. But his long, easy strides outran news of the disaster. Bill's focus and self-discipline had managed to overcome and ignore the strange visual and aural distractions that had plagued him since race's start. He'd passed them off as hallucinations but determined not to fail now with all he and his girlfriend sacrificed to get here. Now though, he found his sense of smell and even taste assaulted mercilessly. Gritting his teeth hard, and try as he might, the stench and tang of rotting death, foul corruption, and rancid bile soon became overwhelming. Moments later he opened his mouth and groaned loudly in disgust and was doomed.

Drawn like sharks to blood, the vocal vibrations exuding from Bill's mouth attracted Ku's reavers. Bill suddenly saw a free-floating monstrosity, like a python snake with a million hairy legs; appear directly in front of him. The monstrosity dived forward and directly into Bill's mouth, eating its way down into his abdomen in a froth of agonizing pain. Bill's last thought was of Betty. He should have proposed to her last night…

To those remaining spectators on the side of the road, unable to see Ku's minions, Bill appeared to slow down to a walk, and then collapse onto the side of the road convulsing like an epileptic having a severe fit. His eyes then turned white and scarlet blood gushed from his mouth and nose as he died.

A sudden influx of police, emergency crews, and shocked and worried spectators all along the run course looked like it might finally bring the race to a halt. All two dozen runners in front of Lyssa were finally being stopped.

High in the air, and still invisible, Ku took stock of the debacle below. The remaining two-dozen runners, still several miles from the finish line, were showing more and more uncertainty in their motion. Death itself was not a prerequisite for failure in this cosmic challenge. All that was required for Ku to win was that the athletes not finish. If they gave up of their own accord, the Earth was lost.

Lyssa, experiencing more pain than she had ever endured in her life, hit the twelve-mile marker and aid station. Downing more water, placing a large chunk of ice in her mouth, and squeezing two sponges over her head, she pushed herself up the 200 yards of Palani Drive and then headed west on the Queen K. Ignoring the throbbing in her right thigh, the stinging blister forming on her left heel, the bruise spreading on her left hip, the itching ache on her left temple, and the steadily draining strength in her limbs, Lyssa somehow kicked it up a notch and increased her speed.

Lyssa soon found herself starting to succumb to the horrible smells and tastes that overwhelmed her. But though she opened her mouth to groan, no sound came forth. The Lapu could not strike the mute.

Lyssa's anger bubbled within herself, and it took all of a life's training to hold it in check. What incompetent idiot had set the third leg right by a landfill, anyway? That had to be the explanation for the insane reek, and worse there was the sudden chaos of foot traffic and vehicles all around her. Race officials had really dropped the ball when it came to security. Several times she had to dodge to avoid oncoming vehicles, vans by their sensory patterns that kept appearing from nowhere. Worst of all were the damn fans and spectators. Four times someone reached out to grab hold of Lyssa, as if to make her stop running, but each time she was able to sidestep them with her excellent reflexes and continue her run. Nothing and no one was going to stop her from breaking this new record and getting her reward money. Not to mention this Sha'Daa of Johnny's, whatever it was. Something terrible would happen if she did not finish and do well. Lyssa had worked too hard and long to be stopped at this point.

Top race officials, targeted by Ku's servants and afflicted with temporary blindness, deafness, or mental confusion as needed continued to ignore any and all suggestions and even demands to halt the competition. Police and others began to act. The surviving athletes in the third leg, the running marathon, had either collapsed or simply given up upon spreading word of mouth on what had befallen the majority of their competitors. The race was finally being stopped.

Except for one woman. A single tri-athlete from Albania was still plowing forward, refusing to acknowledge any and all attempts to communicate with or stop her.

Ku was furious. The last human athlete was less than ten miles from the finish line, and running strong. How could this be, and a female, no less? In the past it had only been the most dedicated shamans, holy men who had spent their entire lives learning to overcome their every sense who had even managed to complete their challenge, the vast majority dying in their final acts of victory. Some how, some way, this female athlete was of an equal class of esthetics.

The death god flew down towards this champion and kept pace mere feet away in the air. Using all of his newly manifested power, he doubled and tripled the force of all the curses his Lapu were flooding upon her. There was precious little time left. She had to be stopped.

According to the race map embedded in her memory, and every bit of data her suit sensors continually updated her with, Lyssa was less than ten miles from the end. She should have felt triumphant at this point, so close to her personal victory, but so many doubts had started to flood her mind.

The chaos in the swim leg, the unusually large number of bicycle collisions and accidents in the second, and finally, the ridiculously large number of road hazards and illegal foot traffic through most of this twenty-six mile, three hundred and eighty five yard run. Johnny had told her it was imperative she finish this race. But why? What had been happening to all of the other athletes around her? Megan had said fatalities. Had people really been dying during this god-awful challenge? What was the reason for it all? The Sha'Daa? Instinct kept her running at her top pace, but Lyssa now began to doubt her own sanity. By the third long incline Lyssa could feel her very muscles screaming for more oxygen and glucose, and still she moved forward.

Ku began to sense a change in this final athlete's demeanor, though it was not enough to slow down her running. Race's end was only miles distant. Panicking, the death god thrust his consciousness down into Lyssa's mind. Why, it asked itself over and over again, why do you not quail at sight of my Mujina? Why do the voices of my Night Marchers not drive you insane? Why do you not voice your horror at the stench of my Lapu? And then looking into Lyssa's mind, Ku finally saw the truth of it all.

Lyssa had been born without eyes, eardrums, or vocal cords. Blind, deaf, and mute since birth, she was a handicapped prodigy of wildly unusual talents. Looking farther into her memories the death god realized, that this woman wore a shroud as sophisticated in its technology as a host of Ku's most subtle spells.

Lyssa hit the stretch of miles that would lead her into The Energy Lab, and just then Ku used all of his power to call down the weather itself. Instantly, rain, sleet, and fierce winds tore at Lyssa whose pace started faltering, though she continued to move forward.

The sudden cold, constant peppering of rain and sleet, and intermediate pressure of wind played havoc with Lyssa's suit sensors. Her sense of direction was growing screwier with every mile that passed.

At one point the wetness felt particularly sticky on her face. Reaching up, Lyssa found that the bandage on her head had fallen off and the cut was bleeding down her forehead and behind her black sports goggles to her lips. Lyssa used her left thumb and index finger to squeeze the cut shut. She couldn't run the rest of the race like this and prayed the small wound would coagulate in just a couple of minutes.

It felt like an eternity had passed when she exited The Energy Lab stretch and only five miles were left to run.

Ku fretted far above. He could sense that this human champion was failing, even mostly exhausted. But why? Why did she continue forward? What drove her?

Miles later Lyssa reached Kona, ran onto Palani Drive, and made the right hand turn after the twenty-five mile marker.

"Just over a mile to go," she thought. The waves of pain that wracked Lyssa's entire body were almost unbearable.

Fear started to form in the back of her mind when once again her encounter that morning with Johnny filled her mind. Johnny, that strange tall man who called himself The Salesman, and his sudden appearance and disappearance right before she had joined the pack on the beach at race's start.

And it was then that Ku finally fully crossed the boundary of Lyssa's conscious mind.

"That meddlesome Salesman, I should have known he was part of this." Ku spoke. "You do not have to punish yourself this way puny one."

A wave of shock ran through Lyssa, though it did not slow her pace. She had actually heard Ku's voice! Though her auditory cortex had never developed enough to ever process sound, had she eardrums, nonetheless she was able to HEAR this voice, and understand it.

"Yes." Ku spoke. "I offer you this…and much more."

Then, Lyssa's mind, which by now with the aid of her race suit's sensor array had formed a rough monochromatic series of shapes and dimensions surrounding everything within a twenty foot radius of her, instantly transitioned into a gloriously bright, colorful, dynamic panorama of Kona. She could see. And instinctively she knew this was real sight. Ku was letting her see the wonder of the world, the palm trees along sidewalks, the blue sky, the greenest of grass, and the glorious Sun in the sky. And then there was the joyous sound of wind in the trees. The cries of seagulls sounded like the most wondrous of music to Lyssa. It was all so beautiful. Lyssa's pace began to falter more.

"Yes." Ku whispered seductively to her. "You will see, and hear, and if you accept my offer, I will finally grant you speech. All you need do is stop this terrible self-punishment. Stop running. When my armies cross over you will be spared, a fair courtesan in my personal court. You alone will live as millions perish within my conquest."

And it was upon this last statement that Lyssa's mind sobered. Millions killed, including Megan. Johnny had told the truth.

"No." Lyssa snarled within her mind. "I reject you."

And instantly the sound and the vision stopped. Lyssa pushed her failing, exhausted wreck of a body forward. She was but five hundred yards from the finish line.

Ku, furious, brought back the fierce freezing winds, and now they began taking their toll on Lyssa's race suit, as over half of the sensors failed. Her own crude sense of monochromatic sight became more and more compromised while the dimensions and boundaries of the road and immediate landmarks became vague, and each step became as much a guess as a movement of surety.

And now, so close to race's end, Lyssa knew what she had to do, and so she pulled out the cellophane wrapped object that Johnny had given her that morning, unwrapped it, and popped it into her mouth.

The horrid flavor of pepper gum burned in her mouth. She spat it out furiously. Betrayal flooded her soul and Lyssa's breathing became ragged as a memory surfaced of her first few days at the local school for the severely disabled, when she was ten. The horrible tricks the sighted children played on her. One, whom she had begun to trust, as she had Johnny, had slipped her gum like this.

A lifetime of suppressed rage and anger ignited within. For over two decades Lyssa had managed to hold back that fury she had always felt deep within herself. The sexual harassment and even assaults by college professors and later bosses, the inevitable betrayals by lovers too condescending and unimaginative enough to think her disabilities could hide their infidelities from her. A whole society of lawyers, bankers, accountants, or even simple housecleaners more than willing to try to take advantage of and steal from her. For twenty-eight years she had chained her deepest and darkest rages at the unholy and unforgivable trick that life and god had played upon her since birth…until now.

"Damn you all to Hell" Lyssa screamed within her mind. "I don't need any of you!"

The flood of scalding adrenaline through her arteries and veins burned away all doubt, cold, and conflicts in her senses.

Lyssa now experienced her surroundings in frightening clarity, and her mind, abnormal engine of extreme intuition and perception that it was, filled her with a blazing, three-dimensional, monochromatic image of the road and everything surrounding her for a full mile. Though not the multi-colored delight that Ku had offered her earlier, Lyssa now saw everything around her with the cold, precise clarity of a gigantic daguerreotype photograph.

Ku felt these changes within her and wailed.

Lyssa took the two right turns that put her onto Alii Drive.

The overhead news helicopters managed to catch glimpses of Lyssa through the bizarre, localized sleet-storm that hovered only yards around her.

Lyssa ran down that final one hundred yards with every last ounce of willpower and effort she could muster. Ku still battered at the periphery of her mind but she paid him no heed. She would finish this race if it killed her. The numbing cold made her legs stiff and she bit her lower lip until it drew blood. This gave her a final moment of clarity, and it was all that she needed.

With a final burst of speed Lyssa crossed the finish line and timing mat, and collapsed to her knees, exhausted and shaking, onto the asphalt.

Two courageous camera crews managed to brave the cold and videotape Lyssa's courageous finish from twenty yards away.

One by one her suit's sensors shut off as the wafer thin lithium batteries finally began running out of charge. Lyssa had just enough time to confirm her triple race times via her Braille wristband timer, 00:27:08 swim, 02:25:18 bike, and 01:31:56 run. She had set a new women's Ironman record at 04:28:16.

Unseen and unheard by the world at large, Ku screamed in agony and terror. In a rage of betrayal, his very essence slowly shredding into nothingness, Ku blazed toward Lyssa at the speed of thought, vowing to kill her moments before he was banished for another ten thousand years.

A mad cackle sounded in Ku's ears. "Cheaters never prosper, Ku. You've lost!" Johnny the Salesman instantly appeared from nowhere. Power such as even Ku had never seen roiled about him. "I own you, rule-breaker." A bolt of pure force flew from the upraised hand of the wildly grinning Salesman and smashed into the death god, flinging Ku into the slope of Kohala.

A deep rumble drew the attention of everyone surrounding Lyssa. Even she felt the vibrations through the Earth. Somehow, possibly through Johnny's nearness, she knew it was the death of Ku and his legions, swallowed in Mother Earth's cleaning magma.

Kohala erupted for the first time in 120,000 years, a mild eruption in the slow way of Hawaiian volcanoes.

As the vibrations lessened, Lyssa fought her way to her knees. "Where's Megan?" Lyssa thought. She prayed her friend had weathered this horrible day to its end. Lyssa, breathing deeply, dug her palm-sized Braille reader/translator out of her left thigh pocket, typed rapidly, and turned up the speaker's volume to full.

As the last of a lifetime of suppressed rage bled out of her soul, Lyssa hoped someone was within hearing distance when she clicked on the reader's continuous playback. The tiny speaker crackled sarcastically while the ground shook as Kohala erupted.

"Hey. Can any of you selfish pricks take a little pity on a poor, helpless blind, deaf, and dumb girl? I need a taxi back to my hotel."

All Eyes On The Hidden Door

HOW EXACTLY DOES ONE GET TO, OR find, the Triple-Six Tavern? The most precise explanation would likely require a five day cross discussion between the World's top ten theoretical physicists. The simple answer is a lot more fun. How do you get to this bar among bars? Why, through a bar, of course. Stop and think for a moment. Every bar, every tavern, and every drinking hole you've ever stumbled on, look around. Remember that odd door you would see in the back. No, not the kitchen, or the bathrooms, or the storage rooms, or even the rear exits. Think about that one extra door that just stands there, unused, and unattended. It appears to be locked, but is it really? It doesn't seem to serve any purpose whatsoever. And sometimes, if you ever return to the bar, when the beer and booze and charming company don't distract your mind, you even believe for a moment that sometimes that very peculiar door isn't even there… like it just comes and goes, based on nothing more than it's own whims. And there you have it.

Silent Hunter

By Deborah Koren

Lieutenant Rick Javers cursed under his breath as he headed, dripping wet, for his quarters. He went on duty in fifteen minutes, and he still had to dry off and change. Laughter from the King Neptune Festival followed him down the hall. Seven of the crew, including him, had never crossed the equator before. Captain Thorn had surfaced *Harpy* just long enough for all seven to be ordered on deck and tossed in the drink, much to the amusement of the attending crew. The XO had even worn a silly King Neptune costume and made a speech for the occasion.

The submarine was already underway again, heading toward the fleet-designated war game grid.

She was the prototype of the new *Odyssey* class attack sub, smaller than the *Virginia* and *Los Angeles* classes. Faster, quieter. She'd sacrificed some firepower, but made up for it with increased sonar capabilities and a new organic skin over the outer hull that absorbed sound waves and camouflaged her signature. *Harpy* had also implemented a revolutionary automation system designed to operate the submarine with less crew. Her crew complement was just eighty-five, including eleven officers.

Javers was pleased they hadn't restricted the crew to experienced officers. Given the experimental nature of the *Odyssey* class, he'd thought they'd want her trial run handled by an experienced crew. But MOS shortage had given him a chance. *Harpy* was his first tour of duty. He had yet to earn his dolphins, and he was the youngest of the three pukes onboard.

He drew to attention as the XO approached, still in his King Neptune get-up. Lt. Commander Beau Sanderson was a big man, and the costume and spiky gold crown perched jauntily on his head made him appear even taller.

"A private word, Lieutenant?"

Javers gestured down the hall. "My quarters all right, sir? Lieutenant Marullo is on duty."

"Fine, fine."

Javers led the way, trying to see past the fake white beard and long wig. Something about the XO seemed off, but he couldn't place it.

Once inside, the man said, "I have something for you, son. Something you need badly."

The man's voice was wrong. Javers froze. "You're not the XO."

The man quirked an eyebrow and grinned, a single gold incisor clearly visible. "I heard they put only the smartest volunteers in the submarine service."

Javers reached for the intercom button. "Please don't do anything stupid. I'm going to call the chief of the boat."

"Step away from that," the man said, wearily. He held up his hands, palms toward Javers. "Look, I'm just here to make a trade with you."

It sounded so absurd, Javers could only stare at him.

The man sighed heavily. "I'm early, aren't I? When is this? Must have got the times wrong. You were wet...I thought...."

"What are you talking about? Who are you?"

"I'll be back, Rick. And then, you and me are gonna do a little horse-trading. The lives of more than just your crew will depend on you." He walked out.

Javers hurried after him. "Wait just a...."

The corridor was empty except for Crazy Ivan, one of the cooks, coming toward him balancing a tray of sandwiches.

"You see a guy in a King Neptune costume heading this way?" Javers asked.

Crazy blinked at him, eyes round in an owl face.

"Never mind," Javers said.

Javers puzzled over the encounter as he entered the maneuvering room. He'd been assigned as engineering department division officer. He fingered his father's insignia in his pocket, the metal cold and comforting to his skin.

Rear Admiral Rick Javers, Sr. had retired just a few months previously, at the same time Rick Javers, Jr. had graduated from Nuclear Power School. His father was one of those officers everyone wanted to serve under. A lucky officer. Sometimes, Javers thought he carried his father's dolphins hoping that same luck would rub off on him. *You show great promise*, Captain Thorn had said when he'd been welcomed onboard, but he wasn't sure whether he'd received the posting to *Harpy* based on his own merit, or his father's legacy. He studied furiously in his off-duty hours, determined to qualify as quickly as possible and earn his own dolphins. But that didn't stop him from keeping his father's in his pocket.

His gaze slid from the main display to the two men he was supervising. Both were on their second tour of duty. Senichi Hamada, eight years Javers senior, was reactor operator and throttleman. He was helping Javers qualify for the engineering watch. Electrician duty fell to Stephens. Engineering officer of the watch was Dirk Canter, a big gruff man who said little, but when he did, Javers knew to listen.

Harpy cruised slowly, with just enough impetus to keep their course, and the command had come back from the control room for silence. Given that the ship's orders were to proceed directly to the war game's designated coordinates, and that over a day's worth of travel remained to reach the outer edge of the square, Javers couldn't help speculating on what the senior officers were up to.

The collision alarm sounded barely a second before an impact jolted the ship, slamming Javers sideways. Pain speared through his head where he smacked the equipment panel, and then — nothing.

"Lieutenant, Lieutenant," a panicked voice called, repeatedly. "Come on, wake up, Lieutenant." It filtered through Javers' consciousness, struck a chord of recognition. "Damn it, Senichi, do something. We need him awake and we need him now."

Something hit us, Javers remembered, then he coughed and bolted upright at the acrid odor of smelling salts. He groaned as the movement made his head feel like it was falling off. "What happened?" he asked.

"Just hang on a minute, sir," Senichi said, and Javers winced as something was pressed against the back of his head. "You've got a nasty gash here. You're bleeding everywhere."

The other man kneeling beside him was one of the co-pilots. Javers couldn't keep the surprise out of his voice. "What are you doing here, Smitty?"

"The skipper's dead, the officers with him." Smitty was Javers' age. His eyes were wide, his breathing too fast. "COB's dead, and Bailey, the radioman. Doc's working on the XO right now. We lost four men in the auxiliary machinery room...electrical fire. Fire's out. Communications are completely out. Mason and Jimenez are working on that right now. Halbert got a distress buoy launched—"

Javers's mind tried to keep up. He had barely managed to register Smitty's first statement. "What do you mean the skipper's dead?" he interrupted.

"He was in Lab One with the off-duty officers, and there was a hull breach in the collision. The room flooded." The crewman gulped in air, then said, "You're the only officer left on the boat, sir."

"Canter?"

Smitty's eyes flicked to Javers' right. The big man lay crumpled in the corner, blood pooling across the floor beneath his head. "You were the lucky one, sir," Smitty said.

Javers tried to absorb the news as he lurched to his feet. The sudden motion doubled him over, and he retched emptily. Smitty grabbed a hold of him, kept him from falling again. "Damn it," he muttered. "Help me forward," he said, and Smitty nodded.

He's a frightened kid, Javers thought. *And what am I? The only difference is I'm an officer. I have to make things right.*

"Damn it," he muttered again. Pausing at the hatch, he asked, "The reactor?"

"Undamaged," Senichi said.

"Get me a full damage report on engineering as soon as you can," Javers said. "You're officer of the watch now."

"Aye, sir," Senichi said. "Keep that bandage on until Doc can take a look. That gash needs stitches. You're still bleeding badly."

Javers nodded and followed Smitty to the control room.

Doc worked on the XO in the limited floor space. Doc was a middle-aged, usually jovial man. He took care of the crew's minor aches, illnesses, and bruises with an unlimited supply of aspirin and bad jokes. The expression on his face now was positively grim. "Lieutenant," he said. "Guess you're in charge now."

"What's the XO's condition?"

"Stabilized for the moment. I need him in sickbay. That was some helluva a collision...we've got contusions and broken bones all over the boat. I sent Joby Fisher to patch up the minor injuries...." He broke off and squinted at Javers. "What's wrong with your head?"

"Took a whack. Needs stitches, I guess."

Doc jumped to his feet, pushing Smitty aside to take a look. Javers flinched as Doc pulled the bandage away. "Yep," Doc sighed. "I'll be back in a bit to take care of this. Try and keep pressure on it, if you can."

Javers said nothing, just moved out of the way as two of the crew opened a stretcher and under Doc's supervision, lifted the XO onto it. Javers said, "Get me a casualty report as soon as you can."

Doc nodded, and the group headed for sickbay.

Javers took a deep breath and tried to organize his thoughts. "Intercom working yet?"

"No, sir," one of the crew called out. "Working on it now."

A glance around the control room showed all stations manned, including Smitty's co-pilot controls. Javers exhaled sharply, then looked at the crewman who was still supporting him. "Smitty, get the damage control reports from each station. ASAP."

"Yes, sir," Smitty said and hurried forward.

Javers looked over at the central combat controls and communication systems, at the monitors and that should have been displaying all the information he needed to run the ship, but were blank. Two crewmen had one panel open, muttering between themselves as they worked on repairs. *God, he thought, is this really happening?* His headache suddenly felt the least of his worries. "Somebody tell me what happened here," he said. "What'd we hit?"

"Sonar picked up a contact," the pilot, Jonah Mikelsen, said. "We were maneuvering for a better listen—"

"Conn, sonar, you'd better get in here quick!" Javers heard Hawk Hammond interrupting urgently.

"Hold that thought," he told Jonah and hurried to the sonar room. "What's going on?" he said.

The burly sonar man never took his eyes off his equipment. "Sierra Six is on the move again."

"Back up to the beginning, Hawk. I was in engineering."

"Half an hour ago we picked up a strange contact. Definitely biologic, but like nothing I've ever seen before. I mean this thing is ten times the size of the biggest whale you've ever heard of. Huge. We designated it Sierra Six."

"Is that what hit us?"

"Lieutenant, if that thing had hit us, we'd be on the bottom, cracked wide open. It spit at us."

Javers clenched his jaw. "Would you care to be more specific?"

"That's what it sounded like, sir. The XO had us ping it once with active sonar, and the sucker reacted like we stung it. It shot something at us. Something organic. That's what hit us. I've got it all on tape. You can check it out, if we ever get a chance." Hawk shook his head. "Never seen anything like it."

"You said it's moving again?"

"Yes, sir. Changing depth, coming up right under a big container ship we've been tracking."

"Can we warn the container ship off?"

The other sonar man, Jenkins, shook his head. "Communications are out. Some kind of electrical surge. And even if we could, sir, those container ships are so big, there's no way it could maneuver in time."

Javers stared at the sonar display, chewing on his lip. "Hawk, you absolutely sure this thing intends to attack that ship?"

"Lieutenant, I'm not sure of anything, but it sure as hell attacked us, and it sure as hell is on a collision course with that ship."

"What do you want me to do about it?" Javers demanded. "Shoot a torpedo at it?"

Hawk didn't answer.

"Distance?"

"About nine thousand yards to our starboard. Two minutes at most to collision."

Javers racked his brain. His first duty was to the *Harpy* and the injured crew. He didn't have a full damage report yet, didn't even understand exactly what had happened, or what that thing out there was. He glanced over his shoulder at the control room. No captain, no officer of the deck, no chief of the boat...his hand clutched the dolphins in his pocket. None of that changed the fact that some undersea behemoth appeared to be attacking a civilian ship and *Harpy* was the only ship around that might be able to stop it. He singled out one of the experienced seamen. "Halbert!"

"Yes, sir?"

"You're officer of the deck as of now. Get us underway toward that container ship. Quarter speed until Smitty gets back here with the damage report and we know what we can and can't do."

Voices sang out all around him, comforting as sailors jumped to follow orders.

"Reyes?" he called to the tall dark-haired man standing at firing control. "I want a firing solution on Sierra Six."

Reyes said, "Already locked in, sir."

"Sierra Six still rising steadily, on course for the container ship," Hawk reported. "Estimated one minute to collision."

Javers swore silently. Sierra Six was far too close to the container ship to risk firing a torpedo. But he couldn't sit by and watch it hit the ship without doing something. Then Hawk's report came back to him, and he had an idea. He said urgently, "Ping it!"

"Sir?"

"You said it reacted to us only when you pinged it. Well, let's get its attention. Ping the son of a bitch, maximum power. Hit it with everything we've got."

Hawk grinned as he switched on the active sonar. "Yes, sir, but you better be prepared to get us the hell out of here." The sound of the sonar echoed through the ship.

Javers called, "Firing control, you still got a lock?"

"Yes, sir," Reyes responded. "Tracking target Sierra Six. Torpedo tubes one and four loaded and ready to go."

"Good."

Halbert approached and lowered his voice. "Sir, we don't have permission to fire. We don't even know what that thing is...."

"I know that," Javers said. "But I want to keep our options open. Just in case."

"Aye, sir," Halbert said.

"That did it, Lieutenant," Hawk said. "It's turning away from...Damn. It just launched four of those spitballs at us."

"Right full rudder," Javers ordered, "increase speed to twelve knots. Take us down thirty degrees." He turned back to Hawk. "Secure pinging."

"Pinging secured." Hawk tugged an earphone away from his ear and said, "Spitballs heading for our last position. Whatever those things are, they don't appear to have maneuvering capability. They are not changing course to follow us." He shook his head. "Man, someone's going to go ape over these tapes. I've never heard sounds like these before." He adjusted some of the dials before him, typed something on his keyboard. "All four spitballs are going to pass by clean."

Good, Javers thought. Now to keep enough maneuvering room between *Harpy* and that thing so they could dodge whatever it threw at them. "Halbert, bring us back to course oh-eight-oh, make your depth two hundred feet. Hawk, what's it doing?"

The burly man frowned. "Sucker turned back toward the container ship right after it shot at us. It's closing in again fast."

Javers's fingers clenched into a fist.

"Container ship's finally picked up Sierra Six," Hawk said. "Propellers increasing rotations, and she's turning." He shook his head. "Too slow, too slow."

Javers knew the instant of collision by the horror on Hawk's face. Those were sounds no seaman ever wanted to hear.

"No explosion, but impact split her in two, maybe three pieces. She's sinking fast, Lieutenant." Hawk's voice sharpened suddenly. "Sir, change course immediately...oh-four-five. I'm losing contact with Sierra Six in the breakup noises."

Javers passed the course change orders to Halbert. "Increase speed to fifteen knots," he added. He didn't dare take her faster until he heard the damage control report.

Hawk said softly, "Container ship's gone, sir. I don't think there was time for anyone to get off."

Javers fumed silently. His training told him to surface, to search for survivors. To stay there until they were found or they got communications working so he could get his own injured crew to a hospital. But his instincts told him to stay in pursuit of the creature from the depths that had damaged his ship, killing at least ten people, and then had destroyed the container ship and her crew. They cruised beneath major shipping lanes. If he didn't stay with this thing, it could attack other civilian ships. Maybe the container ship had gotten a distress call off in time.

And if Sierra Six attacked another ship? *I won't wait until the last minute next time. I'll put four torpedoes into it,* he promised himself.

"I've lost the firing solution," Reyes called out urgently. "Hawk?"

Frustrated, the sonar operator shook his head. "Lost it in the breakup noises. It was on course oh-four-five. For something that big, this sucker makes almost no noise. That's why it got so close to us the first time. We couldn't figure out what it was until we hit it with active sonar."

"Find it," Javers said. "Get me a course that keeps us on its tail." He started away, then hesitated and looked back at the sonar man. "Speculations? Best guess? What the hell is that thing out there?"

Hawk was silent a long moment. He rubbed at his shaved head, then grinned humorlessly and said, "Pardon my language, sir, but I'd call it a mean MF'er of unknown origin."

Javers smiled grimly. He left the sonar shack and walked slowly back to the center of the control room. He saw the looks the crew cast his way, obviously wondering if the puke knew what the hell he was doing. His fingers toyed with the dolphins in his pocket. Hell of a first tour of duty. He didn't have his own dolphins yet, no senior officer to turn to, and he was responsible for the whole ship. No, he corrected himself. Not just responsible for *Harpy* and her crew, but responsible for preventing that creature from harming any other ships in its path. The lives of the container ship crew were already on his head. He didn't want any more.

Halbert stepped up beside him. "We're on course oh-four-five, speed fifteen knots, depth two hundred feet."

Javers asked, "Who's working on communications?"

"Mason and Jimenez. Good men, sir. If it can be repaired, they'll do it."

"I don't want *if,* Halbert, I want *when.* We need communications." Now where's Smitty with the damage report?" Javers had no sooner said it then the aft hatch opened, and the seaman came through. Out of breath, pale, but he'd finally made it.

They were better off than Javers would have guessed. Damage control parties had already rewired what had been scorched in the auxiliary machinery room. The lab where the captain had died was still flooded, but the interior bulkheads and hull plates had held firm and the rest of the ship's integrity remained intact. Ballast and trim had been adjusted by the computers automatically to accommodate the damage. It would take a dry dock to repair the small hull breach effectively, but monitors showed the organic outer skin growing rapidly over the hole ripped in *Harpy's* side. As soon as it sealed over, if the skin was as good as its designers said, he'd be able to take her up to full speed. Reactor, helm controls, maneuvering were all fine. But communications, including the intercom, were still out.

But the worst news was the casualty report. Thirteen men were dead. The XO was stable but in a coma. The remaining crew had suffered multiple minor injuries, mostly bruises, two broken arms.

Sierra Six was traveling at over thirty knots, and Javers couldn't figure how it maintained such a speed. *What the hell is that thing?* he asked himself and could not find a satisfactory answer. Something unknown, that was the only thing of which he was certain. Not even the craziest sea stories held a creature like this. Not that big. The image from sonar was unusual. It wasn't even a streamlined fishlike thing. It had two great appendages on either side of a giant bulbous head. It didn't appear to taper to a fin or anything obvious that would provide propulsion. But it sure as hell moved fast somehow. *Harpy* had external cameras, but on visual mode, the playback had shown nothing more than a big dark blur. Infrared displayed the same unrecognizable image that sonar had given them.

He'd watched the surveillance tapes of the officers' demise as well, the audio off. The visual was more than enough. Hawk had told him how a huge cloud of muck had risen from the deep before Sierra Six had appeared, most likely stirred up by the creature itself. Captain Thorn had grinned excitedly on the tape, testing out equipment and collecting samples through the filtration system in Lab One. *Harpy* was the first military sub to have two biologists and a lab aboard, ostensibly to test the effectiveness of the outer hull's new organic skin while underway. Thorn had called the off-duty officers to join him.

Javers had watched the officers glance up suddenly and knew the collision alarm had gone off. Seconds later, the hull of the sub had buckled inward when Sierra Six's spitball slammed into the sub's flank. The officers were flung across the room. A bank of instrumentation sprayed sparks at the same moment something in the hull gave way and water burst in. The camera lens shattered, and the view mercifully blurred. None had gotten out.

"Conn, sonar," Hawk called out. "Another surface target. Long range. Lieutenant, I think this one's a cruise ship."

Javers swore under his breath, bile churning in his stomach. "You sure?"

"Yes, sir."

"And our friend?"

Hawk hesitated. "I don't have it locked in right now." He pointed to the sonar screen. "I think it's this anomaly right here, but I haven't had enough time to learn its sounds yet. Something that big should be pumping a lot of water through its gills to get enough oxygen. Hell, displacement alone should stand out like a beacon, but I'm not hearing anything. This thing makes no sense. You want to risk active sonar?"

"We have to know. Use the lowest setting possible. So far it's ignoring us. Why? Why didn't it sink us when it had the chance?"

Hawk shrugged. "Maybe it thinks we're a fish."

"What do you mean?"

"I mean we're under the sea and we've got that fancy slime over the hull. Changes our signature. We don't look metallic any more. Food or prey or targets for it appear to be on top of the sea, not under it. Maybe it thinks we're just an annoying fish getting in its way."

"Well, it's got the last part right."

Hawk adjusted the settings on his equipment and issued a single ping. Javers listened to the sound leave the boat, then watched the multiple screens, the waterfall images, and the computer-generated planned position indicator displays. He waited impatiently for the signal to reach the target. Hawk listened silently, Jenkins beside him, both men with their headsets pressed to their ears, their eyes watching the displays, fingers making constant adjustments.

Both men reacted at the same time, and Javers nearly jumped at the overlapping shouts: "Goddammit," from Jenkins and a "Holy crap," from Hawk.

Hawk's broad face contorted with anger and guilt. "Lieutenant, the target has just been sunk."

"What?" Javers barely got the word out.

"I was wrong. What I was tracking was nothing...Sierra Six just ripped the bottom out of that cruise ship. She didn't stand a chance." Hawk slammed his fist down on the console.

"Sierra Six Six Six, more like," Jenkins muttered.

Javers stared unseeing, the anger coursing through him. Barely a half hour had passed since the container ship had gone down. Now...how many passengers had been on that boat enjoying a vacation in the South Pacific? He thought he was going to be sick again, but he fought the nausea down. He couldn't give in to emotions, not now, not with that thing out there hunting for more ships, more lives. He called to Halbert, "Get us up to full speed. Let's see if *Harpy* can best her sea trials record."

As the orders were echoed around the control room, he said softly to Hawk and Jenkins, "You find me that son of a bitch. I'll give you all the speed this ship's got. We've got to close the distance. Sierra Six is *not* going to touch another ship. Get me a target, understood? Active sonar authorized."

"Yes, sir."

Javers stepped back and let them get back to work. He thrust his trembling hands into his pockets and gripped his father's dolphins. He listened to the voices in the control room, just a few steps away, and he marveled at the military structure. Follow orders. Don't ask questions. Even when the officer in command was younger and more inexperienced than they were. For a second, he closed his eyes and wished himself thousands of miles away, back in the States, sipping a beer, watching ESPN. But no, he'd chosen this path. And now his responsibility was laden with guilt. He would stop this thing before it killed again, and he would get his crew and ship back home safely. That was his duty.

He felt someone approaching and looked up to see Doc. "What?" he asked, frowning, wondering what new casualty the man would report.

"Your head," Doc said and held up his bag. "I need to stitch it up, remember?"

God, Javers thought. He'd forgotten all about it. The constant ache had become part of his existence, something to think around, not about. He'd forgotten the reason for the pain. He gritted his teeth and nodded.

Harpy sped through the depths at thirty-eight point five knots. The organic skin had done its job of sealing up the damage better than he could have hoped. It had taken nearly an hour to close to ten miles of Sierra Six. The creature had been within torpedo range for awhile, but Javers didn't want to fire from too far away and give it time to escape. It was a huge target, but it moved surprisingly fast, and he dreaded discovering what kind of evasive maneuvers it was capable of. They had to hit it with the first round of fish.

The creature was back on a steady course…its original course…straight toward the rest of the Pacific Fleet and the waiting war game exercises, bee-lining for more ships to sink. The *Theodore Roosevelt* was there, but though the thought of some undersea creature sinking an aircraft carrier seemed ridiculous, he recalled the mere moments it took for the container ship to vanish. Even if the fleet detected the behemoth coming toward them, it would take them far too long to realize the danger. It was biologic, something to be studied, not something to be feared. Even at that size. And he couldn't warn them. The intercom had been repaired, but the main communication systems were still out. The repair team were taking it apart yet again.

He forced his doubts out of his head. He had to destroy that thing before it reached the fleet.

"Firing solution locked?" he asked.

"Yes, sir," Reyes said. "Torpedo tubes flooded, outer doors open."

"Slow to one-third," Javers said and waited as *Harpy* decelerated. Halbert was watching him, a question in his gaze. Javers ignored him. When the thing was dead, Javers would be the one responsible. He would answer all the questions and charges regarding endangering the ship and crew and the loss of the civilian ships when they got back home. Halbert had nothing to worry about.

Javers held his breath, just for a second, then ordered, "Fire tubes one and four."

"Firing one and four. Torpedoes away!"

"Fire tubes two and three."

"Firing tubes two and three!" Reyes grinned. "As my granddaddy used to say, they're running hot, straight, and normal." His hands were on the controls, ready to correct the course of the wire-guided torpedoes as the need arose.

"Sierra Six still on its original course," Hawk called. "Torpedoes on target. Only propeller noise from the torpedoes right now." They'd already discussed the creature's reaction to active sonar while they were racing after the leviathan and the risks involved if they allowed the Mark 48s to use their own sonar. Reyes had overridden the controls. The four fish were being guided solely by wire.

Javers found his fingers clenching the dolphins in his pocket as Hawk counted down to impact. This had to work.

"It's diving," Hawk said suddenly. "No..." he trailed off, hunching forward over his panels, listening intently. "I think it's turning around, but it's doing it fast. Torpedoes still on target."

Jenkins was counting down, "Ten... nine..."

"Spitballs!" Hawk called out.

"Eight... seven..."

The explosion came early. Both men yanked off their headsets. Javers felt the shockwave rumble the ship, heard equipment rattle and bulkheads shift. Seconds after it passed, both sonar men were attuned to the sea again.

"Too much noise," Hawk muttered, working the equipment in front of him.

Javers waited, saying nothing, chewing on the inside of its lip. *Come on, tell me there's nothing but bits of blubber left to attract sharks...*

The sonar man straightened, his voice urgent, "Son of a bitch is coming straight at us! Seventeen thousand yards and closing. The torpedoes hit the spitballs, not the target."

"Halbert, left full rudder, all ahead flank! Bring us around to course two-six-five." The course would angle them away from the creature's approach, but would keep them from losing contact with it in their baffles.

"Sir, it just stepped on the gas," Hawk said, and his voice changed to something approaching awe. "It just passed forty knots."

Javers felt his mouth go dry.

"Forty-one... forty-three..." Hawk shook his head in disbelief. "Sir, it just passed our flank speed and is still accelerating."

Harpy was not going to be able to outrun it or outmaneuver it. The realization rocked Javers. It had turned its giant body almost instantly to take out the torpedoes with a couple of spitballs. It was ten times their size, and it turned ten times as fast. It didn't seem possible, but it had done it somehow. He had to find a way to evade it or make it lose interest, and he had to do it fast.

"Hawk, how's it tracking us? Does it have its own form of sonar?"

"Not that I've detected. So far it's been reactive only to what we send at it. How it's seeing us... your guess is as good as mine." He paused, then said, "It just passed fifty knots, Lieutenant."

"That's not possible," Javers said.

"Tell that to Sierra Six," Hawk said.

Halbert called out, "Steady on two-six five, we are approaching forty-one knots."

"Distance?" Javers asked Hawk.

"Fifteen thousand four hundred yards. It's changing course too, no, it just shifted to our starboard. I think it's aiming to run parallel with us."

They were running out of time. Javers hurried to the plotting tables. Halbert had the computer feed on and both their own and the creature's course were updating.

"Can we use a decoy?" Halbert asked softly.

Javers nodded. "What if we go dead quiet? Hide under a thermal layer, if we can find one. Will it lose us? Hawk said it's displayed no use of its own sonar."

"Yet," Halbert muttered dryly.

"Conn, sonar!"

Javers snatched up the intercom. "Go ahead."

Hawk's voice said, "It's up to fifty-five knots, and it just launched a couple of spitballs at us. They'll pass well astern, but this thing looks seriously pissed."

Javers looked urgently at Halbert. "We can't outrun it," Javers said. "Any other alternatives?"

Halbert studied the plot again, then shook his head. "We go dead, launch the decoy. If that thing follows the bait, it'll lose us."

"Agreed," Javers said.

Halbert started issuing orders, and Javers returned his gaze to the plot table, watching Sierra Six closing in on a parallel course. The hundred things that could go wrong flashed through his mind as the crew rushed to obey Halbert's orders. The distance between *Harpy* and the creature continued to shrink.

When Halbert reported back all was ready, Sierra Six was just over four miles away. Far too close for Javers' liking. "Pass the order to all hands for silence. Stop all rotations, launch decoy."

Reyes launched the decoy just as the propeller was shut off. *Harpy* coasted.

Javers said. "Come left forty degrees. Make your depth three hundred feet." The orders passed around the room barely above a whisper.

Hawk reported softly, "Decoy proceeding on our previous course. Sierra Six following, distance now six thousand yards."

If this fails, Javers thought, *we'll have almost no maneuvering room.*

"It's shooting spitballs again, one right after another. It's getting smarter too: it's aiming some of them ahead of the decoy. Spitballs are going to bracket the decoy in five seconds."

"What propels those things?" Javers muttered. "Why don't they lose speed due to water resistance?"

No one gave him an answer. Seconds later, Hawk said, "Scratch one decoy. Sierra Six has stopped at the wreckage."

Not good, Javers thought.

Hawk's face scrunched up in confusion. "It's thrashing around or something, making a helluva racket, like it's breaking out the champagne and doing a victory dance, or it's throwing a tantrum."

Even worse, Javers thought. "And *Harpy*?"

Jenkins listened a moment then grinned and said, "We're quiet as a church mouse, sir."

Javers let out a breath slowly. Sierra Six couldn't find what it couldn't hear. They would get out of this yet.

"It's gone still," Hawk said.

Halbert padded over and murmured, "We just leveled out at three hundred feet."

Javers nodded. "Let's keep her—"

He broke off, screaming in agony as something sliced into his mind and exploded. Not a voice, not a thought or an image, so much as a feeling thrust into his conscious. The crew seemed to be screaming with him, or maybe it was only echoes of his own cry, bouncing off mental walls. He could no longer see the control room or the sonar shack; the sheer pain of the mental invasion blinded him to everything.

His focus narrowed, and he tried to push the invader out of his mind. Sierra Six laughed at his efforts, slashing through his consciousness, shredding willpower and emotions. And behind its glee burned a core of malevolent power. It was within Javers, gloating and taunting, and he could neither get away nor dispel the evil presence.

It vanished as suddenly as it had come.

Javers gasped for breath, and each inhalation inflamed the headache the attack had left behind. His heart pounded. He forced open his eyes and stared blankly at grayness. The floor. Sharp pain flared through his knees, and he realized he'd fallen during the mental attack. Wincing, he raised his head and looked around the control room.

It *had* been the other men he'd heard screaming. Like himself, they were trying to pick themselves up. Halbert lay curled on his side nearby, whimpering. Javers touched him on the shoulder and the man reacted as if stung, lashing out with his right arm.

Javers tried to say his name, but had to swallow several times to get his raw throat working. "Halbert. John. John!"

Using the man's first name got Halbert's attention and Javers saw the eyes refocus, leave the evil memory and see the present.

"Get up, John," Javers said and forced himself to his feet.

Javers heard a groan and saw Hawk sprawled nearby. "What the hell..." the sonar man gasped.

"Sonar..." Javers said. He was gratified to see instant comprehension in the sonar man's eyes.

"Help me," Hawk said urgently, reaching for the lip of the console.

Javers hauled the heavy man into his chair. Hawk had to grab twice to get his headphones, but his eyes were already scanning the monitors, shaking fingers reaching for the keyboard. Javers leaned against the back wall of the sonar shack to keep from falling. Jenkins was unconscious, slumped forward over his console. Javers was reaching to shake him when Hawk began swearing.

"It's heading straight at us, distance...Crap! Two thousand yards!"

Javers swore, then ordered, "Secure from silent running. Get us under way." He whirled toward Halbert and shoved him into the control room. "Move!"

Hawk's voice shouted after him, "It's shooting spitballs. I've got four of them coming at our broadside."

"Get to your stations!" Javers shouted at the crew. Most were collapsed on the floor, still stunned, holding their heads. "Someone get on the ballast controls. Halbert!" Javers pushed by him to get at the controls himself.

"Spitballs...fifteen hundred yards," Hawk shouted. "Sierra Six is right behind them!"

Javers lost his temper. "Get the hell on your feet. *Now.* Or we're all dead." He kicked none too gently at one of the crew in his way — he thought it was Jonah, the pilot — and reached around another man just getting to his feet to grab at the two manual valves at the top of the ballast control panel.

Halbert was starting to issue orders. Javers watched him tap the engineering screen to increase speed himself.

"A thousand yards!"

"Hawk, release counter-measures." Javers doubted they would do any good, but it couldn't hurt. He turned the handles and called out, "Initiating emergency blow." The valves sent high-pressure air directly into the ballast tanks, and *Harpy* shot toward the surface. Javers grabbed the console to keep his balance. He caught hold of Jonah's arm, pulled him roughly up into his seat. Nearby, the co-pilot was slowly crawling into his own chair.

"First round of spitballs will pass well beneath us," Hawk called. "But Sierra Six just shot four more, angled at the surface. Eight hundred yards and closing—"

Harpy broke the surface like a cork, and everyone not grabbing onto something struggled to maintain his balance.

Halbert said, "Engineering making for maximum rotations."

The ship shuddered beneath Javers' feet as the sub's screw thrashed the water and they began to pick up speed. He moved to Halbert's side. Their eyes met, and Javers saw the barely controlled terror there. Softly, Javers asked, "You okay?"

A milimetric shake of the head. "What the hell is that thing?" Halbert asked.

Javers' lips twisted into a smile. "Mean MF'er unknown origin."

Before Halbert could respond, Hawk's voice sang out, "Spitballs...four hundred yards!"

"Halbert, get us the hell out of here," Javers said. "Course oh-nine-oh. Take us back down. Depth two hundred feet, emergency dive."

"Two hundred yards," Hawk called. "Lieutenant, it's bracketing our position, just like it did with the decoy. Countermeasures ineffective. We're not maneuvering fast enough to evade. At least two spitballs will impact in... thirty seconds."

The pilot had his controls pushed all the way forward to give maximum angle to their dive as the ballast tanks flooded. The ship drove downward, listing a bit to starboard, with no crew or time to adjust the trim tanks.

Javers slammed on the collision alarm, then hurried to the sonar shack.

Hawk reached over and yanked the headset off Jenkins who was still unconscious. "Fifteen seconds."

Javers waited, every second that passed eating a new hole in his stomach. He knew he hadn't handled the situation right. But he wasn't sure what he could have done differently, other than not engaging Sierra Six in the first place. No one had known how fast that thing could move. No one could have anticipated its mental attack that had left the sub's crew incapacitated when they should have been maneuvering. Not that those minutes would have made any difference. Sierra Six could swim circles around them even if they were at flank.

And where the hell was the Navy? Halbert had launched the distress buoy hours ago. Hadn't the Navy picked up the signal? Why weren't there planes in the air investigating, or ships coming on the double to find out what had happened to the new sub? *Bring on the cavalry,* he thought.

He braced himself as Hawk counted down the last few seconds.

The first spitball hit low and amidships, seemed to skim the bottom of the sub, rolling the ship sharply to port. The second one hit a few seconds later just as the sub started to right itself, striking directly behind the bow. The impact hurled Javers against the back wall of the sonar shack. The control room dissolved into a chaos of thrown bodies and screams of pain.

"All stop!" Javers yelled.

Halbert was yelling back, "Flooding alarms in the torpedo room."

"Sonar's gone!" Hawk shouted from beside him. A cut on his forehead bled down his face. "That hit took out the entire front array."

The ship was sinking nose first. Javers clutched his right arm to his side; his shoulder felt wrenched. He did a quick mental rundown. Sonar gone, the forward main ballast tanks on the port side would be badly damaged. And the bow held the twelve Vertical Launch System tubes that were most likely damaged as well. That was bad. A fire in the missile fuel systems could result in a detonation that would send them instantly to the bottom.

He swore under his breath, then ordered, "Surface the ship." He prayed only the port side ballast tanks were ruptured. If intact, the front starboard tanks would help offset the damage.

"We'll be sitting ducks for that thing on the surface," Hawk warned.

"We're sitting ducks already," Javers snapped. On the surface, at least he could get the crew off.

A third spitball glanced them amidships. Metal crumpled with an unearthly shriek, and once again the men were thrown aside. Javers heard the sound of water spraying and regained his feet without thinking. Water and fire...the two things submariners feared most.

It came from the ladder leading up to the bridge. *Conning tower must have been struck by that last blow,* he thought. Two of the control room damage control team were right beside him, rushing to isolate the leak and prevent any flooding. Cold water sprayed over him, and he wiped the back of his hand across his eyes.

It was not a severe leak, and the damage control team quickly had it under control. Javers left them to it and had just started back toward Halbert when he saw the aft hatch spin open and a man peek in at him. A familiar man, wearing a long white wig, fake white beard, and a lopsided gold crown. Javers blinked, then remembered the incident with the stranger just hours ago. The man had said he'd be back. *He said the lives of more than just the crew would depend on me,* Javers recalled. *How had he known what would happen?* A rush of fury came instantly with that thought...*why the hell hadn't he warned me?*

Javers called, "Halbert, you have the conn. Get us on the surface."

"But—

"Do it! I'll be back in a minute." Javers pushed by the damage control team, yanked the hatch open. He found the costumed stranger waiting in the hall beyond. Javers grabbed two fistfuls of his costume robe and snarled in his face. "You knew, you bastard. I don't know how you knew, but you knew this was going to happen."

"Lieutenant, we don't have time for this. I'm here to—"

"Thirteen of my crew are dead because you knew and didn't say anything!" Javers threw a punch at the man's jaw with all of his rage.

His fist connected with nothing and he found himself off-balance and falling forward. The man had simply vanished. Javers caught himself against the wall.

"You're wasting precious time," the man said from behind him.

Javers spun, mouth dropping open.

The man was straightening his costume, smoothing out the rumples left from Javers' grip. "Yes," he said. "I knew the creature was coming, but not what it would do. I'm a salesman, not a fortune teller."

Javers stared. "You're a what?"

"Salesman. I have things for all occasions...demon-related."

"Demon...?"

"That's right. That rampaging leviathan out there is a demon, from a hell dimension."

"Look, I don't have time for jokes. That thing outside is going to broadside us in about five minutes."

The man heaved a sigh. "It's always about timing. First too early, now too late." The man straightened to his full height. His voice when he spoke again was powerful and commanding, like Javers' father, like the skipper, and Javers jerked to attention despite himself. He couldn't help it. "Lieutenant, I've had enough out of you. You're the one out of time, not me, so you just sit down, shut up, and listen."

Javers clenched his jaw, but said nothing.

"That's better," the salesman said. He pulled out a large bronze coin between thumb and forefinger. "This is a very ,very, very old coin forged in Akroteri for an ancient Greek hero named Agenor."

"Never heard of him," Javers muttered.

"Not all heroes and legends make the history books, and many prefer it that way. He was named for the son of Poseidon. Now, this coin was forged to allow Agenor to call upon Poseidon himself, but he did not use it, and it eventually fell into my hands. Now it's falling to you." The salesman cocked his head and studied Javers. "You know Poseidon? Neptune? God of the sea, god of earthquakes? This coin has the power to call him. Touch this coin against the beast outside, then get the hell out of the way."

It sounded crazy but, then, after the things he had just witnessed, Javers was not prepared to throw away any potential weapon, no matter how ridiculous it seemed. What did he have to lose anyway? He was out of time and out of ideas. He stretched to take the coin. The salesman jerked it back out of reach.

"Sorry, Lieutenant, I'm a salesman, not a loan shark. I need something in return...your father's dolphins."

Javers reached in his pocket and gripped the pin. He didn't even ask how the man knew he carried the insignia. "No," he said between gritted teeth.

"You're going to earn your own, Lieutenant."

Javers laughed. "After this cruise? I'll be court-martialed, dishonorably discharged, and lucky to make Third-Mate on a rust bucket hauling rubber dog crap out of Hong Kong."

"That's the trade," the salesman said. "Take it or leave it."

Javers brought the dolphins out of his pocket, rubbed a finger across them. *They're my luck,* he thought and then wanted to laugh. Some luck for a first cruise. Why *was* he holding onto them? Because he was Rick-lite and his father's dolphins made him feel less insecure? Because he was Dumbo and they were his magic feather?

He thrust the dolphins at the salesman abruptly. "Take them," he said hoarsely. "Before I change my mind."

The salesman plucked the pin from his hand and set the coin down on Javers' palm. It was strangely heavy, cold. The touch of it sent a shiver up his arm. He tried to make out the salesman's features behind the ridiculous costume. Softly, Javers said, "If you're lying about this...I will find you again, I don't care what it takes."

The salesman just regarded him solemnly, said, "Good luck," and disappeared.

Javers blinked, then rubbed his thumb against the coin's raised markings. One side showed a scowling Poseidon, a trident clutched in one hand, a serpent in the other. On the reverse, two dolphins faced each other.

He made a fist around the coin, then scrambled up the ladder and hurried into the control room, closing the hatch behind him. "Status?" he asked.

"We're surfacing, but slowly. Depth eighty feet."

Javers nodded. He felt surprisingly calm. "When you get to the surface, prepare to abandon ship."

Halbert started to object, but Javers turned away. "Hawk, anything?"

The sonar man said grimly, "I've got the towed sonar array paying out now. Sierra Six is closing up on our port side. Range five hundred yards."

"Good," Javers said. He'd ruled out attaching the coin to a torpedo. That thing would just swat the torpedo out of the water with a spitball before it got close. He would deliver the coin the old-fashioned way. The forward escape trunk was just forward of the control room. "Halbert, the conn is still yours."

Javers stepped through the hatch, closed it behind him, his last view of the control room one of Halbert staring at him, mouth open and brow furrowed.

Two men stood watch at the escape trunk.

"Get me an air tank and fins on the double," Javers said. "I'm going out."

"Sir?" one asked. His name was Jesse, Javers remembered. The other was Carl Sontag. Carl was already opening the locker. It was filled with the emergency oxygen masks for abandoning ship. But *Harpy* also carried two sets of actual diving equipment fore and aft. Carl pulled out one of the air tanks.

Javers said, "Hurry," yanked off his rubber-soled shoes and socks, and let them help him into the equipment.

A mental hand clawed into his mind.

Javers groaned in pain as the headache that had never gone away from the creature's first attack flared up. He heard the moans of the two crewmen. A collage of swaggering evil triumph floated through his mind.

Screw off, bastard! Javers screamed in his mind. *Leave my crew alone!*

Sierra Six laughed. Red and black colors, rippling as if viewed through a wave of heat, pulsated through Javers' mind. The coin clenched in his right hand sent a slight jolt through him and the pain of the mind attack seemed to lessen slightly.

Javers squeezed Carl's arm until the crewman forced his eyes open and looked at him. "Get me outside," Javers hissed. "We're out of time."

The man nodded, opened the escape trunk and shoved Javers inside. Water sluiced in, rising rapidly.

The colors tightened, a band of pain encircling his consciousness. Images of steel hulls torn open, bodies thrashing as they drowned. *Your fate*, the creature gloated, though there were no words.

The signal flared green, and Javers spun open the escape trunk hatch and launched himself out into the vast murkiness of the sea. The sub rose beneath him, and he pushed off her deck toward the port side. The ocean surface sparkled, just fifty feet or so above him. *Harpy's* conning tower would break the surface any second. He fought against the colors and the pain that twisted through his head, looked down...and saw it.

He'd known it was huge, but somehow the knowing and the seeing were two completely different things. A dark mass, so broad he had to turn his head to see from one side to the other, stretched beneath him. Three red eyes stared from the middle of its head. The great width of it was accentuated by two giant appendages bulging to either side. It was not smooth-skinned, but seemed covered in some sort of long flowing growth.

It angled slowly toward the limping *Harpy*, taking its time now, taunting them with its psychic power, savoring the approaching kill. The creature seemed to be timing its ascent so that it would be in position to rip out the sub's hull just after the Navy vessel broached the surface.

Javers swam in place. Sierra Six would pass directly over him. He would just have to kick upward, grab on, and hope to hell the Salesman had traded him the right thing. The ancient silver coin radiated warmth against his right palm.

The leviathan swept straight for him, and he tried with difficulty to keep from hyperventilating. He kicked to get closer, to be ready. Then the bow wave from the monster struck Javers, tumbling him onto his back. He nearly panicked as he was sucked downward. Sierra Six was passing by twelve feet over his head, and he couldn't reach it.

The creature continued to pulse mental images of fevered hatred at him. Javers fought against nausea and knew he was losing. He knew the whole crew was feeling the monster's attack, and anger spilled through him. His eyes focused on the black nightmare heading for his sub. He fought the wake the creature generated and swam for his life. Tendrils of plant-like material struck him in the face as he neared the side of the creature and he snatched at them with his left hand. He kicked both legs and pulled himself in. Darkness swallowed him.

His mind throbbed with the colors of destruction. The monster's thoughts constricted around him, and his physical grip on it loosened.

The monster shrugged abruptly, and the motion jerked the tendrils free of Javers' grasp. Frantically, his fingers raked the water. He locked his left hand around a fist-sized mass of the creature's plant-like tendrils. His legs were tiring, but he kept kicking, pushing his way in. The mountainous creature whipped its head toward him, a movement so fast that it nearly ripped the regulator out of his mouth.

He choked on seawater, gagging on the taste of brine and putrid decay.

Out of the darkness, one of the gigantic red eyes loomed, hunting for him. Huge and malevolent, it searched, it stared, and it saw him.

He felt the instant it ceased its mental attack on the crew and bore in on him and him alone. Its presence ballooned in his mind, filling every corner, exploding against his will and his defenses. Breaking through the magical protection the coin had imperfectly supplied up until then.

Javers tried to scream.

It laughed, twisting closer, the eye growing in size until Javers saw nothing but throbbing red and black, mere feet from him.

Javers' grip slackened; he couldn't breathe. His head was being pulverized from the inside out, and he felt his consciousness slipping before the psychic assault. He thought he still clutched both the creature's tendrils with his left hand and the coin with his right but he could no longer feel either. *No more time.*

He gave one last kick with his remaining strength. He punched at the creature, and his right fist sank deep into the Jell-O-like tissue of the creature's giant red eye. Unbearable pain flared in his hand at the contact, and his fingers flew open, releasing the coin a full foot inside the monster's cornea.

The giant eye exploded.

Sierra Six roared and twisted its titanic body into a spin.

Javers let himself be flung free. He wasn't sure if it had actually made the noise aloud or if the roar was in his head. The mental attack had ceased, and he drifted in a soundless haze of lingering pain. He could not swim, he could not feel, his body breathed from habit.

The hell monster thrashed, then abruptly dove. Javers watched from his floating void as the dark bulk drove downward, blending and disappearing into the depths where sunlight never touched. He drifted, his body buffeted by currents. He knew he was still alive, but he could not cross the mental gulf to order his muscles to move. The weight of the air tank and his own body tugged him downward.

Fitting, he thought. *I'll follow it to the depths of hell. At least I won't have to face a court-martial.* He realized then that he did not fear the repercussions of his actions. He feared facing his father, seeing the disappointment, the naked hurt that Rick Javers, Jr. had been unable to live up to his father's expectations.

The current rolled him and instead of the black depths, he saw the brightness of the afternoon sun glittering off the surface waves. *Harpy* was silhouetted against the day, her sleek shape beautiful to him. He couldn't see the damaged bow, but it suddenly didn't matter. She'd survive that. The Navy would put her back together again better than before. She was on the surface, and she was alive. He'd done that much at least. No matter what else happened, she was alive.

A dark form nosed his side. He tried to scream, but his body still wasn't responding. Slowly, the shape resolved into that of a dolphin, its singing intruding on the void he was in. He felt something on his other side and a second dolphin appeared in his field of view. It was whistling at him too.

I can't understand you, he wanted to say. He stared at them, his panic melting away, fascinated by their grace, so different from the hell beast. Both mammals were agitated, urgent.

I can't move, he tried to tell them.

They seemed to figure that out, and suddenly he found himself being bumped upward. They worked in tandem, and together they rose rapidly for the surface.

Not so fast, he wanted to say, *need to adjust...*

He understood their urgency a moment later as the ocean reverberated with the deepest sound he'd ever heard. He felt it pass around him, through him, not an explosion exactly, more like a giant underwater earthquake. He felt the shockwave coming, heard the roar of rising displaced water even in his deafened void.

Swim, you bastard, swim, he told himself desperately and, finally, his limbs started responding.

Then the shockwave hit, and he felt no more.

"Lieutenant, Lieutenant."

The voice called him, over and over.

I've been here before, he thought. *Don't want to be here. Leave me alone.*

But the voice was insistent, and he finally had to respond, just to get it to shut up, if nothing else. He blinked in the sunlight. He was lying on *Harpy's* deck. Every part of him ached badly. He didn't think he could have moved even if he wanted to. *At least I can hear again,* he thought. Halbert and Doc knelt beside him, though there was something wrong with his eyesight. It was blurry, and he couldn't make out their features. Several other crewmen stood nearby, their shadows falling across him.

"...hand is badly burned," Doc was saying. "We need to get him below."

Halbert appeared to be ignoring the doctor, and Javers saw his grinning face lean close. "Lieutenant, can you hear me?"

Javers blinked, tried to nod.

"Dolphins kept you afloat until we could fish you out. Man, you always hear stories, but I've never seen it with my own eyes."

"Sierra... Six..." Javers tried to say.

"Gone. Not sure what happened, but Hawk said it dove and there was some sort of massive underwater earthquake. We felt it up here. Almost tossed the *Harpy* clear out of the water."

The lookout in the conning tower called out, "Aircraft approaching from starboard, sir!"

Two Navy F-18s passed over them, the roar of their engines catching up a moment later.

Halbert laughed. "Now they show up. And don't they look beautiful?"

Javers closed his eyes and found the strength to smile.

Down The Rabbit Hole

ONCE OR TWICE SOME DRUNKEN PTERO-saurs did a cackling flyby of the screaming head-bouncing stage band but for the most part the majority of this on-vacation Triassic flying act seemed happy sticking to their box-seat perches just below the domed ceiling.

Out of the corner of his eye, Bak suddenly spotted what appeared to be a six foot tall white rabbit covered in splotches of red blood, with a half-naked blonde twenty-something woman flung over it's shoulder, sprint through a gap on the dance floor and disappear into one of the Tavern's endless numbers of small shadowy alcoves.

The doomsday clock was now operating at 90% capacity and the majority of the gaming tables had been abandoned for this greatest of all games of chance. The pit boss was standing atop one of the pool tables he had dragged over and was fielding an endless series of cross bets with all the alacrity of a New York stock exchange specialist broker.

"Your name's, Bak, right?"

The non-stop roar of cross talk, laughter, and shouting that echoed throughout the bar, not to mention the slamming rhythms from the heavy metal band on stage, flooded the cavern in deafening cacophony. And yet magically cutting right through it all was the loveliest voice Bak had ever heard. He looked up from filling an endless series of drink orders.

"Who wants to know?" he asked suspiciously, barely able to hear his own voice. Standing across from him was a gorgeous woman, easily six-feet-tall with long, green hair and yellow-gold eyes.

"Call me Daphne," she said, sporting a mischievous dimple on her right cheek. "That's my handle for this lower plane of existence. Johnny gave it to me."

A series of nasty glares from his many wives quickly made Bak aware that his mouth was hanging open and that his eyes had focused just a bit too long on…

"Johnny. Daphne. Right. Right," Bak mumbled. "What was the question?"

"You're cute when you're nervous," Daphne giggled and drew a line across Bak's bald head with her index finger. "Did you know that?"

"Unless you're willing to sign a non-consummation contract right this instant," Bak said, while slowly removing Daphne's hand from his head. "I'd strongly advise you to take a step back." Bak looked pointedly at two of his wives who were already sharpening long Damascus blades. Daphne laughed delightedly.

"I'm tougher than I look big boy," Daphne said seductively. "But I'm on a mission. So I guess we'll have to put off a formal introduction until later."

"Right. So I'm Bak and this is my place," Bak stated. "What's your pleasure?"

"Oooooh, I like the sound of that, but first things first. Here." Daphne placed a shiny piece of metal on the bar counter. It was flat and shaped like a five-pointed star, roughly the size of Bak's palm. "Johnny needs this for a trade, possibly his next and most crucial one. You have to get it to him immediately."

"But…" Bak started. "Why don't you just…"

Daphne shushed him with a gesture.

"I'm on a schedule myself," Daphne said. "A mutual acquaintance told me Johnny's gonna need me in another time. Later, Bak." Just like that, the dreamy statuesque vision with killer hips disappeared into the rowdy, undulating mob that now filled most of the interior of the Triple-Six in what had become the apocalyptic party of all parties.

Popping Dexedrine like breath mints, Bak chugged a small glass of beer and walked behind the long bar counter giving each of his working wives words of encouragement, a quick back rub, or kiss where needed. The beer, booze, and other liquid ingestibles were down to reserve supplies but a quick visual survey left Bak fairly confident the Triple-Six would weather the last couple of hours of this outrageous two-day binge with a few gallons to spare. Out on the main floor his ten zombie bar maidens had their hands full with constant drink orders, rapid calculating monetary and barter transactions, and avoiding the more amorous of the customers. How the hell Emperor Gaius Germanicus of all people had found his way here on this night was beyond Bak's imagination. But wasn't it just like the impetuous Caligula to crash the greatest party of all time. And who else but him would have the audacious temerity to think he could seduce one of the indentured undead.

Bors and Jaxas had found a couple of jeep-sized wheel barrels somewhere and were hauling away corpses from the grudge pit frantically trying to keep up with the ever increasing piles of body parts and cadavers. It seemed like every two beings in existence with a violent disagreement had decided to drop into the Triple-Six this evening to settle matters. The floor of the pit, with its ever-growing splatters of multicolored gore, was looking like an impressionist titan's used palette.

But the biggest headache of all came from Bak's wife, Maribel, the Triple-Six's Madam, who kept yelling her outrage that every nook, cranny, alcove, and shadowy corner of the giant cavern was now playing host to innumerable erotic liaisons, and thus taking business away from the brothel tents. As far as Bak was concerned, however, anything that let off steam in this building pressure cooker was not a bad thing.

Bak took a moment to examine the exotic object Daphne had given him, eyeing its sharp edges and nasty looking points. He took a deep breath and let it out slowly. He was about to try something he had never done before. In fact, it was the first time in over three thousand years he had felt weak in the knees. Nodding to six of his nearly exhausted wives and doing his best to ignore their angry stares, he abandoned his post and bulldozed his way in the general direction of the bathrooms. He then made a strategic error, attempting to save time by directly crossing the dance floor. Bak instantly came into contact with one hundred head-butting five-foot-tall salamanders slam dancing to Metallica's *Seek and Destroy*.

Five bruising minutes later he stumbled to an uninhabited shadowy alcove to the far side of the restrooms. Johnny's crevice was difficult to see, though. Some smartass wizard had placed a temporary spell on the overhead illumination crystals that were now strobing in psychedelic unison with the stage band.

Bak contemplated the sliver of shadow for a moment and had an instant inspiration. Raising the chunk of metal, he walked slowly forward, "Salesman. I've got a trade for you."

An explosion of light blinded Bak for a few seconds. He felt the ground shift under himself momentarily. Then everything went black.

Deathstalk

By Bruce Durham

KLAANGG! "WHAT WAS THAT?" asked Petty Officer Alice D'Amico.

Lieutenant William Hamlyn sat slumped in the canvas seat beside her, fingering a Celtic cross attached to a thin silver chain draped around his neck. "It's a Sea King, Petty Officer. It does that."

D'Amico swallowed, her hands coming together into a nervous ball. "I hate strange noises. Strange noises equal crash. I hate crashes."

Hamlyn hid a smile. Across from them Leading Seamen Fraser James and Brad Ferguson grinned and exchanged looks. They were veterans of episodes like this.

Hamlyn turned to face his second-in-command. The pretty young woman peered at him anxiously from under her green helmet. A dusting of freckles flanked a pert, slightly upturned nose while downturned lips evoked a sense of perpetual sadness. Brown eyes paid homage to her Italian ancestry. Hamlyn saw the clenched hands and took pity. If there was one constant after countless missions with the PO, it was her abhorrence of flying, though Hamlyn suspected it was, in part, an act. Flashing a reassuring smile, he said, "I'll go check, okay?"

Finding his balance in the mildly buffeting machine, Hamlyn approached the cockpit. The Sea King's sensor operator, Master Corporal Brenda Tran, was already involved in an animated conference with both pilot and co-pilot. Wedging his body beside the specialist, he said, "My ears are burning. Talking about me?"

The woman shook her head, "Oh, no sir."

"Good. So what's up? We been ordered back to the NATO Response Group? Another search for that Yank submarine? What was it again, the *Harpy*?"

"No sir. We're, ah, having mechanical problems. Nothing to worry about."

Hamlyn's lips twitched into a smile, "Words like mechanical and problem in a Sea King doesn't instill confidence, especially in the middle of the Indian Ocean."

"Really sir, it's nothing to worry about."

"Is that so? My PO is ready to pee herself. And it would be embarrassing if my *Search and Rescue* team become the subject of its own search and rescue. Catch my drift?"

"I catch your drift, sir," Tran stood and motioned Hamlyn away from the cockpit. She leaned close, "We're having trouble raising the *Toronto*."

Hamlyn lifted an eyebrow.

"Normally we'd divert to another vessel but, well, we can't."

"The mechanical problem?"

"Yes sir. But honestly, it's nothing to alarm your command over." Offering a vaguely comforting smile, Tran returned to her station beside the cockpit.

Hamlyn frowned. One quarter of his veteran team was *already* alarmed. Standing between pilot and co-pilot, he leaned forward for a better view out the chopper window. The *Toronto* was just ahead. The state-of-the-art *Halifax* Class frigate sliced effortlessly through a sheen of blue-green water, the numbers 333 stamped boldly on its light gray hull, "We okay? I heard you can't hail my ship."

The pilot, Captain Jeremy Slack, looked at him, "You heard right. Probably a glitch."

"You're not sounding too confident."

The co-pilot, who had been talking into his headset, turned to Slack and shook his head before returning to the controls. The helo slowed as the frigate loomed close, the letters 'TO' emblazoned on the bottom edge of the turf green flight deck.

"I guess we'll find out," Slack said. "Better buckle up. We're landing."

Hamlyn nodded and made to turn, but something caught his attention. Something seriously out of place. His eyes swept the deck. "Where's the crew?"

Slack looked, "Don't know," he paused, as if considering an alternate course of action. Shaking his head, he said, "We really have no choice, Lieutenant. We have to land. Back to your seat, it could get bumpy."

"I think we'll ready our weapons," Hamlyn stated before returning to his seat. D'Amico raised an inquiring eyebrow as he engaged the seat belt. "We may have a situation, PO. Have the men ready their side-arms."

D'Amico signed to the leading seamen. Ferguson and James, both in their mid-twenties and similar in height and build, were veterans of countless boarding missions with both Hamlyn and the petty officer. They trusted each other implicitly. Even so, the order they acknowledged raised obvious questions, as was evident on their puzzled faces.

The Sea King began its descent. The horizon slid past the window as the wheels touched down with a firm jolt. The motor whined and the rotors slowed.

James was first to the cargo door, throwing the latch and pulling it along greased runners. Ferguson leapt the short distance to the flight deck and assumed a defensive position, his 9mm SIG-Sauer P225 in hand. Hamlyn and D'Amico came next. James followed.

Hamlyn scanned his surroundings. They were deserted. "Cover me," he said, and cautiously approached the open hangar.

A figure appeared, stepping from the hanger's dim recess. A stranger, dressed entirely in black. His long trench coat swept the top of his polished shoes. A stylish fedora sat atop an apparently clean-shaven head. From under its brim a set of close-set eyes observed, their corners crinkling with mirth. A long nose hooked over a set of thin lips, lips that twitched into a grin, revealing a gold tooth.

Hamlyn halted, "Identify yourself!"

"I'm the Salesman," the figure replied, and spreading his arms expansively, continued, "but you can call me Johnny."

Hamlyn's gun dropped a notch, "What?"

"Should I repeat myself?"

The gun went up, "The crew. Where are they?"

Johnny laughed without humor, "Now that is the mystery, eh?"

Hamlyn raised a hand and motioned his team forward.

D'Amico joined him, "Sir?"

"Secure laughing boy to the rail. Ferguson, James, check the hangar."

The seamen padded to the hangar and abutted the wall beside the gaping entrance. James nodded to Ferguson, who entered the dull interior at a wary crouch, pistol gripped in both hands. James followed.

D'Amico reached for the Salesman's arm, but Johnny stepped back, "I have something of interest." He held up a small, flat box. A DVD case, "You understand the gravity of this situation, yes?"

Hamlyn said, "Not really."

"Then you'll want answers," Johnny offered the item, "This will help. For a small trade, of course."

D'Amico reached again and took his arm above the elbow, "Why not just tell us?" She tugged hard, twice, and then released him, her face a confused mask, "I can't budge him, sir. He's like a slab of stone."

Hamlyn frowned. Who was this throwback to the 1930's, and what part did he play in the crew's disappearance? Indecisive, he waffled from playing the trading game, forcing answers or proceeding alone. He decided against option three. Something was wrong, but he didn't have enough data to risk barging ahead. Nor did he suspect a bullet to the kneecap would produce results. Sighing, he decided to play the game. For now. Lowering his gun, he asked, "What's the trade?"

The Salesman's face split into a wide grin, "Thats the spirit." He touched a finger to his lips and mumbled, "What to trade, what to trade? A loonie. That's it. I will trade this package for one of your loonies."

In a flat voice Hamlyn said, "You…want…a loonie. For what's in your hand? You could be out of luck."

The Salesman gestured toward a pocket on Hamlyn's blue uniform, "But I'm not. You carry five dollars and thirty eight cents in loose change: one loonie, two toonies, one quarter, one dime and three pennies. That toonie looks sweet, but I'll settle for the loonie." Once again the Salesman offered the case. He advanced a step to bring it closer.

D'Amico sighted her weapon, "Take another step and I'll shoot."

The stranger bowed slightly and touched the brim of his fedora, "I'm sure you would, my dear." He winked and returned to Hamlyn, "Loonie?"

The lieutenant drew his lips into a thin line, reached into his pocket and counted the change. Five dollars and thirty eight cents, just like the man said. Hiding his surprise, he tossed over a copper-colored coin.

The Salesman snapped it out of the air and held it between finger and thumb. "Heh, will you look at that? The coin has a loon on it. Loon. Loonie." He shook his head, a lopsided grin spreading across his face. "You Canadians."

"Yeah, we're a country of comedians." Hamlyn motioned with his fingers."You got what you wanted. Now hand over that DVD."

The Salesman tossed the case and returned to inspecting the coin.

Hamlyn examined the DVD. The title on the splash page read *Hellraiser*. He flipped it over, read the blurb on the back, "What's this supposed to tell me?"

Johnny appeared crestfallen, "It's in the title. I thought you would… oh dear."

Ferguson had appeared at the entrance, one hand braced against the wall, his face ghostly pale. Bending over, he threw up.

James called from the hangar in a strangely neutral tone, "Lieutenant, you'd better come have a look at this."

Hamlyn hurried over to Ferguson, shouting, "Be there in a minute." Over his shoulder he said to D'Amico, "Keep an eye on our guest."

The woman's voice raised a notch.,"What guest?"

Hamlyn turned. The Salesman had vanished, "Where is he?"

D'Amico spread her hands. "Don't know, sir. I only took my eye off him for just a second. Honest."

Hamlyn scanned the flight deck. No Salesman. "This is getting weird, PO. Really weird. Okay, go brief Captain Slack, and then keep an eye out in case laughing boy returns. I'll see what spooked James." Hamlyn knelt beside Ferguson. "Christ man, you look like crap."

The seaman was on his haunches, elbows across his knees, face flushed and mouth slick with bile. He tried to speak, but could only point at the hangar entrance.

Hamlyn placed a comforting hand on Ferguson's shoulder, and then with a hint of unease, entered the dim interior. Immediately he detected an acrid smell among the ever-present odors of machine oil, fuel and salt.

Blood.

He saw James.

The leading seaman stood by a port door. Beside him was a workbench. "Over here," James said in a voice barely above a whisper. "Watch your footing."

Dark stains streaked the floor, coalescing into a solid, dry pool at the end of the workbench. Something odd lay on it among the tools, something Hamlyn had missed when he first entered. He approached, and what he saw twisted his stomach into a heavy knot.

An arm, severed above the bicep, its meaty fingers curled into a claw. The bloody, blue uniform was shredded where the jagged flesh had been torn. The sleeve was rolled to the elbow, and Hamlyn found himself drawn to the wristwatch. The secondhand marched on, oblivious.

"That's not everything, sir," James continued, "the rest of him is in there, or at least, most of him."

Splayed against a staircase beyond the port door lay the remains of the sailor; legs crooked, faceless head lying unnaturally on one shoulder, chest and belly ripped open, ribs exposed, entrails coiled in the seat of his lap.

James shuddered. "What's going on, sir? No one should die like that."

Hamlyn ran the tip of his tongue across dry lips and fought the urge to run. Instead he took a deep breath, held it, and slowly exhaled. Something was indeed going on, and as horrifying as it appeared, he was duty bound to find out. Taking another deep breath, he carefully scanned the remainder of the hangar, relieved to discover no additional horrors. He looked at the DVD still clutched in his hand. *Hellraiser*. He'd seen it. Good horror flick. Had some memorable scenes. But its meaning here eluded him, and he tossed the case on the workbench. It came to rest against the severed arm.

Raised voices erupted on the flight deck, Captain Slack barking questions and D'Amico shouting for calm. Hamlyn motioned to James. "Let's go."

D'Amico was hunched beside the kneeling Ferguson, one consoling hand on the seaman's arm while Slack stood over both, face dark with fury.

Hamlyn joined them. Quietly he said, "A word, Captain?" Together they moved to the starboard rail. "There's a body in the hangar. Torn up bad."

Slack nodded curtly, "I managed that much from your man. Petty Officer D'Amico also spoke some nonsense about a salesman and a DVD. Lieutenant, what the hell is going on?"

"I wish I knew. The Salesman appeared from the hangar. The DVD was a horror film. Said it was a clue. Then he up and vanished. Into thin air."

"You said vanished?"

"Yes, Captain. Damnedest thing."

Slack rolled his eyes. "No one just vanishes." He paused, waiting for the lieutenant to supply a logical explanation. Hamlyn remained silent. Slack scanned the flight deck for himself. Seeing nothing, he asked, "Was this Salesman the killer?"

Hamlyn pondered that before shaking his head. "I can't see it. No. No way. Trust me, the body's bad. Looks like a bear mauling."

Slack digested the information, jaw working soundlessly. He stared over the ocean, taking time to gather his thoughts. Finally he sighed. "Very well. Take your team and get to the bridge. I'll remain with the Sea King and oversee repairs. If the worse happens we'll just have to take our chances with it. Meanwhile, I'll inform the NRF of our status."

As they returned to the group, Hamlyn said, "We'll use our PRCs to keep in touch until I determine the situation."

"Very good." Slack tilted his head toward Ferguson. "Will your man be all right? I'd send Tran with you, but I need her here."

"He'll be fine. Won't you, Leading Seaman?"

Ferguson could only nod.

Armed with MP5s and Remington 870 shotguns obtained from the Sea King, Hamlyn led his team along the port side of the *Toronto*. The bridge was located forward of their position and up a level. To reach it they had to pass through a corridor running parallel to the hangar, cross the missile deck and climb a ladder.

Moving cautiously, they had expected the worse, but saw nothing more than instances of drying blood. One such dark smear stained the bulkhead leading to the bridge door. Hamlyn motioned Ferguson and James to stand ready while he gripped the latch and pulled. The steel door swung wide and the seamen rushed in, shotguns leveled. D'Amico and Hamlyn followed.

The bridge was a disaster. Blood splattered the walls and windows, spread over the consoles and spilled across a table laden with charts. The upholstery of the captain's seat was shredded, much of the bridge equipment damaged or destroyed. Navy ballcaps and green helmets lay scattered across the floor. A helmet, the word *Bridge* written across its front, sat perched on the helm console.

Hamlyn stood speechless at the sheer display of violence. Beside him D'Amico gagged into the crook of her elbow. James, seemingly unaffected, moved slowly toward the starboard door while Ferguson leaned heavily against a wall, eyes unfocused.

The PRC squawked. Hamlyn pressed the send button. "Rescue One."

Slack's voice crackled into the stillness. "Report. Over."

Hamlyn looked at D'Amico. His second in command had removed her helmet to expose brown, close-cropped hair. She wiped at her damp brow and returned his look. "You okay?" he asked.

She nodded, and managed a weak smile. "Good to go, sir."

He triggered the PRC. "The bridge is deserted, Captain. I'll try SHINCOM before I continue the search. Over."

"If things screw up, return a-sap. Over."

"Will do. Out." Hamlyn went to the captain's seat and peered through the window. The *Toronto's* bow gently rose and fell as the frigate sliced through blue-green water stretching to the horizon. He glanced at a digital readout overhead to check speed and course. The display was shattered. So was its partner further along the bridge. He said, "See if you can raise anyone, D'Amico."

"Sir." The petty officer moved to the shipboard integrated interior communications system. Taking the receiver, she punched several buttons. "Anyone on *Toronto*, respond to the bridge." Her voice carried across the deck. The silence on the bridge became palpable as they waited. She repeated the message. After the fourth attempt, she shrugged. "It doesn't look-"

A voice burst from the speaker. "Get away. While you can. Destroy the ship. Go."

D'Amico grabbed the mike. "Who is this? I repeat, who is this? Report."

Silence, and then, "Go. Destroy the ship. Sink it, before they-" The voice cut off, though the line remained open. A sound like nails on steel flooded the bridge, followed by a long, deep growl and an abrupt scream.

James broke the stunned silence. "What the hell was that?"

Ferguson stepped away from the wall and eyed a nearby hatch leading to the bowels of the ship. "I say we listen to him." He started for the portside door.

Hamlyn snapped, "Easy, Leading Seaman. We're not leaving until we're damned certain we know what's going on."

Ferguson paled. "What's going on? Isn't it obvious? Something took out an entire crew of over two hundred men and women. What in God's name can the four of us can do that they couldn't?"

Hamlyn stared hard at the seaman. Ferguson was on the verge of losing it. Still, he had a point. A glance at James and D'Amico saw them relatively composed. He looked at the floor to collect his thoughts. His forehead creased. "Any of you seen shell casings from small arms fire? Anywhere?"

D'Amico glanced at the floor. "Now that you mention it, no."

"So tell me, how can a ship be overwhelmed without so much as a shot fired in defense? With all this state of the art equipment there should have been ample warning of an attack."

James pursed his lips. "Makes sense. So what are you getting at, sir?"

Hamlyn blew air through his teeth. "I'm not sure, but I'm thinking the crew was so completely surprised they had no time to arm. Whereas we," Hamlyn brandished his MP5 sub-machinegun and looked directly at Ferguson, "are."

A hint of color returned to Ferguson's face. He looked down at the Remington in his hands and hesitantly said, "That still doesn't explain what happened."

"Does it matter? So far none of this makes sense, but it's still our duty to investigate. We heard a voice. There's no reason to think there aren't survivors. James, what's our present speed? We may need to hit the engine room first."

James looked at the broken overhead displays before walking to a console. "Ten knots, sir. Bearing three-oh-two. Just a moment." He lifted a helmet to relocate it. Something fell from the webbing to strike the deck with a sound like an overripe melon. He jumped back, the helmet tumbling from loose fingers. "Oh shit. Oh shit."

Hamlyn rushed over and stopped dead. On the floor lay the top half of a human head, sliced cleanly below the nose. Its shaved scalp displayed an intricately patterned tattoo. The eyes were wide, locked in the final seconds of primal fear. They were blue.

Several minutes passed before Hamlyn could convince everyone, including himself, to commence their search. Cautiously they stepped through the aft door and explored the balance of the level. Their search turned up no more bodies, just continued signs of violence.

The sweep completed, Hamlyn informed Captain Slack they had secured the level and were ready to descend to one-deck and the communications room. Slack acknowledged, and then added the mechanical problem on the Sea King had been identified and repairs were under way. Meanwhile, he had contacted the NRF. The NATO fleet confirmed they would steam their way once the strange situation with the attack submarine *Harpy* was concluded. Until then the *Toronto* was on its own.

Not encouraged with the update, Hamlyn ordered his team to proceed.

James led as they descended the staircase to one-deck, his footfalls wringing a creak of protest from the ribbed metal, each sounding like a claxon in the eerily quiet ship. Touching the floor, he checked the corridor. No movement. However, a long, bloody smear trailed its length to the Communications Room, as if a body had been carelessly dragged. He swallowed as he spied a leg protruding from the Comm room door, like some grisly doorstop. He waved the team down.

D'Amico and Ferguson took defensive positions along the corridor, allowing Hamlyn to join James by the Communications Room. A quick inspection revealed the leg was severed, torn from the hip, its sticky dark blood having pooled around the ripped flesh. Hamlyn signed to James. The seaman raised his Remington and nodded. Hamlyn kicked open the door and James charged in, Hamlyn following. Nothing greeted them, save signs of struggle, splattered blood and damaged equipment.

Breathing a sigh of nervous relief, James whispered, "This is insane."

Hamlyn could only nod before retreating to the hall. There had more rooms to check before the level was considered secure. They would start with the CO's cabin.

Minutes later they regrouped, having found no sign of life. Hamlyn reported his progress to Slack as they gathered at the entrance to two-deck. Once again, James led the way down.

Two-deck was equally deserted, though signs of struggle were everywhere. Blood on the floor, wild splattering across the cream colored walls, bloody hand prints and body parts. Lots of body parts.

They moved toward the bow, striking starboard through the dark confines of the Operations Room until they reached the weapon's workshop. A 9mm SIG sat locked in a vise. Several tools lay strewn on the floor.

Hamlyn knelt beside a twenty-four inch pipe wrench half coated in blood. Something about it had caught his attention. Hefting its weight, he set it on the workbench and puzzled over the ribbons of purplish flesh and crushed feathers wedged in the jaws.

D'Amico leaned in for a look. "What the hell is that, sir?"

"Don't know, PO. Someone put up a fight, though." Hamlyn motioned toward the stern. "Let's move."

Crossing to port, they entered a corridor. To their right was a series of administration rooms. Beyond those a bulkhead door led to a row of officer's cabins. Every room was inspected, each member taking a turn as first in. Each proved empty.

At the end of the hall Ferguson and D'Amico took position on either side of the final cabin. With a nod from Hamlyn, James pushed open the door. Ferguson stepped into the darkened room.

Movement erupted from within the quarters, a deep growl and the sound of bodies colliding. The shotgun went off, its blast deafening in the tight confines of the narrow passage. Ferguson screamed.

Hamlyn rushed in, and froze. Ferguson lay on his back, fending off the snapping jaws of a creature unlike anything the lieutenant had ever seen. The thing was reptilian, man-sized, its skin coloring a mottled purple. Black and red feathers ran across the muscular shoulders, down the arms and along its ridged spine. The arms ended in hooked claws. The mouth on its elongated head was extraordinarily wide, displaying twin rows of serrated teeth. With a guttural snarl it reacted to Hamlyn's entrance. Hamlyn roused himself from his surprised state, sighted the MP5 and fired. The rounds struck the creature in the head and across the shoulders. Dark blood sprayed the walls, desk and bed. Its growl rose into a high-pitched shriek before it slumped heavily across Ferguson.

"Get this damned thing off me," the seaman shouted, pushing hard against the lifeless bulk.

Hamlyn laid his gun on the bed and bent to help. D'Amico and James crowded in, both talking at once. D'Amico found a light switch.

Aided by Hamlyn, Ferguson used his boot to kick free of the creature. James helped him to a seated position.

Hamlyn motioned with his thumb at D'Amico. "Watch the door." Taking up his MP5, he knelt beside the creature. Its skin had been rough and cold to the touch. On closer inspection he saw it had a layer of semi-translucent scales, like those on a fish.

Ferguson was propped against the bed, breathing heavy, arms and hands lacerated and bleeding, the creature's blood splattered across his face. His protective Kevlar vest sported a savage gouge across the chest. Luckily it had prevented physical damage.

Hamlyn grabbed a pillow, removed the case and handed it over. "For the blood. Once we secure this level we'll treat those cuts in sickbay."

D'Amico poked her head in. "Lieutenant, I hear something."

Hamlyn joined D'Amico in the hallway. "Where?"

The petty officer pointed toward the stern. "That way."

Hamlyn listened. After a moment he detected faint sounds, a strange skittering like bone on metal. It grew louder. He pictured the claws on the creature in the room and felt a lump of cement settle in his stomach. "Ferguson, James, let's go. We're out of here."

They assembled in the passage as the first growls reached their ears.

Hamlyn eyed the injured seaman. "You good to fight?"

Ferguson cocked his shotgun. "Yes sir."

The lieutenant jerked his thumb toward the bow. "Then you two provide cover from the end of the hall." The seamen acknowledged and retreated to the corridor entrance, each taking position on either side of the bulkhead door. Hamlyn touched D'Amico on the sleeve. The woman looked up at him, eyes wide with nervous anticipation. "Relax, PO. We've been through worse. Remember that Somali boat in the Gulf of Aden?"

D'Amico laughed, uneasily. "How can I forget? Near thing, that." She paused as the sounds grew louder. "But with all due respect, Lieutenant, the Somalis didn't have claws and pointed teeth."

"Good point. Ready, PO?"

"No."

"Neither am I."

A creature entered the corridor, closely followed by four more. Each of them scrambled and clawed to be second through the narrow entrance. It should have been comedic.

Hamlyn and D'Amico opened fire. The steady retort of the sub-machine guns contested with enraged howls as bullets riddled the alien bodies. Spent shells pinged off the walls and bounced along the deck. Three of the creatures fell within a dozen feet of the entrance. The fourth lunged forward, bounding like an enraged tiger, finally brought down in a sliding mass at their feet.

Hamlyn's MP5 clicked. He snatched another clip and shouted, "reloading."

D'Amico stepped up to protect him. "Hurry. I'm almost out."

The remaining creature had paused, wary of the lethal, unfamiliar weapons. But, when another chorus of growls signaled reinforcements, it snarled, bared its teeth and charged, only to fall lifeless as D'Amico emptied her gun. "Reloading," she cried.

Hamlyn slammed his clip home as two more bounded in. Beyond those another wave swarmed outside the bulkhead door.

James bellowed from behind. "Down!"

Instinctively, Hamlyn dropped to one knee, his free hand pulling D'Amico ungracefully on her ass. The shotguns boomed. An alien head exploded into dark mist. The other collapsed with a gaping hole in its chest.

Hamlyn scrambled to his feet.

"Let's get out of here," James shouted.

Hamlyn pulled D'Amico up and dragged her through the bulkhead door. Kneeling, he aimed and fired back down the corridor into the seething mass of creatures. James and Ferguson joined in, shotguns blazing. D'Amico reloaded and added her firepower to the thunderous conflagration.

Minutes later Hamlyn lowered his weapon and raised a hand. "Cease fire." Beside him James and Ferguson hurriedly loaded fresh shells into their Remingtons. D'Amico reached for another clip.

The corridor was thick with dead creatures, their dark blood coating the walls, ceiling and pooling on the floor. The air was heavy with the odor of hot brass and gunpowder.

Hamlyn strained to detect any sound over a high-pitched ringing in his ears. He shook his head, exasperated. "Anyone hear anything?"

James cupped his ear, "I can barely hear *you*, sir."

Hamlyn frowned and stared hard down the corridor, wondering if there were more to come. He decided to postpone the search. "Back to the bridge. We'll regroup and plan our next move. Let's go."

They entered the bridge to find the Salesman in the Commander's chair, feet braced against the forward window, twirling the loonie around his fingers like some deft magician.

Hamlyn was not entirely surprised to see him. Striding to the first aid kit, he popped open the latch and tossed James disinfectant and bandages. "See to Ferguson. D'Amico, keep an eye out." Setting his MP5 on a console, he removed his helmet and wiped the grime from his forehead. Finally he acknowledged the Salesman. "What the hell do you want?"

Johnny stood, his feet hitting the floor with a resounding thump. "What the *hell*? Very good, Captain."

"Lieutenant."

"Whatever." Johnny paused as he inspected Ferguson, James and D'Amico. "I see you met the enemy. Commendable you all survived. Very commendable. So, when do you return?"

Ferguson held out his arms as James cleaned the cuts. His face was a study in controlled discomfort as he growled. "Who exactly is this guy, Lieutenant?"

"Good question." Hamlyn strode up to the Salesman so they stood nose to nose. He crossed his arms. "What's going on?"

The Salesman crossed his arms in return. "Sha'Daa."

"Sha-what?"

"You have little time, so I'll make this short," Johnny said. "Hell has come to earth. For forty-eight hours. Beginning last midnight, barriers between the dimensions thinned and unleashed the very horrors that have served as your myths for countless thousands of years." The explanation was met with dead silence. Johnny raised both eyebrows. "Well?"

Hamlyn frowned. "I think it's time we got off this boat." He reached for the PRC.

The Salesman held up a thin-fingered hand, a warning gesture. "You can't."

"Just watch."

"You don't understand."

Hamlyn snarled, "There's a lot I don't understand. For starters, creatures from other dimensions."

"Demons."

"Huh?"

"They're demons, technically speaking."

"Thanks for the clarification, not that it makes a crap of difference." Hamlyn snapped his fingers. "Say, here's a thought. Seeing as you know so much about this, why don't you deal with them?"

"That's the rub, Captain. I can't interfere, directly. I can only offer support through trades."

Ferguson approached from the opposite direction, his arms tightly wrapped in bandages. "You've been a fat lot of help so far, even indirectly."

The Salesman's tone turned defensive. "I told you what to expect on the flight deck."

Hamlyn snorted. "With a DVD? What kind of help was that?"

"It prepared you."

"Like hell it did."

Ferguson asked, "What was the DVD, Lieutenant?"

"*Hellraiser.*"

The seaman pursed his lips. "I suppose in retrospect it makes sense." He fixed the Salesman with a withering glare, voice rising in anger as he said, "Though you could have given us something solid, like *details on a fucking piece of paper!*"

"Ferguson's right, you know," Hamlyn agreed. "So tell us, what do we not understand?"

Johnny perked up. "What you seek is aboard your ship. In your engine room, to be precise. Clearly it was fortunate this event occurred on a vessel."

"You have a penchant for wandering off topic. But okay, humor me. Why was it fortunate this event happened on a vessel?"

"Isn't it obvious? These demons have no where to go. They can't swim. That's why they gather material."

"Material," D'Amico echoed. "What for?"

The Salesman spun on her and flapped his arms. "Why, to summon a brother that can fly."

Hamlyn didn't like where this was headed. "Exactly what kind of material do they gather?"

"The crew. They gather the crew. It's a requirement for the ceremony. Not nice. Not nice at all."

The bridge fell into an awkward silence.

The Salesman adjusted his long coat, leaned back against the bridge window and inspected his fingernails. Unexpectedly the PRC lit up, Captain Slack's harsh voice jolting the team from their dark thoughts.

Hamlyn keyed the send button and updated the Sea King pilot. He held nothing back.

There was a moment of silence before Slack's response crackled. "Are you shitting me?"

"You can come see for yourself."

This time the reply was hesitant. "Then I advise we abandon ship and let command decide how to handle this."

Johnny shook his head. "No time. Trust me. No time."

Hamlyn cursed softly. He keyed the PRC. "Stand by, over." His gaze swept the team, taking their measure. James was a study of determined calm, a state Hamlyn wished he shared. D'Amico swallowed before meeting his eyes, her nod barely perceptible. Ferguson stared at the deck, shifting from foot to foot. The firefight had returned much of his spark, but he remained torn. Hamlyn said, "You want to guard the Sea King, Ferguson? We won't think less of you for it."

The seaman chewed his lip. His eyes flitted from James to D'Amico. A sigh and a shudder, and then he relaxed. "No need, Lieutenant. Let's kill them."

Hamlyn turned to the Salesman. "So what do we do?"

"We trade."

"That's it?"

Johnny spread his hands in a placating manner. "It's the best I can offer. The knowledge I provided about the Sha'Daa is a freebie. I can allow no more."

Hamlyn drummed his fingertips on a console.

"It was a show of faith," Johnny continued. "You must trade if you wish to succeed. Assuming you survive."

James cracked, "Thanks for the vote of confidence. Let's get on with it, eh Lieutenant?"

Hamlyn sighed. "Okay Johnny, what do you have?"

The Salesman reached into his long coat and produced another DVD. "This for that toonie of yours."

The lieutenant reached into his pocket, produced the silver and gold colored coin and swapped it for the DVD. He read the title out loud. "*The Abyss.*"

Ferguson repeated, "*The Abyss.* Took place underwater, right?" He scratched the back of his head. "How's that supposed to help?"

James said, "I'm betting it's the title. Abyss. Like a door or portal. How else could these things appear out of nowhere with such complete surprise?"

The Salesman nodded.

Hamlyn set the DVD on the console. "And it's located in the engine room. So what do we do when we find this abyss?"

Johnny produced a third DVD and pointed at Hamlyn's neck. "For that knowledge I require something of greater value. Your cross."

Hamlyn instinctively touched the Celtic cross. "I can't. It was a gift from my mother."

The Salesman clasped his hands before him, like a priest beginning a sermon. "She died of the disease you call cancer," he said, nodding in understanding. "Hard to part with, I agree." The DVD disappeared inside his coat. "Sad that is. Good luck then, I believe the expression goes." Johnny walked slowly to the port door, tipping his black fedora as he passed D'Amico. "Ma'am."

Hamlyn shouted, "You son of a bitch. You go on about saving the world and then have the nerve to walk when you can't get what you want?" He jerked the cross and chain from his neck, tossing it on the Commander's chair. "Take it, you bastard."

Johnny spun about, his face splitting into a wide smile as he clapped his hands. "Oh good," the DVD reappeared and the exchange made. "Now I must truly be off."

"What the-" Hamlyn began.

The Salesman vanished in a curling wisp of smoke.

Ferguson said in a small voice. "Did you see that?"

James growled, "Nothing surprises me any more. What's the DVD, Lieutenant?"

Hamlyn hesitated, rattled not only by what he had witnessed, but what he had given up.

"Lieutenant?" The seaman asked again.

Hamlyn looked at the case. A thickly mustached James Coburn, brandishing a gun, stared back, "*Duck, You Sucker.*"

"What?"

"*Duck, You Sucker*" A distant memory twigged. "I saw this movie years ago. Coburn played an Irishman, had a trench coat full of dynamite." He returned again to the case. "Yes. *Duck, You Sucker.* Also known as *A Fistful of Dynamite.* That's gotta be it. That's how we close the abyss."

"With dynamite?" Ferguson asked.

"Not dynamite. C4." Hamlyn grabbed the PRC. "We'll need to reach the armory first, but we can do it." Quickly he outlined his plan to an incredulous Captain Slack. After a minute the captain grudgingly agreed. Hamlyn stowed the comm device, slapped on his helmet and grabbed the MP5. "Everyone locked and loaded?"

Hamlyn and his team returned to the hallway where they had first encountered the demons. Gingerly stepping over and around the remains, the soles of their boots grew sticky from the blood-coated deck. Once free of the passage, they reached the small arms magazine and spent several minutes replenishing ammo. D'Amico loaded several bricks of C4 into a messenger bag and pocketed detonators and safety fuses. Fully armed, Hamlyn led the team to a staircase that accessed three-deck, the next level down.

Three-deck held the galley, a series of administration offices, crew's heads, cafeterias and mess halls. Upon reaching it, a scan of the immediate surroundings revealed the expected blood and body parts, but no sign of movement. Hamlyn decided to forgo securing the level in lieu of locating the portal. With the hatch leading to the engine room before them, he hand-signed to proceed.

D'Amico paused, cocked her head and whispered, "You hear that?"

James grunted. "Yeah, I hear it. Sounds like pounding on a door."

Hamlyn took a last look at the hatch before reluctantly nodding. "Let's check it."

The team cautiously traversed three-deck. Twice the pounding ceased and the team took defensive positions in anticipation of attack. An attack never materialized, and the arrhythmic noise resumed. As they neared the bow they heard deep growls accompany the incessant pounding. Hamlyn stepped through a bulkhead door and peered around a slight bend in the corridor.

Two demons stood before a closed door, snarling with frustration as they pounded on the metal in a vain effort to force it open.

Looking over his shoulder, he motioned D'Amico to watch the rear and waved James and Ferguson forward. When the seamen joined him, Hamlyn moved aside so they could see what they were up against. James nodded to Ferguson, and gave Hamlyn the thumbs up.

Both men stood and advanced down the corridor. The demons spotted them, growled and charged. Shotguns boomed, followed by a throaty click-clack before both weapons boomed again. The creatures jerked with each impact, dark blood exploding from several ragged holes. One demon struck a wall and dropped to the floor, the other sprawled backward to land in a crumpled heap. Each seaman selected a prone target each and unloaded one final shot into the oblong heads.

James shrugged when Hamlyn approached. "Just to be sure."

The lieutenant ignored him and rapped on the bulkhead door with the butt end of his MP5. "Anyone in there?"

The latch moved and the door swung open, revealing a large man with a sweeping black mustache, the name Malhotra patched over his left breast. He clutched a metal pipe in one meaty hand. Malhotra broke into a wide grin. "About time someone showed." He spotted Hamlyn's rank. "Sir."

Hamlyn peered beyond the man's bulk; saw more than two dozen faces. "How many with you, Sergeant?"

"Thirty-two, sir. Four badly injured."

"Weapons?"

Malhotra smacked the lead pipe into the palm of his hand. "This and some other tools, sir. Best we could do. They surprised us."

"You weren't the only ones."

"We were lucky to make it this far. Several didn't. Had to leave them in the hall." Malhotra's brow wrinkled. "You come across them?"

Hamlyn shook his head. "You're the first survivors we've found since our arrival." He saw no need to mention the man in the hangar. "I was hoping you could tell us more."

Malhotra shrugged. "I wish I could, sir. What now?"

Hamlyn quickly outlined events leading to their rescue.

Malhotra shook his head. "Hard to believe, if I didn't see for myself." He leaned close to Hamlyn's ear and whispered, "Of course you know exploding C4 in the engine room could cripple the ship, if not sink it."

"I'm well aware of that, Sergeant. It's a chance we have to take. Now get your wounded up to sickbay and arm yourselves. I want you to secure all decks above us. Nothing leaves this boat."

Malhotra nodded. "Aye sir. And you?"

"I have a mission to complete. We'll take you as far as the staircase." He unholstered his 9mm SIG and handed it over. "Take this."

Leading the survivors, Hamlyn and his team reached the aft staircase and waited until the surviving crewmembers had ascended to the second deck.

With the last of them safe D'Amico said. "Something odd, sir."

"What's that?"

"Our gunfire should have attracted more demons. It didn't. Why?"

Hamlyn pursed his lips and eyed the hatch down. "I guess we'll find out. Ready?" Heads nodded. James took lead.

As they moved into the aft engine room, the smell of oil and stale sweat warred with an overriding odor of blood and death. Body parts were numerous, discarded in a way suggesting they were torn from their victims in some cruel frenzy.

It took all of Hamlyn's self-control to ignore the grisly vista and focus on the task at hand. He moved slowly, stepping carefully, and soon detected a flickering light that cast a kaleidoscope of colors off the ceiling, walls, pipes and metal fixtures. He raised a fist and the team behind him silently dropped to one knee. Another quick signal to wait, and Hamlyn cautiously edged forward to peer around a cabinet.

He saw the portal. The abyss.

The rift between worlds was roughly circular in shape and about ten feet in diameter. An outer ring of crackling energy supplied the wildly divergent light display. The colors muted as they spiraled toward a pitch black center.

The black began to shimmer. An outline appeared, wavy at first, then gaining substance until it resolved into a demon. It stepped from the portal and abruptly turned right, disappearing behind a series of storage bins. A moment later it returned, carrying the partially dismembered body of a crewman. Oblivious in its task, it re-entered the portal and was swallowed by the blackness.

Hamlyn shuddered. This explained the lack of bodies, just as the Salesman had said. Turning, he signaled D'Amico to prepare the C4. Returning to the portal, he saw another demon appear and follow the path of the first. As it slipped back into the void with another body, he struck on an idea. He waved for the petty officer.

D'Amico crab-walked to Hamlyn. "Sir?" she whispered.

He took the messenger bag from her. "Watch."

D'Amico did so as another demon appeared. Spinning on her heel, she gagged, her face flushing red.

Hamlyn waited patiently, placing a reassuring hand on her shoulder. When D'Amico had regained some composure he said, "There's a delay between each trip. I'm going to rig this to a body so it'll blow when one of those bastards enter the portal."

D'Amico wiped her sleeve across her mouth. "Will that do it?"

Hamlyn grinned. "It's what the DVD implied." Turning serious, he said, "Of course, there's only one way to find out."

A hand reached out to touch his arm. "You be careful, sir." D'Amico's eyes bored intently into his.

Hamlyn smiled and pointed at her mouth. "You missed a spot." Turning to face the corridor, he waited for the next demon to come and go. Clutching the messenger bag tightly, he said, "Cover me." The lieutenant stepped into the narrow engine room corridor and rushed toward the portal. Within feet of the storage bins, the black pit shimmered. Hamlyn's eyes darted to either side and saw no cover. "So much for timing," he mumbled. Swinging his MP5 free, he dropped the messenger bag and kicked it aside.

A demon appeared. If it could show surprise, it hid it well. The thing growled, bared its serrated teeth and bolted back through the portal.

Hamlyn straightened. *That* wasn't supposed to happen.

James shouted, "Better retreat, Lieutenant. It could be going for reinforcements."

Hamlyn half turned. "I'll…"

A shape exploded from the portal, striking him a glancing blow that sent the lieutenant hard into a conduit. He felt searing pain in both chest and back as he slumped into a seated position. Frantic shouts erupted from his team. Shotguns discharged. D'Amico's MP5 responded with stuttering bursts. A man screamed. James. Images flashed past, more demons, more gunfire, then silence.

Carefully lowering his head, Hamlyn examined his chest. The Kevlar body armor was severely scored. He suspected several ribs were cracked as well, if not broken. Whatever had burst through the portal was unlike the others: larger, faster and stronger. Was that the next stage the Salesman had referred to? He looked over at the portal. It had to be closed. Now.

Gathering his legs, Hamlyn tried to stand. The pain in his chest flared. Each breath became a painful gasp. He groaned and slid back down.

There was movement in his peripheral vision. A demon returning to kill him? No, D'Amico and Ferguson. The petty officer looked bad; one arm clasped to her side, a deep gash running from cheek to jaw line. Ferguson, limping, was far worse. Jagged cuts scored his legs and blood welled freely from a deep gash across one thigh.

D'Amico's voice came as a croak. "You all right, sir?"

Hamlyn grimaced. "Better than you. What happened?"

"Whatever came through was different. Our bullets did squat. Banged us up real good. Lucky it didn't stick around to finish the job. Lucky for you we killed the bastards that followed."

"Where's James?"

"Dead. Gave a good accounting when the demons came through, but they swarmed him. We couldn't do anything about it. Too many."

Hamlyn nodded and looked away. "See where it went?"

"Aft. And there's something else."

"What's that?"

"It had wings."

"Damn. We can't let it get off the ship. Help me up." Once on his feet, Hamlyn found his breathing easier. He heard the faint sounds of gunfire coming from above, "D'Amico, get to two-deck. See if the crew's having better luck. If not, we'll have to alert someone."

The petty officer hesitated, her look of concern for Hamlyn obvious.

Hamlyn said, "I'll be all right. Honest."

D'Amico smiled weakly and hurried off.

Hamlyn turned to Ferguson. The man was deathly white. "You're not looking so good."

Ferguson managed a thin smile. "I've felt better. Where'd you drop the C4, Lieutenant?"

Hamlyn gestured to where the bag had fallen.

Ferguson retrieved it, checked the fuse, and then pointed down the corridor. "You better go, sir."

Hamlyn frowned. His gaze shifted to the blood-soaked pant leg, and realization dawned.

Ferguson nodded. "I think it nicked the artery, sir. Won't stop bleeding. Go. Please. Go before something else comes through that damned door." On cue, the inky black center began to shimmer. The leading seaman sighed. "Will you look at that? Wish I had that kind of luck in the lottery. Now get, sir."

Hamlyn hesitated, but knew there was no reasoning with the seaman. He raised his MP5 in salute. "It's been an honor, Ferguson."

The seaman nodded, turned and limped to the portal. His first step was tentative, but with stoic effort he gathered himself, clutched the messenger bag, and strode forward with purpose. His body faded to merge with the growing shimmer. Moments later the black hole erupted into a blinding white light.

Hamlyn shielded his eyes. The brilliance grew painfully intense, and then the abyss folded into itself and winked out. No sound of an explosion. No debris. It simply ceased to exist.

Stepping painfully, Hamlyn moved aft, stopped at the broken body of Fraser James. The seaman lay surrounded by several dead creatures. D'Amico was right. He'd given a good accounting.

D'Amico and Sergeant Malhotra met Hamlyn on the second deck. The sergeant held a C7 in the crook of his left arm and presented Hamlyn's 9mm SIG. The lieutenant holstered it with a nod of thanks and turned to his PO.

D'Amico held a bloody cloth pressed to the side of her face. "Glad to see you made it, sir." She looked beyond him.

"Ferguson didn't," Hamlyn confirmed. "But he destroyed the portal. Now, where's that demon?"

"Making for the main deck. The crew is doing their best, but bullets only irritate it. There's one thing in our favor. It's bulky. It's having trouble worming through the hatches and bulkhead doors."

"Has the NRF been alerted? Captain Slack?"

"Yes sir, on both accounts. Even the carrier *Teddy Roosevelt* has responded."

"Good. Sergeant?"

"Sir?"

"Head to OPS. Gather anyone you need. See what systems you can get online. That thing must be stopped at all costs."

"Yes sir. Where will you be?"

Hamlyn reached for the stair rail. "Up top, buying time, with any luck." He took one step, sucked in a deep breath and asked in a pain-wracked voice, "Alice, help me, will you?"

The howls of the winged creature greeted Hamlyn as D'Amico helped him push through the portside bridge door. The scent of the ocean filled his nostrils as they moved aft along the open deck, past the chaff dispensers and to a metal railing. Below them, the demon burst through a set of double-sized doors.

The creature was large and sturdily built; a mature version of the things that had initially invaded the frigate. Unlike its smaller brethren, this one had wings and a tail. The oblong head titled back as it roared its victory, free of the confining corridors of the ship. Turning slowly, it faced the vast expanse of the Indian Ocean. Great, leathery wings unfolded and flexed.

Hamlyn raised his MP5, knowing it was a forlorn hope. Clenching his teeth against the pain in his chest, he emptied the clip into the broad, feathered back. D'Amico fired round after round from her 9mm SIG, the ammunition from her own sub-machine gun long exhausted.

The demon roared and swung about, its long tail swishing ponderously. Head tilting, the coal-black eyes fixed on its source of irritation. With another thunderous roar, it spread its wings, bunched its muscular legs and pushed off to hover, glaring down at Hamlyn and D'Amico. The wide mouth opened to reveal razor sharp teeth. Hamlyn reflexively put his arm around the petty officer, but the demon turned, as if these mortals were beyond contempt, and with a mighty down stroke, launched across the water and away from the ship.

Hamlyn released D'Amico and slammed his fist on the rail. "No, damn it." Desperately casting about, his eyes settled on a .50 caliber machine gun mounted between the chaff dispensers. Pushing his pain aside, he rushed over and found it still loaded, possibly abandoned during a practice session when interrupted by the attack. "D'Amico," he shouted. With the petty officer acting as loader, Hamlyn sighted on the demon and released a hail of five and one half inch shells. The bullets struck, a steady torrent that stitched a path across its massive body, ripping loose a bellow of pain.

Hamlyn let free a hideous laugh. "Don't like the fifty, eh? Here, have some more!" Spent shell casings tumbled to the deck as the lieutenant felt a surge of hope. The heavier caliber was having a definite effect.

The demon roared and banked toward them.

"Here it comes," D'Amico shouted. Her good arm swept around Hamlyn's waist and pulled. "Come on."

Hamlyn glanced over his shoulder, measuring the distance to the nearest door. They wouldn't have time. He pushed D'Amico hard to the deck; with luck it would only see him. Screaming defiantly, he pressed the butterfly trigger, knowing it wasn't enough. The fifty didn't have the power to kill it.

The air suddenly erupted with the drone of a thousand angry hornets. Shocked, Hamlyn looked aft. Though hidden from view by the exhaust funnels, he knew what had generated that sound: the Phalanx, a 20mm Gatling gun designed to destroy enemy missiles, capable of firing 4,500 rounds per minute. He'd bought enough time for the crew to get the weapon on line.

The large caliber rounds tore mercilessly into the demon's scaly hide. Jerking and twisting from the onslaught, shredded fragments of its massive body struck the ocean in an ever-growing hail of flesh and bone. When the Phalanx ceased its bloody work, what little of the demon remained hit the water with a heavy splash.

Hamlyn, covered in a spray of black blood, pumped his fist, pointedly ignoring the pain from his brief celebration. D'Amico picked herself off the deck and, placing her arm around his waist, gently led him to a nearby staircase. She sat beside him.

"Looks like Malhotra came through," Hamlyn managed to say. "Seems I'll be standing the crew a beer."

"Only after you visit sick bay, Bill."

"Bill...?"

A familiar voice exclaimed, "Nicely done."

Startled, Hamlyn and D'Amico looked up.

Johnny the Salesman stood before them, a wind gust shifting the tails of his black coat.

"What do you want?" Hamlyn snapped.

The Salesman clapped his hands. "To offer you congratulations. Mankind owes you a debt, you know. You should be proud."

"Too many died. Not much to be proud of."

"The deaths were regrettable, yes. But think on this. If events had unfolded differently, the hellspawn would be loose upon your world. At least take comfort in what you accomplished."

"And what about the dead? What happened to them?"

A gleam entered Johnny's eye. "Would you like to trade for that knowledge?"

Hamlyn reached for his pocket. "What will it cost?"

Johnny's wide smile revealed a gold-capped tooth. "Your sanity, Lieutenant. Only your sanity."

Don't Hide The Madness

WHEN THE AFTER IMAGES FADED FROM his eyes Bak stood up and looked around. For the first time in four thousand years he'd stepped out of the confines of the Triple-Six.

"Amazing," Bak marveled. He stood next to a five-foot diameter hole in the floor. Some how some way he had fallen "up" into this place.

Bak then looked about himself and his jaw dropped, for he was standing within the largest warehouse in all of existence. Packed massive shelves stretched off infinitely. The treasures Bak beheld took his breath away. Here was the hoard of a thousand dynasties, the machinery of tens of thousands of wondrous inventions, and priceless artifacts from every single culture across the history of humanity. Bak himself was wealthier than a dozen Roman emperors, but here was an abundance of riches that left him feeling impoverished.

The ground underneath stretched everywhere, like a membrane of polished black obsidian. Moving across it was like walking across the night itself. Overhead lay jet-black nothingness with neither ceiling, nor sky, clouds, nor stars in view. No lamp or torch or overhead light was on display, yet somehow, some way, everything was well lit. And then Bak heard the laughter.

It began as a series of short giggles and snorts. The direction the sound came from was hard to determine, and Bak found himself jogging for several minutes in one direction, only to back track and start all over. Again and again he found himself covering hundreds of yards only to realize the Salesman's laughter was beginning to fade. And with each stretch of aisle covered, the distraction and siren call of wondrous object after wondrous object displayed on each shelf became almost overwhelming: the complete contents of the lost Library of Alexandria; King Agamemnon's looted treasure from Troy; a set of chess pieces each as large as a human with half carved from mastodon ivory tusks and the rest from giant chunks of golden amber; it just wouldn't end.

And then Bak found him.

Rounding one wide aisle Bak came to a sudden halt. Confronting him was the most unexpected of scenarios. All of the many lanes and aisles that comprised the otherworldly warehouse ended in a huge clearing, the center of the spider's web. And sitting in the heart of this mostly empty expanse was an early 20th century Edwardian living room. Gas lamps illuminated beautiful oak furniture and cabinets that all rested upon a large lovely Persian rug. There were no walls.

Kneeling next to a beautifully carved coffee table, and dressed as always in his black coroner's suit with long dark trench coat and fedora, the Salesman shook and shivered in near convulsion. At first Bak thought the mysterious man was wheezing, until he realized it was a series of intense and exhausted giggles that poured from Johnny's mouth.

"By the mighty Aruru," Bak prayed. "Johnny."

Johnny suddenly sensed Bak's presence and looked up, his eyes nearly bulging from their sockets and his lips stretched in an inhuman rictus.

"Bah, ha, ha, ha, ha, ha, ha, Bak!" Johnny spouted. "Ha, ha, ha, ha, you wonderful, bald little man, he, hee, hee, hee, hee, hee, you really shouldn't be here you know." Johnny wrapped his arms around his own midsection, almost as if through sheer physical effort he could force the uncontrolled laughter back into himself.

Bak slowly approached to within a few feet of the Salesman, keeping his hands to his sides. He'd seen Johnny in action a couple of times over the millennia, defending himself from some pretty impressive supernatural bar toughs, and the result had left Bak with a most respectful appreciation of what Johnny was capable of.

On the rock floor, several feet beyond the far side of the Persian rug, a beautiful woman with long black hair and cat-like eyes lay bored and manacled within a tiger cage.

"Tippy-toes, tippy-toes, easy as it goes Bah ha ha, ha, ha, ha, Bak." Johnny spit out. "Oh Bak-meister if only you could see the look on your face, ha, ha, ha, ha, hah. And keep your eyes off Sajella. She has a nasty habit of seduction, old friend."

Bak slowly drew the metal star shape out of his left pocket, grateful for the moment as the points of the damned thing had cut through the fabric of his blue and green robes to repeatedly stab his left thigh. Bak could not take his eyes off of the spectacle that was Johnny, The Salesman. For with every bout of laughter, Johnny convulsed as if from a series of minor seizures. Johnny's skin, actually his whole body, was warping, stretching, from odd angle and extension then back to normal, like a life-size stretch Armstrong doll which Bak had once sold as a souvenir to some silicon based life-forms from the Andromeda galaxy.

Bak leaned forward and set the flat, metal star on the ground.

"Daphne said you would need this for your next sales-trade," Bak said nervously. "Wasn't even sure you would be here. Figured it was worth a shot, trying to catch you between missions."

Johnny's eyes widened at sight of the device and he struggled to stop laughing for a few moments.

"Oh Johnny likes, yes he does, oh he does," Johnny said. "My last trade, don't you see, yessiree, ha, ha, ha, ha, ha…"

Sweat streamed down Bak's forehead as Johnny's eyes locked on his.

"And so you see my curse, Bak, the immortal bartender, inheritor of Xanadu. This geas laid upon me by a council of those you would worship as gods, gah, ha, ha, ha, ha, ha." Johnny giggled. "For this is not my form, or norm, no, no, no, no, hee, hee, hee, hee. Johnny is not a head and torso with two arms and two legs, Bak-arolli. For ten thousand years I have been fuh, fuh, fuh, forced, against my will, to maintain this unimaginative and petty collection of protoplasms."

Johnny's revelations didn't just unnerve Bak, they were beginning to terrify him. But he couldn't move. Johnny's magnetic eyes locked him to that spot, forced to listen to this unimaginable being's ancient confession.

"Whole millennia unable to transubstantiate," Johnny panted. "But something's gotta give, oh, yes oh yes, tick-tock, tick-tock, bick Bak, bick Bak, ha, ha, ha, ha." Johnny's face and skull started stretching into and out of shape. "But not this body. Oh no, no, no, no, no, hee, hee, hee, hee,. Johnny's mind, yes, his mind, his mind, his mind, ha, ha, ha, ha."

Johnny started swaying back and forth and still Bak could not break the spell that rooted him to that spot.

"Decades Bakky, ha, ha, ha, ha, sometimes centuries, Johnny goes without a spell of madness. But the Sha'Daaaaa, Bak, the Sha'Daa, ha, ha, ha, ha, ha, ha. Oh, the strain Bak, the strain, hee, hee, hee, heeee."

"How long will this spell last, Johnny?" Bak asked.

"THIS spell? Ah, ha, ha, ha, ha, ha, ha," Johnny laughed louder than ever. "It's only beginning, bartender, only beginning, the wind before the storm. Now leave, ah, ha, ha, ha, ha, ha, ha. Run my friend. Run." A streak of worry filled the Salesman's voice. "You cannot survive my madness. No human could…run!"

Johnny's head leaned back and a terrifying howl of laughter burst forth.

And the trance that had held Bak snapped, and he spun around. Out of the corner of his eye Bak could see Sajella quaking in fright with both her hands pressed frantically over her ears.

Bak strained his brain and ran as fast as he could, desperately retracing his passage back through this maze.

"Bah, ha, ha, ha, ha,"

With every stride, Johnny's maniacal laughter grew in strength, loud furious cackles that sounded more hyena than human.

"Run, Bak. Bah, ha, ha, ha," Johnny's hair-raising shrieks and wild screams pursued Bak as his heart hammered within his chest.

As Bak finally approached the exit Johnny's insane laughter grew to a clashing cacophony that filled the air with resonant tendrils of pure madness. Bak felt dizzy and his eyesight began to grow blurry. The last few steps before he half fell into the jagged doorway were the longest of his life.

Reach In The Acid

By Jordan Ellinger

THE FIRST MONITOR CODY POWERED ON at Aitken Crater Lunar Base showed a man standing on the surface of the moon without a space suit. Face twisted in pain, eyes bulging slightly from decompressing, his arms jerked upwards like those of a puppet guided by a particularly cruel master. Shoulder-length hair swam in the microgravity, blossoming from his scalp and temples. Alone on the barren desert of the lunar crust, he shuffled towards the base, a thousand pin pricks of stellar light behind him. Clouds of lunar dust marked his footsteps.

Cody shivered as he stared at the monitor. He turned to his partner Lt. Colonel Matthew Schneider. "Matt…" he began, turning back to the monitor. The lunar surface was empty. Not even a footprint showed. Had he imagined it? "—Never mind."

"What?" Schneider looked up from the blue plastic binder that he'd been thumbing through. "LOG" was written in Sharpie on its side. Schneider had made a beeline for it as soon as they'd entered Aitken Base. Nestled in the bottom of Aitken Crater on the Far Side of the Moon, the base was an impressive achievement. A collection of domes manufactured from lunar concrete, it nearly filled the floor of one of the moon's most massive craters, hiding in the shadow of massive corrugated walls of bedrock.

Matt had flicked on the monitor hoping that it was part of some internal closed circuit that might give him some clue as to the fate of the base's personnel. Instead, he'd seen a man where no man could possibly be. He hesitated. What could he tell Schneider? That he'd hallucinated some kind of living corpse? Not a chance. Schneider was a former test pilot. He'd served in the Gulf; so comfortable in a space suit he looked like he'd been born into it. Schneider was the "rescue" part of "rescue mission".

Matt was the other part, and he was pretty sure Schneider already had a low opinion of him. There could have been two astronauts on this mission instead of one astronaut and one civilian specialist. If the base hadn't been radiating a very specific kind of radiation—the kind upon which Matt had done his dissertation—Schneider could have swooped in, rescued the base personnel, and come back to Earth a hero. Instead, Cody was pretty sure that Schneider thought of himself as a babysitter. No use confirming the man's suspicions by confessing to hallucinations. Not unless they got worse.

He shrugged off Schneider's question, and concentrated on searching the rest of the room.

They'd entered Aitken base through a small airlock near the crater rim. Blueprints given to them by NASA showed a larger service entrance closer to the centre of the crater, and another one beyond that, but they'd elected to enter by the closest airlock in order to determine as quickly as possible why the base had suddenly gone radio silent.

The airlock had opened into a small storage room. A waist-high table ran around the perimeter, filled with electrical equipment. Several blindingly orange extension cords had been bundled together and duct taped to the wall where they fed a bank of monitors.

A small fridge hiding beneath a bulky microscope contained several mould samples in shallow plastic trays. An IV bag containing either beer or urine hung from a rack in the back. On the second shelf, a cube of yellow gelatin sat on what looked like a half-eaten hot dog. The dog was beginning to come apart, almost as if it was being digested.

He found a console and tapped in a few commands to reboot the base's servers, bring them back to operational status. As the two astronauts moved through the small storage chamber they could hear distant generators coming to life.

"Judging from the state of their refrigerator, this area of the base has been deserted for several days," said Cody. "Still plenty of places they could be," he added hastily.

Instead of answering, Colonel Schneider leaned into a speaker on one of the consoles and pressed a button. "Attention all personnel of Aitken Base: If you are able, please report to your primary airlock."

Cody shifted uneasily. His hallucination still bothered him. He couldn't shake the feeling that they were alerting *something* to their presence.

When there was no answer from the intercom, they moved deeper into the base, Schneider in the lead, Cody following up behind.

The door to the next room slid open, revealing a suffusing white glow. Trays of wheat grass extended for hundreds of feet in either direction, their narrow green stalks waving gently in a breeze simulated by huge overhead fans. Several space suits hung on the far wall. Too large, obviously, to have fit comfortably in the storage room by the airlock, they stared at Cody with the empty gaze of dead soldiers.

Six empty spacesuits meant that no one had left the base.

"The helmets are damaged," said Schneider. Cody moved closer to the suits. He hadn't noticed from a distance, but each faceplate had been tampered with in some way. They were smeared, partially melted. No holes were visible, but the next person to take one into the vacuum of space would suffer rapid decompression as the thing blew clean off their face.

Metal crashed behind him and he spun around. He saw nothing but an endless sea of gently swaying wheat grass. For a moment it felt like something passed close by, just out of sight. He looked at Schneider, but the Colonel was still examining the spacesuits.

"Did you hear that?"

"What? Some kind of static on the radio?"

Cody sucked air in between his teeth. Of course, with his helmet still on, he couldn't hear a thing except the gentle hiss of the radio. Except that he had heard metal hit concrete like it was two feet away.

He tapped his helmet then shrugged. "Must have been a malfunction."

But he knew in his heart it wasn't. There was something very wrong. He sank to one knee and peered under the plastic tables, past the forest of watering hoses. He bit his lip. The colors were just slightly off. Above the tables, green was green, but beneath them, green was chartreuse.

Sitting on its side, still rocking slightly, was an old-fashioned tin watering can. A chill swept up Cody's spine. With all this automation, who would need a watering can? Worse, what could possibly have disturbed it?

He felt a wild urge to run out of the green house. Instead, he stared into the wheat grass for a long moment. When nothing appeared, he slowed his breathing and forced himself to relax. Perhaps this was just some mild form of claustrophobia brought on by being confined to a spacesuit for the past three days. The base would settle into the crust just the same as any other major structure, especially in a crater that was almost mantle-deep.

When he turned around, Schneider was gone. He'd been examining spacesuits and now he'd disappeared, as if he'd simply ceased to be. The airlock they'd come through was too far away, and he'd have seen Schneider if he went for the one that led further into the base.

"Matt?" Cody stepped back. A spacesuit pressed against the back of his gloved hand. He felt a dull point where there shouldn't have been one and turned.

He gasped.

The spacesuit had six nipples. It hung like a sow in a butcher shop, nipple cavities distended, the rest of it horribly human. The lights had dimmed and shadows played around the base of the suit, ugly shadows that whispered things just below the range of human hearing.

In the space between blinks, the lights brightened and Schneider was again standing next to him. "They appear," he said, "to have been exposed to moderate heat, or perhaps a mild acid."

Ignoring him for a moment, Cody spun around. The field of wheat grass looked like nothing more than a field of wheat grass, and, dropping to one knee again, Cody saw that the tin watering can had disappeared.

"What's wrong?" asked Schneider, following Cody's line of sight.

Cody forced himself to take a breath. "Matt. I… I gotta tell you something. I think I have space sickness."

Matt stared at him for a second, then cracked a smile. "Nice one! Space sickness! Did the guys at mission control put you up to this?"

"No, I—" What did he tell Matt? That he was hallucinating? Did he believe that himself? He remembered the feeling of the spacesuit's nipple under his hand. The *feeling* of it. How could that be a hallucination? "I think there's something going on here. We need to be careful."

Schneider's brow crinkled. "Are you sure you're okay, buddy?"

"Yeah," said Matt, keeping his face as neutral as he could. "If the spacesuits are all here, that means the base personnel must be somewhere in the base's interior. Let's keep going."

The next room was blessedly small, more manageable. It was some kind of storeroom for the hydroponics next door. Bags of fertilizer and soil, spare seeds. Beyond this was an eating area, then another lab.

As they searched, turned up room after empty room, Cody's sense of alarm began to grow. The menace he was feeling from the base wasn't natural. They weren't alone here. They were being watched by something that hated them with a terrifying intensity.

His thoughts turned to his wife and son—Dylan was only three. Radiation be damned, he wanted nothing more at that moment than to hop into the Lander and blast off for home. He needed to tell Schneider. Maybe he'd understand.

"Matt, there's something wrong."

Schneider stopped. "What's wrong?"

"I think," said Cody, thinking fast, "someone should go back to the Lander and try to get a hold of mission control."

Schneider saw right through him. Cody didn't know what was worse, the sense of dismay he saw in Schneider's eyes, or his half-hearted attempt to cover it up. "Sure. You do that, buddy. I'm going to keep looking for the base personnel."

As Schneider turned to go on, Cody saw the next doorway flicker. It opened into a hallway like any of the hallways they'd already passed through, but the colors were off, washed out, sinister grays and shadowy blacks. The sense of dread was overwhelming, but Matt didn't seem to feel it. Cody had to stop him. "Don't go in there!"

Schneider paused, then rounded on Cody, fury in his voice. "How did you get past the psychological screening? Or don't they still test for yellow? I got no respect for cowards. You run back to the Lander, and let the real men rescue the base personnel."

He stood for a minute, then he dismissed Cody with a wave, stepped through the doorway, and disappeared.

The base was utterly still.

"Matt?" Silence. Nothing but the hiss of the radio. "Schneider?"

The doorway leered at him evilly.

Cody's heart was in his throat. He needed to get away. Panic overcame him and he ran. Doors flashed by him, monitors, microscopes, supplies. He ran like an animal, clawing his way past life support apparatus, pounding on door panels until they slid open

When he stopped, he nearly wept.

Schneider had reappeared, standing ahead of Cody. He was no longer in a hallway, not where he should be. He was in a storage room, staring at the ceiling.

"Matt?"

Schneider didn't move. Worse, he looked… grainy, distorted, as if Cody was seeing him through an antique camera lens.

"Matt?" he called again, and realized he was wailing. But Schneider remained frozen.

Cody's mind churned, spewing up dozens of terrible things that Schneider could be staring at up there on the ceiling. Base personnel, torn apart and mounted like trophies? An alien creature with a stalk of hypnotizing eyes? Whatever had worn the spacesuit with nipples?

There was only one other door in the room, and Cody barreled towards it. He needed to get away from Schneider.

The next room had to be some kind of command centre. A wall-sized monitor stared down from the opposite wall. A U-shaped central control panel sat in the middle of the room, flanked by several smaller, more specialized stations. There was more instrumentation in this room than there had been in the Lander.

A nearly translucent cube measuring about ten feet to a side dominated the room. He'd found the crew. Each was frozen, deep in the cube, in a position of abject terror, their expressions twisted in various positions of pain and dread, mouths agape, eyes blinking slowly, pupils heavily dilated.

One of them, the tallest, with a lean frame and hideous smile from which jutted a gold tooth, hung by his wrists so that he loomed above Cody like a crucified man. The flesh of his cheeks looked half-digested, revealing strands of muscle and the angry white cord of the tendon that bound cheek to jaw. Nothing about him moved except the soft in-out of his breathing and his dark eyes, still mostly intact, which focused on Cody eerily. A disgusting image of the partially digested hotdog flashed into Cody's mind.

The cube lunged at him, a tangle of arms and legs all jammed together, churning like an oncoming storm behind a gleaming wall of some substance with the consistency of gelatin.

Animal instinct propelled Cody backwards. He hit something hard and metal mid-thigh and fell backwards over a chair, landing hard on his back and shoulders.

Though no part of the cube appeared to propel the creature, it advanced towards him like boiling mud. He rose in a panic, hampered by the weight of his suit and pack, and stumbled backwards towards the door.

He was going to die. His hand fumbled for the door button but patted empty steel. This monster was going to absorb him like it had absorbed the base personnel. Only half a meter lay between him and the cube, not enough space for him to turn. His hand swatted at the space where the door button should have been.

The monster hit him with the force of flung pudding, pressing him gently into the bulkhead, lifting him to his toes and then into the air. If he'd thought he couldn't be more afraid, he was wrong—his reserves had barely been tapped. A scream bubbled up and erupted. Soon he was screaming and couldn't stop.

The half-eaten man's face was inches away from Cody's helmet. For a microsecond, their eyes met, Cody's wide with terror, the other's filled with anticipation and glee. Then it spoke, its voice a choir of pain. Further back in the gelatin every mouth moved in unison. "You'd make a nice mid-afternoon snack, boy, but, lucky for you, I'm full." The gelatin drew back and Cody's feet found purchase.

For an instant, he sagged with relief. Then his faceplate, blurry already with residue, began to bubble like an overheated film reel. He yelled again, tearing away the clasps and flinging it into a corner.

The dissolved man's eyes followed the helmet as it bounced on the lunar concrete. "You probably needed that."

"Who are you?" asked Cody, still panting. "How can I hear you?"

The man in the cube smiled his hideous smile. Cody could actually see the tendons that drew back his cheeks. "They call me the Salesman, Dr. Cody Magnus, Professor Emeritus at Cornell, husband to June and father to Dylan. I'd shake your hand, but…" He trailed off, and looked meaningfully at the gelatin that surrounded him.

Cody stepped away from the wall, circling until he stood in the centre of the room. There was at least one console between him and the jelly creature. "Are you with the base personnel? Are they all in there?"

With the most minute shake of his head, the Salesman blurred the translucent material of the jelly. "Afraid so. They found this thing out there on the lunar surface and brought it back to the base. 'Course it wasn't nearly this size then. Kitten-size, puppy-sized maybe. Soon as it hit the old O2, it blew up like an ex-beauty queen at an all-you-can-eat buffet, and—like that same beauty queen—started dining on whatever it could find. They ended up barricading themselves in a storage compartment. There ain't, however, no place you can hide from a creature without a spine. It came through the ventilation duct."

Cody's face twisted. The Salesman's flippancy in describing the death of the base personnel was almost more horrifying than the deaths themselves. "Why didn't it absorb me?"

"Maximum occupancy," said the Salesman. "No vacancy. Gotta wait for one of us to check out before you can check in."

Were the others, like the Salesman, still alive? It was a chilling thought. He knelt, trying to catch the eyes of the frozen bodies, but it seemed that the jelly was thicker in certain areas than others, and he could never quite meet the gaze of any of the crew.

"Can I save any of you?" he asked. Or, at least put a bullet in your brains, he thought silently.

"Don't know if I care to be saved at this point," said the Salesman in his choral voice. "I was kinda partial to my cheeks and once they dissolved, my self-esteem went right out the window. Whoever who said it was tough being bald never dealt with life without skin."

The Salesman's mad complaint drew Cody's attention back to those corroded cheeks, and a fresh wave of revulsion swept over him, but it also made him take a closer look at the figure in the jelly.

"I recognize you. I saw you on the monitor when I entered the base. You're not with NASA are you? Who are you? What are you?"

"I told you. I am a Salesman—the door-to-door variety to be exact. If you'll press that button, I'll show you what I mean."

The button he indicated was faintly backlit. Cody's finger hovered over it. Did he trust this man, this creature? A label above the button read "exterior lights", but what if it was the airlock release? No, it couldn't be. The Salesman would also die. He decided to press the button, but be ready for anything.

The giant monitor before him flickered to life, displaying the monochromatic lunar surface. A second later, floodlights swept the away shadows, revealing three giant stalagmites, each several hundred feet high, jutting out of the floor of the crater like a grasping hand. A perfect triangle, there was no way that formation was natural.

"It's been radiating neutrinos for at least six months. Your people found it when NASA turned on the Solar Express at LaGrange Point 1."

This was Cody's mission. If Schneider had been sent to rescue the base personnel, Cody had been sent because NASA had detected a pattern in that radiation, one that hinted at a sentient origin.

The Salesman's gaze flicked up and around, darting to different points in the Jelly. "Your astronauts found this creature at the centre of yonder formation. They had one of the robots go out and pick it up, bring it in through the utility hatch in the green house. They marveled at its properties. Even in the vacuum of space it retained its temperature and consistency."

The jelly crept closer to Cody. He stepped away from the console, maintaining his distance.

The Salesman seemed not to notice. "None of them suspected what it was until after lights out. Only when they awoke with jelly in their mouths, muffling their screams, did they realize what they had brought upon themselves."

"What is it?"

"A probe from Hell."

Cody closed his eyes then reopened them. He found himself staring stonily at the gateway. Three pillars. Three fingers attached to a struggling hand surging out of the lunar surface. Small details—knobby joints, pock-marked skin—lent the rock the appearance of something living, something unnatural. If the Jelly was a probe from Hell, then surely…

"It's a doorway, isn't it? Out there?"

"A door to another universe," replied the Salesman. "Like many doors, it is meant to be used—in this case, every ten thousand years. Behind this particular door lies a Thing. When the Sha'Daa arrives, as it surely will within hours, this Thing will seep out of the gateway and coat the barren surface of the Moon with its filth. When your children look up into the night sky they'll see a blood red moon and know that their daddy isn't coming home."

"Jesus Christ."

"Not quite."

"The Sha'Daa? Is that the name of the Thing?"

"No. It is the name of *a* thing. The Sha'Daa is the weakening of the barrier between dimensions. It is a thousand points of light over every continent and planet in the solar system, through which can travel Things That Don't Belong."

"Every planet?"

"Indeed."

Good Lord, these things were coming to Earth. June and Dylan. An image of them suspended inside the body of the jelly alongside the Salesman flashed into his mind, his little boy with specks of ivory showing through rotten cheeks. He had to warn them.

June's dad was 14th Infantry out of Ft. Drum, several hours north of New York. There'd be no place safer than a military installation.

He raced to the base's communication panel. The monitor was black, but a little yellow button in its lower corner brought it back to life. Four graphs sprang up, occupying separate quarters of the screen. All were solid, dead lines.

"If the radio worked, don't you think Houston would have heard screams of agony while this thing was eating their astronauts?"

Cody's fist slammed down on the panel. "Dammit." He spun on the jelly. "You said you were a Salesman. What do you sell?"

"Keys. A key is usually associated with the opening of a door, but in reality, a key is merely a switch that changes the *state* of the door. If it is locked, a key will unlock it; if it is unlocked then a key will wrap it up tight again. I have a key to yonder door, and I will give it to you for free. But it won't avert the Sha'Daa. It will merely avert it *here*."

Cody had never met a Salesman who gave stuff away for free. "All right then. You've made me aware of the door crashers, and I appreciate that. Now what are you actually selling?"

"I can fix the radio."

"Done."

"Don't you want to hear the price?"

"Anything you want…"

"I want your Lander."

Cody sat down hard in the radio terminal's swivel chair. "The Lander? What could you possibly want with the Lander?"

"The things I desire sometimes have no value beyond that assigned by their owners. The Lander has enormous value to you, doesn't it?"

"How am I going to get home?"

"Ignoring for the moment that you have no helmet, if you left right now, this very second, it would still be three days before re-entry. Your wife and child will be long dead by then. The door is ajar—only a crack for now—but it *is* ajar, and the stream of neutrinos has increased a million fold. I think you'll find that any radio transmission is impossible. Except through me."

Cody stared at the divots in the concrete ceiling. So he could leave the Moon, but June and Cody might be dead by the time he splashed down. Hell, if there really was a demon apocalypse, there might not be anyone to pick him up. Or he could warn his wife and son and they just might find sanctuary at Ft. Drum.

The base was self-sufficient, wasn't it? He could live here comfortably until a rescue mission could be mounted.

"Deal."

Immediately, the radio console flashed to life, the line graphs developing peaks and valleys. A tone blared over the speakers, followed by the gentle beeps of an old fashioned tone dial. The line clicked. *You've reached the Magnus family. Please leave us a message after the beep.*

"June! June, I need you to take Dylan over to the 14th. Stay with your father, and don't leave the base until I come for you. This is an emergency. You've got to trust me. Maybe it looks like there's no reason for it now, but this is not a practical joke. If you love me, please do it."

The second beep cut the message short, and he sagged back into his chair. A thousand things might go wrong, but at least he'd tried.

Now he just had to stop the Moon from turning red, rescue Schneider— if that were at all possible—and wait for rescue. He recalled the way that Matt had been staring at the ceiling in the storeroom and shuddered. Maybe he'd slipped into another dimension—the kind of place where spacesuits had six nipples. If so, he was beyond Cody's ability to save.

"You mentioned a key?" he said.

The Salesman's gaze flowed up to the large monitor that dominated the exterior wall. Cody stood, squinting in order to get a better look.

A small figure stood perfectly still next to the closest spire. It wore a NASA spacesuit, but its helmet was cradled in the crook of its arm. Its head was bare. Cody thought at first that it was some kind of mannequin, a fake, but when he dialed up the magnification of the monitor it became apparent who it was.

"Schneider," he whispered.

Matt's eyes were frozen shut. Frost crystals caked his skin and hung from his eyelashes. His cheeks bulged outwards, as if they'd been distorted by the vacuum of space seconds before they'd frozen in position. His hair, once a chestnut brown, had turned completely white.

"Your key."

Fear welled up in Cody, followed quickly by cold fury. Cody shoved himself from the console, sending the chair bouncing slowly away in the microgravity.

"Did you kill him?"

The Salesman's eyes glittered implacably, but he said nothing. His silence only fed Cody's rage. Cody picked up the chair and leapt at the jelly, the cold metal rising and falling again and again and again.

The jelly barely moved. The best Cody could do was carve a medium sized glob off a corner, which lay in a mound nearby. He dropped the chair. He was fighting a carnivorous fondue, and the Salesman was buried too deep within to harm directly. Fighting it was pointless.

"You can't save your friend, but you can still close the gate. Prevent the Sha'Daa in this little corner of the universe. Otherwise, this base and everything in it will be obliterated in under an hour. A few hours after that, the Thing will build a giant chrysalis, and when it emerges… well, the full Earth calleth."

"So what can I do about it?"

"You need to go out there and do what your monkey ancestors have been doing for the last two million years. Dance."

"Dance?"

"Of course. Your species evolved the ability to talk maybe fifty thousand years ago. When the Sha'Daa came at the dawning of your species they couldn't debate it away, now could they? They enacted their spells through dance. Every culture on Earth has ritual dances, many of them with roots in the dance of the Sha'Daa. You must dance the Sha'Daa. Think of your friend Schneider as 'Simon'. Just do as Simon says."

Cody sagged to the ground and put his head between his hands. "I can't go outside. I don't have a helmet and all the ones in the base have been melted by that overgrown flan."

"That *is* a problem."

The Salesman's blank tone infuriated Cody. He felt his face flush and found himself glaring at the lean figure in the ooze. Neither of them said a word, the only movement between them the gentle rise and fall of the Salesman's chest.

Wait! That was it. Stunned, Cody climbed to his feet and crossed to the lump of jelly he'd carved away from the block in his fury. It had maintained its shape, seeming to defy the pull of the microgravity. Where there should have been a puddle there was still a lumpy shape wobbling on the floor. Cautiously, Cody removed his gloves and brushed his hand along it. His hand tingled but didn't burn.

Didn't the Salesman say the base personnel had been devoured by the jelly weeks ago? They'd barely been digested. Whatever mechanism the jelly used must be primitive in the extreme, designed to cause maximum discomfort over a period of months. It was possible it fed on fear rather than flesh, immobilizing its prey and then letting them taste freedom on the other side of the gel.

Cody cast about the control room and spotted a first aid kit on the wall. Inside was some gauze, anti-septic, a knife, and a transparent plastic mask with which to administer CPR. He removed the mask, cut it in half with the knife, then smoothed the corners of the halves until he had something roughly eye shaped. He palmed these, and then retrieved his helmet.

The faceplate had melted clean away. Clearly the jelly could concentrate its acidity when it chose. Cody looked through the monitor at the figure waiting for him at the doorway—the flash-frozen body of his fellow crewmember. Sure, he had only the Salesman's word that the Sha'Daa was coming in the next few hours, but the evidence to back him up waited out there for Cody to join him.

He reattached his glove then headed back to the corner of jelly he'd carved off with the chair and scooped it into the helmet. It bulged slightly out of the hole left by the missing faceplate, but it seemed to display an unnatural ability to maintain its shape—and its consistency in the vacuum of space. So the Salesman had said.

He pinched the makeshift goggles he'd fashioned out of the breathing apparatus between cheek and brow. The plastic wasn't completely transparent, but he could see through it—and hopefully it would protect his eyes.

Helmet clutched in both hands, he looked over his shoulder at the Salesman. "Is this going to kill me?"

There was no answer, simply a brooding stare, lips pressed into a line. The truth was it didn't matter if it did. Cody had no choice.

He took in breath after breath, hyperventilating, terrified of the ooze in his helmet. It is one thing for a prisoner to know that the key to his cell lies at the bottom of a vat of acid but quite another for him to reach inside and take it.

Cody *needed* to reach inside.

He needed to reach *inside*.

One last prayer, and then he tipped the helmet over his head and waited for the pain.

It didn't come. His skin felt irritated, confined, and itchy, but not burning. And he could see! The command centre was extremely blurry—maybe the equivalent of 20/200 vision, but he could still make out shapes in a general sense.

Now the hard part. The Salesman had been breathing, and he'd seen movement from the base personnel. He could only assume that the Jelly was somehow oxygenated. He knew divers who'd practiced liquid breathing on extreme dives. More than a few suggestions proposed by some of his colleagues to avoid the tremendous acceleration of rocket launches involved highly oxygenated liquid breathing apparatus. It wasn't a completely outlandish idea.

If he had all the time in the world, he would have studied the jelly and determined its properties like any decent scientist. Hell, clinical trials were always a good idea weren't they? But he didn't have all the time in the world. He had under an hour. And he was out of ideas.

His first breath was terrifying. His drowning instinct kicked in immediately, but the next breath came easier, and the next after that was almost normal. He'd taken his most terrible risk. Now he needed to stop the Sha'Daa.

He made his way over to the airlock, found the door control and opened it.

There were two buttons on the other side—the "Cycle" button and the "Open" button. He paused, experiencing his second "moment of truth". He hit "Cycle" and saw the Jelly ripple as powerful jets suctioned the air through nozzles in the wall. Soon, the jelly regained it consistency and he knew that he must be standing in a vacuum. He wasn't dead, and the jelly had retained its shape and consistency, just as the Salesman had described.

He hit the "Open" button and stepped onto the lunar surface. Grey regolith crunched underfoot. Above him, shadowy crater walls encircled a canopy of stars. The stone fingers loomed over him, and in their shadow lay the gate. It was a pool of blackness deeper than shadow, wriggling like something alive. Like something in pain. Nearly the size of a backyard swimming pool, Cody knew that when it grew enough to touch each of the fingers, he would be in trouble.

Schneider's facial features were nothing more than a smear through the jelly. Matt turned and began a circuitous path around the fingers. Cody was reminded of the way the Salesman had moved the first time he'd seen him. Jerking like a puppet with a particularly cruel master. He could almost see the Salesman back inside the base pulling Schneider's strings.

Cody followed because he had to, eyes on the ground, taking care to follow Matt's footsteps exactly. Ancient martial artists were told to visualize painting Chinese symbols with their feet as they practiced their moves. Perhaps that had been inspired by this practice. Schneider's steps shuffled, one foot sliding, the other tapping the ground and then reversing.

Nearly a third of the way around, Cody made the mistake of looking into the doorway. A tiny finger of shadow had stretched out and connected with one of the stone pillars. A small sliver had opened between worlds, and what he saw nearly made him lose his step. Pink things wriggled against each other, *man shaped things* with the thin, semi-translucent limbs of fetuses, they howled bellyaching screams and ate each other, strips of flesh hanging from their jaws.

Babies with large snake-like veins coiled around their temples, legs protruding from the sides of their heads, squealed with cries that sounded frighteningly like the real thing. Like maggots on a steak, they crawled on the surface of a still larger creature, so large that Cody could make out no individual feature save the curve of a mouth so large it stretched out of sight.

The crying was the worst part. Bypassing the vacuum, transmitted directly to his brain through some arcane mechanism, a thousand voices screamed in pain, crying out in Latin, in Urdu, in modern English, all in a chorus where every word blended with its neighbor and yet was terribly distinct.

Each sight was more hideous than the last, and each held Cody's attention unbreakably long moments. He nearly missed a step, pausing at the last moment to reposition his foot.

They were two thirds around when the jelly began to burn. It felt at first as if the skin of his face had completely dried out. The pain progressed to that of a bad sunburn and then to outright pain. Ahead of him Schneider moved just as mechanically as ever, not varying his pace or speed.

Following him became an exercise in pain. Acid slowly dissolved the breathing apparatus that shielded Cody's eyes. Footstep after footstep he followed, his face on fire. He imagined himself running back to the airlock and pulling off the mask only to find there was nothing left of his face but a grinning skull. Every breath threw pain up his nostrils and down his throat. He choked and coughed, unable to draw a full breath from the noxious gel.

Schneider stood several feet in front of him, unmoving.

Cody nearly cried out in relief. Was he done? Cody ran the last few steps. As soon as he stepped in Schneider's last footprint, the Moon shuddered, and a bass roar tore through the crust like an iceberg tearing through the hull of the Titanic. Something terrible pressed against the barrier between universes, throwing its unfathomable weight against it, but this time the Titanic would not be sunk. The bulkheads held.

Cody took only small enjoyment from his triumph. The pain was becoming too intense. He couldn't take it anymore. He was done.

He bolted for the airlock, hopping across the lunar surface-a slave to the micro gravity. As soon as he crossed the threshold, he slammed a fist into the "Close" button. Powerful airlock fans began to fill the room with oxygen. As soon as he could hear their motors, he ripped off his helmet.

The gel stayed glued to his skin.

Moaning, he pulled his fingers across his face, but he was only able to scoop away a handful at a time. The once transparent jelly was stained pink by the first layer of his skin. The gel was everywhere, in his ears, in his eyes, in his mouth muting his screams. In desperation, he reversed the flow of the fans and hurled himself against a wall, pressing his face hard against the intake vent.

Motors howled as air was sucked from the room with the force of a hurricane. The jelly, pressed up against the intake, began to ripple and pull free. Rivers of flame stretched across the back of Cody's head and ears, centering on the intake vent. Jelly oozed past his cheeks and into the vent. He vomited and it was as if someone had pulled their arm out of his esophagus.

He still couldn't breath.

His eyes bulged out of their sockets and he realized that the jelly was gone, but he was in a vacuum.

Blindly, he groped for the door button, but it wasn't there. His knees gave out and he slid against the door. His skin had stopped hurting. His vision began to grey at its edges. His hand trembled and he couldn't stop it.

Suddenly, the fans kicked on. Wind brought back the pain, but his vision cleared slightly. Instead of a dark blur, he saw a white blur that must have been lights from inside the station.

The airlock door slid open, and a figure crouched before him. He recognized the choral symphony of the Salesman, but this time, it didn't sound like the base personnel speaking in unison.

It sounded like the voices from the gate.

"Congratulations, Cody, you did it. In two hours, your wife will arrive home with your son, hear your message, and go straight to Ft. Drum. There they will wait out the apocalypse and—if others like yourself have also succeeded in their tasks—emerge days from now to a changed, but still human world."

He felt a hand cup his ruined chin and nearly screamed in pain as it was roughly yanked upwards. For a moment, his vision cleared and he met the Salesman's golden gaze.

"I've got to go now, Cody. I've got to help the others close their own gates." The Salesman rose. His cheeks were solid and clean, his skin unburned. He must have stepped out of the jelly as soon as the gate had closed, and now it was as if he'd never been swallowed. The Salesman hesitated. "You can't brush up against forces like these and remain unscathed."

Something moved behind the Salesman, and the lights dimmed as they passed behind the solid lump of jelly that the Salesman had left behind. Base personnel still lay twisted within it being slowly digested, but now that the Salesman had left it, there was a man-shaped hole in its front.

Cody realized in horror that it hadn't eaten him when he'd entered the base only because it had had too much to digest. Now that the Salesman was departing, it had room for one more. His fingers tightened into a fist.

"No!" he moaned, but the Salesman was gone. "No!" he howled into the empty base.

One last thought occurred to him as the Jelly advanced. His face broke into a smile, charred and chapped lips pulled back over teeth rendered nearly translucent by the acid.

He laughed.

He laughed with all the roundness and gusto of a man who's just understood a joke he's been pondering for weeks.

All this time he'd been afraid of death.

He reached up and hit the airlock button one more time.

The Memories And Dreams Of Time

WRITER'S FORMED A SUBSET OF humanity that stumbled into the Triple-Six Tavern on a regular basis. All manner of them, authors, playwrights, historians, poets, columnists, lyricists, philosophers, screenwriters, you name it. Dante, Lord Byron, Edgar Allen Poe, Jack Kerouac, F. Scott Fitzgerald, F. Paul Wilson, Hunter S. Thompson, the first Homer, John Lennon, Confucius, Roger Zelazny, Charlie Kaufman, Hillel…the list went on and on.

The most interesting writer Bak had ever served a drink to was Howard Phillips Lovecraft. Stumbling into the Triple-Six, already half-plastered from imbibing at a non-descript Providence, Rhode Island drinking tavern, Howard gawked at the absurdity of the Triple-Six's bizarre architecture and headed straight to the main bar. Bak found himself engaged in a rambling wide-reaching discussion on history, politics, philosophy, religion, psychology, and mythology with the fantasist. Hours later the two men found themselves entering dark territory.

"I've lived a long, long time, Howie," Bak proclaimed, taking short quick puffs from his huge white dragonhead meerschaum pipe, "but I gotta say that even now, after all I have seen of death, the horror of life, suffering, I still don't have any real insight into why men are such wretched creatures and why we are worthy of existence."

Howard frowned and polished off his sixth shot of aged Kentucky Bourbon.

"Mister Bak, good sir," Howard said. "The most merciful thing in the world, I think, is the inability of the human mind to correlate all its contents… some day the piecing together of dissociated knowledge will open up such terrifying vistas of reality, and of our frightful position therein, that we shall either go mad from the revelation or flee from the light into the peace and safety of a new Dark Age."

The writer slid off his barstool, managing to stay on his feet. "That is not dead which can eternal lie," Howard said as he bowed, "and with strange aeons even death may die."

And with that final esoteric pronouncement Howard staggered off towards what he thought was the men's room only to reappear moments later nonplussed beneath a miserable rainy Providence, Rhode Island night.

Need

By C.J. Henderson

"Necessity is a better pain-killer than thinking."

— Vauvenargues

"HELLO, EDDIE. HAVING A BAD DAY?" The question was, for any that understood the situation, somewhat laughable. For Mr. Edward Milius to be having a bad day was not an unusual thing—it was the norm. Ultimately, all of Eddie's day were bad. For as far back as he could remember. Second marriage, first ... this job, that job, one dead-end shuffle after another, those two years of college—useless—high school, grade school, little league, home life, the hospital, that slick ride down the birth canal ... forty-eight years of bad. Not terrible. Not inhuman. Not wretched. They were survivable. The very familiarity of their level of pain made them easy enough to endure.

They were not torturous, after all. They were simply bad. And ultimately, most everyone can find their way around that which is merely bad.

For Eddie, solace from his woes had come in many forms. Over the decades of his misery he had alternated between a variety of reliefs. Beers stolen from his father's garage refrigerator had come first. Stronger alcohol had followed. Marijuana had been a favorite, combined with his first salvations to various degrees had done the trick for years to come. Numerous chemicals in pill form had found their way to him later, too many for his brain to recall at that moment except as a variety of colors and plastic tastes. Often taken in not-recommended combinations.

"Do ... do I know you?"

There had been blotters chewed for the concoctions soaked into them, there had been needles injected, burning substances inhaled, powders snorted. Again, sometimes as beloved diversions on their own for months or years, sometimes only for a singular moment of experimentation—taken in a jumble of mixes too devastating to Eddie's increasingly fragile form for him to recall. Not that it mattered. Bourbon and cocaine? Heroin and coffee? Dexedrine Spansule and waffles sprinkled with powdered sugar and Seconal?

There had been a lot.

For many, it might have been too much. Overwhelming. Not the stimulants. They had been taken in manageable enough quantities. No, it was the despair that he had been fighting back—the creeping, sucking hopelessness of the modern age he had been working so very hard to keep from washing over him and leaving him drown on some forgotten beach. So far, he had done a reasonable job of keeping it together, of not surrendering to the inevitable fatigue which took so many. And he knew why.

"Of course you know me, Eddie."

It was unfair to say that every single day of Edward Milius' life had been bad. Or, more to the point, that he himself felt they had all been bad—one's perception of any moment being the key to their memory of it, of course. There had been that one good day, that one good day when Glory Baker had said "yes" to him. She would go to the prom with him. She, the beautiful and graceful cheerleader, would be seen on the arm of a science club geek. She had said she thought it would be fun. That—*that*—had been a good day.

His one and *only* good day.

"Everyone knows me."

Eddie stared at the fellow before him wondering, where had he even come from? There before him, at that exact moment—on a Sunday—Eddie's one day off. His one day to not be bothered by anyone or anything else. Wasn't life hard enough? His shit job, his lousy pay, barely enough for food and rent and ... well ... whatever pain-relief was close enough at hand and within his budget at this or that particular time—

The guy did seem familiar, however. As Eddie's eyes narrowed, he searched his memory. He wasn't certain ... somehow the man in the trench coat felt just a bit too tall to be anyone he knew. And, who wore a hat like that anymore? Like they walked out of some fucking 40s movie? Some pimp with a thing for blacks and browns? But then, there was the gold tooth. He knew guys with gold teeth. Lots of dealers had gold teeth. They weren't usually white guys, and they usually had more than one. Still, maybe—

"Are you ... are you ..." a name swirled into his mind from some distant beyond, "... Johnny?"

"Bingo, Eddie my boy. Exact-a-mundo. Eye on the prize. A number one score. Excellent. Yes, yes. I am Johnny. Johnny the Salesman. Dealing in merchandise from here and there, far and beyond. An exotic array of products, a veritable deluge of marvelous one-of-a-kinds the likes of which no one has ever before beheld in one location. All brought here, before you, this bright and shining Sunday morning, so that you—Edward Milius—might have your heart's desire."

"Yeah," answered Eddie, skepticism tainting the tone of his voice. "And what would that be?"

"Only you know the answer to that question, my fine gentleman. Like every other biped scuttling across the face of this world, only you know your heart's desire."

Eddie felt a chill despite the increasing temperature of that summer morning. He had gone to the park because he had wanted to feel the sun for once. There had been no breeze, no cloud had passed overhead. And yet, he had felt cold. Felt it again when he looked into this Johnny guy's eyes.

Maybe, he thought, you're gettin' the shakes. Maybe you do need somethin' this mornin'.

The night before had been rough. Nothing on the television. Seven hundred channels. Seven-fucking-hundred goddamned shitass channels of nothing. Nothing that mattered. Nothing that interested him. Just the same relentless shit. Nothing worth eating in the damn apartment, either. Nothing to drink, to smoke, to snort—nothing. Everything had run out. Everything was gone—

That's why you came to the park, where all those with gold teeth gather, a voice from the back of his brain whispered. Admit it. Payday yesterday. You're flush, and feeling like crap.

It was true. It was not a withdrawal feeling-like-crap Eddie was experiencing. No—as had come and gone so many times throughout his life, he had been clean for several weeks. It was something that just happened to him, on occasion. Sometimes the booze and drugs got boring. And why not? He had certainly gone through his bouts of addiction, found himself in alleys he did not know, places he did not remember entering, circumstances he did not understand.

One by one he had extricated himself from those moments. Every time he had gotten himself under control enough to survive once more. To escape the horrible ... once more. For a while ... back to where things were merely bad. As on those occasions, he had recently, again, drawn one of those proverbial lines in the sand and managed to stay behind it for quite some time. The memory of Glory, and his one good day, always helped with that.

How could it not?

But, hey, his mind whispered to him, you've been good for a while. Longer than usual. Maybe we should check out this Johnny nutjob. Find out what he has. I mean ... what could it hurt?

"So, what're we talkin' here, man?"

"Whatever you want, Eddie. Whatever you want?"

"Come on, don't waste my time. Get real. Just make an offer. Tell me what you're movin' and let me think about it."

"I did make an offer, Eddie. The offer I always make to each and every one of you. I have, here, right here, within the confines of my trench coat, whatever you might desire. Whatever you want, Eddie. What ... ever ... you ... want."

Suddenly a touch angry, Eddie snapped;

"Whatever I want. Whatever—anything in the world. There in your damn coat. Get real."

"Oh, I'm real, Eddie. As real as a lit fuse, but your time is running out with every sputter and hiss." Johnny leaned against a tree next to the bench upon which Eddie had taken his refuge that morning. Staring down at him, offering him a smile, he added;

"But I came to make a deal, or at least an offer. But it's not really a valid bargain if you don't believe me. So ... one time special. Proof. I don't extend such a deal-sweetener often. Name something that would convince you, Eddie. You don't have to accept it in trade. How could you, you don't know what I want yet."

"What do you mean?"

"What I mean is, dear sweet Mr. Milius, is I want you to name something which, if I were able to wave my hands and produce it for you, that thing, the sight of this as-yet-to-be-named object would be enough to convince you that I could produce anything in the world that you might want ... for what I want."

"Anything...?"

"Try me."

"I could say 'an ocean liner' and you would make an ocean liner, not a kid's toy, but a boat big enough for a thousand people just appear. Solid, not a mirage. Fifty thousand tons of metal pulled out from inside your coat?"

"Try me, Eddie."

The ball was in his court. Crazy gold tooth guy had upped the stakes about as far as they could go. And, he had to be crazy. Had to. He had just promised the impossible. Eddie could name anything, anything in the world—a herd of elephants, a partridge in a pear tree, a fleet of fire trucks, Abraham Lincoln, a million gallons of lime jello—

The problem Eddie was having, however, was that the salesman did not seem crazy. He talked that way, acted that way, made those kinds of promises but, he did not seem crazy. When Eddie looked into his eyes, he saw ... control. He saw amusement as well. Arrogance. Although the man looked to be somewhere between twenty-five and forty, his eyes bled with age.

"Anything?"

"Anything ... but time is running out. Choose or lose."

"Okay, fine, smart guy. I'm not even going to make it hard for you. You don't have to pull no brass band out of your pocket, or a space station out of your shorts or nothing nuts."

"Then, what will it be? My one time offer? Just to prove I'm the real deal?"

Eddie sucked down a deep breath, held his mouth closed for a moment as he thought, then finally said;

"My third grade report card."

Without a word in return, Johnny reached inside, his fingers snaring something within his breast pocket. Pulling a manila envelope three by five inches in dimension, he handed it over for inspection. Eddie opened the envelope and removed its contents—finding his third grade report card in his hand. Not a facsimile, not a clever copy, not just any third grade report card.

It was his third grade report card.

It was the right school, the proper teacher with the exact spelling of her unusual name, the correct grades. But there was more. The paper's color was the specific shade he remembered. It had the right feel, the right weight. The ink was the color it was supposed to be—the ink printed on the card and the ink that came from the pen of his teacher.

But there was more.

There was the coffee ring, or more correctly, the five sixths of a coffee ring, there on the front, where his father had set his mug down, covering the upper left-hand corner. Trying to not make a mess of the table to keep Mrs. Milius in a good mood, but too sloppy, too careless, in his attempt to set the cup down properly to accomplish even that one small task. Mr. Milius had rarely succeeded in making his wife happy.

But that was beside the point at that moment. The salesman had proved his point. Without delay, he had managed to produce the most random thing Eddie could think of which he be certain was the genuine article. And that scared Eddie more than a little. Because he had burned his third grade report card. It did not exist. At least, it *should* not have existed.

"Now, Eddie, would you like to make a deal?"

Eddie gulped down a breath of air, his eyes going as wide as possible. He stared at the report card for a moment, then dropped it. Suddenly he was frightened, although he did not know exactly why. What, he asked himself, did he have to fear? He had been offered anything he wanted. Anything in the world. By someone who had just proved he could provide it. It—

Whatever "it" was.

Whatever he wanted.

"You're serious," asked Eddie, to which a smiling Johnny added;

"Oh, my good man, I'm as serious as cancer. Now tell me, what do *you* want? What can I provide for you this sunny morning? What is that one thing you simply must have—whatever it might be in the entire universe ... please, tell me now, Edward Milius ... what can I do for you?"

Eddie found himself trembling in the ever-warming rays of the sun. Why did the salesman frighten him so? He had promised him anything—*anything*—and proved he could deliver on such a promise. All Eddie had to do was ask for something, and it was his. Why was he so worried? For once in his long, rotten, useless life, finally something had broken in his favor. At last, he was going to get his. All he had to do was ask for it. And it would be given to him ... just like that.

No, a whisper came from the back of his mind. Not given. Salesmen don't give things away, do they?

He was right. He had only been promised that his gold-toothed friend could get him anything he wanted. For a price. That was what had Eddie so worried, he realized. He did not yet know the amount on his price tag.

"How much?"

"How much for what, my good and wonderful friend," asked Johnny. "How can I charge you if I don't know what you want?"

"I want a lot of things," admitted Eddie. "Maybe even that's part of my problem. But I don't think you're goin' up to everyone you meet today makin' this offer. I think you want somethin' from me. So ..."

Eddie gulped, his mind freezing over with fear. He did want to ask the salesman for something. Many things. Impossible things. But ever since he had remembered there would be a price for his magic wish, he had begun to wonder if maybe he had suddenly met someone he had believed until that morning to only be a myth. Straining to keep his teeth from chattering, he asked;

"Are you the Devil? Are you after my soul?"

Johnny smiled. It was a thing half built from amusement, half from pity. His voice growing quieter, he answered;

"No. I'm not Satan, or any other name referring to the fellow you mean. Nor after your soul."

"Okay," answered Eddie, feeling better, but still suspicious. "So, what do you want?"

"You're a clever guy, Eddie. More so than you give yourself credit for being. I do want something from you. And in exchange for it, I will give you anything in the world. Or out of it, for that matter. You can have anything you want if you will but give me your memory of Glory, or the day she said 'yes.'"

Eddie's eyes narrowed. What was the salesman talking about? How could he take his memory. He had a moment of panic, thinking that a part of his brain was about to be removed, but Johnny held up a hand, adding;

"Rest assured, Eddie, nothing bad will happen to you. Once you're happy with whatever you ask for—say, one hundred billion dollars—I will simply snap my fingers and you will no longer have the joy of that moment."

"You're sayin' I won't remember Glory at all?"

"No, no. You'll remember her, you'll remember her accepting your offer to take her to the prom. You'll remember the fact that it was her father that forced her to break the date, that it had nothing to do with her affection for you. It ... well ... it simply won't mean anything to you anymore."

Eddie stopped, his mind revolving around all he had just been told. Somehow, he believed the salesman. Knew he spoke the truth. And if that was the case, what was he waiting for? He was safe. He could have anything. All the drugs ever—enough to last a lifetime. Money—the salesman had said so. A hundred billion if he wanted. Hell, why not two? Or three? Or a trillion? Why not? Why not, after all his miserable, bad days, could he not trade the memory of one good one for everything he had ever dreamed of? For everything he deserved?

"So," asked Johnny, stretching his right hand out toward Eddie, "do we have a deal?"

Money, power, drugs, sex—anything, or ... everything. He could ask for it all. He could ask for the planet. The solar system. The galaxy. The universe. That was, after all, the definition of "everything," wasn't it?

Wasn't it?

Looking into the salesman's eyes, he knew it was. And he knew, somehow he just *knew* he was right. All he had to do was ask, sacrifice a bit of feeling and he could possess all matter, all energy—all of time and space, every crumb of the cosmos eternal, back to the beginning of time and onward into the future. All he had to do was—

"No."

Johnny tilted his head to the side, his eyes narrowing as he studied Eddie. Staring into the man's small, mortal eyes, thinking not so much of their deal, but another, he asked;

"Just one last chance, Eddie ... are you *sure?*"

Tears washed Eddie's face, dripping over his cheeks, down his neck. His voice catching, his words blurred by his lack of air, his nose suddenly clogged with phlegm, he stammered;

"I can't ... Glory ... she liked me. She really did. It was her father—"

"I know ..."

"I had a chance," blubbered Eddie. "I coulda been someone with her. I coulda, coulda been happy."

"You are happy when you're with her," answered Johnny. Turning away, he began to walk off into the trees following a path Eddie could not discern, throwing over his shoulder;

"You're always happy when you're with her."

And then, he was gone. Leaving Eddie less alone than he had been in years.

"You saw."

Coming from most anyone else the pair of words would have formed a question. Johnny was not asking the thing before him anything, however. Fibers in the side of the greenish, purple mass vibrated, separating molecules at varying speeds until it could manufacture a noise approximating closely enough human speech so that it might answer.

"I saw."

"Well then, there you have it. You lost."

The shapeless form kneaded itself, twisting in a manner that showed a mix of acknowledgement, frustration and a wondering respect. Known by many names across a staggering number of dimensions, older than the concept of substance, the brooding horror attempted to locate the mistake in its thinking. He had selected Eddie out of all humanity in much the same manner the human had picked his third grade report card.

He did not go for the most obvious, pathetic life on the planet. Where was the sport in that? Besides, if the salesman had no chance of winning, why would he play? The pulsating thought-with-flesh had thus picked a random wretch out of all the wretches the modern world had to offer. Knowing everything about everything, it had delighted at Eddie's one worthwhile memory. Knowing the taste of it would be divine, that it would give the monstrous blob of substantial imagination the insight that would allow it to cleanse the Earth of wretched mankind once it reached that shore, it had agreed to Johnny's wager.

Why not? With the Sha'Daa approaching, the human's morsel would give it the spark it needed. And what did the salesman want if he lost? A bauble. A mere nothing.

Already tired of Johnny's presence, the bubbling slather of insubstantial reality paid the salesman his due and dismissed him. On the way outward from the horror-thing's dimension, Johnny peered into his hand, daring to gaze upon his payment. He had risked the life of the earth, people, bees, crabs, coconuts, paramecium—all of it, gambled on Eddie's humanity, to win what he now held.

It was a dazzlingly beautiful thing, to be sure. Old as the idea of cold, essential as oxygen, as destructive as a noble thought, every aspect of it bespoke one of a kind work of the finest craftsmanship. Fire pinned and gleaming with gold and silver cable, mounted with, when stopped to actually look at in closely enough, a glistening, quite wicked-looking ebony proboscis, it was a multijeweled mechanical masterpiece, an unholy marriage of form and function, brought together in a final blasphemous ordinality taking the form of a tattoo gun.

Johnny smiled. There would be another wager in ten thousand years, of course. There always was, but for now ... at least ... the Lumedi was restrained.

Donnybrook

THE PARTY HAD SOMEHOW MANAGED TO grow even more rowdy, now very nearly at full frenzy.

The heavy metal band cranked out a particularly joyous take on Iron Maiden's *Run to the Hills* on the main stage.

Three thousand humans, extraterrestrial aliens, vampires, zombies, and inter-dimensional demons were crowded into the gaming pit all gazing in awe upon the doomsday clock now operating at full capacity. Every single one of its inner workings was clicking, spinning, bouncing, and swinging in blurring rhythms. Every two minutes the infernal device would set off a series of six bone-shaking gongs that would set the crowd off to cheering, crying, cackling, and howling.

Bak looked up toward Maribel's tents and saw that his poor, overworked bride had simply given up; her employees' activities had spilled out into the bar proper which now consisted of equal portions of dancers, gamblers, grudge-pit competitors, and orgy enthusiasts.

Bak struggled with all his might to get to the main bar counter. Folks were packed in tighter than Tokyo supertrain commuters and they were all undulating to the hair band transitioning to a crazy rendition of Atomic Rooster's *Death Walks Behind You.*

Bak shoved, elbowed, punched, and kicked his way back to the safety of the rear of the main bar which not only contained his nine wives and all his zombie barmaidens, but Bors, Jaxas, and the two dozen Irish bruisers he had hired twenty-four hours earlier as extra security.

"There you are." Maribel said with angry accusation. "The counter's protective spell is barely holding this mob back."

Bak took a moment to catch his breath and take in the spectacle of the party of all parties in his establishment.

Three explosions of light appeared in the air above the main serving tables. Tendrils of molten flame turned a couple of dozen patrons into human torches within seconds. Hundreds piled into the already packed dance floor, game pit, grudge pit, and up the cavern walls to every available outcropping or alcove. Several Flaggra demons tried to leap over the bar only to slam painfully into the invisible barrier.

Slowly, the flames resolved into three large, burning globes which floated twenty feet in the air. The smaller two were red and green in color, the large one was blue. The red globe suddenly dropped to the floor. In seconds it morphed into a fifteen-foot tall auburn monstrosity roughly humanoid in shape and packing more armor than an Abrams tank. It lifted its right leg and brought it down upon one of the granite tables, shattering it like so much cheap carnival glass.

"Show yourself," the monstrosity bellowed. "Come forth, Salesman."

"Bors. Jaxas," Bak yelled out.

The two massive bodyguards looked at the intimidating monster on the main floor and then at each other.

"Boss," they said in unison. "We quit."

"Salesman," The red terror yelled even louder. "Appear or we will level this place."

"Smile when you call me that, stranger."

Every head turned as Johnny strode from his alcove and across the empty dance floor. The burning green and blue globes continued to hover in the air as Johnny stopped about twenty feet from the steaming, scarlet intruder. Bak stared at his friend intently but could see no signs of weakness or any other aftereffects from the Salesman's recent bout of insanity.

"Well, if it isn't the much vaunted Malachondrian. Lord of Chaos, King of Evil, Champion of Death, and primping Hell God of just one more dimensional backwater," Johnny spoke with thick disdain. "Far from home and your bootlicks, aren't you?"

"I knew it," Malachondrian laughed. "Your reputation precedes you, tough guy. Rumor had it this was your sinkhole."

"That's watering hole you deific moron," Johnny said. "What's your beef? And make it quick. I've got a pressing appointment."

"Pickings are slim on that pathetic water ball," Malachondrian chuckled. "Besides. Kuan Ti, Yama, and I aren't looking for petty conquest."

The last comment brought a smile to Johnny's face, as if he had just caught on late to a big joke.

"You realize that I am prevented from engaging in direct intervention in the Sha'Daa, Mal," Johnny said. "By those even you should respect."

"This place ain't Earth, you putrid peddler," Malachondrian spat, "and I've got a rep to build. Let's see what you got, fallen angel."

Johnny took two arrogant steps forward and rounded off with the much larger hell god. "I've been holding back for ten thousand years, big boy. I'd say I've earned this."

Thousands of patrons stared in awed silence at the confrontation in the center of the cavern. The doomsday clock echoed six loud gongs. It was now sounding off every minute on the minute. Unnoticed by Johnny and the hell god, Bak frantically scrambled around the backside of the bar counter desperately looking for various pieces of hardware.

"Die," Malachondrian yelled as a swath of red fire exploded outward from his eyes and upon the Salesman. Seconds later the smoke cleared to reveal…nothing.

"So hotshot," Johnny said.

Malachondrian spun toward the voice only to find his barrel-sized jaw connect with Johnny's diminutive fist. Malachondrian lifted off the floor arcing fifty feet through the air and furiously impacted against the upper wall. He burst into disintegrating red fragments that fell upon and instantly torched Maribel's abandoned tent city.

"And the liberals called it a victimless crime," Maribel moaned.

"Strike one," Johnny said.

Frantically slapping pieces of metal together, Bak couldn't help but notice that a shimmering blue veil seemed to envelope the battleground his main floor had become. And in that moment he realized Johnny was using a large portion of his own powers to shield the tavern from the vast majority of destructive, deific energies that were being released by these demi-gods. Johnny's blue energy field most likely dwarfed Bak's defensive bar spell by several orders of magnitude.

Instantly, the green globe of fire dropped to the floor. In seconds it grew into the shape of an emerald nightmare that looked like a cross between a spider and a Tyrannosaurus Rex.

"Kuan Ti, I presume," Johnny smiled. "Rumor has it you were spawned from a spring break romp in Earth's Triassic age."

The doomsday clock gonged six times.

"Mal never could guard his flank," Kuan Ti giggled with a creepy rasp. "And you should consider me the ultimate Green River Ordinance, Salesman."

Bak rudely shoved two of his wives aside as he hauled a steel box with shoulder straps up onto the counter and started fiddling with a small lever at its base.

Triple bolts of lightning flew from Kuan Ti's jade colored tongue striking the floor where Johnny had been standing a split second earlier. Several more bolts followed the Salesman as he pin-wheeled high into the air, all the time drawing closer and closer to the hideous hell god.

Kuan Ti roped out one of his many-segmented hairy legs and slammed Johnny to the ground. The hell god rushed forward and stretched its giant maw wide, displaying six-foot long teeth.

"Now Salesman," Kuan Ti howled. "I will…"

Johnny stretched his own mouth open to an inhuman yawn and bit down on the restraining appendage, instantly cutting it in half. He jumped to his feet and leaped upward and into the monstrosity's mouth, disappearing from sight. Even Bak, focused on his construction project, stopped in shock.

Kuan Ti started rocking and wailing. The suspense was overwhelming and short lived. Kuan Ti's chest cavity burst outward in a spray of multicolored gore as Johnny tore through the otherworldly digestive tract. The deific corpse slumped to the floor. Johnny made a show of straightening his fedora and trench coat, both miraculously showed no stain or sign of wear.

"Strike two," Johnny said with a glare.

The last and largest of the three burning globes, the blue one, slowly dropped to the floor. In seconds it grew into the shape of perfectly proportioned twenty-foot tall woman, naked, hairless, buxom, and possessing slightly Asiatic features. Yama bowed to Johnny. Colored a dark sapphire from head to foot, the death god was almost too beautiful to behold. Held tightly in Yama's right hand was a glistening black mace.

"Public decency laws aside, Sweetie," Johnny said. "I don't take kindly to bullies messing with my friend's place of business."

"Long have I admired your honorable crusade, Salesman," Yama spoke with a gorgeous lilting voice. "Coyote, Jack, Raven, Kokopeli, Anansi, Seth, Loki, Prometheus, so many brave names over thousands of years."

"So you're a celebrity stalker with a cobalt fetish," Johnny said. "I'll give you my agent's cell phone number right after you leave."

"But I," Yama continued unfazed, "will always think of you as…Nommo."

Johnny's eyes grew wide in realization. "You," he spat accusatively.

"Ill met underground," Yama giggled like a giant child. "Do you like my latest incarnation? Not bad for such a dramatic demotion from the higher ranks. And now I will end your mighty crusade, Salesman, destroying you just one trade away from completing your final penance. Funny, isn't it? That she who you robbed of the azure flame of sentience, she who suffers as one of the fallen for your crimes, is the one who brings all of your actions to naught?"

Johnny turned his head to the side and slowly spit. Then he stood tall, arms to his side, and made eye contact with the towering Yama.

"Well," Johnny said. "Are you gonna draw that mace, or whistle Dixie?"

Yama screamed and charged. Johnny leaped into the air and slammed into the giant's torso with such force that both beings fell to the floor. Yama's mace skidded several feet away.

Yama and Johnny wrestled back and forth across the ground, crushing Bak's ancient granite furniture like so many flimsy sand castles.

Three times Yama struck Johnny with a couch-sized fist and each time the Salesman returned the favor with double-fisted haymakers. Each connecting strike echoed through the bar like the loudest of thunders.

"Maribel!" Bak yelled. "Drop a six-foot section of the barrier where I'm standing when I give the signal."

"Are you crazy?" Maribel screamed.

"Just be ready," Bak said. The bartender pulled the straps of the device over his shoulder.

Out on the main floor, twin beams of sparking pulsating white light shot from Johnny's eyes, striking Yama's chest and staggering the god of death. Four more optical blasts pummeled the blue monster, forcing her to one knee.

Yama snatched up her shiny black obsidian battle mace and intersected two oncoming blasts of energy. A frothing blue force wave resonated back along the twin beams and struck Johnny. The Salesman was knocked backward, skidding to a stop near the main bar, clearly stunned. In that moment the sparkling blue energy field that had surrounded the main floor disappeared, confirming Bak's fears that Johnny had divided his own power reserves to shield Bak and all his patrons during this divine combat.

"Now, Maribel," Bak grunted.

Yama rushed forward.

"Hey bitch," Bak yelled from behind the counter. Yama came on, frowning at the little mortal with the strange metallic contraption wedded to the main bar.

"No shirt, no shoes," Bak depressed the selector switch, "No service."

Yama towered over him as Bak squeezed the trigger.

Yama began the downward swing of her battle mace when Bak unleashed hell. Firing at a rate of four thousand rpm, the mass of flying ordnance from the GE minigun brought the rampaging death god to a complete halt. Bak had taken the added precaution of having an eclectic mix of ammunition created for his pet weapon. The minigun poured out a random smorgasbord of depleted uranium armor piercing shells, clergy blessed silver bullets, crushed petrified wood shotgun shells, diamond shot, and 23rd century mini-titanium flechette grenades.

Yama barely had time to look shocked as she was torn completely in half. The minigun fell silent, ammo exhausted. Yama's upper torso fell over like a felled redwood, her eyes still and preternaturally white. A group cheer roared through the bar as hundreds of patrons jumped around, hugged each other, and resumed their debauchery. Wealth quickly changed hands as it was confirmed that the death god had absolutely left this plane of existence.

Bak stripped off the feeder pack and leaped over the counter. Johnny forced himself to sit up. Bak grunted and helped the Salesman to his feet.

Looking at his bartender with new respect, Johnny gave Bak a slight bow. In the background, the doomsday clock let out its string of six gongs. It was now sounding off every thirty seconds. Bak handed Johnny his fedora.

"No offense, Johnny," Bak said, "but you look like shit."

Johnny smiled, "You're seeing me at my worst, Bak buddy. But I've got more trades to complete. The Earth ain't won yet." Johnny took a moment to dust himself off. His trench coat displayed several tears and rents.

Johnny started walking toward one of the rear cavern entrances but stopped suddenly and turned his head.

"In ten thousand years I've never said this," Johnny said, "I owe you one."

Bak chuckled, "No sweat Salesman. Besides, I'm just a temporary pharmacist with a limited inventory. Good luck."

And with a nod and a wink Johnny dragged his exhausted form into the shadows.

Horsemen

By James I. Wasserman

HELL SPAT OUT THE FOUR HORSEMEN of the Apocalypse and in this time and place they were: Mr. White, giver of traitorous gifts, Mr. Grey, who slew with lies, Mr. Red, the blade-wielder and their captain, and the greatest monstrosity, Mr. Shadow, incarnation of Death…

Detective Yuki Federhof saw a cigarette through the rain and the darkness of the alley near their car. She heard gibbering and giggling in a language other than English.

"You see that?" her partner Bill Pritchard asked.

"Yeah," Yuki said.

Bill grabbed her arm tightly.

"I don't like it" Bill said. "Might be a trick. Go around and up the other entrance. Flank him."

"But…"

"Now." Bill was her senior partner. Yuki followed orders.

Bill jumped out of the car and slowly moved forward. Yuki was already running around the front of the abandoned warehouse. It would take her about thirty seconds to get in place. Then they'd stomp this creep. Bill moved forward into dark.

The burning point became two.

A man ripped out of the blackness, clothed in a red suit and tie, holding a huge knife. Just past the killer's legs Bill could see the slumped remains of a female victim, and what he had thought to be the tip of a cigarette were eyes, glowing like coals.

"What the…" Bill cried.

He fell back, raising his shotgun and getting off two clean, center mass shots. They were ignored.

Bill screamed as the dark man stabbed him savagely. Blood, crimson in the darkness, spurted out.

Yuki, screaming herself, sprinted up the rear of the alleyway firing blindly. She was sure that at least two of her bullets had struck the assailant, but before her very eyes he shuffled away and disappeared into the rainy night.

Her partner lay dead at her feet.

Under the damning light of day, the only blood and other evidence found would show that only she, Bill, and the female stabbing victim had been there that night. Not a trace of the man in the red suit would be discovered.

In the Acropolis Diner, a middle-aged, balding man, dressed in a winter coat, sat alone in a booth. "I didn't deserve it," he said, arms wrapped around himself. Other restaurant patrons ignored the strange man.

"They beat me," the man babbled.

A man in a gray suit sat down at Wintercoat's table.

"Who are you?" Wintercoat looked at the gray-suited man.

"It's more important that I know who you are," Gray replied.

The man in the wintercoat gritted his teeth. "They told me I was stupid."

Gray nodded. "I know they did. And they're here, all around you, the people that victimized you."

"They did this to me," he agreed.

The man in gray nodded. "And they deserve punishment."

Suddenly, Wintercoat rose, pulling out an Uzi.

"No," the manager shouted as gunfire erupted.

The man in gray walked over the torn bodies and out of the diner.

"It's been a banner year for World Pharma, gentlemen," Dr. Plenary said, smoothing his hair back.

The World Pharma board members watched him with varying expressions. He glanced at the other VP, Dr. John Vothe from the Nexus division.

"Just sum it up," urged another executive.

Dr. Plenary grinned widely. "Well, sales of Cycloril and Benatril have reached their peaks. The cancer treatments have proven quite the successes."

"And the virus?"

"Harmony will be destroyed once its usefulness has expired."

Dr. Stein looked uneasy. "Could you be more specific?"

"Yes," Dr. Keller said, "considering we all know its potential and the motivations of your company."

Plenary frowned. "I assure you that the Nexus Division has no plans to make it a product in and of itself. It was only used to generate cancers for the cancer fighting drugs to be tested on."

"The drugs are on the market now. We're sitting on something potentially catastrophically dangerous here," Stein said.

"There's still a potential for further investigations."

"Such as," Dr. Stein challenged.

"What if the drugs don't work like they should? What if we could develop further cancer treatments?"

There was silence in the room.

"Perhaps we should all sleep on it," Plenary suggested with a chilly smile.

After the board meeting, John Vothe and David Stein sat in the cafeteria. Dr. Stein stared at the small silicon chip under the skin of his right wrist. "Peace and harmony to the world," he muttered.

"Ironic," Vothe said, "naming an airborne virus that causes accelerated cancer, Harmony. Still its led World Pharma to Cycloril and Benatril, the most effective anti carcinogens in history."

"I still don't like it." Dr. Stein said. "I don't trust Plenary. He's out of the biowarfare part of Nexus."

Vothe nodded.

"I have this feeling that something terrible is going to happen," Stein said.

"Lots of terrible things are happening," Vothe answered. Sirens sounded in the distance, as they had all day long.

"Yes, and that's what makes me nervous, madness around here, with Harmony present."

"Is it safe?" Vothe asked.

"I don't know," Stein returned. "This security device, the codex," he fingered the metal edge beneath the skin of his forearm, "is unique, every board member has a piece and without all of them you can't access Harmony. Still, I think we need to press Plenary on this issue."

Yuki Federhof stared at the television in her apartment as if waiting for a revelation, but there was nothing new.

"And Carol Fenner, age 32, was found dead after two police officers, acting on an anonymous phone tip, arrived on the scene. She'd been stabbed fifty-two times. Also, the first of the two officers on the scene, Detective Bill Pritchard, died trying to apprehend the assailant. The killer is still at large."

I wasn't fast enough, Yuki thought, tears swelling up in her eyes.

"Eyewitness Detective Yuki Federhof described the killer as a man dressed in a red suit and tie. Anyone with information regarding the case is encouraged to phone the police on the toll free hotline…

"This has been only one in a spate of vicious murders today in Boston."

She slapped the television off. The world was going mad, fifty murders in the past few days. And the police had one lead and one lead alone- The Man in Red.

You monster, Yuki thought. You took Bill. I'll get you somehow.

Incompetent, she heard whispered back in her mind, you are my meat.

The phone rang ominously. Yuki picked it up.

Five hours later, in the Hospital, Yuki gripped the locket she kept under her shirt and prayed.

The madness of the past twenty-four hours was tearing her apart. First her partner was killed just feet from her, and then two hours later a madman in the Acropolis Diner gunned down her mother along with so many others. Yuki longed for revenge but the perp who had killed her mother had turned the weapon on himself. Her mother lay in the morgue, and with the city was degenerating into chaos, she couldn't even arrange a funeral.

Concentrate, she thought, there is something more going on here. All your life you've seen patterns, networks where others couldn't. It's why you became a cop instead of a college professor or code breaker in the military. You know there's one here.

Answers from surviving witnesses flowed chaotically through her mind. Was this connected to the man in red? She mulled over the one unexplained fact. A man in a gray suit had spoken to the killer just before everything went mad. Had he egged him on, somehow? Was this mystery man as much to blame as the loner who had opened fire?

Yuki pulled up CNN on the Internet. "Killings continue. Police baffled by random violence. A spate of disasters and conflicts have broken out worldwide with confused reports-"

Yuki's phone rang. "Hello."

"Yuki- it's Mike."

"Are you still in town?"

"I'm getting out soon. Too much insanity is going on. We're heading for our place in the country to fort up there. Come with us."

"I can't, Michael. Not until I find out what is going on."

"Yuki, I'm sorry about what happened. Your partner. Your mother. It's insane. There's something going on and it's bad. The world's going mad."

"Sorry, Mike but thanks. You're a good friend."

"OK. Look, take care of yourself and stay put. If you change your mind, bring food and any spare weapons." Yuki's ex-husband hung up.

Yuki pulled up CNN again. There had to be a pattern to the violence and a network behind it.

An hour later Yuki sighed as she stared at the pile of fresh files in her inbox. There'd been fifty-two murders in Boston, and at each an eyewitness fingered the same perp: a guy dressed in a red suit, burning eyes and a large knife. Each victim was stabbed fifty-two times. The worst serial killing in history and no one was anywhere closer to solving it.

They couldn't even keep up with interviewing all the victims' families.

The killings appeared random: first a slaying of a man's fiancée, then anyone from street winos to old men and women, all in the dark of night.

She thought about her partner Bill. The attack came from nowhere–he'd been walking into that dark alley when the Man in Red struck.

Then came the restaurant massacre. This one was less of a mystery, the madman gunned down the patrons then turned the Uzi on himself.

Yuki pulled a necklace locket out from under her shirt and gazed at the photo of her only son, Joshua, accidentally drowned in a public pool five years ago. "I love you, Josh. But mommy's not gonna be able to think about you for awhile. I have to get this bad man."

Yuki stood up from the computer trying to shake off a headache from a day of non-stop hacking and searching. Other odd crimes were multiplying rapidly. But it was the descriptions of the perpetrators that clued Yuki. The Man in Black wasn't the only force operating. A Man in Gray was causing terror as well. Perhaps even a third, a Man in White, who gave gifts that then led to violence. Was the Man in Red who killed her partner mixed up with them?

She decided to step outside for some fresh air, looking at the neighborhood around her. There was no one in sight. After a few minutes Yuki sighed and walked back into the Precinct office.

"Care to talk business, Ms. Federhof?"

Yuki jerked back. A man stood inside the doorway, a dark figure in a trenchcoat and hat. He hadn't been there a moment ago.

"It's Detective Federhof. Who are you?"

"Just someone who'll give you something you need for a modest price."

"What?" Yuki said.

"This."

Yuki found she was holding an old book, bound in mahogany leather.

"Ever hear of Zeno's paradox?" the man asked.

"Of course," Yuki said, "I've got an M.S. in mathematics. You throw a rock at a tree. Each time you cut the distance in half, the rock never reaches the tree."

"Paradoxes can be very useful, they may save you."

Yuki flipped through the yellowed book. Symbols, Greek and other, stared back at her.

"Why do I need this?"

"You will. I just need something in return."

"What's that?"

"A locket."

Yuki scowled. "How did you know I had that? Who are you? Are you the man in black?"

"No, fortunately for you. I assure you, you need this."

"But why…"

"Remember how you found your son floating in the deep end of the pool? That scream you felt deep inside you? All your efforts to revive him? How you blamed yourself. Spurned your husband for some deep inner fear that some part of you would somehow destroy him also…"

"How," Tears filled her eyes. "How do you know this?"

"Because I do." he said. "Now please, the locket."

Yuki looked down at the locket now in her hand. From somewhere inside a certainty came that this was what she needed to do. As if of it's own volition her hand with the locket extended to the man in the broad-brimmed hat.

Pumped full of coffee, Yuki stared at the map on the wall. She'd nailed down three patterns of crimes. There seemed to be three perps on the loose, each connected to one crime spree.

Red, white and gray. The Man in Red did direct murders, over fifty now. The Man in Gray gave false information, which led to catastrophes. In the Man in White crimes, people committed arson, demolition and murder. All they remembered was a man in a white suit, who gave each a gift. One man claimed his terminal cancer had been healed by a pill that the man in a white suit gave him. He'd killed the Archbishop afterward claiming the Archbishop had given him the cancer in the first place.

The map revealed a pattern to the Man in Red murders. The thumbtacks on the map formed a sign, the shape of an inverted pentagram. There were two spots left. Yuki had little time to lose and no backup as the city and perhaps the whole world descended into chaos.

Plenary spoke to his mirror in the office bathroom. "I saw defeat in my dream."

The image wavered in the mirror and turned white.

"You won't lose," White said.

"I fear it," Plenary said.

"Some work against our masters' plans," the Man in White said. "You must act soon. There have been many unexpected reversals. The Sha'Daa may fail yet. Arrange the meeting, early in the morning at the end of the summer solstice. Get the Codex from them. Use the gift I gave you."

"Yes."

The image wavered to gray. "They called you sick. See what deceit these infidels bring? Follow your great destiny, and then a new order will be established. You will lead this new world."

"Yes, my lord."

The mirror wavered to Red, "Kill! Kill! Kill!"

"I will kill them."

The reflections faded.

He picked up the phone. "Dr. Stein, it's Dr. Plenary. I need to call a meeting. We have issues to discuss."

"Yes, we do."

"We'll meet early in the morning, at the end of the summer solstice and discuss the future of our little opus."

"The summer solstice? That's tonight. What does that have to do with anything?"

"I want everyone there."

"I'll make the calls."

Yuki watched stories coming off the press like some kind of recurring nightmare. People were being slain everywhere. The city was going to hell. And it wasn't only in Massachusetts, either. Something had happened in the sewers of New York. Other strange things were happening in places all over the world–Britain, China...

Yuki cared only about the Man in Red. The world could burn so long as it lit the way to that giggling, gibbering beast.

She knew she couldn't wait for approval from her superiors.

Suddenly, Yuki felt someone behind her. She spun around. In the dimly lit apartment was the man with the trenchcoat, sitting at her kitchen table. His face was the same, not evil, it was young and old and wise all at the same time.

"You again!"

"Don't mind me," the man said.

"Who are you?"

"A salesman." The man smiled.

Yuki grabbed a nearby fireplace poker and swung. Nothing was there.

A voice came from behind her. "Let's cut to the chase here, Detective Federhof."

"Why are you here?" Yuki asked.

"I see you intersecting more than one probability nexus in the very near future. I've come to give you another item. You'll need it. No bullet or knife can bring the Man in Red down." The Salesman took an item from his coat, a sturdy black flashlight.

"I need something in return. Your wedding ring."

Yuki froze.

"The divorce went through last week."

Yuki found herself unable to move. "The ring?"

"Yes, the ring," he said. "Michael is in love with another woman. She's pregnant with his daughter. He was going to tell you about their upcoming nuptials the day your partner was murdered. He'll never return to you."

Tears welling up in her eyes, she traded.

Over the next two hours Yuki plotted out the crimes and found the patterns. The crimes linked together by lies. She printed out a map. The points on it illuminated a symbol, a question mark. The period at the bottom of the symbol was missing. After two days of hell, murder, mayhem, and this- must be the final spot.

Yuki's map led to an old, deserted clock tower. She had an odd feeling of emptiness.

No fellow cops, no tactical team would help her. All her evidence was circumstantial, and completely fantastic. No sane person would ever believe her assertations. She was the chosen opponent of the Men in Colored Suits.

Somehow, though, she felt comforted by the old, yellowed leather-bound book of mathematical proofs and laws. It promised reason and order in a universe now empty of them.

Yuki put on an old navy peacoat, jammed the book in one pocket, the flashlight in the other, and readied for her foolhardy journey into the unknown.

Yuki walked through Union Square near midnight. The next thumbtack, if the pattern would be followed, ended up here. Under her coat, she had Bill's sawed-off, 12-gauge shotgun in addition to her 10mm Browning and her dead father's K-bar strapped to her leg.

A woman's scream echoed from an alley beside an old, deserted night-club. She drew the shotgun and raced into the darkness.

The Man in Red stood over the ravaged carcass of what had been a middle-aged woman. His face was twisted, primitive with glowing eyes that had never been human. "Hee, hee, hee!" he giggled, pulling the bloody knife out of the woman's torso.

Yuki fired the shotgun, center of mass. Red fell backward. As the knife flew from his hand, viscous liquid spurted out and he squealed.

That's not blood, Yuki thought.

The Man in Red rose, his chest dripping a black tar-like substance. He stopped giggling and deeply inhaled. The tar retracted into his chest, and the red suit reappeared, unscathed.

"Sweet Heaven!" Yuki cried, too shocked to fire again.

"Heaven, Heaven," he mocked and lunged. Yuki was slammed backwards into a wall, sinking to the ground.

The creature scooped Yuki up and tossed her down the alley. He turned back towards the monstrous knife on the ground.

Yuki pulled her 10mm from his holster. Still on the ground, she fired.

"Die, you sick bastard." Yuki emptied a full clip into the beast's head. He roared and the tarry substance sprayed as pieces of his head blew off.

"Gotcha!" Yuki snarled. Dropping the empty automatic, Yuki stumbled to her feet and pulled the K-bar. The monster spun.

She swung the K-bar, gashing his arm. The appendage fell to the ground. Yuki ran for the shotgun.

The Man in Red picked up his arm and fixed it back on the stump. The arm moved like it had never been wounded, and he reached for the monstrous knife.

Yuki raised the 12 gauge.

Suddenly, wind gusted and a bright light flashed. Globes of light appeared in the alley and coalesced into a man in a black trench coat and hat, a wild grin on his face.

The Man in Red shrieked and fled.

"Detective Federhof," the man said.

"You." Yuki stuttered. "Are you following me?"

"Looks like I didn't anticipate this encounter. You're lucky I dropped by..." His grin widened, exposing a dazzling gold incisor.

"What the heck was that thing?"

"A demon."

"Impossible."

"You tried to kill it, didn't you? And your partner Bill, yesterday. No bullet nor knife, ma'm. No bullet, no knife."

"Who are you, really?"

"Johnny, also known as The Salesman."

"Look Johnny, what is going on here?"

"I have what you need." The Salesman took out a pair of pliers. "But as you already know, it comes with a cost."

"Why would I want a pair of bloody pliers?" Yuki's head swam. "And what have I got left that you'd want?"

"You'll need them. But I need something in return."

"What?"

"Your jade earrings."

Not the earrings. They were her only connection to her long dead mother.

"Yes. I need them. They mean a lot to you, and thus to me."

"My mother's earrings for a pair of pliers?" She looked at them, undistinguished and a bit rusty, with jaws for wire-cutting.

"Yes."

Yuki's eyes filled with tears, but somehow she knew that it was what he needed, and made the trade. As quickly as he appeared, Johnny was gone.

Five hours later Yuki walked around the deserted precinct, holding three thick files she'd assembled on the "Three Colors." She thought about her mother, and how she had traded the weathered jewelry for a rusty pair of pliers. The earrings, her locket, her wedding ring. It seemed a betrayal, as if her last piece of motivation, her last tie to humanity was gone. Like she was somehow being shorn of all her emotional ties… and weaknesses.

There was one more thumbtack on each of the Red and Gray shade maps. One completed Red's pentagram, one the dot of a question mark that was Gray's symbol.

In the background the radio intruded on her musings. "And in the midst of the terror in the city, World Pharma, still plans to push its new cancer drugs…"

"Well, John," another voice said, "at least something good is going on."

Something nagged at her, something she'd seen in a file. World Pharma, the pharmaceutical company that had been in the news for its revelatory new cancer drugs. She'd been there before, talked to the president, a Dr. Plenary? The address of their new 52 story headquarters in Boston was 52 Willowcrest, famous for being built in 52 days. Bingo. That was a link to World Pharma: 52 Victims, 52 stab wounds. Red's legacy. It was near early morning…almost on the two-day anniversary of the first crime. It was significant, somehow, and there wasn't much time.

Vothe and Stein stood outside World Pharma, in the light of a nearby streetlamp.

"Something's seriously wrong here."

Vothe nodded. "Indeed."

Stein sighed and shook his head. "You are with us on this, right?"

"Like you said, Plenary's a loon."

Stein nodded. "I've spoken to a few others: Johnston, Hammersmith, Leeds. I think they'll support us."

"Good."

The two looked up at the massive concrete building. It was dark, except for the top floor conference room.

Another scientist appeared in the darkness.

"Dr. Hammersmith." Stein addressed the tall, gangly man in his forties with the ubiquitous black tie and gold-rimmed glasses.

"Do we know what's going on here?" Hammersmith asked.

"Plenary is inside." Stein said.

"Then lets not keep him waiting." They made their way through the silent building to the boardroom to find the others already there.

"Sorry to call this meeting so late." Dr. Plenary said.

"Let's get on with it." Dr. Stein said.

"Well, it has come to my attention that certain people believe my judgment is impaired."

"There is a growing feeling that we should end our partnership with the Nexus and destroy the Harmony virus." Stein said.

"Well," Dr. Plenary said with a crooked smile, "I had no idea I had a coup on my hands here."

"Not a coup. A vote of non-confidence." Stein said.

"I'll tell you what. I'll pour us all a drink–I've got some Macallan 25 and some Pellegrino for the non-drinkers. Give me an hour to convince you and if the feeling is still the same, I'll step down."

The board members chatted amongst themselves as Dr. Plenary mixed and passed out the drinks.

"To Harmony," Plenary said, drinking his own scotch. The rest joined in.

"Now, we wait." Plenary said.

"Wait for what?" Dr. Stein asked.

Suddenly, Hammersmith grabbed his stomach. He began convulsing, and fell to the floor.

"Jesus Christ!" Dr. Leeds exclaimed, moving to help Hammersmith. Leeds bucked and suddenly threw up blood. Others began falling.

"What have you done-" Stein rose to his feet. Blood ran from every orifice. Beside him Vothe's head struck the table.

Plenary smiled. He dangled a small vial in front of his dying colleagues, laughing. "It worked, just as the masters said."

Plenary took out of a knife. One by one, he cut the codex pieces from each dead executive's arm. He beamed at the star-shaped steel card the codexes formed.

John Vothe raised his head from the table. "Nice work," he said.

"What? Why aren't you dead?"

"You've done well with Mr. White's gift. Now it's time to leave things to the big boys." He seemed jovial.

"But the masters-"

"Your purpose has been served," Vothe said.

"I saw them. The three masters. I did as they asked."

"Yes, my lieutenants." Vothe gripped his sleeves. From each, a long silver knife protruded. Plenary stepped back. Vothe, leapt over the table and threw Plenary into the bar, smashing his head on the glasses. Vothe swung the two blades and Plenary screamed as the knives tore open his gut. Vothe crossed the blades so they gleamed in the light.

Yuki headed down to World Pharma on her shadowy lead. The city had never been so dead. She saw corpses lying limply on the roads or dangling from trees. Cars were abandoned, some with the windows smashed.

Something was going to happen at World Pharma. She knew it.

As she pulled into the empty parking lot, Yuki saw lights on the top floor. She felt as if spiders were running over her skin. It seemed there were whispers everywhere, just below the level of hearing. She heard the word, Sha'Daa.

Here goes, Yuki thought. She stalked through the glass building doors, gun at the ready. Inside it was dimly lit. She walked up to a row of marble elevators and rode to the top floor. Oaken doors led down different passages. She saw a light peeking from underneath what appeared to be a conference room door.

Yuki kicked the door. Inside, the room was floored with bodies. Another man, who Yuki recognized from the news as the president of World Pharma, lay as a bloody cross on the ground, arms sliced off, head contorted in a scream, blood leaking from chest lacerations.

"Hello," came a strong, commanding voice. The man wore a black and gray suit with a gold-and-black tie.

"Who are you?" Yuki asked.

The man grinned.

"Did you do this?"

"Indeed, though I did have some help."

"You're the final one. I knew...

Dr. John Vothe stretched his arms out, two blades extended.

Yuki fired, remembering the Man in Red's invulnerability.

Vothe laughed and leapt at the detective.

Yuki dodged. "No bullet nor knife, eh?"

"You're pretty good. Put everything together."

"Those fiends...the three shades? They were like you, weren't they?"

"They are the means: White for treachery, Gray for deceit, and Red for war, I am the end, Blackness and Death. We snuck into your world weeks ago.

All our work has been building to these two days. We shall open a doorway to our plane of existence. This is the time of The Sha'Daa!"

Vothe brought the knives up; flames ran down the blades as he lunged.

The pliers, rusted but glinting in the light, fell from Yuki's slashed coat.

"I see the hand of that hateful Salesman," Vothe snarled, looking at the pliers. Black wings stretched from Vothe's back as a mottled tail emerged, extended, and struck an off switch. The room went mostly dark, barely illuminated by the overhead lamps in the hallway outside the office. "Mr. Red. Kill her."

A burst of giggling spewed from behind Yuki. Suddenly she was falling forward, pushed, tumbling on the office carpet.

Mr. Red stood over her. He appeared as Yuki remembered, suit pristine, face gleaming with rabid lust, his shining teeth, eyes glowing with rage. "It's almost time."

"What are you?"

"The Red blade in Death's hand."

With a simple swoop of its claw-like hand, the demon threw Yuki against the nearby wall.

"You're the last," it said with unholy glee. A dark, mottled tail wrapped around Yuki. She felt it crush her bones, and the pain became worse. Somehow, she stayed conscious. A revelation struck her. It only operated in darkness. The Man in Red clings to the dark, in alleyways and places long forgotten.

She fumbled in her pocket and drew the flashlight the Salesman had given her and hit the button. The flashlight was impossibly bright. It seemed to refract from the walls, growing brighter by the second.

Mr. Red shrieked as it was speared in the light. Yellow and orange flame erupted from it. It twisted, flailing and dropped Yuki. The demon's white shirt melted away, exposing a red body, a mass of contorting spines. A huge hole that ate the light opened behind the demon which fell into it. Voices boomed, trumpeted, sounding its doom.

FAILURE, a voice, more like a solid, piercing thought. Then it was all gone.

Bill was avenged.

Vothe ran forward, his flaming knives thrust at Yuki. Vothe flinched and screamed.

Yuki suddenly realized that the two flaming knives had passed through her, yet she felt no pain.

Vothe drew back. There was a palpable shift in the room, in the air, in the world.

"You...you can't kill me." Yuki gasped. The jigsaw collected in her mind. She saw a brief vision...Mr. Red, screaming in pain and flying through a portal.

He can't kill me, Yuki thought, he can't kill me because the monstrosity, Mr. Red, who gave him that power is dead.

"Look, little girl, run back home. I have important things to do." Vothe snarled.

"Try and kill me now, whatever the hell you are." Yuki taunted.

"As you wish. Mr. Gray," Vothe shouted. "Kill her."

Mr. Gray stood at the side of the doorway to the office and glowered at Yuki.

"Who are you?" Gray demanded.

Before she could respond, a frantic man ran through the doorway toward her with a briefcase in his hand, wearing a pullover and jeans. "Where is the devil? I heard it was in here."

It's his final strike, Yuki thought, Gray's last victim.

Mr. Gray shouted, his voice somehow more powerful, louder, but with a hint of desperation.

"KILL HER! SHE'S THE DEVIL. KILL HER BEFORE SHE GETS YOU!"

Yuki's assailant charged her. She side stepped the clumsy man, and sent him colliding into the nearby wall, still dazed.

She moved toward Mr. Gray.

Mr. Gray waved his hand.

Suddenly, the office room widened. Yuki realized that although she was now running toward Mr. Gray, she was getting no closer. The room twisted and turned up and down as if in an M. S Escher drawing.

"In a society of problems, where are the solutions?" Mr. Gray taunted. "If everything I say is a lie, wherein lies the truth?"

Yuki stopped running. She steadied her mind, grabbed hold of the arm of an office chair and concentrated. The illusion vanished. She found herself close to the demon. Gray was smiling now, perfectly white teeth gleaming.

Gray waved his hand again. There was a loud pop and Yuki blinked. When she opened her eyes, she saw several dozen gray figures, laughing.

Yuki remembered the book. She reached into her backpack.

Axiom, Law, Hypothesis.

She threw it at the demon.

Gray caught the book. He took it into his tentacles, babbling more lies.

Yuki thought about the paradoxes, solutions, the equations in the book.

Absolute, concrete, truth.

Gray looked at the book. Alarm spread over its face, strange wisps of light danced around him. Symbols–Greek, mathematical, sigmas and psis flew around Mr. Gray forming a circular wall.

"There is no Truth," Gray bellowed, dropping the book. The characters froze into a glass wall around him. Gray couldn't move, each tentacle touched by a symbol burst into flame.

Suddenly, Yuki was shoved aside. The mystery man had returned and slammed the case he was carrying into Yuki's ribs.

Darkness started to surround Yuki. "You don't have to do this," Yuki called in her haze of pain. "That thing. It's not human. It's a liar. A farce, brought on..."

"You're the devil!" the man said.

"Just look at it!"

The assassin did and his jaw dropped.

Yuki swung her fist for all she was worth at the gaping man who dropped to the floor. Pain lanced through Yuki, her hand throbbed in agony from the sloppy punch.

Above her Gray spun around like a tornado. "No, I cannot fail," he screamed.

The shadows coalesced into a gaping black maw in the air forming a portal. Wisps of smoke drifted out and began to pull Mr. Gray in. "No! I need time! Time solves all!" Mr. Gray's image split apart with an ear-splitting crack and disappeared into the maw.

All that was left was a playing card, the ace of spades, which drifted to the ground.

52-pickup, Yuki thought, C S Lewis was right, in the end all they are is a small meanness in creation.

Vothe staggered. Symbols, giant symbols, danced around him. He screamed in pain and the shadows grew thinner. "Not again!"

Another shade was dead. The Gray demon burned.

For a moment, Yuki looked down at the unknown man who had attacked her. He was unconscious.

Yuki pulled out her pistol. She now stood between Vothe and the back-door exit of the conference room. Gun at the ready, she faced the demon.

"What happens at the end of the summer solstice?" Without Gray, Vothe could no longer lie. "Answer me. Who and what are you?"

"I am the Fourth Horseman of the Apocalypse, Mr. Shadow, death incarnate. The four of us descended upon the Earth last month as a last measure by our Masters to ensure the success of The Sha'Daa."

"What is the Sha'Daa?"

Shadow quivered in anger, but answered. "The Apocalypse, you fool."

Yuki grinned broadly. "How do I destroy you?"

"The Salesman has given you the means," Shadow said. He roared and gusts of unbelievably foul air shoved Yuki aside. Vothe fled the conference room. When Yuki followed she ran into a closed steel door.

A voice sounded in Yuki's head. Perhaps it was the last thing that could have shocked her this day, her son's voice...

Think, Mommy, think.

"Josh! My God is it you?"

Yes, mommy, think!

"The pliers."

Yes, mommy, the pliers.

"What about them?"

You're good at this, mommy, you think about them.

"I'm not that good. I lost you, didn't I?"

Do it for me, mommy. I'm closer now. Bad things are happening.

"I tried CPR but couldn't bring you back to life."

You need to concentrate now, mommy.

"Okay, I'm thinking."

He told you his name.

"Who-"

Yes, that's right.

"His name was Mr. Shadow."

That's right, mommy.

"Shadow? Like the three shades."

Come on, mommy! I know you can do it!

"What is its flaw? Black to light? Lies to truth?"

Yes, mommy, yes!

"Shadows."

Yes, Shadows. Shadows need light as Death needs life.

"Shadows need light?"

Yuki ran the opposite way, remembering a room she'd passed on the way in. A painted arrow on the wall indicated Main Power. The hallway wound into a big green generator with many wires crawling across the walls. She noticed a thick bundle of wires with warning signs all around it. Main Power–Do not engage. How would she use the tool without getting electrocuted? Surely the generators would blow.

What do I do?

Mr. Shadow headed towards the security doors to the top antechamber. In one hand he held the codex card, gleaming in all its glory.

The Sha'Daa draws to an end.

"Whistle while you work," he said, smiling. Finally, the last vault was in front of him. If Plenary had done his job right, there would be enough explosives in the conference room to spread Harmony deep into the atmosphere.

He slid the codex into the door's keyhole. Alarm bells, sirens placed on the top and the sides of the door, screeched loudly as the door opened.

"Hallelujah." Mr. Shadow said, looking in the center of the white, metal room at a bunch of vials covered by glass and a control panel. He approached the pedestal and looked through a small glass window at the Harmony virus. Shadow carried his vial of glory carefully into the conference room and placed it on the desk.

Yuki saw the red light of the emergency power turn on. "Blast!" She looked around the dank room then stumbled around the hallway. She passed the Main Power sign, heading down another corridor Yuki approached the wires with the Salesman's pliers and some rubber gloves she'd found. With a deep breath she began cutting. Sparks erupted.

"Now, if I remember correctly?" Shadow said, moving part of the bar aside, it folded in half at the mirror. There was a safe inside and his claws punched in the code. Inside a small computer display: Emergency Detonation Protocol.

Suddenly the lights went down. "No," Shadow screamed. Lights flickered out and he fell into the ground. He became the shadow that he'd never cast.

"AAAAAGGHH!" the demon screamed as he was sucked into the floor. Shrieking sounds came from all over. Shadow tried to pull himself free of his own shadow. An instant later; he was bathed in red light. Emergency power had activated.

"HAAHAHAHAAHA!" Shadow pulled himself out of the pool of inky blackness he'd become moments earlier. He walked triumphantly to the safe and entered a code. "Here goes, you stinking monkeys," he said, pressing the button. The display read Emergency Protocol Activated. Thirty seconds remaining.

"I love this part," the demon crowed.

Mr. Shadow, Captain of the horsemen, stood at the crest of victory, whistling as he watched the countdown. He poured himself a glass of Glenmorangie scotch. Suddenly, a rift yawned over Mr. Shadow. Screaming and giggling came from within.

"I would speak with you, my Master," Shadow said.

Finish your work, a giant voice replied.

"I want to know what happens to me after."

Your purpose will be done.

"I was kind of hoping I could stick around."

I see I have given you too much sentience. This is my mistake.

"You uncorked the monster. Now you have to decide what you're going to do with me."

You are a Horseman. Once the destruction of this plane succeeds, you will return to us.

"I will not be devoured."

It is all you will have.

"I want to exist."

You will be taken apart and put together in an unholy quest when you are needed.

"I'll do as you ask, Master, but we will speak of this again."

Yuki raced into the emergency generator room, a bunch of large green boxes labeled Auxiliary Power. She pushed through the door and looked around for a wire. There was a glass box surrounding a fat red wire labeled: Emergency Access Only. She smashed it with the pliers.

"Come on, come on," Yuki muttered as she slipped the pliers under the wire and cut.

Emergency Protocol Halted. The red lights in the building failed.

"No!" Shadow began falling into himself again, sinking into the floor as if melting.

The doorway opened and Yuki leaned in. "Nighty-night, you scumbag," she said.

Tentacles flapped. "Ggghhh, I have not failed, ggghhhh," the boiling puddle said.

The detective noticed the void that had opened beside the last vestiges of the horseman entity. It's sickly green light did not help Shadow.

"Failure," a million voices screamed. She could see something within the void.

Screaming and weeping faces of villains, young and old, burned in fiery ruin.

"From Hell's heart I strike at thee," a voice hissed from the hole.

What did that mean? Yuki wondered. Then she spotted the vial on the table. Snatching it up quickly, she threw it into the hole. But she'd come too close. A tentacle speared her chest. She pulled herself off the spear of flesh before she could be pulled in. Suddenly Shadow was gone and the floor was just a floor.

Yuki staggered to the window, blood pouring from her wound. *My job's done. I did it. The thing's dead, or at least back from whence the bloody monster came. Regardless of what happens to me, I did it.*

A figure appeared in gleaming light. But this was no angel; it was the Man in White, last of the Horsemen. But its image was eroding, dying as the last seconds of the Sha'Daa wound down. "You will die, Detective."

Yuki stared in contempt.

"I can help you, but you must hurry. I can give you life again."

"No deal."

"But you'll die! Take my hand."

Yuki felt the life draining away from her but spurned Mr. White's hand.

The surviving horseman dissolved in despair.

Yuki looked out the window. Day was coming. Whatever horrible crisis had befallen the world was done. The Sha'Daa, the Apocalypse was thwarted. Hopefully her ex, Mike, and his girlfriend had survived. Yuki lay down, content, her vision fading at the edges. "Joshua, son, are you there?"

Yes, Mom, time for you to come with me now.

"Good, son. There's nowhere I'd rather be."

Last Call For Alcohol

N HOUR AFTER JOHNNY, THE SALESMAN, had survived a showdown with three Hell Lords, the Triple-Six Tavern was repacked to capacity. The doomsday clock gonged constantly, and several reliable mystics confirmed that mere minutes remained of The Sha'Daa and that the outcome was still uncertain. No word had gotten back to Bak from the Salesman, but the immortal bartender did not expect any. Johnny had the mark of doom on his brow when he left the Tavern earlier, and Bak found himself wondering if his oldest friendship had come to an end.

The place was a mess, but Bak and his staff and family had done a respectable job of clearing away the more manageable portions of debris, including two very distracting death god corpses.

Up on the main stage a West African drum band was pounding out a heart lifting rhythm that somehow managed to stay in sync with the resounding apocalyptic clock.

Deciding that his patrons had earned it for sticking around throughout the recent ruckus, Bak shouted aloud.

"Final round, on the house. Last call for alcohol."

Hundreds charged the long bar counter.

Bak and his exhausted wives worked furiously to fill drink orders from the last of their reserve supplies.

Following an instinctive cue, Bak, his wives, workers, and all the patrons present began shouting out a countdown starting at one hundred. The doomsday clock, on top of its constant gongs, had begun to glow a bright yellow.

"Ninety five, ninety four, ninety three…"

Bak frantically poured five brews off tap, mixed three Kahlua and creams, and slid four rum and cokes down the bar to his left. Maribel yelled out loud for more olives.

"Fifty, forty nine, forty eight, forty seven…"

Expectation filled the Triple-Six like a growing nuclear chain reaction.

"Bak, I made it," a friendly voice yelled out.

The bartender looked up and across the counter at a robust seventy-two year old man wearing a dust-covered early 20th century suit, dapper bow tie and displaying a dashing grey mustache.

"Gwinnett, you ornery bastard," Bak laughed. "Where you been?"

Both men were practically screaming to hear each other over the tavern wide countdown.

"Modeling sombreros," Gwinnett chuckled. "Gimme a brew."

"Thirty, twenty nine, twenty eight…"

Bak scooped out the last two mugs of ale and handed one to the elderly writer.

"How about a toast old friend?" Bak said raising his own mug.

"To Bacchus," Gwinnett saluted. "A convenient deity invented by the ancients as an excuse for getting drunk."

"Nineteen, eighteen, seventeen…"

"Praised be the fathomless universe," Bak shouted, "for life and joy and for objects and knowledge curious; and for love, sweet love."

Both men downed their drinks.

The doomsday clock sounded out one long unending hair-raising gong.

"Twelve, eleven, ten…"

What would the future hold? Bak wondered. Would Johnny survive his final confrontations and sales trades? Would the Earth outlive the latest Sha'Daa? How would all this affect business?

"Eight, seven, six…"

Bak took a deep breath and let it out slowly. He had existed for four thousand years, and still he found himself fearing death and desiring more of reality. He had a loving family and a job that gave him no end of pleasure and purpose.

"Five, four, three, two…"

Life was good.

"One."

The doomsday clock flashed a brilliant bright green and disappeared.

Every single patron in the Triple-Six Tavern joined their voices to shout out one final exclamation, one footnote to the greatest party in the history of existence, held in the trendiest and most famous bar of them all. And this last word burst forth, where it is said by many to echo throughout all time and space and eternity.

"Sha'Daa!"

— THE END —

Visit

SHADAA.COM

for all author biographies, the secret history of

this chilling franchise, and the inside

low-down on all the books in

Michael H. Hanson's

Sha'Daa™ series

(including those currently in the works)

and how you can order them.

The Sha'Daa is
coming.

Are you ready?

Excerpt From SHA'DAA: Pawns

SHLEY BIT HER LOWER LIP AND RAN her eyes suspiciously around her crowded shop. Vampires haggled with one employee over the value of a lovely gold and sapphire laden crucifix. One family of Alpha Centaureans desperately tried to purchase a laminated interstellar passport. Ancients were cashing in any antique in their possession for whatever gold and silver they could carry out. Demons of all varieties were lining up to hit the sacrifice altars. Ordinary humans were stocking up on esoteric weapons, and time-travelers were dithering aloud about divesting themselves of any and all objects that could be labeled anachronistic. This growing crowd rubbed shoulders in unusually large numbers. Ashley had not seen this diverse a group of customers within her shop at any single time in, well, ever.

Ashley locked eyes with Johnny, struggling not to get lost in the twin pools of endless blackness that were his pupils.

"Not for nothing, but five centuries I've worked this counter, and you've never brought me a treasure like this," Ashley said, "and now, all these customers, all these trades and sales, not to mention the rush on sacrifices… what the hell is going on?"

Johnny leaned forward and whispered a single word mere inches from her face.

"Sha'Daa."

A chill like an icy stiletto shot up through Ashley's spine.

"Ohhhhhh shit."

To read more, look for *Sha'Daa: Pawns*, arriving Spring 2014.

Copper Dog Publishing LLC

OUR IMPRINTS:

Pumpkin Hill Press

To find out more about our imprints
and our upcoming releases, visit our website:
www.CopperDogPublishing.com
or our Facebook page:
www.facebook.com/copperdogpublishing